SEAL TEAM SEVEN BOOKS 6&7 QUINN AND DEVON

JORDAN SILVER

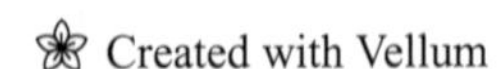

FOREWORD

Diplomacy…bullshit wrapped in a sweet tongue. The ancients call this guile. It's used by men with dark hearts who seek to destroy…trust no one.

1

KELLY

~

"Where are you taking me?" I struggled against the restraints as I tried to take stock of my surroundings. My heart was still beating too loudly in my ears and the tinny taste of fear lingered in my mouth.

I held my breath as best I could and strained to hear what was going on around me over the vicious thumping of my heart. That saying 'blind fear' is very accurate. It felt like all my senses, especially that one, was on have the fritz.

I worked my jaw when I realized I was gritting my teeth too hard to stop myself from wetting my pants and it was beginning to hurt.

My body was tense, poised and ready to take flight, but I couldn't have moved even had I not been tied up and immobilized. Fear held me in its grip so hard that I'd become almost paralyzed with it.

I concentrated on slowing my breath down if only to stop the unhealthy racing of my heart, and started to settle down once I realized that there was no immediate danger.

It took a sec for my mind to send that message to my body, but my limbs soon started to relax, bit by bit and the pain eased from my limbs.

Once I finally got my bearings I used my shoulder to feel the place where I now leaned, and the ridged pattern of the hard cold steel gave me some idea of where I was or at least what I was being held captive in.

It felt like one of those old rusted containers down by the tracks that my friends and I had liked to goof around in when we were younger.

This couldn't be good. That sickening feeling came back with a bang and was now full blown terror. I was headed hard towards panic mode as the air got trapped in my lungs.

The fear threatened to choke me and I came very close to passing out, but my natural fighting instinct prevailed and I fought the feeling until it passed again.

'Fear is your greatest opponent. Never give in, you fight it with everything you've got.' I heard my daddy's voice in my head and never wished for him more. 'If you can defeat fear you're still in the game.'

It was one of his many mantras that had seen me

through even the most harrowing situations. Though I've never found myself in anything approaching this magnitude before.

Still, one of daddy's life lessons was that my life was worth more than anything I could ever face no matter who or what. As long as I remember that, it would be the catalyst I need to get me out of anything. The survival instinct he called it.

He also taught me that no man on earth had any power over me, nothing more than what I was willing to give. The reminder gave me a much needed second wind and a resurgence of determination, which helped to relax me even more.

I regulated my breathing as best I could, using all the exercises I'd learned. I tried going into a meditative state but it was no use, too much panic, but at least the mind numbing fear was now gone.

I opened my eyes in the darkness, a lot calmer now, but still no closer to an answer as to how to get the hell outta this mess.

The space was pitch black and it took some time, but once my eyes adjusted to the dark I saw that I was indeed in a container; one of the long ones semis and freight trains haul.

There were no windows and the lone door was at the other end, what seemed like a million miles away. For some reason this scared me more than if I'd woken up in a room somewhere. At least then I'd know that I was still local, close enough for daddy to find me.

This could only mean one thing though, I was being transported somewhere. That thought made my chest tight and that overwhelming need to pee came back full force. My tummy was already hurting from holding it in.

I started shouting again though I was sure my captors couldn't hear my screams through the metal of my prison and over the rushing of the wheels as they sped through the night.

It felt like they were going at least ninety in this death trap. Pretty sure at this rate we'd be past the city limits in no time, if we hadn't already. Away from everything I know and everyone who could help me.

I swallowed the rising panic as the enormity of my situation finally kicked in. I'm on my own, can rely only on myself, and I haven't the faintest idea what the hell is going on.

What I'd erroneously thought was a sick infantile joke at the hands of my friends just a short while ago, has fast become something far more sinister.

I clenched my legs tightly together so that I didn't wet myself as the gravity of the situation came crashing down on me. This is the stuff nightmares are made of.

An urban legend, that you and your friends tell one another late at night in the dark to scare the crap out of each other.

What I wouldn't give to be at one of my best friend Connie's crappy sleepovers, or trapped in some too real dream.

The flop sweat pouring off me in the enclosed space was a solid reminder that this was no dream. Still it didn't seem real, a bit incongruous if you ask me. Stuff like this just doesn't happen to people like me.

I've always avoided trouble, had always been a model child and even now in my third year of college, I had yet to give my parents anything to seriously worry about.

Okay that's probably bullshit. Dad has lamented time and again that my antics would send him to an early grave, but he's the king of exaggeration.

Really Kelly? You're thinking about this shit now? I knew it was my mind's way of protecting me from the true horror of my situation but I also knew I couldn't afford to linger there for too long.

Instead I closed my eyes and concentrated on beating back the fear that was insistent on taking me over. "Step off bitch."

I flexed my shoulders, as much as I could while being trussed up like a hog going to market and let my mind go blank.

Daddy had taught me a lot of neat tricks, what he calls survival exercises, and they've never been needed more than at this moment.

I'm blind yes, don't know where I am, where I'm

headed or who snatched me, but this was one of those things I'd been trained for.

All I have to do is remain calm and use whatever resources come my way when they let me out of this death trap. I'm a fighter, I know how to use both mind and body to get out of any situation.

I kept repeating that over and over to myself until I felt my body relax. As the fear receded and my mind began to clear, anger reared its head, good. Now I know I'm back in the game. If fear is a great defeater, controlled rage has always been my friend.

Rage reminds me that I am human and have certain inalienable rights that protect me from assholes who seek to do harm. Rage gives me added strength when I need it, and boy do I need it.

I let the rage build until it was at a nice simmering boil just beneath the surface. My training was finally kicking in. Daddy always said in certain situations a good head of anger can get you a long way, as long as you can control it and not let it control you.

Anger reminds you that you're still in the fight, that you still have a chance. Anger doesn't throw punches like a pussy, but has some power behind it.

I went through my mind and pulled out everything daddy had taught me from the time I was a little girl. While other parents were teaching their kids not to take candy from strangers, daddy was teaching me how to kick a stranger's ass.

With my thoughts finally in order, I worked on my breathing and getting my body under complete control. Each time my mind drifted to the end of this road and what that might be, I dragged it back from the brink.

No matter what, I will fight 'til the end. If nothing else I will make daddy proud by not giving in too easy. Maybe that could be my epitaph. 'She put up a valiant fight.'

Of course I wanted to curl into a ball and cry until he came and got me, but I could hear his strong reassuring voice in my head. Yelling at me to use everything I had in my power to survive. Fresh tears started as I envisioned our nighttime ritual from my youth.

Ever since I was old enough to remember, daddy would tuck me in. Whenever he was at home that is and not off saving the world.

He'd sit next to my bed and read to me, before brushing the hair back from my face with his reassuring hand. I loved that best. It always made me feel so safe, loved.

Then he'd lean in close and kiss my forehead before whispering in my ear, what a precious person I am. How no one was better or stronger. How I could do and be anything I want, because I was made special and there was only one me.

Those words always made me feel taller, stronger

braver. Like I could take on the world. Thinking of him and mom, the strength they'd tried to instill in me, made me all the more determined to fight. Though my mind struggled to sway from one thing to the next, I fought to concentrate on the here and now.

There was no point in wondering 'why' this was happening. No point in berating myself with 'what ifs'. Now was the time for me to formulate a plan that would see myself coming out on the other end of this thing, with myself intact.

The chances of me being able to talk myself out of this one didn't look too promising, so it's elbows to ass time as daddy would say.

Since my abductors were out of sight for now, the best I could do was plan for what came next. I've always done dry runs in my head of what I would do if I found myself in any kind of life threatening situation, but I had nothing for this scenario.

I'd always envisioned myself fighting off my assailant and kicking the shit out of him. But I'd never imagined anything remotely close to this shit show.

My mind wandered again and I recalled my day from the time I woke up this morning until now. It sure hadn't felt like today was the day I was going to die. So I won't, I refuse to. Back to work Kelly, don't be maudlin.

Since I didn't have much to go on, I just kept repeating the same questions in my head over and over, as the wheels of whatever vehicle was hauling this thing sped through the night, heading to who knows where.

The one question that stuck out the most is, just what the hell is going on? How could a person just going about their life, minding their own business, end up in a situation like this?

I guess it's a myth after all that if you live your life a certain way, avoid murky situations, and just be an all around decent person you'd avoid evil. Thanks to dad I've never been that gullible, though I did operate under the assumption that at least part of it was true.

Even with my straitlaced lifestyle, I still knew to look over my shoulder and to be super vigilant about my surroundings, especially after going away to college.

With all my years of informal training, and the instilled self-preservation that my parents had taught me, security was ever uppermost in my mind.

I never in a million years would've seen myself here, in the belly of a container, at the mercy of obviously unscrupulous men.

It was the surprise and suddenness of the attack that had caught me off guard and led to my being here. Had I been aware from the get, they would've never got the drop on me.

Silly me, because I was back in my hometown where the streets were usually safe, and everyone knew each other, I'd let my guard down.

One minute I was leaving my best friend's home on the way back to mine after a night of girly fun and games, and the next someone was putting a bag over my head and dragging me off.

At first I'd thought it was just one of my silly friends playing a trick on me, though this one was a little out there even for them. Besides they usually kept the scarier pranks for around Halloween, which was months away.

They usually pull less macabre tactics when they want to torment me with their teenage antics on a day-to-day basis.

I'd been expecting them to pull some kind of stunt to welcome me back into the fold, so though I was caught asleep at the wheel, it was all in good fun.

After the initial shock had worn off I'd cussed at my friends in between bouts of laughter and trying to catch my breath. I even started to tell them how cool it was that they'd finally found a way to get the better of me after so many failed attempts in the past.

I was all set to congratulate them on getting one over on me after years of me having the upper hand in the pranking game, but my alarm bells had started ringing.

Usually they'd be laughing and high fiving each other, while speaking in those stupid B-movie monotones meant to strike fear in the heart. But this time they were quiet. Too quiet!

I'm not sure what finally alerted me to the fact that

these weren't my friends out for a night of fun. Maybe it was the haste in which the men moved, the lack of giggles and snickers that usually accompanied my friends when they were up to mischief, or their smell.

Their sour scent hadn't been one I recognized. And then one of the men had spoken and I knew for sure I'd never heard that voice before.

The voice was gruff, the tone harsh and menacing. It struck fear in my heart and my knees weakened and gave out so that they had to drag me. Once my brain started functioning again every horror movie I'd ever seen came flashing across my mind.

I tried kicking out at them as they flanked me on both sides, screaming bloody murder, doing my best to escape. Then a hand came around my throat hard enough to crush my larynx and the screams remained trapped in my lungs.

It's funny, but you never know how you'll truly react in certain situations no matter how much you try to imagine or prepare for it. I have to admit I never thought I'd bitch out though.

Not saying that I did then either, but by the time I knew what was going on I'd lost too much ground to bounce back. Not much I could've done with my head covered and my hands restrained anyhow. So I moved onto door number two; use your head.

I couldn't for the life of me think of why, or what I'd done to bring this on myself. But I guess when you're not expecting trouble it's hard to comprehend when it finds you out of nowhere.

I did the whole retracing my steps in my head thing, thinking maybe I'd pissed someone off without being aware. People are touchous as shit these days and it doesn't take much to set most of them off.

I'd been home for the last few days and hadn't had any run-ins with any undesirables as far as I know, and I hadn't pissed anyone off at school enough to have them follow me back here to settle a score.

Most of the guys I've had to let down easy in the last three years became very understanding once they met my dad, and there was no one else who could be holding a grudge that I am aware of.

Our family home is in one of those small towns where people usually drive through on their way to somewhere else. No one had moved here since about the early fifties.

The families who lived here, population about three thousand, all knew each other either by name or sight, and had been here for the past three generations or so. I was sure I didn't know my abductors.

It could be someone from a few towns over. From what I've heard the place has been going down hill since my high school days. For a town that's as small as ours, they sure have been having their share of crime in the last ten years or so.

Drugs were usually to blame for most of them, and I

wondered if these men had somehow mistaken me for someone else. Maybe that's it, just mistaken identity.

All those thoughts went through my head in what felt like hours but could only have been a matter of a few seconds. We were moving really fast at this point and I remembered always hearing that you never get into someone's car when being abducted.

That it was best to fight to stay where you are. I opened my mouth to scream but fear had muted me. I swallowed hard a couple times until my tongue was no longer clinging to the roof of my mouth in abject terror.

Once I finally found my voice I tried screaming again, even trying to reason with them whoever they were. Obviously they had the wrong person and all that was needed was for me to convince them of that.

I told them as convincingly as I could that I was the wrong person that I had no money on me. All the things I hoped would cause them to drop this and let me go.

When nothing worked, when they didn't even acknowledge me but kept moving, I finally accepted the inevitable, that I was in deep shit.

I'd done my best to get away even though struggling took all my strength and left me breathless. But that was before the prick in my arm had silenced me for good.

2

KELLY

~

Now I've awakened here in the belly of a dark, dank container, and every depraved act man had perpetrated against man since the beginning of time played itself out in my head.

That's the flip side to having a daddy who protects you from everything and tries his best to give you all the tools you'll need to stay safe. Some day he'll have to tell you just what the hell it is he's keeping you safe from. My daddy, being who he is, never sugar coated shit for his only daughter.

I wanted to scream, throw up and go back to sleep so I could wake up from this nightmare, but there was no shying away from reality. This shit is happening in real time and if I don't come up with something, my life is never going to be the same again. I know the odds though, and they're not good.

Is this it then? Is this the end of the line for me? But why? Isn't there supposed to be some kind of logic to life? Why should these people, complete strangers no less, get to decide what course my life takes?

This isn't fair; I refuse to let this happen, to be a victim. I will not be a victim. DADDY! I screamed for him in my head as tears of frustration gathered in my eyes when I tried once more to free my hands and legs that were tied, without success. I hate these zippy tie things, they seem so innocuous but they sure are very fucking useful at doing this shit.

To think that I'm going to die because of something that cost less than a freaking quarter. I rubbed my skin raw against the hard plastic before slamming my heels into the steel bottom of the container in abject frustration.

Life isn't meant to be interrupted like this. People don't have the right to fuck with you just because. I used my usual mantra to keep that rage of fire burning as I tried fruitlessly to free myself.

Once I'd tired myself out with my efforts and could no longer hold myself upright, I slumped against the side of my prison and fought back whimpers. I swallowed around the lump in my throat, which was raw from my earlier screams, and willed my useless tears away.

I needed to preserve my energy anyways for whatever

was going to come next and tears are very exhausting. Suck it up little girl. What's done can't be undone and this is your new reality. Some asshole has thrown you in the back of a metal coffin like he owns you. What're you gonna do about it?

My mind was full of all the shit I could do to an opponent, if my hands weren't tied. In my head I wreaked all manner of vengeance against my enemies, but really I'd like to be home raiding the refrigerator and being a regular pain in the ass as I'm fondly known around my house.

Do my parents even know that I'm gone yet? How long have I been here? There was no way to gauge the time from within the deep darkness and my hands were tied behind my back so looking at my watch if it was still there was out of the question.

The thought of my parents and what I was leaving behind had the tinny sickening taste of fear returning. I vacillated between bouts of unadulterated rage and back to the scared little girl who just wanted her mommy and daddy to keep her safe.

One minute I wanted so badly to crawl into a ball and cry my heart out, but in the next I knew that wouldn't get me out of here. Think, Kelly, think. I kept telling myself over and over while fear nipped at my heels and clawed its way up my throat.

I did my best to push it aside, and try to remember

everything I'd ever read, or heard about abductions and the best way to react. Over the years daddy had drilled into my head everything I needed to do if such a thing should occur.

I'd always felt that I was prepared for anything from all his teachings, but now realized that the mind and body doesn't necessarily work that way when you're in actual danger. What a time to learn this shit.

In between the bouts of fear that burned a hole in my gut, my mind wandered to all the things I had put off doing. All the things I'd been too afraid to try or told myself there was plenty of time to try later; so many lost opportunities.

I'd watched my friends over the years, starting in middle school, through high school and now college, take risks, spread their young wings and try new things, while I always stayed in the shadows.

Because of who my daddy is it was hard for me to get away with half the shit my pals did, and I learned at a very young age not to even try. The one constant in my life from my earliest memory to this, is my need to make daddy proud of me in all things. My behavior has always been exemplary where it counts.

So while the others were being wild, untamed teens,

I'd relied on my wild overactive imagination, and had enjoyed many an adventure there in the recesses of my mind. But not once have I ever had the courage to try, to dip my toe in the waters of rebellion. Now it may be too late.

My heart raced sickeningly in my chest at the thought, and the bitter taste of bile lingered on my palette. I wanted to rage at the unfairness of it all. What had been the point?

Weren't good little girls supposed to be absolved from things like this? Doesn't it say that if you live your life a certain way you will never face some of life's more horrible atrocities? What a load of crap.

All those years of being the good girl had led me here. All those times I'd been overly cautious and bore the brunt of my friend's jokes when I was once again the voice of reason, trying to talk them out of whatever hijinks they were plotting to get up to.

And tonight they were all at home, safe in their beds, while I was the one in the clutches of who knows what.

My mind shifted to thoughts of my family again, my mom and daddy, aunts, uncles, cousins. And the fact that I may never see them again. Tears streamed freely down my cheeks as I saw my mother's face in my mind's eye.

Will I ever see it again in this life? Will my daddy ever tease me, pull my hair and call me pumpkin again in that way he has that always made me feel safe and loved?

It's amazing what you think about when your life is in

imminent danger. But I think those are the things I would miss if I never get back to them. Like hell I won't see them again, I will not let them take my life.

I forced myself to think positively, not to give in so easily to despair. Whoever my captors were they're still just men. Men can be bested if you use your head. More of daddy's tenets.

I tried to boost my spirits, telling myself that I will find a way out of this once I got rid of the shakes and could think clearly again.

I psyched myself up and told myself to fight whatever this is with all I've got and not just give in. There had to be a way out, there always is if you think hard enough.

My mind flashed to a story I'd read years ago when I was too young to understand the severity of the situation. It was the story of a young girl, one much younger than I am now.

A girl who'd been taken from her bed in the middle of the night. A family torn apart, a city on edge as the nation watched. That girl had found her way back home. I too can do the same.

The thought gave me solace and I held onto it for as long as I could, keeping the fear at bay. I'll bide my time until I get the lay of the land so to speak, and then I'd go from there.

I won't fight them until I was sure I'm in a position to

win. Any opportunity that arises I'll take it, no matter what I have to do to escape this horror.

That's a girl Kelly, keep thinking ahead don't look back. I felt my inner strength build and left the defeatist attitude in the dust. My daddy has been preparing me for this day ever since I got a firm grasp on the English language. Both mentally and physically.

I can hold my own in a fight, fair or otherwise. Right now I couldn't use my physical strength since the enemy was not in sight, so I'd have to rely on my brain.

With that thought in mind I tried to sort out the situation. They'll have to untie me at some point, unless they planned to kill me right away. My pulse raced with that new horror until common sense prevailed and I convinced myself that had that been their intent, I would be long dead.

No, this was something else and I didn't need too many guesses to figure out what that something was. The news has been full of trafficking stories in the last few months. I never imagined I had to look out for anything like that because of my lifestyle. And for all I know I could be way off the mark.

Bottom line, it doesn't matter what awaits me at the end of this ride. I'm in a fight for my life. It's me against them, and who the fuck, is them? Oh that anger was boiling away now and I was ready to throw these hands, but the fuckers were out of reach.

I decided it was best to preserve my mental energy and get some rest for as long as I could so that I could spring into action when the chance arose. I settled back against the side of the container and closed my eyes.

Instead of my horrible circumstances I let myself imagine a time after this, when this was all over and done. First thing I'm gonna do is live.

I'm going to find me a guy just like my daddy. Strong, kind and honorable. We'll settle down in a small town like the one I grew up in and have a million babies.

He's going to love me the way my daddy loves my mom and our little girls are going to be his joy. I'm never going to know a moment's fear again and our lives are going to be picture perfect.

I held that picture in my head and it became so real I could almost believe it. It had the added benefit of slowing down my heart rate and I actually felt the excitement of falling in love.

The little daydream gave me hope. The only problem was I had yet to meet anyone that came even close to living up to that image. But for now it was enough that I hold onto the hope that it might still, be possible.

My heart was no longer beating in my ears and maybe that's why I finally heard it. I held still and stopped breathing again trying to hear it more clearly, to make sure it wasn't just my imagination.

The sound was faint but I thought I heard something

other than the rushing of the wheels beneath me. It took me a moment to realize there was someone else here with me.

At first I thought it might be one of my captors left here to keep watch over me, but as I strained to listen, it sounded more like weeping.

"Who's there?" Why am I whispering? They must know no one can hear me since they removed my gag. The body on the opposite side moved as if to get away from me.

I tried to see in the dark interior, but my eyes refused to adjust. I started to shake, I don't know why. Maybe because the presence of another human being brought it all home.

The sound was coming not too far from my left, soft pain filled moans. I'm guessing they'd been drugged same as I and was now waking up. I turned in the direction of the noise and strained to hear more.

The person had stopped at the sound of my voice and I imagined someone biting into their lip to stifle the sound of their tears. Heartbreaking.

"Hey, are you awake?" I kept my voice nice and calm even though inside I was screaming. My only answer was another moan and then as if the floodgates had opened up, I heard more movement coming from my other side and all around me. There were more than two of us in here.

Shit! Please don't let that be Connie or any of my

other friends. The thought of my girly friends being caught up in this sent new fear racing through my heart.

I knew that even if it wasn't, I wouldn't be able to leave whoever was in here with me behind to face a fate I didn't want for myself. That was something else daddy had taught me. Never leave a man behind. Crap!

3

QUINN

~

I jumped straight up in bed with my heart racing, glock in hand, body in fight mode. I listened for any kind of sound as I scanned all four corners of the bedroom with my gun arm extended.

What the fuck was that? Still caught in that place between sleep and wake I couldn't immediately decipher if the disturbance had been internal, or something that was physically here with me.

My gut was tied in knots and I felt fear like I haven't since I was a kid. There was a strange hum in my ears and my breath stilled in my lungs as I tried to get my bearings.

With my training I would've known by now if there were anyone else in the room with me. There wasn't, but I still couldn't shake the feeling that something was very wrong.

I listened very carefully and there was no sound, but still everything in me screamed extreme danger. I could almost taste it, and all my signals were going off full blast.

Some fuck was wrong, my hackles were raised and my skin prickled. All the signs that I was having an episode.

It had been so long since my 'gift' had shown itself that I didn't readily accept that that's what this was though, plus we weren't in the field and that shit hadn't shown itself anywhere but there, in a long fucking time.

Once I ascertained that the room was clear I shook my head as I tried to pinpoint what it was that had awakened me. There was nothing in the rest of the house when I did a walk through.

No sound coming from outside where the dark night peeped through the windows. I checked the security monitors surrounding the compound but as expected, all was quiet.

Back in the bedroom I did another quick check as that feeling of dread persisted. I had the curtains Danielle had installed pulled back and the window lifted to let in the night air.

Maybe a small animal or something had got too close to the house, but a quick scan of the ground below showed nothing, no disturbance.

Not even the leaves were moving in the still of the eerie predawn Georgia morning. It was too early for the birds, and the crickets had long been asleep. So what the fuck?

I exhaled and flung myself back down on the bed and sent out feelers, testing my surroundings. Ty the ass likes to call them my spidey senses but they've saved his worthless hide a time or two and were usually on point.

Nothing! At least nothing I could see, but my senses were hardly ever wrong and that shit was screaming loud as fuck. I squinted into the dark trying to call to mind the last thing I'd seen in REM.

I felt unsettled when I couldn't recall what I'd been dreaming about and that feeling of, 'knowing', lingered over me. Well shit! I cleared my mind and listened.

I was very aware of the irregular beating of my heart and the sickening cramp in my gut. Someone belonging to me was in trouble and I can't for the life of me figure out how or who. Everyone I love is right here, safe and secure. Or was this an omen of things to come?

My blood zinged like a live wire beneath my skin and I rubbed my arms as I tried to listen to what my senses were telling me. It had been a while since I'd got that little tingle in my senses.

In the last few years it had only shown up when we were in the field and never in my everyday life. Granted things were a bit tense around here lately with all the bullshit my brothers and I had been dealing with, but somehow this didn't feel as if there was a connect.

That shit doesn't scare me, we've dealt with worse. The only difference being, that this time, it was personal and we had the women and my niece to protect.

Still, my brothers and I knew what we were doing, and as dangerous as the situation was, we weren't too worried. Not yet!

I let myself relax all the way and with my eyes closed, tried to read my surroundings. I'd done this shit a million times in more hostile situations and it had never failed me once.

When nothing was forthcoming, I got comfortable and went back to sleep. I woke twice more with the same results until I started to get pissed the fuck off.

Some shit was definitely wrong but for the first time in my life I couldn't get a bead on it. That sense of danger lingered and I checked the security I don't know how many times until I was convinced that everyone was safe.

Another quick walk around outside just to be sure, turned up nothing. And when I finally broke down and called each of my brothers to check in, they'd all assured me that things were fine on their end. Except Ty who told me to fuck off and Devon who wanted to come over in case some shit was up with me.

I laughed at Ty's grumpy ass and refused Dev's offer. I

probably should've let him come on over since I was sure he'd spend the rest of what was left of the night worrying.

I knew I was right when he called me half an hour later and I lied and told him I was just feeling unsettled because of something I ate.

After he got through confirming that Ty was indeed right and I was most definitely bitch made, he hung up. At least he was no longer worrying about me.

I awoke a little later, still with that unsettled feeling in my gut. I felt like I should be moving faster, like there was something that needed my attention. It made no sense.

For the first time there was no direction to follow, when always in the past I at least had some idea of what the fuck.

That zing in my blood had become a strange crawling sensation beneath the surface of my skin. I looked around outside and all seemed calm, so I was once again assured that at least my family wasn't in any immediate danger.

I was on high alert once I left the house in the early hour between night and day, when everything is still silent and the light is barely peeping above the trees. This is usually my favorite time of day. It's peaceful and undisturbed; not today though.

The others were still in bed as I made the rounds

around the perimeter just to be safe, before making my way to the gym we'd built on the premises.

A look at my watch showed it would be another hour at least, before they stirred. I'd like to be there myself but unease had run me from my bed.

4

QUINN

~

I thought of the CO as I did my laps in the indoor pool. Swimming helps me to relax and clear my head when it gets too hot, or when something keeps rattling around in there.

It wasn't long before I felt the stress begin to leave me and my limbs became more relaxed and pliant as the tension eased.

Only in the water do I feel this at peace. An old woman once told me that it was because of my 'gift'. Apparently those things are all connected to the elements or some shit.

I could do without this 'gift' as she called it, though it has helped me out a time or two in the past. And then there're the times when it's a right pain in the ass; like now.

From the time I was a very young kid, before my dad tried to beat it out of me, I had a very strong sixth sense. Apparently it's something that ran in the male line of my family. Some Celtic shit that had been passed down since the days of the druids or some fuck.

Fuck if I know, I grew up on the streets of Chicago where shit didn't lean to the supernatural but more survival of the fittest. I wish I would have told my boys that I hung with back then about this shit. My ass would never have made it out of the south side.

I always knew I was different, and somehow knew this difference wasn't something to be shared. It could be because of my dad's reaction the first time I mentioned 'seeing' something that wasn't there.

He'd freaked the fuck out and I can't remember if the beatings for that particular infraction started then or some time later. Whatever!

It didn't matter what the asshole did, that shit just kept on coming. Sometimes I would just know things, things that no seven year old should know or have any knowledge of.

That's the earliest recollection I have of this shit, when I was about seven and trying out for little league. I remember seeing this kid bleeding from the head and somehow knowing that it was going to happen that day.

Not understanding of course, I'd told my mom who was sympathetic and tried to reassure me. I remember it had led to a heated discussion between my parents and then dad had been pissed off and slammed out of the house only to return later, drunk.

That's when he'd yelled at me and told me never to do that shit again. That's when I first started to hate my 'gift'. Not because he yelled, asshole was always yelling. But the look on his face I'll never forget as long as I live.

As I grew older, I got so good at ignoring my 'gift', that after a while it seemed to have disappeared; but apparently the shit was just playing possum, because it came back full force in my teen years.

It was a source of great confusion back then. How could the thing that warned me not to follow Johnny Spinner back in eighth grade, the same Johnny Spinner who'd lost his life playing duck-duck goose on the train tracks that same day when I listened, be such a bad thing?

But that look on my dad's face was never forgotten and being a kid who lived for his dad's praise and approval there was no choice.

So, I spent a lot of time as a young boy frightened and confused, and as I grew older I'd try to hide that shit until I came to hate it. As far as I was concerned it was something to be ashamed of. I mean if my old man hated it so much there must be something wrong with it right.

For the majority of my life up until the time I met my

brothers, it was some shit that I wasn't too keen on sharing with the rest of the world's population and had gone to great lengths to keep buried.

Of course after meeting Lo and the others who'd joined up a few years ahead of me, there was no way I was telling these tough as nails motherfuckers about my little hiccup.

If I'd hid that shit before it was damn near imperative that I annihilate it now. I could just see the six of them laughing their asses off or worst, telling the CO.

So all through training I'd kept that shit to myself even though for some perverse reason it seemed to choose that time to be even more of a pain in the ass.

I remember the first few weeks of training it was a constant companion and once I realized I couldn't shake it so easily this time, I dealt with it. I guess if you're going to put your ass on the line everyday it was a nice little side bennie every once in a while, but I worked hard at keeping it under wraps.

If it helped me to excel, well hey. But it took more than that to get me through that shit. All through training as I built my physical strength, my gift grew right along with it-it seemed and it was getting harder to contain.

Still I was feeling pretty good that after months with my brothers they hadn't picked up on my 'knowing'. And then I'd outted myself when we were going on a particularly sketchy raid. That shit had been riding my ass all day and I'd put it off as long as I could.

We'd recently been teamed up together after I'd kicked major ass in BUD training and it was only our third or fourth run. No way did I want these bad-asses knowing that I was a damn freak of nature.

We were in the Congo on a rescue mission to extract the son of a diplomat who'd got himself kidnapped. The family was more than willing to pay, but that's not how this shit works. You start paying off these fucks it would never end.

It was our first extraction but we'd done drills until I could run them in my sleep, and we'd been in tougher situations together a time or two by then. I was just hitting my stride and beginning to feel like I belonged, that I was part of something worthwhile.

We were getting Intel from one of the locals that the CO had been assured was on the level, but something just didn't feel right in my gut. As we moved through the night deep into the jungle, that feeling persisted until I could no longer ignore it and I caved in and got Lo's attention.

I'll never forget his face when I told him we were walking into a trap. He'd studied me like he could see into my head. Then without question he'd alerted the others.

Long story short, the local ended up with a broken neck and we went in and got the kid using my 'gift' as guidance. When we got back Lo had confronted me in front of the others.

I was embarrassed as fuck, but they seemed more impressed than repulsed when he finally dragged the shit out of me. Of course he convinced me we had to tell the CO.

I was nervous as fuck, still a young man of about twenty back then and had finally felt like I belonged somewhere. I'd heard the others talking over time and knew that most of us came from fucked up beginnings, some worse than mine.

I was terrified that the CO would use this as grounds to kick me out, but things had gone in a whole other direction.

Instead he'd called us all into a meeting and after grilling my ass like a suspected terrorist skell he'd praised me for my abilities. At first I'd thought he was making fun of me, but the reactions of the others had soon set me straight. They'd actually thanked me for saving their lives.

Apparently the CO had learned too late that the local guide had been compromised and there was no way to pull us back. He'd been mounting a second team to go in after us.

That was the night they became my brothers in heart. It was from that moment on that the seven of us just clicked into place for me. That was a lifetime ago now and we'd come very far and had faced some serious shit together over the years that had only made us closer, stronger.

As time went by we became more than just a team. I don't remember us ever being apart even when we came back stateside after that. Lo had decided to take our training a step farther and since we were a motley crew of semi orphans, we all just seemed to fall into brotherhood.

Before that I was more of a loner; still have a bit of the lone wolf in me. The navy hadn't knocked the stubborn out of me and I'd say for sure if not for my brothers, my ass wouldn't have made it out of the sling a time or two. But since we 'semi retired' I've calmed the fuck down like ninety percent.

Lo has a lot to do with that. He knows each of us almost as well as we know ourselves. That's why he's so good at being our leader in the field and why we still trust him to call the plays now that we're home.

Before the CO left us this place, we'd hole up in some beach town somewhere or a cabin in the mountains when we didn't feel like dealing with people in our downtime.

We'd always planned to stay together when we got out, and the CO who always seemed to know everything, and had played a bigger part in our lives than just that of a commanding officer, had made that possible.

I pulled myself up out of the pool and dried off as I pushed the weirdness of the night from my mind and thought of my family. Though we were all roughly the same age give or take a year or two, we'd all fell into certain roles as easily as if we'd been born to it.

Logan was a born leader and protector. Connor's his wingman and the rest of us just found our place and took up position with Lo at the helm.

We've had very few losses over the years, and through them, because of our bond, I'd grown into someone I could be proud of.

Since dad was an asshole of the highest order and mom had been long gone by the time I signed up, it was my brothers with whom I'd shared my greatest achievements.

The kid who'd been aloof and withdrawn, who trusted no one but himself, had learned to trust, not just the men I fought and bled with, but the man who'd led us.

It was easy for me to take a step back and let Lo do his thing because I knew when it was needed he had no problem letting the rest of us take that position. We all played on each other's strengths.

He'd given Cord the reins this last go around which thank fuck we'd all survived. That boy is just a little bit touched if you know what I mean and there were times in the last couple weeks when things were touch and go.

Thank fuck he has his woman to keep his ass on his toes now and the rest of us can catch a break. We'd dodged a few bullets there and were facing yet more bull-fuckery in the not too distant future, but the rules of our game had changed a hell of a lot.

We were all keeping it on low keel for the sake of the women, but had it been just us, we would've fucked shit up already, consequences be damned.

That usually involved leaving bodies scattered to fuck and back. But now with everyone becoming family oriented and shit, we're having to find new ways and means.

Plus, this shit was on domestic soil, something we've never had to deal with before, not like this. We were treading new waters with this one.

5

QUINN

I don't know if it's divine intervention or just plain happenstance, but I find it more than just a little strange that in the midst of all this bullshit, my brothers have been dropping like flies. That shit so far, has been an adventure of a whole different bent.

I'd never seen them in love before. I don't think any of us ever even gave thought to the possibility. The kind of men we are, love just never seemed like it would ever be in the works and I think we were all cool with that.

But since we moved here something shifted in the wind or some fuck and boy has this shit been all kinds of entertaining.

Connor was the first to go, and he needed to be first.

That's one crazy motherfucker. The danger with Con is that he seems calm as fuck, but beneath that veneer beats the heart of a true beast.

His quietness hides a deep-seated hatred for all the things we stand against as warriors. He, like the rest of us, believes in honor, courage, commitment and the fair treatment of everyone who deserves it.

I'd say he's probably the toughest nut to crack. So I guess it was only natural that once he took the plunge the others would follow suit.

Logan is right behind him in the crazy stakes, but he has a little more control. His shit is like ice, but he can keep it contained and do what needs to be done.

Zak is outright-nuts. He loves hard and it's even harder for him to forgive. But when he's on your side you know you're safe, you're gonna make it out of whatever situation you're in.

Ty, well, Ty is the baby of our little family even though he likes to pretend he's the big dog. Maybe it's because out of all of us, he got the shittiest deal in life and that's saying something.

But no matter what the rest of us suffered at the hands of others as children, nothing beats watching your mother murdered by some asshole, not knowing if said asshole was gonna come for you next.

So, we're all very protective of him though none of us

would say that shit out loud. On a good day he's probably the most softhearted of us. But he's also the loose canon, the one most likely to say fuck it, break rank and off a motherfucker.

I guess you can say he's the brother who says and does the things you wish you could, but training holds you in check. He slips his training like a snake sheds its skin and don't give a fuck. Good times.

And then we have Cord, Mr. Master of all he perceives. No one really knows how deep that fuck runs, we just know that with him in our corner, whoever comes at us are gonna have to come hard as fuck.

Each of us have put our lives on the line for the others a time or two and would do it again without a second thought. Together we make a formidable team of bad-asses.

Devon is the silent creeper. He holds everything close to the vest, stays pretty much to the background taking in everything until it's time to strike. I'd die for each and every one of them, and now the women they'd brought into our tight little circle, and of course our baby Zak.

I grinned at the thought of my precocious niece who has us all wrapped around her little finger. My gut tightened up a bit when I remembered that my sisters were pregnant and we were in the middle of a shit storm.

We've had to protect women before but under very

different circumstances. There's a big difference between shielding girls and women in a school in Kabul that was under threat of being bombed because some asshole didn't think women should learn shit, and having that shit happening in your own backyard, with women that are now family.

The situation still gives me pause, but I can't say that I would wish for things to be different at this stage. I can't imagine them not being here, part of the fabric of our lives.

My brothers are happy and after the shit we'd seen together in the field, I can honestly say, they deserve every bit of that happiness. I'll do whatever it takes to see that nothing and no one fucks with it and them.

It hadn't been easy at first, had taken some getting used to for the rest of us each time another one fell. It had been just us guys for so long that suddenly having the care of females was going to take some reorganizing on our part.

Females take up a lot of fucking space, both physically and mentally. Men of honor know that shit and have to deal accordingly.

Though we'd built our homes to accommodate family, I don't think any of us ever really expected things to happen this quick after we settled down here. Now we're down to just Devon and I being the last holdouts.

I'm not sure how to feel about this shit, other than it

makes me nervous as fuck. From what I see none of the others had been looking for love and happily ever after. But the shit sure did seem to find them out of nowhere, and that's the shit that was making me antsy.

Personally, I never thought there were any women out there suitable enough, in the sense that any woman taking on any one of us would have to have a strong constitution and be just as tough. She'd also have to put up with six nosy over bearing brothers who'd protect her with their lives.

Not the one of us is easy and our standards are high. But, as with everything else in life, my brothers have chosen wisely and my new sisters fit right in with us. It's getting so I don't remember what our lives were like before they became a part of us.

The whole dynamic has changed and as if by silent agreement, we've all adjusted our ways to make things run smoothly. If I have to jump in every once in a while to bring peace between one or the other of the couples that's fine. Even their fights are funny as shit.

It's good to see what I'd be up against if I ever did take the plunge, though I'm convinced I'd have more sense than the rest of them. For fuck sake you'd think they were the first men to fall in love.

I've never seen grown men, men I knew were hard as they come, cave, whine, moan and groan like this lot. And now with the baby here and the pregnancies that seem like the status quo around here these days, they're just pitiful.

As happy as I am for them, I don't see myself walking down that same path though. Sure I get lonely sometimes, and watching the way my brothers are with their women might give me the wants once in a while. But that shit's not for everyone.

I'm more than happy to be the big brother and the proud uncle to the many nieces and nephews I foresee in my future. I'll just stand watch over them and make sure their lives go untouched by the world's assholery.

It seems almost as soon as I'd left the water my senses reignited and I knew this shit wasn't going away anytime soon. I decided to get a head start on wrapping up the equipment we were taking along with us as an excuse to avoid the others once they were up and about.

They'll be up soon and I wasn't looking forward to breakfast where we all gathered around together and everyone got into everyone else's shit.

The last thing I needed was one of them or their women looking too hard at me.

By the time they were up and about I still had no answers for what the fuck was nagging at me so I kept that shit to myself and did my best to appear like all was fine in my world.

If I knew what the fuck it would've made a difference but since I was still in the dark I saw no point in making them worry as well. The last thing they needed was my shit to deal with on top of everything else they had on their plates.

I avoided the questioning looks as we went about the business of packing up, but that feeling gnawed at my gut all day without letup

Okay, I've had enough of this shit. I've been out of sorts all day, still not able to shake that feeling of gloom.

All morning and into the afternoon I've racked my brain trying to figure out what it could be, if maybe there was something we were overlooking. But after going over and over our preparations there was nothing out of order.

It didn't feel as if it was directly associated with the shit we were dealing with no. Somehow it seemed more personally directed at me, and not one of my brothers, but that was the only thing I was certain of.

I still couldn't quite put my finger on what it is that has been plaguing me since I rolled out of bed. I've steered clear of the others as much as I could since waking up this morning, especially Lo, or at least I tried to.

But my brothers aren't known for keeping their noses out of shit and we're all so in tuned with each other, when one is off someone else always knows. I was definitely off.

I figured it was best to lay low until I knew what the hell was going on, but knew I wouldn't be allowed much time to myself if anyone even suspected that some shit was wrong with me.

If one of my brothers didn't sniff me out, one of my sisters will, sure as shit. So it was easier to just lay low under the pretense of being busy.

I did my part to get us ready to head out, which was another thing that was fucking with my head. I knew it was the best deal for the women and baby Zak, but I wasn't convinced that our place wasn't secure enough. Still, I wasn't willing to take any chances and neither were the others.

Mancini seems cool enough but I'm about looking after my own. Not that I don't trust him. From what we've seen so far he's as straight as they come, but for as long as it's mattered it's been the seven of us taking care of shit.

The trafficking shit had drawn in others that we'd known before, like Law and Creed, and by extension Mancini and a few others had been brought into the fold.

This is the reason why here lately our little family has been steadily expanding, not only to the women my brothers were set to marry, but our friends, old and new, who've also been caught up in this thing one way or another.

For a split second I wondered if perchance my unease had something to do with one of these new acquaintances, but easily brushed it aside.

There was no shaking the feeling that it was all about yours truly. For that reason it was almost easy to push it to the back of my mind as I did the shit I had to do.

There isn't much I fear, if anything, so as long as nothing and no one was fucking with my family, I'm good.

Whoever, whatever this is, I'll deal with it. For now I was only making myself crazy trying to figure the shit out and that was no help to anyone.

Instead I brought my thoughts back to the fuckery that we were ass deep in the middle of. The man at the center of it all is someone I have great respect for even though he's gone. He'd played too big a part in my life, in all our lives, for him to ever not be a part of it, even in death.

I played around with the idea that maybe it was him trying to talk to me from the great beyond, but since my 'gift' had never worked that way before, dismissed the idea. Then again this whole experience was unlike any I'd dealt with in the past so who knows.

Maybe the old man was trying to guide me from the grave. Too bad I don't believe in that shit. It was hard enough accepting this sixth sense I've had since childhood. If I had to deal with some new anomaly now in the middle of all this bullshit I'd lose my fucking mind.

When lunchtime rolled around I made an excuse and continued working while the others went on ahead. I couldn't eat now if you spoon fed me the shit

6

DEVON

I looked back at Quinn once before following the others to Lo's house for lunch. I can't put my finger on it, and he's so good at camouflaging shit when he wants to that it had taken me a while, but something's up.

Ever since that early morning phone call I knew he was hiding something but had let myself be convinced otherwise.

I was tempted to go back and get that shit out of him, but the baby distracted me when she met us at the door.

She babbled away about something or the other that only Ty understood and the rest of us became bystanders to their continuing saga.

I don't care how hard you are, nothing melts you

faster than a tiny tot with attitude and a chip on her shoulder.

She read Ty's ass but good. The rest of us got a few eye rolls and finger shakes, but he was her mark no doubt. It was hard not to smile at the two of them and their antics.

Once he picked her up and cleared the way we made it inside where the women met us with smiles that for once weren't hiding some shit that they'd been up to.

It usually takes less than five minutes to read the room, but they're getting sneakier everyday. With Vanessa in their midst, teaching them tactical maneuvers and shit, it won't be long before they have us completely snookered.

"Umm, something smells good." Lo made his way over to Gaby and wrapped his arms around her from behind.

The women were bustling around the kitchen with their usual laughter as they spread platters of food on the table.

Since greedy ass Ty was preoccupied I thought it wise to dig in before he remembered that he was hungry.

There was a lot of kissing hello and whispered words, followed by the women's giggles, followed by belly rubs and hand swats. The scene of domesticity still took some getting used to.

I was also amazed at the skill with which my brothers

switched gears from plotting the demise of fuck-nuts who dared breathe the same air as us, to rubbing barely there pregnant bellies and whispering sweet nothings in their women's ears.

I'd seen my brothers in many lights over the years and I have to say this shit is borderline comical. I doubt the boys knew they had those sappy looks on their faces as they practically ran their women around the room.

As with everything else, they showed no shame. Warrior Con was at this very moment looking like the biggest sap as he tried conning Dani into sneaking off with him. At least I think that's what all the whispering and head shaking in his corner was about.

If Quinn were here the two of us would give them shit for the PDAs, but it didn't feel the same on my own. Asshole threw me to the wolves.

I didn't have time to wallow in the injustice of it all because Zak's voice rang out with a hint of fear that almost stopped my heart.

"Zakira, NO." He was halfway out of his seat and every adult in the room went on high alert. The baby, who had been messing around the stove while no one was looking, had big fat tears in her eyes as she looked at her daddy.

I imagine his yell had scared her more than anything when her lips started to tremble and the first tear fell. Oh shit!

“Dude what the fu…” Ty snatched her up while giving Zak the stink eye. He cooed to her on the way out the door, her little arms wrapped snuggly around his neck.

We all looked at Zak for an explanation. He shrugged and sat back down on his chair. “Ty put her down for two seconds to say hi to Vicki and she went for the pot on the stove that quick.”

We all relaxed and sighed in relief that he’d caught her before anything happened to her. The room went back to bustling bedlam and I was congratulating myself on avoiding my sisters’ machinations so far.

If their men could keep them occupied for the rest of the meal that would be great, but I wasn’t kidding myself that this shit would last.

If they’re not meddling in my shit they’re not happy. Thank fuck the conversation focused on the baby and all the ways and means she finds to get into trouble.

“You do realize none of us are ever going to be able to discipline our kids with Ty around right.” Connor grabbed a biscuit and buttered it for Dani as everyone else took their seats.

The way he broke it in half and placed piece in front of her without even thinking, is one of those things that make me thankful as fuck that we had this, even though a year ago the shit was a foreign concept.

“We’ll scold and he’d placate and we’re always gonna be the bad guy.”

"Or you could look at it as our kids will always have an ear they can bend. They'll always know that there's someone on their side no matter what." "I won't worry about it; kids know when they're loved. Don't worry Con your little girl's gonna love you no matter what, even when you go all caveman on her."

Zak grinned and dug into his food with one hand while holding Vanessa's with the other.

"I'm not having a girl, I'm having all boys."

There were lots of groans and pleading going around the table as each of my brothers piped in on the preferred sex of their offspring.

Ty is the only one that doesn't seem scared shitless by little girls. Could be because they had about the same mentality who knows. If he was here he'd be ragging their asses for sure.

The conversation was light and playful with not even a hint of what we'd been up to this morning. The women knew we were leaving soon and they knew a little about what was going on, but we've been sheltering them from the worst of it as best we could, which hadn't been easy.

They're all naturally inquisitive, or as their men put it, nosy as fuck. I'm pretty sure, though they deny it, that my brothers have been sharing pillow talk. I've seen these women in action; no way they aren't syphoning information from their men. Either that, or Vanessa has been doing Intel recon.

And my brothers, these once fearless leaders, were putty in their hands. They just didn't seem to know that shit yet. When they weren't making my skin itch with their lovey-dovey bullshit, it was fun watching the dynamics between them.

Every last one of them were whipped as fuck, including Tyler who still thinks he's unscathed. Cord is the one who surprised me the most. There's going to be hell to pay when he finds out that Susie is the one in control. She has him eating out the palm of her tiny little hand.

I relaxed a little at the comical conversation, only once looking out the window towards the mansion where Quinn had stayed behind. I'll give him 'til the end of lunch and then I'm kicking his ass until he tells me what the hell is wrong with him.

The others didn't seem to notice, but that could be because everyone was so tensed up about the move we were about to make. Not to mention all the new players on the field. This would be the first time the seven of us have worked with nonmilitary unknowns this closely on an Op.

We'd dug into Mancini, as much as it's possible to dig into a spook or whatever the fuck the guy is. And though we're all agreed he's our kind of people, it's still not easy for us to just put ourselves in someone else's hands; especially not when the storm was raging all around us.

For the women though, it was probably the best move.

Not that we couldn't protect them, but with everything else we had on our plate and as far reaching as the shit seemed to be, it might be good to have a little extra help while we hunted assholes.

Ty came back inside with the baby who'd calmed down to the sniffles. He was still looking at Zak like he wanted to shoot him when he took his seat with baby Zak on his lap.

She said some shit to him that he understood and he put her down after wheedling a kiss from her. The guy is such a sap.

She made her way to her daddy on toddling legs and stood at his knee. Zak pretended not to see her as she clasped her hands and peered at him from beneath her lashes.

All eyes were on her as we held our laughter. This is one of her more famous tells. She does this when she knows she's guilty as shit but she wants you to be the one to cave.

Not sure which of her parents she inherited this from. Could be either one of them since they're both sneaky as fuck.

When he still didn't look at her, she poked his knee with her finger and batted her lashes at him when he finally gave her his attention. "What can I do for you Zakira?"

Without an answer, she climbed into his lap with his

help of course, and started lecturing him. She laid her head on his chest, picked one of her feet up between her hands and played with her toes through her socks.

He tickled her little girl tummy and she giggled and lifted her head to kiss his cheek. All is forgiven.

"Traitor." Tyler mock growled at her and she went into fits of giggles. For some reason, the conversation centered once again around children and who was going to be the best dad and uncle, with Ty of course claiming the prize for both.

We teased him about his book reading, that is until Dani busted Con for doing the same thing. The others were soon all toppled by their women one by one. My brothers are reading baby how to books. Damn!

I remember a time when all or most of our conversations were about war or some other sick shit that only a handful of people in the world knew anything about.

But five grown men were actually arguing about some shit that like I said, even a year ago wasn't on our radar. The thing is, I think they were serious and so did their women who all looked at me like 'do something about this freak show'.

I just shook my head and laughed because hey, these fuckers are crazy. How I ended up with this band of misfits is anybody's guess, but from the day I got picked for the team it's been like this.

As someone who prefers watching from the sidelines

it was easy to see the camaraderie between these men, to sense that underlying thread of trust and mutual respect needed for a team such as ours to exist.

As one of the last to join the ranks, and me being who I am, I'd tried distancing myself in the beginning. Even though the CO had drilled it into our heads that in order to work together as a team we had to damn near live in each other's skin.

It was a new concept for me, trust, plus I had a problem with authority as well, and a chip on my shoulder that no one was gonna knock off. I wasn't about to trust none of these jokers and no amount of half ass inclusion attempts was going to make me think any different, or so I thought.

I was still questioning what the fuck I was doing in the navy back then. I'd joined up because it was something to do and when you don't give a damn if you live or die, the armed forces is about the best gig going. I guess I didn't think shit through well enough, didn't quite get what signing up would entail.

Everyone usually cut a wide berth around me and I had kind of a reputation for being an asshole all through basic training. But that was before they teamed us up after my stint in BUDs and sicced Lo on my ass.

It wasn't just the chip on my shoulder that had kept a cold distance between me and everyone else. It was also the preconceived notions that many had.

Lo had been the first one there to look at me and see just me. I tested him hard as fuck in the beginning, but my brother never wavered. That's Logan for you. He only sees team he doesn't give a fuck if you're part android. And the fucker is relentless.

7

DEVON

When I first joined up no one thought I would make it as a SEAL. There's a myth going around that the 'brothers' can't cut it, can't make the grade. I'm a straight up mongrel.

Mom was black and dad was Italian. I had the best of both of them in me and though I was as light as my brothers there was no hiding the fact that I had some Grade A black blood in me. Not that I ever tried.

Anyway, that myth died a hard fast death when I showed up. Never tell me I can't do something, or that I'm not good enough. That's just the catalyst I need to fuck your preconceived notions in the ass.

I aced that shit and left my naysayers in the dust.

When I was chosen for this particular team though, motherfuckers were looking for my grandfather.

They couldn't believe a little black boy from the streets of Detroit had made it and done it in such a big way. So of course to them, I had to have had help.

When they realized that I'd done that shit on my own merit and strength of character, it didn't sit too well with some. Fuck…them.

I didn't hold that shit against them, I never did with anyone who acted like that. Who has the time? I myself hadn't expected to shine among the thousands of other young men and women, some of whom were seriously vying for the position when I'd just been pissing around.

But it was their disbelief and the way some of them just dismissed me like I didn't count, that in the end pushed me to be better, not just good, but fucking A awesome.

By the end I actually learned to enjoy it and have a little pride in myself. I'd finally come home, but fuck if I wanted any squatters in my abode.

The CO was probably the first adult I'd ever encountered since the death of my parents that I thought was worth a damn. No matter what shit I threw at him, he never let the fuck up, never once didn't have my back, and believe me I tried.

I tested his ass at every turn, was an insubordinate fuck on more than one occasion, but he refused to give up on me even then. He'd discipline my ass for sure, but he was always there the next day riding my ass to do better.

His 'boys' had to be the best in the history of the SEALs and no piss-ant little snot nosed brat was going to mess with his program.

I never had shit easy in my life, not since the day both my parents died together in a car crash. My life ended that day. The happy teenager who'd known love and support was suddenly set adrift in the world on his own.

I'd never been close to any of my relatives since both sides had a grievance with my parents' relationship. It's sad to say in this day and age that that shit was purely racial and made no sense to the two people who loved each other like their next breath.

They were the ones who taught me to see beyond color into the heart of a person. My dad was always fond of saying, out of hearing of mom of course, 'Son, there're fucked up people from all walks of life. I've seen enough shit to know that-that race shit don't matter. Like the man said in Needful Things, 'Let God sort 'em out.'

He was an upstanding man who was full of heart and loved his wife and son unconditionally. Losing him, losing both of them, was a blow that I hadn't really ever recovered from.

The uncle I was forced to live with for the four years before joining up hadn't helped matters any. I think the fucker only took me in for the sole purpose of tormenting me for whatever slight he believed my parents guilty of.

After dealing with his special brand of care after their passing and I was left at his mercy, I'd grown a new hard shell. That shit was titanium and nothing was ever getting through it again.

I'd locked my heart off from ever feeling anything resembling love again. It took me years to realize that that was just anger and pain from my loss. After these fucks had sledge hammered my walls and wormed their way into my good graces it was a wrap.

I laughed along with them and their silly arguments now, knowing that it was just their way of letting off steam and taking a load off from the hell we've been dealing with just lately.

This too was something new I was learning to get used to. It was a side to them that I'd never seen before, this softness when it came to their women. None of us had ever had a woman for longer than a one-night stand as far as I can remember.

We'd had a creed, which we held to until we retired. Then Con fell and fell hard and the shit set off an avalanche. I've been in some shit with my brothers but this shit takes the cake and I'm not talking about the fucks trafficking shit off the pier in our backyard.

No, I'm talking about the rate at which these mother-fuckers are falling. Ty with his pussy whipped ass swore it would never be him, now Quinn and I are the only ones left standing.

The thought made my gut tighten but I wasn't sure if that was from fright or want. I never let myself think about shit like that, but every once in a while it sneaks up on me and I wonder.

Then I come back to my senses and accept that no, as much as we're alike these men and I, we differ in one way. We've shared pretty much everything else for the past ten plus years, but this is the one place I can't follow my brothers. The one journey I cannot take.

I can never open myself to that kind of emotion again. I'll face anything else, but to have something that means that much to me existing in this fucked up world, no fucking way. I've seen too much. But damn they make it look so good. Maybe…

No fucking way! I dashed those thoughts as quickly as they appeared and went back to sharing in their fun even if it was from the outside looking in again.

After lunch we needed to get shit done but of course my brothers piddled around, not wanting to leave their women who had them wrapped neatly around their little fingers.

I guess they knew their women and understood that if left unattended for too long they'd get up to mischief so I couldn't begrudge them an extra hour or so. Though I wish Quinn was here to take some of the heat off my ass.

While the guys were bullshitting I noticed a hushed mum coming from the other side as we sat around Lo's living room. I took a quick peek and sure enough they had me in their sights. My sisters be looking at me like they got plans for this shit, hell fucking no.

I'm bobbing and weaving like a son of a bitch in this fuck. I kept my head turned but kept them in my peripheral playing like I can't feel them staring holes in my damn skull.

It doesn't take a genius to figure out what the topic of conversation is in that circle. That would be the same thing it's been for the last week or so since Cord that fuck lost his damn mind.

If Lo and Con wouldn't ride my ass I'd go into hiding. But ever since we figured out that the Desert Fox was involved in this shit those two have been worse than old women on the fucking rag. No one was allowed to go off by themselves.

"What Dani?" I couldn't take that shit anymore. I looked up at her just as Nessa plopped the baby down on my lap. Yeah, like that's gonna work. The little one was just as bad. She took my face between her hands and stared into my eyes before she started lecturing my ass to death. That's her only speed, tears or lectures; she's her father's kid for sure.

"Nothing, we were just wondering you know…" Dani

answered as she shrugged her shoulders, and I played the role.

"Wondering what?" My idiot brothers were just sipping their coffees not saying anything about their nosy ass women meddling in my shit. There was no sense in looking to them for help because I know whose side they're on.

"Isn't there anyone in town that you like?"

"No." I find that it's best to keep this shit short and to the point because these women are sneaky. I slip up and say the wrong thing they'll have a line of women for me to choose from by nightfall.

She pouted like it was a grave injustice that I wasn't in an all fired hurry to get hitched. I was about to turn them onto Quinn's ass when Gaby changed the subject to wedding preparations.

From the pained look on Lo's face I knew that was my out. I grinned and passed the baby back when the others got up to leave with the excuse that we had shit to do, which wasn't a lie.

We beat feet to the door blocking out the whining and complaining that came at us hard. You'd think these grown men hadn't stared death in the face a time or two before, the way these women have them running to get out of the line of fire.

"Some fuck's wrong with Quinn." Ty dropped that little nugget as soon as we cleared the door. His words had all heads turning in his direction. Lo of course was the first one to address his statement.

"What do you mean?"

"He's doing that shit he does when we're in the field. You know, like he's hearing and seeing shit no one else can." That gave the rest of us pause as we looked around at each other.

Damn. What now? I knew something was off but didn't think it was anything that serious. I'd even started to put it off as just him overthinking the move we were about to make.

He does that shit sometimes until the rest of us want to pull our hair out by the roots. But if it was his special gift there was nothing good at the end of that fuckery.

"Dev."

"On it." I picked up the pace and jogged ahead at Lo's unspoken command. I should've done better. If Ty was spooked enough to mention this shit then it must be bad.

We all try to stay on top of each other and though I'd felt the change in my brother the last day or so, with so much going on, unless someone was bleeding or dying there was no time to dwell. Plus, I figured when he was ready he'd let me in on whatever was eating away at him.

The call in the early morning had given me pause but even then I never guessed in a thousand years that it was this serious.

Quinn tries to play down his ability to get glimpses

into the future, but I for one am extremely grateful for that shit. It saved our asses more than once.

The only thing is that shit only seems to show up when there's some sort of danger, never a harbinger of good.

8

QUINN

~

I leaned back against the steps of the CO's mansion with my eyes closed and the hot Georgia sun warming my face enough to distract from the ass-fuckery that was going on inside my head.

The others should be coming back from lunch soon and even though they'd been gone for over an hour, it still wasn't long enough.

That feeling beneath my skin had now become a raging inferno. The sense that I needed to move was strong but I still had no idea where the fuck I was supposed to go. The longer it lingered the more positive I became that the shit was personal.

If we were in the middle of an Op I could whittle shit down if I wasn't shown where the danger laid outright.

It's rare, but every once in a while my 'gift' likes to fuck with me and leave me guessing. In those cases I could usually work my way around to the truth but there were two things hindering me this time around.

One, I was absolutely certain that this had nothing to do with what we were dealing with here in regards to the traffickers and whatever hell Khalil was cooking up.

And two, my heart never stopped beating me to death this whole time, that's new. And since there's no one beyond these walls that I give a fuck about, the shit is confusing.

Had it been anyone here I would've seen the aura. That's some weird shit that I don't want to get into so I won't, but suffice it to say, I know it's not one of my family members. So who?

And why instead of the few seconds it usually lasts, has this shit stayed with me for hours? Maybe I was losing my mind, maybe the stress of the last few months was catching up to me.

That and being here where the old man had spent his life away from us. We never talk about it much, but I know we all feel his loss every day that we're here.

It was probably best that I don't think about that shit now, not with all the mystery still surrounding his death. But boy do I wish he was here.

I heard Dev before I opened my eyes and peeped up at him just as he reached my side. He towered over me with that look on his face I knew only too well. My time had run out.

"What's eating you bro?" That was not a passing question. I shoulda known one of them would corner me sooner or later. I'd seen that look Ty threw me when he came by with the baby earlier. Sometimes it sucks having brothers who knew me so well. Dev just might know me a little better than most.

I smirked at the realization that each of us had our mediator or handler if you will. When Ty loses his shit, Connor calms him down. When Con goes batshit crazy, Lo brings his ass back and vice versa.

When something gets in Zak's ass, Cord is the one to figure it out. With Cord, it usually takes all of us, and Devon and I have each other.

"I'm good." His 'don't fuck with me' glare said he didn't believe me one fuck. It wasn't like I could just brush him or any of them off, that shit doesn't work with this bunch.

Plus the truth is, had it been any one of them acting the way I am I wouldn't let up until I knew what was wrong with my brother.

There was another side to this thing as well, another reason for our extreme vigilance, and I would hate it if I was giving them reason to worry needlessly.

We've known way too many of our fellow servicemen and women who took their lives when shit got too tough.

PTSD is nothing to play around with, and we've all been each other's therapist in one way or the other over the years.

Used to be there was a stigma attached to anyone who admitted to having that shit. Some people had lost their tridents, career ended, all because they sought a little help to keep the demons at bay.

I think it's another reason we worked so well together in the field and back here at home. Lo would never let any one of us hide that shit, and neither did the commander when he was alive.

It wasn't always easy to sense that shit in others, but being as close as we are, always in each other's space, it would be damn near impossible to keep that shit hidden for long.

So far we've all been spared but it could happen to anyone at anytime. I guess the fact that the seven of us came from fucked up beginnings shielded us a bit. Maybe that's the reason the CO put us together way back when, who knows.

My brother looked tired, we all did I'm sure. Things have been moving kinda fast in some aspects of our lives and still others were dragging ass.

Our lives seem to be on a constant wheel of change. Now that Dev and I are the only ones left standing since Cord took the plunge, I think we've both upped our over-protectiveness a couple notches.

We'd both decided that it was our job to pick up the slack now that the others had women with children on the way and Zak already having Zakira.

Of course we didn't share this with them, it was an unspoken deal between the two of us. We're both very protective of the happiness behind these walls and would do anything to see that our family stays safe. But the truth is none of us could've expected the rate in which that family would grow.

It wasn't hard accepting these women into the fold, the guys had all chosen well thank fuck. If they'd ended up with undesirables we'd of course have made it work, but it was good that we all got along as well as we do. The way we live on top of each other it would've been hell if they weren't a perfect fit.

I've watched them form a bond, my five sisters, and I know that that's a big part of the reason why things run so smoothly here. I'm sure my brothers pay such things no attention whatsoever.

For them it's just a given that their women would get along. They won't ask, more like demand if it came to that. But from the beginning the easiness between them was almost as strong as the one between us men.

I wasn't surprised either by the strength of the love my brothers bore their women. I know we're all passionate men, so how could they be any other way.

But the swiftness still left my head spinning, and has

my mind going in directions it ought not to. I don't ever see myself in that happy position, no matter how in weaker moments I may wish it.

Nonetheless I'm exceedingly happy for all of them and though none of them have made it down the aisle as yet, as far I'm concerned they're as good as married.

I don't see any ring or piece of paper making them any closer than they already are. I'm sure my brothers already consider themselves married, even if the women were always knee deep in wedding plans.

I don't think we're gonna have to wait too long on the whole ceremony brouhaha anyway no matter what the hell else is going on. From all the grumbling around here lately, it appears the girls had taken about all they were gonna take on that front.

I'm afraid if something doesn't give soon, there will be hell to pay. And on that thought, I finally sat up and gave him an answer.

"Nothing Dev, I just feel…off. Like that feeling you get before the other shoe drops." He clapped me on the shoulder and took a seat next to me. "You wanna go for a run?"

Yeah, maybe some more physical exercise might clear my head. Somehow I didn't think so though, and besides I didn't feel like leaving the grounds, not until I got a handle on things. Not until I was sure where the danger lay.

"No, I don't want to leave the others unattended. I need to stay close to home today." That was the only thing I was sure of. Which only added to my unease. I couldn't see the threat, but I knew it was close to home. I won't leave them unprotected.

My brothers had their attentions divided between ending the threat posed my the Desert Fox and their pregnant women. I can do no less than to stand guard over all of them. To stand between them and whatever was coming behind this thing that's plaguing me.

He didn't question me, but I could see the worry in his eyes. I hated that more than anything. Everyone else was holding their shit together under pressure.

If this shit chose now to act up, I don't know what the fuck I would do. Unless it gave me some answers soon I just might lose my fucking mind.

It had never left me hung out to dry before, and that's where the fear came in. Because I couldn't see the danger this time, just sense it as it drew nearer, it basically had me by the balls.

Even though I'd nixed the idea of leaving the compound I did need a change of pace. I needed even more to erase that look from Dev's eyes.

"What did you guys have for lunch?" I changed the subject in a bid to get his mind off of me. "Never mind that, make this the last time you leave me alone with that bunch."

From the look on his face I knew he was talking about our new sisters. It was enough to lift the gloom and make me bark out a laugh.

“What happened? Did the wittle girlies scare the big bad sailor boy?”

“Fuck off!” He punched my shoulder which only made me laugh harder. Seems that none of us can escape the women.

Each one of us, whether we’d admit it or not, have a healthy fear of the girls when they band together on one of their schemes. There was no need to guess what they’d done to him to put that look on his face.

“It was brutal bro.” He mock shivered and told me what the couples had been up to at lunch and how Lo had saved his ass just as the women started to go in on him.

“I’m dead ass brother, you cannot leave me to face that shit alone again. Our so called brothers are more than happy to throw my ass to the dogs as long as it keeps the heat off of them. If we’re not careful they’ll have us both in a noose before long so you can wipe that grin off your face.”

He was spot on with that one. Since we’re the only two left the women think it’s their sworn duty to marry us off. There’s no help from their men who are only too happy that their soon to be wives are on our asses instead of theirs.

Of course neither of us would say or do anything to hurt their feelings when they start their meddling shit.

Not only because Lo and Con would have our asses if we did. But because neither of us would hurt them for the world. But it can get pretty sticky sometimes when they get that bone between their teeth.

I can just imagine his flop sweat over lunch. Just as I can see Lo hightailing it out of there when they started in on the weddings.

It's just too damn funny, seeing my brothers in their new roles of husbands and family men. I'd seen each of them in battle mode and knew what they were all made of.

Now they were as soft as they were hard, but only when it came to their women. I never believed that such a thing could be possible. That hardened warriors could have it in them to be that… gentle.

Sometimes watching the interplay between them makes me wish for things I know I can't have. I wouldn't admit this to any of them, but I'm a little jealous.

I never thought I would want what they have, never believed I could have it. But they make it look so easy, so right. It's hard not to build dreams around 'what if'.

I'd been a loner for most of my life, until I met my brothers in fact. We were all so alike that it was easy to think our lives would always take the same path.

We thought we were happy as we were. It was enough to serve our country and stick together as we always did.

But I'd bet the guys would say they'd never known true happiness until they met their women.

I wouldn't blame them; it's obvious that the women had opened a new chapter in their lives and just when they needed it. Shit had got really heavy these last few years. It seemed like the more evil we fought, the more cropped up.

Now it looked like some of the men we'd trusted to have our backs were dirty as fuck. For men who'd already seen the worst the world had to offer, it was just another knock.

So having the softness of a good woman could only help I guess. And so far the five of them seemed to be happier and the women at least took their minds off all this other shit if only for a while.

It had been just us for so long though I had begun to think none of them would ever get married and settle down.

They never showed an interest, and that was the part that keeps me looking over my shoulder. Ever since we moved to this town, it seems you don't have to go looking for love, the shit just finds you. And it's been finding them at an alarming rate.

We'd made a pact never to marry while we were still in, which had made the question null and void. We had a good reason for making that promise to each other.

After seeing what being away from their wives and

children had done to some of our colleagues, not to mention what it does to you when you have to tell someone that their loved one wasn't coming back. None of us wanted to have to do that to each other. Too fucking heartbreaking.

So I'd been perfectly fine with the way things were, just me, and my six brothers. We'd started a business just like we'd planned and thanks to the CO we had this place where we could all live together like we'd wanted after retirement.

For the first year things had stayed the way they always were. And then the guys started getting shanghaied.

I have to admit that they make this being in love shit look good. With our track record it stands to reason that one day I'll be joining the ranks of the whipped and clueless just like the rest of them, seeing as how we all seem to follow one another in whatever venture is on the menu. But that won't be for a long-long time if ever.

Although this kind of happiness wasn't in the works for me any time soon, I was happy for my brothers. Because of them I had more family than I ever expected to have, including a niece that already owns my heart. I'll let that be enough for now. As long as they were happy I could deal.

Some people may not understand our bond, but my

mother couldn't have birthed a son that would mean more to me than these men that I've served with.

Ours is a bond I'm sure will never be broken no matter what. I never had that with any of my so-called relatives in the past. And that was part of the glue that held us all together. The thing that had made us as close as we are today.

Each of us had our own fucked up childhood story to tell. And we'd all found what we needed in our little makeshift family. Nothing was going to change that, and if our family was growing, then so much the better.

After taking my mind off of my worries for a minute, regaling me with the exploits of the rest of the family, Dev left. "I got shit to do bro, can't hang around here with your lazy ass all day."

I gave him the finger as he got up to leave and watched him jog back the way he came. Huh, that was easy but I'll take it. It's not every day that one of them leaves shit alone, like dogs with a bone every last one of them.

That's part of who we are, we look out for one another even if it means crossing certain boundaries. Then again we have none, not when it comes to each other.

9

QUINN

I let myself relax now that I had dodged The Spanish Inquisition, and thought of what we had left to do before we could head out. There was no telling how long we would be away, but hopefully it wouldn't be for too long.

This thing seemed to have a long fucking reach though, and with the tangos involved, there was no telling where this mess would go before it was all said and done.

I hated that my family's lives were put on hold, because of outside interference. It's funny that the one thing we had promised each other, had avoided so effortlessly the last ten years or so, had come back to bite us in the ass.

We never wanted any woman we chose to have to go through the horror of war, of having to wait for their man to come home. Never knowing if he would indeed be coming back. Now they're stuck in the middle of something dark and ugly because someone, an old nemesis, had brought the war to us.

If I could stand in front of this, protect them from it, I would do it in a heartbeat. But now the situation had spread beyond anything we could've imagined right here in our homeland, and right in our own backyard to boot.

If we were the types to do half ass jobs then sure it would've been over from the moment we suspected that our CO had been murdered. But we've had to put our own personal need for vengeance aside for the greater good.

There was a very serious evil being perpetrated beneath our noses and I know that like me, my brothers hadn't fought for our country just to have assholes pulling that shit on our turf.

It's not easy holding back and not just going in and taking out the ones we already knew were guilty. But if we got this shit wrong we had more than each other to think about. The backlash if we struck and missed would be horrendous.

It's obvious that Khalil chose the old man's hometown to do his dirty deeds as a fuck you to him and us. But there had to be more to it, something we're missing.

There were too many better options for him and his cohorts to use to run their human trafficking ring, so why here? Why such a hard on for the CO? It was personal, but why? How?

It would be easy to take it at face value that he was just sore about the old man always sending a team to fuck with his shit. But we'd gone after others before and after him and never before has the shit followed us back here.

And that was another worry. How the fuck did he ever find out who we were? Or who the CO was for that matter? That right there was the kicker, the thing that made it so easy for us to accept Mancini's offer.

It was obvious that we'd been compromised. SEALs don't even talk about the fact that they're SEALs. We don't even really talk about a job after it's done, because the shit that our team was called on to do was always top secret.

Countries could be destroyed, regimes toppled if our lips got too loose. Then we'd have one of our own coming after us to silence us.

That's one of those things that those in the know like to keep as well hidden as possible. That's how we know that Khalil had help from the inside. Someone who was close to the old man as well as others in high places.

It's not going to be easy taking care of them all without setting off an international fuck storm, but I won't stop until we do it. I'm not about to let them win, fuck that.

I sat up when I heard footsteps headed my way. I should've known when Dev walked away that easily that something was up. When he came back with the others in tow I wasn't surprised.

"Let's go I hear a run is in order." Lo held his hand out and pulled me up from my perch on the steps. I eyed the rest of them as they lined off behind him in the 'don't fuck with me' pose. Arms folded, legs spread, and a scowl.

"Couldn't keep your mouth shut could you?" Dev shrugged his shoulder at me and we turned to follow the others. "Come on, a nice run on the beach will do you good. Plus it would give us a chance to see what, if anything is going on down there."

"I could've sworn I turned down this offer." I scowled at Dev but he of course ignored me. "Stop bitching brother you know the drill. One of us is off all of us are fucked. Here comes the handler." He moved ahead as Con took his place beside me.

There was no point in arguing so I just fell in beside Connor as we headed for the gate. I guess he got stuck with babysitting duty. They must think I'm really fucked if they were siccing him on me. Lo is our fearless leader in all things military, Con is the one who deals with the more personal disruptions.

"What about the women?" I looked over at him as we

jogged out of the yard and headed for the water that was a mere hundred or so feet away. Damn that felt good.

"They're fine. Davey's with them and everything's on lockdown. If anyone gets too close the silent alarm would warn us don't worry." The truth is I knew that without asking, but this feeling of impending…something, was fucking with my rationale.

We jogged along the beach going in the opposite direction from where we knew the tunnel ended. No one watching would have the first clue that we even knew that shit existed, but it was broad daylight and we didn't want to seem too obvious. On the way back we'd be able to see what if anything was going on down that end.

There were a few locals getting some sun, most of whom waved or said hello as we passed by. That was a vast difference from the welcome we'd received when we first relocated here.

They didn't know what to expect from seven bike riding tattooed men who were built like trucks and always had a stern expression on their faces.

Thankfully the old man had had a few pals here who took it on faith that if the CO had left us his place then we must be the salt of the earth, as he was.

They'd blazed the trail to the others accepting us and now with four of my brothers marrying local girls it was pretty much a cinch.

We even stopped and had a quick chat with a few who

knew and were constantly asking about the goings on down by the pier at night, but as usual we played it down.

A few of the old timers had almost got themselves in trouble by trying to tackle the suspicious activities in the past and we'd made a promise to protect them from themselves.

We just gave them the company line that we were on top of it and will let them know when or if we found anything. That seemed to satisfy them and we went on our way.

Connor went back to lecturing my ass and the sweet burn in my legs was welcomed. It had been too fucking long since we'd taken the liberty of a good hard run.

I was beginning to relax a little. The breeze from the water, the sun shining down in all its magnificent glory and Con talking shit next to me as we pounded the sand was working.

It was good to feel the sea air on my face as we ran flat out. It had been a while since we'd come down here for anything other than a stake out.

We had all this beauty right in our own backyard and hadn't really had the time to enjoy it before this shit fell on us.

Most of my sisters had grown up here and this was a luxury they'd freely enjoyed in the past. Now because of their entanglements with my brothers they couldn't even step foot out their front door without an armed guard.

It was getting to me so I can only imagine how the others felt, having to curtail their women's movements. And since the women's last attempt at mutiny I'm sure they won't be seeing outside again for a while.

Hopefully this place Mancini was dragging us off to would allow them some freedom, especially little baby Zak.

My poor niece was being held hostage by these fucks and she wasn't even two years old yet. I'm fucked if anyone's gonna fuck up her childhood the way mine had been.

Nope, better not go there now either, my insides were fucked up enough as it is, no need to add fuel to the fire by dwelling on just how pissed I am about the situation we were in.

The mood was light and I could hear my brothers ragging each other as per usual. Ty the runt was popping off shit about stamina and old men. Cord tripped his ass in the water causing him to cuss a blue streak, which was good for a round of laughs.

And then we turned around and headed back the way we came, facing the location of the tunnel, and a tight fist wrapped around my heart and squeezed.

"Quinn." I looked up at Con's shocked voice as I bent over with my hands on my knees and tried to catch my breath. It felt like I was about to fucking die.

I shook my head because I couldn't speak and for

some unknown reason there were tears gathered in my eyes. My skin felt hot and my head swam, my vision blurred in and out.

Something had me in its grip and had I been a lesser man I would've been scared as fuck. I looked toward the tunnel and the direction of the house we'd raided just a few short months ago, which now felt like years.

There were too many people laying about so once the others gathered around us I kept my unease to myself. "It's nothing guys, just a little winded."

Their eyebrows went up because they knew to a man that this was little more than a walk in the park for any of us. Lo shook his head when Ty started to question the truth of my words.

Like a bull in a China shop, Ty isn't very good with subtleties. And when he got worried as he so obviously was now, his patience tends to fray.

It was burning a hole in his tongue I could tell, but he held in whatever it was he wanted to say. Of course Lo gave Connor who stepped in beside me the 'look' as we started running again, back towards the compound.

Con glanced at me and away. "You've got 'til end of day." I knew what that meant. I'm surprised he was letting me slide that long. But what the hell was I going to tell him, them?

I don't even know what the hell this is myself. Ergo my reason for avoiding them, which I was doing a fine job of until asshole Dev had to open his trap. This shit made me unfit for any kind of company.

Shit, and we're expecting the others soon. For the past two days we've been waiting for Lyon to make up his mind whether or not he was gonna make the move or not.

I guess he wasn't as malleable as the mafia don thought. In the few conversations we'd had with him in the last few days, in between the 'what the fucks' he'd let it be known that he wasn't pleased with the idea of running like a bitch as he put it.

Mancini had tried talking some sense into him, but that didn't work. Now he was on his way there to drag him out of his cave. Good luck with that.

It's a good bet that no one gets Colton Lyon to do shit he wasn't inclined to. He may not have served in any military service, but he has the heart of a true warrior. Natural instinct I guess.

Thinking about his shit helped to clear my mind and ease the racing of my heart a bit. I knew that whatever this was, my brothers had my back, but I didn't want to drag them down with me.

"Is it a vision?" I thought he said I had 'til end of day? I shook my head, not quite ready to try to explain. Always before I could tell them exactly what I was seeing. This time I wasn't seeing shit, just feeling. What the fuck was I supposed to do with that?

"I didn't think so, you would've said. You're not sick,

we were all cleared last checkup. Any ideas?" Dammit. If I tell him to leave it the fuck alone he'd only get the others involved, that or knock me on my ass.

Plus none of us were ever any good at keeping our noses out of each other's shit. "Nah, I can't get a bead on it. I know it's not one of us, that's all I know." I didn't tell him that it was someone close to me though, because who the fuck can that be?

We made it back home and the feeling let up a little but didn't evaporate as we went back to getting shit ready to leave later tonight when the others showed up, if they ever came.

I was sure of one thing now though. Whatever was fucking with me had something to do with that tunnel. I'd put bank on it.

10

KELLY

I feel sick. Whatever they'd injected me with had a nasty lasting side effect and left a horrible taste in my mouth.

I was able to see the others now and my heart sank. They'd brought us to a house and locked us in a room chained together against the wall.

The smell of fear was heavy in the room. Someone had peed on themself and there was a scent of feces as well in the air.

The girls were all my age or younger, most of them looked to be no more than fourteen or fifteen. My mind reeled with all the implications of this.

I didn't know anyone here, but we all had one thing in common; dread. It was written on the faces of each and every one of us.

I looked around the room, no one was saying anything, but it wasn't hard to guess what they were thinking. I fought back the fear and tried to remain calm.

There's never any situation you can't get yourself out of if you use your head. My daddy taught me that, in fact it was like a mantra for him when I hit my teen years and was allowed out of the house without his or mom's supervision.

"Does anyone know why this happened or where we are?" I kept my voice low so that it didn't carry outside the room. I was amazed that it hadn't shook with fear and nerves.

I'd already made up my mind that I was going to take control. From the looks of my companions they were all too scared to think straight. Or so I thought.

"How the fuck should we know? Aren't we chained here just like you?" A hiccup followed that outburst from one of the younger girls. She looked Latina, about fifteen and beautiful.

She was too pretty to be here facing this horror, they all were. What a strange thought. Why is it that we never think shit should happen to beautiful people? Save that one for later Kelly. Now is not the time to pick apart stupid shit.

"You don't have to bite her head off, she was just asking." One of the others answered but the fear in her voice was evident.

I wish I had something to say that would make the situation better, but the first girl was right. We were all in the same predicament, so unless I had a solution there was no point in asking unanswerable questions. Something else my daddy had taught me.

I looked around the room for anything that could be of help, but it was depressing. We must be in a basement because there were no windows.

"I heard one of them talking when they thought we were asleep." I turned in the direction of this new voice. She was an attractive girl about my age. Frail stature with wide eyes and a look of innocence that was rare these days. The words pampered princess came to mind.

"What did he say?" I turned to her as much as my chained body would allow. "He said something about having to use a different safe house and that the place was hot so they'd have to be careful. And then something about a tunnel."

She shivered after imparting those words and though they shed no new light on our predicament, at least it gave me something to think about instead of dwelling on the fear that was now threatening to choke me.

I found myself wanting to remember everything as if one day soon I'd be telling this unbelievable story to someone else.

I guess that comes from living in this age of technology where people would rather video record something than step in to help. We've all learned to disassociate from reality. Because surely this couldn't be my life.

I tried moving her words around in my head to make sense of them, but in the end it was no use because I still didn't know where we were.

We'd arrived here under cover of night and had exited the truck in some underground garage and led straight here to this room.

The water and sandwich they'd placed beside me was still untouched and will stay that way unless they force fed it to me.

My mind flashed to my family and what they must be going through, but as with all the other times that happened, I brushed it aside. I had to think. Now was not the time to get lost in despair.

My daddy had been and will always be a navy man and he'd taught me how to protect myself. All I need is a chance any chance and I'll take it.

I already knew there was no way out of the thick iron chains they had around my wrist and ankles so I will have to use my wits.

When the door opened and one of our captors entered, it burnt a hole in my tongue not to call out and demand to know where I was and why I was here.

That was the female in distress thing to do, it was

natural. My daddy didn't raise no female, he raised a fighter.

I struggled to remember everything I'd learned about being in this situation. Most of it was common sense so it wasn't too hard, though a heavy dose of Sun Tzu wouldn't hurt.

There were only but so many avenues opened to me here however. Usually I'd go with know your enemies but that one wasn't going to work here since I didn't know how long I'll be here or how many of them they were.

My other favorite is attacking my enemy's alliance with his friends, but that wasn't going to work here either so I was gonna have to wing it.

I didn't waste my time even as the others around me asked all the questions that were stuck in my gullet. Instead I watched the man whose face was half covered by a bandana.

He was maybe four inches taller than I. Short by male standards since that would only put him at about five foot seven to my five-three. He wasn't overly muscular but he wasn't scrawny either. In short he looked nonthreatening.

It doesn't matter. I've thrown men twice his size, no sweat. When he growled at the girls to shut up I caught his accent and tried to place it.

Definitely American, from somewhere in the mid-west. I forced myself to relax when his eyes finally landed in my corner.

I could see from the way his eyes crinkled that he was smiling behind the cotton he had covering the lower half of his face.

I had the urge to move back even closer to the wall to escape his leer but forced myself to stay still. I dug my nails into my palms, which were out of his line of sight.

I didn't hold his gaze for long but instead stared down at my lap. It wasn't wise to stare down a wild animal in these types of situations lest they interpret it as a challenge.

I didn't flinch when he came to stand next to me; a size nine shoe or there-about. Scuffed work boots, brown. Jeans frayed at the edges and covered in grease stains.

"Why you ain't eat that sandwich girl?" If this were an old western this fool would've spat a wad of chewing tobacco on the ground.

Instead he pushed the paper plate closer with his boot. I fought my baser instinct to tell him to go fuck himself. Asshole!

I reached my chained hand out and lifted the bread and whatever was in the middle of it to my lips still without acknowledging him. Leave him guessing.

He might have the upper hand when it came to the physical right now, but I'm sure I could take this dolt in the thinking game with half my brain cells on idle.

I took soft bites and spent an inordinate amount of time chewing. If I ate any faster I'd throw up and no way am I going to show any kind of weakness in front of this jackass.

"Cat got your tongue girl? I know you can talk, I heard you scream. Or maybe that's the only way you know how to communicate."

He knelt and reached out as if to touch me. Now here you'd be tempted to glower this asshole into oblivion… and I can't believe the things I'm thinking at a time like this.

Instead of the bitch brow that I'm famous for, I gave him a smile. Not a come hither, not that of a simpleton; but one designed to make him wonder if I'm about to give him the ride of his life or take his nuts and feed them to the dogs.

He got the message alright. And in the split second where he forgot that I was chained and couldn't get at his inbred ass, he was the one moving back. What a sitzpinkler!

I didn't smirk at him in victory, but went back to slowly chewing whatever it was I was eating. I couldn't taste anything beyond the fear. Daddy where are you?

He'd always taught me that no matter what no matter where, he'd always come and get me. I never stopped believing him. Now would not be the time to start.

Graduate of the year finally remembered that he was the one with the upper hand and tried to regain some footing by acting tough, but I'd already seen him flake.

He'd cowered before a chained female. I knew it and he knew it. Weak!

I refused to look at him and instead pretended great interest in my food while he searched for something to say.

I ignored every word that came out of his mouth. There was no rule saying I had to talk to this cuntbucket. Oh dear heavens, now I'm beginning to sound like my daddy. I could almost hear him saying, 'give him hell honey, until I get there.'

"You won't be so high and mighty when the big man gets you." That one got my attention. The big man. So they were taking me to someone in particular. To be sold, ransomed?

Daddy had never shielded me from too much. Whatever he could share in fact from his time in active service, he'd shared with mom and I. So I knew there were some people out there who might have it in for him.

Although he never shared names and places, he always made sure we knew that although he'd made our world as bright, loving and safe as it was, there was another element that existed right outside our door.

My daddy isn't the most trusting guy in the world. Everyone is suspect until he no longer thought so. I'd have to say mom and I were about the most well prepared females for all man-made disasters because of that.

We knew every martial arts technique, or most of

them, not to mention Krav Maga, which was pretty much all you needed to kick major ass if your hands weren't chained to a wall.

Asshole in chief had a lot to say and some of the others started weeping softly. The more they cried the more pissed off I became, which was good. I'm gonna need that when I kick his ass.

While he was focused on them I studied the hallway beyond the door he'd left open. I couldn't hear anything beyond these walls and no one was moving around out there.

Had they left him alone as watchman? That might work in my favor. If I could talk him into removing my chains to go the bathroom maybe… but he can't be that damn stupid. And even if I overpowered him, what about the others? I can't leave them here chained up like dogs.

No, until I knew where the others were I couldn't make a move. I pushed the chewed bread into my cheek with the rest to spit out as soon as he was gone. How was I to know if he'd drugged it or not?

I brought my attention back to him as he taunted the already scared young girls like the bully he was. With each word he exposed more and more of his weakness to me.

The others may not realize it, but I knew that any grown man who had to go to that much trouble to instill fear in already traumatized females was nothing more than a scared gutless douche nozzle. Without the chains he probably wouldn't have dared step foot in here.

One thing was certain, this was not their first time bringing girls here. The chains were very secure and were made especially to fit smaller wrists and the room had obviously been occupied before. But it was also the ease with which they'd carried out the operation that said they were naturals.

I took all this in as he returned his attention to me and tried to get me to react. I gave him another look this one a more vapid rendition of the first.

No trouble here sir. I'm just dumb with fear. Asshole! If my hands were free I'd rip his balls off and feed them to him. I guess he felt his manhood was intact which is what I wanted him to think as he turned and walked away.

The room was quiet as he left and the tension thick. Someone whimpered in her throat and yet another tugged at her chains in vain.

"Don't do that, you'll only hurt yourself. Save your energy." I directed my statements to the young innocent looking girl who looked like she just wanted to be home in her bed, safe.

"Energy for what? Don't you get it? These men are traffickers we're never going to get out of this." The Latin queen answered me again and I nodded.

"That might be half true, they may be traffickers, but we're not out of the fight yet." I didn't say any more just then because I had to think. If it were just me I could concentrate on myself, but there were others here younger than I, I'm not leaving them behind. Not if I can help it.

11

KELLY

~

We were there for hours getting to know one another between bouts of fear and tears. The tough Latin queen from before turned out to be the softest when she broke.

All she wanted was her mother and all I wanted was to get across the room so I could put my arms around her and offer comfort.

The waiflike kid never stopped whimpering but no one told her to shut up because we all knew what she was feeling. I was suddenly more upset for them than myself.

They were still so young, some of them no more than babies. What the fuck did these sick fucks want with them? As if I didn't know.

"Let's exchange names and hometowns in case we get separated." I kept my voice steady so they wouldn't know

I was afraid. One of us had to be strong for the others and it appears that was gonna be me.

"What good's that gonna do?" It was the Latin queen again. I looked at her with steady eyes.

"Because we're getting the fuck outta here one way or the other. And if I get separated from any of you I wanna know who I'm looking for then maybe that could give me some idea of where to look."

I saw the flash of hope before she buried it. I know morale is just as important as physical strength so I kept at it. "Now we're all gonna use our heads and think. Whatever you were before today, whatever your thinking, we're in this together."

"If one of us escapes then we need to know what to tell the cops. Best case scenario we all make it out together." Good, now they weren't looking so beaten and the snivels from the other corner had stopped. Well kinda.

My adrenaline was kicking in and I just knew I wasn't gonna die today. There were five of us in that room. I don't know how, but somehow I'm gonna get us all out of this.

All I needed was that one chance. I guess mom is right, I am my father's daughter as she's always accusing me of whenever I get what she calls 'difficult'. Bring it on motherfuckers.

"So go ahead." I got the little lights of hope that I'd been aiming for from the younger girls. The other one who was about my age gave me a look like she wanted so badly to believe, but she knew it was bullshit. I warned her with my eyes not to say anything and she looked away dejected.

The more I listened to them the more stern my resolve grew. I wasn't meant to die this way. I had things to do, dreams to fulfill.

I'll be damned if Ricky Jarvis groping me in the funhouse on our seventh grade field trip was going to be my one and only foray into sex-land.

Poor Ricky had gotten a bloody nose for his troubles and I'd come away with a healthy distaste for anything male. Pig.

More time went by and the fear was now mixed with anxiety. After listening to the others I knew there was a pattern here; that this hadn't been by chance. They were all daughters of men or women who'd served.

I didn't mention my suspicions to the others, but I was ninety percent sure this had something to do with daddy and his service. If he knew someone was after him there was a good chance he'd know where to look for me.

I comforted myself with that thought, but knew it was a long shot. If he'd known he'd have kept me under lock and key.

I scanned the room once more for anything, any way out. Since there were no windows the only light came from the sliver that leaked through beneath the door from the one out in the hallway. I hadn't shared my plans to try an escape with the others, but I was on the lookout for any opportunity.

I heard the drone of voices out in the hallway and strained to listen. All I got was something about a trip to California but they could've been talking about a vacation for all I know.

The next time I heard the key in the door I knew this was it. I braced myself and prepared for whatever. A few hours had gone by so it might be night outside, and since they were worried about this safe house, maybe they were in a hurry to move us.

There were two of them this time, the second one built much bigger than the other. I concentrated on working the kinks out of my hands and feet to get the blood flowing again once freed, and winced at the pain.

I felt hot and sticky and I needed a bathroom break like yesterday but didn't want to bring unnecessary attention to myself by asking. I was amazed when they actually offered before leading us out into the hallway.

The men stood outside the door while we took turns in the stall that had been set up like that of a girl's middle school restroom.

Not many houses with that little attachment I'm sure, something else to make note of. I took a deep breath and psyched myself up to be ready for anything as it became obvious that we were indeed on the move once again.

If I thought I was afraid before, nothing prepared me for what I felt when we stepped from what felt like a hundred foot tunnel into darkness and smelt sea air.

That could mean only one thing; we were leaving the country most likely by ship. Well that puts a different spin on things.

QUINN

After our run we went back to getting things together so we could leave. Each of us had a duty to perform to make sure that the compound was secure.

It had been getting dark out when we decided to do a last walk through of the mansion and that's when Cord found a book with codes. Codes that only the seven of us, and the man who wrote them would understand. I took the book and moved to the secure computer with the others following behind.

It was a bit of a shock to see the words as they unfolded on the screen. Not just the meaning, but it was like hearing from the old man again. Like he was reaching out from beyond the grave and the eight of us were going to work on this last job together. I knew my brothers felt pretty much the way I did, gut punched.

The codes only left us with more questions than answers and now we were left wondering who the people the commander mentioned were. We were pretty sure the 'he' was the Desert Fox but had no clue who the 'she' that he asked us to protect could possibly be.

That made the shit worst. If the old man was going to such lengths to protect her identity then she must be of importance to what was going on here.

At least we knew now that the CO had definitely known about what was going on-on the water and had been making moves to put a stop to it. He wasn't dirty, like some had tried to make us believe.

Not that any of us believed that shit for a minute. The old man was made of better stuff than to be on the wrong side of this sick shit.

He also knew about the tunnel that we'd found, he'd got that far. After the shock of finding the codes had worn off it was decided that we would blow the tunnel and put it out of use instead of waiting. We set the time for later tonight and went back to work.

I needed a hot shower to wash the cobwebs from my head but that shit wasn't about to happen any time soon. There was a new urgency in the air now too, like we didn't already have enough on our plate.

There was some talk about how to deal with the

women when it came time to leave as we wound down from the day. Five grown men were now brainstorming on how to control their women just so we could leave and take care of business. It was good for a laugh at least, listening to them talk.

They still believed they were the ones running shit. One good thing about being stuck babysitting my sisters is that it's given me an inside look at how their minds work. When it comes to the fight between the sexes, my money's on the women hands down.

The talk switched somehow to whose woman was the most trouble and who had the most control over their respective mate. Devon and I shared a grin and just shook our heads.

In my mind I was thinking, 'look at them. They're so funny these brothers of mine.' They haven't got a clue.

I listened with a smile on my face as Tyler got the rest of them going with his shit. Since I'm the sucker they've been leaving stuck here with the women more often than not, I could tell them they're full of shit, but why bother? It's more fun watching them tear their hair out.

Ty is the funniest one of all. Mr. Big-shot is as whipped a motherfucker as I've ever seen. Though he's still deluding himself that he's the one in control.

Poor Dev and I have been trying our best to keep the peace while the rest of them lose their damn minds, and I for one, am praying that my day don't come no time soon.

On the one hand, it would be great to finally have what my brothers have found, that shared love and affection that's so evident between them and their chosen women. But then I think of the headaches each and every one of them has to deal with and I back the hell off.

"You listening to this shit?" Dev came up beside me to watch the show.

"Look at the shit eating grins on their faces bro. You think we'll ever have that?" I didn't miss the hint of longing in his voice. Like me, he hides it well, but I imagine he might be feeling the need every once in a while too.

"You feeling the urge brother?" I looked at him out the side of my eye. I wonder if he'd notice that I skirted his question. The truth is no matter what goes on in my mind, I'm not completely sure.

Sometimes I find myself on the fence. Out of nowhere I'd get that burning urge for a woman of my own. And every time baby Zak lays her little head on my chest, I want one of her too. That's when Ty lets any of us near her; damn baby hog.

"I'm not sure that's for me brother." I hated the ring of sadness in his voice. We all knew where each of us came from, the shit we'd endured as kids, so I knew why he might feel that way. It was okay for me to feel that way about myself but not my brother.

Of all of us, he needed someone to love and be loved

most. Whereas the rest of us had had shitty or neglectful parents, except for Ty who'd lost his mom tragically, Dev's story was a horror. It hurt me to the core to hear him say such a thing.

"You're wrong brother, it's because of what you suffered that you'd be the perfect husband and father." There was such a look of hunger in his eyes that it was a shock that I'd never noticed it before.

Oh he wanted this alright. I also knew his stubborn ass would fight it with every breath in his body because he didn't think he deserved it. Or that somehow he wouldn't live up to his responsibilities which is bullshit.

Now that I'd seen that look, I'm going to make it my mission in life to see that he never lets the opportunity slip through his fingers if it should arise.

I'd have to work on him first though because he can be a hardheaded son of a bitch. I knew just how to get him too. "If you don't do it then I won't either." He gave me one of his looks.

"Don't be an ass Quinn, you can't deny yourself happiness because of me I won't have it." He looked towards the others to be sure they weren't sticking their nose in.

"Fine then, it's settled, we'll both go for it. If asshole Ty can be domesticated I say we can too." The laughter lightened the heavy mood and we moved to join the others.

It was already going dark outside by the time we broke. “Whose place are we eating at tonight?” I liked this new arrangement. Before the women came it was a toss up as to what form of swill we’d be eating with each of us taking turns.

“Zak’s.” Ty with his greedy ass keeps track of these things. “Let’s go round up the girls, have dinner then we’ll go take care of the tunnel.” Cord with his newly whipped ass was almost out the door after that suggestion.

“Looks like the danger’s passed.” No one had to guess at what Logan was referring to as we watched Cord cross the yard.

“Thank fuck, you assholes need to calm the fuck down, too damn hyper. Next time one of you go the fuck off I’m putting something in your food.”

“Look who’s talking, Ty you’re full of shit.” Logan laughed at his misguided ass.

“What’re you talking about? I never acted like a caveman. Zak was damn near certifiable, Con was a bitch to live with and our fearless leader here had a strong case of PMS with his bitch made ass. Of course that one is fucking nuts so his shit is to be expected.” He pointed out the door at Cord. “But me, I was the only one who kept my cool. I never went full asshole.”

“You’re also the only one who had to be medicated.”

Devon deadpanned and the rest of us howled with laughter, while Ty gave us the finger and stomped out the door. He had a point though. This last meltdown of Cord's was something I could do without for at least another week.

That's another thing about these new relationships my brothers are in. Not a day goes by that one of them isn't having to corral his woman for some misdemeanor or some shit, or losing their damn mind because of something their woman did, and the rest of us are left having to calm their ass down.

12

QUINN

~

"Get a move on, I'm hungry. Fucking women didn't let me eat today with their staring shit." Devon rubbed his gut and yawned.

"Now you know how I feel when I'm left riding herd on them."

We were walking the yard making sure shit was secure before we headed to dinner. Lo's over cautious that way especially with the girls here.

"We've got a long night ahead of us, I can feel it." I almost asked him what he meant but I was sure he was talking on the same level as the shit that's been messing with my ass.

"Had a lot of those lately."

"Yeah well I'm done with this fuckery. As old William

Shakespeare once said, I'm ready to 'cry havoc and let slip the dogs of war.' He all but growled at me.

Wonder what the hell crawled up his ass and died. He and his mercurial moods were nothing new to me, but this time I didn't have to think too hard to figure out what was bothering him.

Now that the laughter was gone it was back to the reality of what was staring us in the face. The codes I'd decoded earlier, and hearing from the CO even if it was just on paper, had fucked with all our heads I'm sure, even though we were holding it together for now.

No one had really said anything about it yet, but the fact that the old man knew something was coming at him and the new realization that we'd deliberately been kept apart when he needed us, is going to be heavy on all our minds for a while. We'd never let each other down before, and it kinda felt like we'd failed him when he needed us most.

When we thought he'd died of a heart attack it was barely acceptable, but knowing that some fuck had done him, none of us were going to rest until we avenged him.

Not to mention the fact that some asshole had sent us into a trap that was meant to end our lives when we were blind to all that was going on. Knowing Lo, they already had a target on their backs.

Everyday there's something new for us to muddle through and the hits just keep on coming. That shit's not easy when you don't know the rules of the game or the players. For every ten steps we take forward, we're pushed five back.

I had no doubt that just as in the past, we'd figure this one out together. But the shit was aggravating as hell. We're soldiers, we follow orders and get shit done.

There's always a trail to follow so we know there's a beginning and an end. This shit just seems to keep going around in circles.

But I should've known that beneath the laughter Devon was hurting. The old man had meant a lot to all of us, but there'd always been something special between him and Dev.

He'd been the hardest nut to crack believe it or not, the one the CO had spent the most time bringing into the fold. That hard shell he'd had wrapped around himself had taken a lot of long drawn out convos between the two men.

Not that we hadn't all spent our fair amount of time bending the old man's ear, but for Dev with the old man's passing it's as if he'd lost two fathers in one lifetime.

"You okay brother?" I looked ahead to the others as we walked in step.

"They fucking killed him. I wasn't sure, even after we suspected, I was never a hundred percent sure until I read that shit today."

"I know brother and we're going to fix it."

"When I find the motherfucker responsible for this treasonous bullshit I'm gonna hatefuck his ass with a Billy-club wrapped in sandpaper." Ouch. I clapped his shoulder as we moved to catch up to the others. "We'll take turns."

The only good thing to come of all this is that I hadn't been plagued with my new dilemma for a few hours now. At least these new developments were helping to keep my mind off my own shit.

This puzzle needs to be solved yesterday, but like I said, each time we think we've made progress, some shit else pops up and we're back to square one.

Ty is right about that too. I too have grown tired of feeling like we're going around in circles with this thing. Knowing the CO, whatever the fuck we're missing is right under our noses. He always did like to make us work for it.

I wasn't worried about us figuring shit out, but time was not our friend and lives were being destroyed. It was a sobering thought.

"It stands to reason that we're being watched. If the old man was in that deep, whoever's running this shit-show stateside will have us in their crosshairs." Devon continued as he flexed his shoulders and rotated his neck like he was ready, to spin up and go live.

There was still so much that we didn't know at this point that it was hard to make any definitive moves and that's the frustrating part. It's also a given that if we're being watched, they're already monitoring our communication, or trying to.

Not that they could follow our trail, but it pays to be super cautious until we knew more. And quite frankly this shit was bigger than us. We didn't have the navy behind us on this one.

I guess it was good that Mancini and the others were onboard. We have excellent resources, and our gear can't be hacked we made sure of that. But Mancini had proven that his shit was even better than ours, which is saying a hell of a lot.

For a 'civilian', Mancini's shit is ice and his resources seem to be never ending. His network plays beneath the radar and does not have to adhere to the same restrictions we did as military. From what we'd seen so far, his Intel wasn't too shabby either and this game is all about who knows what, when and where.

It's the first time we'd let an outsider get this close and now we have not only him, but Lyon, Law and Creed. The last two we've worked with before on an Op or two, but never before have we enlisted the help of unknowns. It was a testament to the mettle of these men that we'd even consider it.

He's also a loose canon, but not on the same par as Ty, he's too fucking smooth for that. Lyon, now he's a different story. I don't think he plays by anyone's rules and from what I've seen so far his shit makes Tyler's seem juvenile.

It's going to take a while to get a handle on our new friends, but so far they seem to fit right in with our motley crew of fuck-ups.

We crossed the yard in silence and met up with the others. I'm sure he put his game face on same as I did before we walked through the door.

It's an unspoken rule that we don't let any of this touch the women, and though Dev and I were the only ones left standing, that shit was as important to us as it was our brothers.

We're all responsible for the women and this shit ain't something they should be worrying about. Though unlike their men I happen to know they know way more than they let on. I guess Zak forgot that Vanessa was special Ops, or he's pretending to.

13

QUINN

~

Dinner was noisy as per usual and afterwards we sat around laughing and talking with the women while Ty was being his usual asshole self, keeping us all entertained with his antics.

We were just a family having an evening together with the baby being passed around or more like she was making the rounds, getting her hugs and kisses from all her aunts and uncles; fighting sleep. That kid hates bedtime.

Every once in a while my mind would remind me of what laid ahead of us tonight, what it meant, what it signified. Everything we do from here on out is for the old man it goes without saying.

Closing the tunnel the men were using to traffic the

women wouldn't put an end to their evil, but it would be a first step to stemming the flow of that shit in our own town.

We'd all fought for the freedom of others in other countries, I'm fucked if I'm going to see anyone enslaved in mine.

The fact that the waters off our own backyard were probably the last of their homeland these girls and women might see left a bitter taste in my mouth and a burning rage in my gut.

I turned it off and listened to the light banter between my family. Baby Zak and Ty were the stars of the show as usual, and was just what we needed before all hell broke loose in the next coupla days.

I listened with half an ear as the tingles in my gut came back full force as the night wore on. Thankfully I didn't have time to dwell as it was getting close to crunch time. I wonder what excuses the boys will use this time to get away from the women?

The girls started talking weddings and I knew it wouldn't be long before the exodus begun. Nothing gets my brothers moving faster these days than the women and their wedding plans.

Lo was getting ready to make the call when his phone rang. We all held our silence as he listened. These days every time the phone rings it's cause for action.

We were already heading for the door before the call

ended. Lo hung up and turned to the rest of us.

"Mancini, the others are here." Thank fuck, time to rock and roll.

We headed to the gate and watched through the security monitor as a caravan pulled up outside. I'd forgotten how many of them they were.

Lyon and his brood were first in line, followed by the only two men we'd known of this bunch before we were all thrown together.

Law and Creed had their women with them as was expected and then there was Mancini and a coupla unknowns. I listened to the men say hello in their own special way.

Which meant insults from Lyon and the usual ragging you can expect when grown men who had way too much testosterone got together.

The women and children went off to be with the others at Zak's place and the men fucked around with bullshit until Lo's phone went off again. He walked away to take the call but this time we knew there was nothing good on the other end of that call when he came back.

"That was our guy on the inside, something's going down. Quinn what the fuck?"

I'd been watching Logan as he came back toward us and something hit me in the gut.

This time I knew I couldn't ignore it any longer. I smelt something in the air, don't know what the fuck it was and since this was the first time I'd been hit by this phenomenon I didn't have time to investigate. The need to move was strong though, that much I knew.

"We have to go NOW." Cord said something about securing the women and took off as the others looked at me.

"What is it brother?" I looked at Dev but wasn't really seeing him.

"I don't know, something…" I ran flat out towards the beach not knowing why just knowing that something was calling me there.

My senses tingled and I could still scent that strange odor on the sea air. It wasn't something I could explain, but somehow I knew that I was the only one who could smell that shit.

There was no one on the beach as far as I could tell but the sense of danger was getting stronger. Only this didn't feel like the usual shit we'd get ourselves into. This shit felt personal. Every sense in my body had come alive and was on full alert.

"What's up bro?" I hadn't realized that I'd stopped until Ty asked that question. I still wasn't sure myself, but something inside me screamed to go into action and I felt my inner beast crouch ready to spring.

What the fuck? I actually envisioned that shit in my head. I shook my head to clear it as my brothers gathered around me. "What are you seeing Quinn?"

I didn't miss the looks that passed between the others that were not part of our team but now was not the time to be shy about my little anomaly.

"Something's going on. I've felt it since last night. No-no-no." I rushed to assure Logan when he looked back towards the compound.

"If anyone was in danger I would've said something before now. This, whatever this is, it's about me. I just don't know how or what."

"That's a stupid fucking thing to say. If it's about you it's about all of us. We'll talk about this shit later. Lead the way."

KELLY

Yep, we're on the beach. I smelt the water before my feet hit the sand once we cleared the tunnel. The fact that we weren't blindfolded was worrying; we weren't meant to come back.

I looked sneakily around for anything that could be of help while trying to keep an eye on the men who were leading us out.

There was no one on the beach at this time of night, but I understood why they hadn't shackled us again.

It was obvious that there were houses around in the distance and there was a chance some unsuspecting soul might come waltzing by.

The threats they'd made to silence us if we cried out may have scared the others but it was just the chance I was hoping for.

The farther away we walked from the tunnel the more I wanted to turn around and go back to my prison. I knew that whatever was waiting for me at the end of this trip was going to be worse than anything I'd faced so far.

It's strange, but I'd held it together this long and now all I wanted to do was break. I cried for my mom and dad and the fact that I may never see them again. I felt the loss as I stumbled on the sand causing one of the men to glare back at me in the moonlight.

There were more of them now but I didn't know how many since we weren't allowed to look around. I heard the soft whimpering cries of Cara, the Latina girl who'd melted enough to tell me that much earlier.

I tried telling myself that all those self defense classes my dad had taught me could not have been for nothing, that I was going to find a way to get us out of this; all of us.

I was ready to try anything as I glanced along the beach ahead of us one last time, and that's when I saw them. From this distance I couldn't make them out but I was sure someone was there.

We were headed in the opposite direction from where the people were coming from and I knew this was my only chance. If we got any deeper into the darkness and with the fog coming in, they'll never see us.

Without giving myself time to think I kicked out at the man closest to me, and started running towards the silhouettes in the distance. "Help!"

My screams got lost on the wind and I felt tears of fear and finality cloud my vision as one of my captors caught up to me and tried dragging me back.

I dug my heels in the sand, which wasn't the easiest thing to do and scratched and clawed at him in a bid to escape. I don't think the others had seen what I'd seen so the good thing was that they stopped their forward progress to watch instead of carrying on with the others in tow.

My legs almost gave out when I heard feet rushing our way but I didn't stop struggling against his hold. He too had seen the on-comers and I saw him struggle with the decision of whether to leave me and go or try getting me back there kicking and screaming.

My heart was beating too fast for me to think, but there was only one thing on my mind. I'd die here before I let him take me.

14

QUINN

After Lo gave me the go ahead, I set off down the beach in the direction of the tunnel. I looked through that hazy fog that sometimes settled on the beach at night trying to see anything, my senses leading the way.

My heart almost gave out when the moonlight shone through the fog for a split second and I saw something up ahead in the distance.

"What the fuck is that about over there?"

The guys stopped next to me and looked through the fog that was rolling back out, and we could now clearly see a man and a woman up ahead.

It was hard to tell from this distance if they were struggling or playing around, but something didn't feel right. My senses screamed and my lungs filled as I heard the word 'go' loud and clear coming from somewhere deep inside.

"What the fuck?" My feet started moving before my brain had time to send the message. My heart beat out of time and there was a strange ringing in my ear. Someone or something was screaming at me to hurry and there were tears in my eyes for the second time that day. What the fuck!

I heard my brothers and our friends behind me as we raced towards the scene but I was well ahead of the pack. It only took one look once I reached them for me to know that something was definitely wrong here, and I went into beast mode.

I kept my eye on the female, or rather the female form, since it was too dark to see the person that well. But I saw enough to size up the situation. That fire in my gut was a full on five-alarm blaze now as I moved in closer.

I literally wanted to break his fucking neck, could feel his flesh and bones beneath my hands; I think I heard the snap. Fuck me, I think my 'gift' had gone feral.

In reality I had moved in between them as much as I could and was pushing him back away from her. He refused to release his hold on her, but I could scent his fear.

"Hey asshole, let her go."

"Stay out of it this has nothing to do with you." He tried making his voice sound tough but he wasn't fooling anyone least of all me. He looked around as if expecting someone to come to his rescue, the girl meanwhile never stopped trying to get away from him.

"Fuck that hands off." My brothers had caught up by now and I had my hand in his chest pushing him back while trying to free the very obviously frightened young girl with the other.

Something, there was something about her, but I'm pretty sure I've never seen her before. My senses had gone into overdrive and my signals were all kinds of fucked up. I had the urge to hold her, this unknown girl, and the need to kill him.

I finally wrestled her away from him and kept my body between them facing her with my back to him, shielding her with my much larger frame. That scent was coming from all around her and though I still had no idea what it was, I understood the affect it had on me.

My vision swirled and I saw the world in color, bright vivid colors. There was a warmth beneath my skin that had nothing to do with the atmosphere. I shook my head to release myself from my thoughts, time to focus.

"What's going on here sweetheart, you know him?" Still couldn't see her that clearly but this time it was because her head was hanging as she rubbed her arms where he'd held her too tight I guess. I could see more of her now and a few things registered at once.

She was shaking, half naked and cold; and she was

tiny as fuck. Second, although they were well away from the tunnel when we caught up to them, I wasn't sure they hadn't come from there. I got a bad feeling in the pit of my stomach; that and rage, the likes of which I've never known.

My brothers and I have been staking out this place on the down low for a few months but the fuckers always seemed to be one step ahead of us, which was beyond frustrating.

We'd found the tunnel sure, but we had yet to see anyone using it. I wasn't sure if this had anything to do with that, but as far as I'm concerned even if this douche was her boyfriend he had no right to be treating her this way. And then she spoke.

"No I don't know him, he…he..." She retched and I barely jumped out of the way in time to avoid being puked all over.

"Hold him." I shouted to the others before I turned back to her and gave her the bandana from my back pocket to clean up. I removed my jacket and wrapped it around her shaking shoulders.

"You're going to be okay now, you're safe." My skin felt hot and itchy but I ignored it as I left her side again. "Stay here!"

I approached the asshole who was now surrounded by the others. "Who are you asshole and what were you doing with her?"

"She's my girlfriend."

"She doesn't know you-you lying fuck try again before I call the cops."

I had no intentions on calling the cops. I was more interested in snapping his fucking neck for putting hands on her. Again, what the fuck? I looked back at her and felt that burn under the skin shit happen again.

"The others." She started to run back in the opposite direction and I moved to stop her still without touching her. She'd been manhandled enough for the night. Still I had the strongest urge to put hands on her. Instead I concentrated on her words. "What others?" I looked in the direction she'd been headed in and only then saw the silhouettes that had been buried in the fog.

It looked like people were moving quickly away from us, but it's not that easy to run on sand unless you've had training. "We've got this, stay with her."

Mancini, Lyon, Law and Creed turned and headed down the beach moving swiftly and silently. The fool who'd been trying to drag her away was still making noises but I couldn't hear him any longer. No, my full attention was on her.

The moon had chosen to stop playing peekaboo with the clouds and fog and I could see more of her. The sound of my brothers' voices as they questioned the skell faded as if they'd walked away but I knew they hadn't they were still right there. My eyes were planted on her face, her eyes especially, and everything inside me settled for the first time in forever.

I moved towards her as if in a trance, leaving the asshole to my brothers. If I was fanciful I would believe there was something magical going on here, but even with my… whatever the fuck it is that happens to me, I'd never believed in this shit. I felt my knees weaken and my cock go on full throttle; this can't be real.

It was the family curse, that thing my old man had tried to snuff out of me until the state had taken me away after the last beating when he almost killed me.

I had a million thoughts go through my head as I stood there looking down at her in the moonlight and I felt new wetness gather in the corners of my eyes

Even as I felt it happening, as I felt that knowing like I'd known her my whole life, that feeling that we were meant, it made no sense. I'm a SEAL for fuck sake, I don't believe in this shit.

Okay the premonition shit I can't do anything about, that shit just shows up when it wants to, does its thing and moves the fuck on. But this, this was another ballgame altogether.

The legend ran through my head on a reel. It was believed that the men in my family not only had the 'gift' of second sight, but they were also cursed or blessed depending on which way you look at it, with the ability to know their mate on sight.

It was her that I'd been scenting, on the wind. Not her perfume if she was wearing any, but her skin, her natural pheromones.

I blocked out everything else, not that I had a choice. I was in the grip of something. That fear and uncertainty that had been riding me was no longer there, but the fire still burned; for a different reason this time.

Still I didn't believe, didn't want to believe. For a man like me who'd restructured his life, who'd trained himself to be a warrior, this was some fairytale bullshit. But I couldn't seem to stop myself from moving in. Up close and personal.

Knowing that she must still be scared out her fucking mind, I reached out my hand slowly, as you would when facing a cornered animal that had been taken down. As soon as my hand touched her electricity ran up my arm. "Fuck!" I jerked away in surprise and stared down at her.

She finally lifted her head and I saw her face more clearly for the first time. Sheer beauty stared back at me and something in me went in and out of time. I lifted my hand to her cheek and rubbed my thumb gently back and forth across her soft flesh. "Mine." The fuck?

It felt as if I was walking through Jell-O, nothing felt real. It was only when I dropped my hand from her face that the world came back into focus. This all happened in a matter of a few short seconds and when my head cleared a little the other's voices came back loud and clear.

Logan had the asshole in a headlock, pulling him back while I could hear the others making their way back. But I was more interested in what had just happened here. What the fuck was that?

I think I pushed her away from me, I can't be sure, but the next thing I knew she was stumbling and I caught her against me. That was all it took.

I picked her up in my arms and started heading for home at a dead run. I could hear as if from a distance Connor and Cord calling after me but I knew I couldn't stop. It was Logan who told them to stand down, he understood. I knew he did when I heard his muttered 'its about time' on the wind.

As usual, Lo knows the story only too well as he's in the habit of dragging shit out of us. Even things we try to keep hidden from ourselves. He's the only one who knows about this part of my 'gift', because the shit's too embarrassing to share with the others.

I ran away from them and back the way we came, carrying her lightweight like it was nothing. She didn't even question me, just clung to me with her face buried in my neck.

There was no longer any fear in her. Somehow I knew I would've felt it, sensed it. It was as if she knew too. I wasn't sure if she was supposed to. It's been a while since I'd heard the old legend, and much longer since I'd stopped believing in it.

I didn't take the time to explain my strange behavior, what would I say? Hey, I know we just met but I'm pretty sure you're my life mate? She'd probably laugh in my face.

It didn't matter anyway; I was no longer in control, whatever was inside me had taken over. Something had me in its grip, hard.

Everything in me, all my raw senses, were focused on one thing, her, getting inside her. Swear to fuck it was almost a compulsion. Having her this close wasn't helping as the protector in me warred with the animal that wanted to take her down on the nearest flat surface and mount her.

In the back of my mind I heard rational me asking this out of control beast what the fuck he thought he was doing. All of society's bullshit etiquette went out the fucking window in a heartbeat.

Whatever I'd learned about being a gentleman when it came to the opposite sex was dashed to pieces and all that was left was the most primal urge to fuck.

My dick was hard as fuck and I kept running as fast as I could until we were a good distance away from the others, holding her safely and protectively in my arms.

I was having some sort of out of body experience. Never before in my life had I endured such a rush of emotions, as though everything I was, everything I'd ever been, came down to this moment in time.

I didn't even make it back to the compound. A feeling of such intense lust hit me that I stumbled and almost fell to my knees. I looked around with my senses open until I found a hidden spot well into the dark.

I pulled at her clothes as she stood in front of me wordlessly, not making a sound. Some rational part of my being was telling me that this was wrong, that she'd just been through something horrible, but the thing that now dwelt in me wasn't about to stop.

I took her down to the sand and covered her body with mine. My pants weren't even half way off before I was feeing between her thighs with my fingers. Need pounded away in my chest and my cock was harder than I've ever felt it before.

There was something riding me hard, something that overshadowed my judgment and pushed me forward even when somewhere in my head I asked myself what the fuck.

There was a strange ringing in my ear and her scent was everywhere now until I couldn't breathe without breathing her in.

If she'd cried out, fought me, I would've pulled back, at least I hope so. But she didn't struggle, instead she looked up at me with those bright eyes as if she understood when I didn't. I knew I was in a the grip of something that was bigger than I, something I'd long dismissed as a fable. But this was no fairytale.

I felt like I needed to get inside her in the next second or die. That's how desperate she made me feel. Once my cock was free I slammed into her and caught her scream in my mouth.

I've never been that careless with a woman before, but now that I was inside her the madness seemed to be fading away, just a little. The beast was still crouched inside, teeth bared but he'd stopped growling.

I pulled back just a little with my hand around her throat holding her in place, almost as if I expected her to fight me. I got my whole cock in her tight little pussy and she opened her legs and accepted me. Now I could breathe again, now I felt whole.

I heard the beast inside me settle down a little once the heat of her pussy wrapped around my throbbing cock. But now there was a new madness beating away inside me.

'Mate' I heard the word like an ancient whisper on the wind and that's just what the fuck I did.

As the fog started to clear from my head I felt her nails in my back and the cool night wind on my skin. She moved with me, our bodies seeming to know each other, perfectly in sync.

I pushed my cock into her tight sweetness over and over and she took me. My thrusts grew wild and I wasn't sure I wasn't hurting her. But I couldn't stop, I had no control left. Something else was at the helm and it wanted in deeper.

I pulled out and put her on her hands and knees before me, and slammed my cock back into her hard, going deep with one stroke. She cocked her ass and pushed back against me as she cried out.

I placed a hand over her mouth as I pulled her back on my cock with the other on her flat stomach and rode her like a rutting bull, while something chased me. Some deep dark mystery that had awakened inside me.

I wasn't fucking, and I damn sure wasn't making love, no, this truly was a mating, and she was my only mate. I knew it down to my soul. It was her all along. It was my mate who'd been calling out to me because she was in danger. I'd felt her before I even knew her. I knew it as sure as I knew my own name.

My cock grew longer, harder with my thoughts as I fucked into her warm supple body. I sank my teeth into the flesh of her neck and marked her as the hardest orgasm of my life slammed into me with such force a veil fell over my eyes.

Our bodies locked together. Her pussy tightened and clenched as if milking the seed from my cock as it emptied into her. I turned her head roughly and gave her my tongue so that the roar that had built in my chest wouldn't escape into the night.

My cock refused to go down but I was worried the sand might scratch her knees so I pulled out once again and put her on her back before slipping back into her wet heat.

I ran my hand over her body, hefting the weight of her breast while the other hand held her nape as if holding her in place for me.

I caressed her body, pushing her top and bra up over her breasts so I could feed on them as my still hard cock moved inside her. I didn't even know if she'd cum, so I set about seeing that she did.

I fucked her slower this time now that the beast had been fulfilled, and felt her pussy quiver and her legs shake as she coated my cock with her pussy cream while I had her tongue in my mouth.

"That's my girl." I kissed her lips and she accepted me without question, and the last of the madness evaporated like the fog. The kiss was almost as wild as the mating and I wondered fleetingly if it was always going to be like this between us. I'd be dead in a week and so would she.

Her eyes stared into mine when I finally lifted my head to look down at her. "Welcome home baby." I rubbed her cheek with my thumb as she smiled and stretched with me still inside her and swear to fuck I was ready to take her again.

But then I heard the others coming back and reality hit me like a brick upside the head. What the fuck Quinn?

15

QUINN

I pulled out of her and knew that it was her blood I felt on my cock, mixed with my seed and her natural juices. I didn't have time to check the damage, I didn't want the others seeing us like this, so I fixed my jeans and picked her up in my arms and started running again.

I only calmed down once we reached the gate and she was safely away from any danger. I let us in and once inside I finally looked down at her and found her just staring up at me.

In fact she was staring at my ink. "You're navy." Her eyes flitted up to mine. After what I'd just done to her this is what she wanted to know?

Now that the fire had abated I felt like an animal. I

have never in my life treated any woman the way I just did her and it didn't matter that I didn't seem to have any control back there, like something had come over me.

It was on the tip of my tongue to apologize, to explain, but again that voice in my head startled me. This time it simply said one word that seemed to make it alright. 'Yours.' Oh fuck, no wonder the old man was afraid of this shit. Instead of trying to figure this shit out now, standing in the middle of the yard, I answered her question.

"Yes." I stared down at her almost having to hold my breath because her scent was making me crazy and as much as my body screamed at me, I knew I couldn't fuck her again. Not until I'd seen the damage I'd already done.

"Thank fuck." Her head fell back on her neck; she'd fainted.

I roared; at least that's what the others said it sounded like on their way back to the compound. I heard their feet rushing towards me as I stood just inside the gate. The door to Zak's house flew open and the women filed out with Vanessa in the lead like they were expecting trouble.

Another time I'll remember this shit and laugh. They made quite a picture as they rushed across the yard, but that's not what I found so comical. It was the fact that the women were armed. I don't think my brothers realized.

Dev reached me first and I barely saw Mancini and the others as they lead a group of people across the yard in the opposite direction. My eyes followed and my blood heated when they fell on the asshole that'd been manhandling her. I wanted to finish him, but I had to see to her first.

"What the fuck Quinn." Dev looked at me hard. I just looked down at her as an answer and he got the drift.

"She hurt?" His hand came down on my shoulder as if in support. I fucking bared my teeth at him and had to hide that shit by lowering my head. He was too close to her. What in the fuck!

"Fainted." The word came out as a growl.

"Okay let's get her inside with the others, we're going to question…"

"No, she stays with me." I actually shifted my body so he couldn't touch her and he held his hands up and backed away slowly.

Lo and the others had already walked over to their women and was settling them down and ushering them back inside to safety. Everything around me seemed to be going in slow motion and my head kept going from hot to cold and back. My emotions were all over the place, my thoughts fractured.

"Okay brother, you need me?" I'd started walking towards my house with him on my ass. "No, I'll take care of her and then I'll be there." He veered off and followed the others towards the little cottage next to the mansion and I continued inside. She was still out but her breathing was normal.

I laid her on my bed and stood back to study her. Shit, she should've been up by now. I checked her over but found no wounds or anything to say that she was hurt, other than the marks on her arms that were left by the asshole's fingers digging into them.

Had I hurt her, had I done this? Shit, yeah you did Quinn. The mark on her neck was just beginning to form and I saw where my five o'clock shadow had marred the skin of her breasts. Damn, I don't even remember taking her into my mouth.

I wanted to mount her again and had to fight for control. She's out cold Quinn what the fuck are you thinking? That's just it, I wasn't. I'd lost control of the situation, more to the point, something inside me, something I didn't know was there, had taken over.

Her eyes fluttered but did not open as I was putting her shirt back in place. That need to mount her grew stronger the longer I sat there. The blood sang in my veins and I could hear my heartbeat in my ears. I was super fucking aware of everything.

The lights in the room that I'd slept in for over a year suddenly seemed brighter, even the colors of the bedspread were more vivid. And her beauty, fuck. I'd never seen anything so beautiful in my life.

In my head I heard the word 'yours' over and over, and 'take'. If my cock stayed this hard around her all the time I'm in trouble. I tried reasoning with whatever the fuck was in my head, she needed rest after her ordeal and I needed to make sure I hadn't torn her little pussy with my cock.

Now that I had her here in my bed I saw how small she was, how dainty, and wondered how someone that tiny could handle what seemed to be growing inside me for her.

I knew I would have to leave her soon, there was bound to be a shit storm waiting for me beyond this door, and the others needed me. But I couldn't bring myself to get up off the bed where I sat beside her. The thought of leaving her so soon after taking her was like severing a limb.

I knew I was in trouble, that I needed to get a handle on this thing whatever it was and fast when all I wanted to do was cover her body with mine and drive into her. Was this shit supposed to last forever?

At some point today I'm gonna have to take a serious look at what this was between us, but right now, someone had hurt her and the man in me needed to rectify that shit. I'ma have to shed some blood.

The anger came back full force as I remembered what I saw on the beach, the way he'd been handling her. I looked down to see that my hands were shaking, both with rage and adrenaline.

I looked back at her face, so delicate so perfect, and I'd taken her down in the sand like a beast. Damn!

Her eyes slitted open the slightest bit and she did something I'd never seen outside of BUD training. It was the way she came awake, her senses open and alert as she held still and kept her breathing even as though still asleep.

She didn't move an inch, something that took a lot of training and control given the situation. My lips twitched as I looked at her. Someone had taught her well. Then I remembered the question she'd asked before she passed out.

A quick look at her hand showed no wedding ring and the sick feeling that had started brewing in my gut eased a little. I knew she'd been a virgin when I took her, I'd felt the membrane tear and give beneath my cock. But maybe…

"Who's in the navy?" I clenched my hands so I didn't reach for her in anger. She'd been handled enough for one night. But the thought that she had a man, someone who loved her enough to teach her that trick made me want to flip my shit.

Her beautiful eyes opened on mine and she stared right at me for a second before lowering them again. There was still a little bit of fear and tension in her, but I sensed her ease as her eyes went to the ink on my arm, and I awaited her answer.

"My dad. Admiral Kyle McCullum."

"What did you say?" My heart beat sickeningly in my chest. She finally lifted her eyes back to mine and I caught my breath.

I'm sure most people just see sparkling blue orbs when they look into them, but me, I saw fire and ice, passion. And something that seemed to call out to me. It took all my control not to climb on top of her and sink back into her heat. What the fuck!

"Admiral Kyle McCullum." Fuck, that's what I thought she said. That sick feeling started up again in my gut, but this time it had new teeth.

As much as I wanted to keep her here, I knew that she was part of the puzzle, I'll have to share.

"Speaking of which, I need to call my dad, he's probably batshit by now." I raised my brow at her salty language but held my tongue. She held her hand out to me.

"Phone. My abductors didn't let me keep mine." She

spoke as if we were sitting across from each other having lunch.

Wasn't she going to bring up what I did to her? I know why I was acting like a caveman but why wasn't she cowering in fear?

Now that the lust had loosened its grip I saw what I had done in a whole new light, and though I didn't regret it, I would understand if she had some questions.

"Why aren't you afraid?" It didn't make sense that she was being so blasé. By rights she should be screaming, shaking, something. If not because of what I'd done to her, then because of the fact that some asshole had abducted her.

Instead her voice was steady and her body relaxed. I've known grown men who couldn't pull that shit off in the same situation. It's one thing to be taught that shit, that kind of discipline, but the girl was a natural, it was ingrained.

She was good, but not that good, so I didn't miss the slight tremble in her arm as she kept it held out between the two of us. She studied me; I mean really studied me, as if she was reading my body language. Good girl.

"I'm scared shitless, but I have to hold it together, my daddy didn't raise no bent shit-can." I laughed outright, the first real laugh I'd had in a long time, and found myself rubbing my hand over my chest where my heart was talking shit to me.

I pulled her up from the pillow and held her head against my chest, a totally involuntary move. I couldn't help myself. Fuck if she didn't feel like she belonged.

"What's your name sweetheart?" Now she was the one laughing. "It's a little late for that isn't it?" I knew what she meant. I'd fucked her like I owned her and now I was asking for her name.

Still I didn't feel the need to apologize, like it was my right. I squeezed her. "Answer me!"

"Kelly, Kelly McCullum." She actually cuddled into my chest like it was the most natural thing in the world and the raw edges of my mind started to piece themselves back together.

That move spoke volumes, it meant she accepted and I wished again that I'd paid more attention to the family legend.

I couldn't remember if she was supposed to be aware of me as I was of her. She certainly seemed accepting, compliant. But how much of that had to do with what she'd been through the last day or so?

My emotions were on a rollercoaster ride. One minute I felt intense tenderness and the next I just wanted to put her under me and pound my cock deep.

I could see, feel and taste her. The others were waiting, she needed taking care of, but the need was stronger than all of that. I moved onto the bed with her still clutched to my chest.

"I need you again, don't turn me away." At least this time I was giving her a choice. She didn't even hesitate and I felt like I'd fallen into a dream or an alternate universe when she opened her arms to accept me.

I lifted the shirt over her head and tore at her bra before I took her nipple into my mouth. They felt familiar in my hands when I hefted their weight. She was perfect, like she was made to fit in my hands and the beast came fully awake again.

Her hands on my head, holding me in place, accepting me, calmed the beast and I growled around her flesh as I chewed and tugged gently with my teeth.

I pulled at her shorts and threw them over the side of the bed before cupping her pussy heat in my hand.

I left her nipple and licked my way down between her thighs. Her scent washed over me and when I tasted her on my tongue for the first time I had a thirst unlike any I've ever known.

I wasn't eating her pussy, it felt more like I was consuming her essence. I drove my tongue into her and those cute little sounds she made spurred me on to do more.

Lifting her ass I my hands I pulled her harder onto my tongue until my teeth grazed her clit. I licked sucked and nibbled the succulent little nub until it stood erect, before driving my tongue back inside her heat.

She moved against my mouth as I ate her pussy hard,

her juices flowing down my face. I'd never tasted anything like her; sweet, fresh, mine.

When I'd had my fill of her juices I pulled my tongue from her body and moved up between her thighs until my cock lined up with her newly opened pussy slit.

This time I could see her eyes, see that she was with me when I slipped into her. Now that I wasn't completely blinded by lust I could feel how tight she was, how perfectly she fit around my cock.

I wanted to go slow, to show her that I wasn't always a beast, but that fire started in me again and I knew it was a lost cause. "I'm sorry baby, hold on."

I had to cover her mouth when the screaming started because I sure as hell couldn't stop pounding into her. Her legs wrapped around my hips as she took me and I delved into her heat over and over as my cock pierced her like a battering ram.

She sucked on my tongue and her pussy clamped down around my cock and I swear I saw stars. Has pussy ever been this good?

Have I ever felt this connected to a woman before? I knew the answer was a resounding no. As I fucked in and out of her I knew that the woman beneath me would be the last I ever share this with. The last I'd ever want.

When I came this time I stayed in her, on her until our breathing came down and rational thought prevailed. I knew there was a whole lot I needed to be doing, but I hated the very thought of leaving her.

I was obsessed, maybe possessed was more accurate. I knew I could spend a whole week buried inside her like this and it still wouldn't be enough. I couldn't stop my hands from moving all over her as if learning her body.

I spent a long fucking time kissing her while my cock went down to semi hard. If I could I would stay buried inside her for the rest of the night, but I had to go kill the fucker that had manhandled her.

16

KELLY

Oh holy night! What was that? I was still trying to catch my breath when he got up off the bed and headed into the bathroom.

I flexed my toes to make sure there was still life in other parts of my body, besides the sweet throbbing between my thighs.

The first time on the beach, I think shock and adrenaline caught me up in the moment. But this second time here on his bed I was very much aware.

This was so out of the norm, like nothing I would ever imagine myself doing. I mean who does this? But somehow I felt right letting him do those things to me.

There was something about him, something so

compelling. I felt it the first time he touched me. It was as if everything inside me came alive.

Like turning on the lights and rides at a carnival that had closed up shop for the season and was now reopening.

My heart was beating me to death and a million questions went through my head, not least of all, what must he think of me, letting him do this not once but twice?

I'm not stupid, I've spent my life hearing the story of how my parents met and knew that what I felt, no one else needed to understand; I did. But would he think me loose?

I could fool myself that it was just a reaction to being alive when my life had hung in the balance these last few hours, but I know better.

I wouldn't have wanted this with anyone else but him. There was a sense of knowing, like we'd known each other in another life, another time.

"Oh shit, what's your name?" I blurted out the question when he walked back into the room. My face lit up like a wildfire as I pulled the sheet higher under my chin.

When he laughed a swarm of butterflies took flight in my tummy and all semblance of embarrassment left me. He's gorgeous, good heavens, have mercy.

He leaned over the bed and kissed my nose and it was the most precious thing. "Quinn, my name is Quinn." I touched the slight stubble on his cheek and my heart filled with warmth.

"Hi Quinn!" We laughed together as he picked me up from the bed and took me into the bathroom where I could hear the water running in the tub.

My heart was light and happy in a way it has never been before and I remembered the promise I'd made to myself while captured. I was going to find me a man like my daddy. I just hadn't thought it would happen this soon, or in this way. Maybe dinner and a movie first?

I was too happy to care how it had come to be, but then I had a sobering thought. What if it was nothing more to him than sex with a pretty willing girl? What if this was something he did all the time?

My heart sank and I felt sick to my stomach. If he was anything like my daddy he could never.

I took a quick look around the spacious room, looking for anything female, and seeing none, I breathed a little easier.

My eyes widened when he stepped into the steaming water with me still held firmly in his arms and lowered us both, with me settled on his lap.

He washed me, like washed me everywhere. My face was back to being red and I buried it in his neck. How can I be this embarrassed after everything we'd already shared tonight?

But somehow this seemed more intimate. I should probably put a stop to it. After all I'd been raised to be a 'good' girl, and this was definitely not the way a good girl would act.

But dammit, he was everything I'd ever said I wanted so why not? He was ringing all my bells loud and clear.

He was hot, had a kickass body and best of all he was navy. At least daddy would approve and that was half the battle.

I lost my train of thought when he turned me around on his lap and sat me on his hardening length. And then he growled at me, "I want you again." Oh shit that's sexy!

He licked my neck and shivers ran through me making me tingle in all the right places. And when his teeth bit into my flesh I felt my body soar as I lowered my hips to meet his.

I knew he was marking me and for some reason, though I'd once smacked the dog snot out of someone for trying this same trick in high school, with him it made me feel sexy, wanted, owned.

My nipples hardened and my insides quivered as I felt him fill me up. I was super aware of everything about him, about us. Like the way his hands felt on my ass as he lifted and lowered me on his dick.

We even moved perfectly together. Like a dance we'd practiced time and again. What was it that he'd said on the beach that first time? Welcome home? Yes, that's what it felt like. Like I'd finally come home.

My thoughts splintered when he shifted his hips and touched something deep inside me and I went flying over the precipice. He pounded me through my orgasm and kept going until it built again. I think I fell in love or at the very least, very serious lust.

I knew about sex, I'd heard enough stories over the years to know what it was supposed to feel like, and this wasn't it. No one had ever described this feeling of dying a little from the sheer pleasure.

I felt strong, alive, beautiful, all that just from having his hands on me, roaming my body as if he couldn't get enough. And his thick length pounding away inside me almost out of control made me feel powerful.

Surely I wouldn't feel this way unless it was meant to be. There's no way there was anyone else on this earth that could make my body sing like this.

I had no doubts in that moment that this was right. Knowing me the doubts will come back full force once he was no longer pounding away inside me. But now, right this minute it felt so right.

I felt my body tighten as lights went off in my head and I screamed just as he gripped me hard around my middle and growled as I felt his body explode inside me for the third time.

Was a body supposed to feel this much pleasure?

Who can survive it? My neck had no strength and my

head dropped onto his shoulder. "You doing okay there baby?" Okay he's got to stop.

Even his voice was having an affect on me and the way he talks. It just went straight to my heart and between my thighs where I was still throbbing. I had enough strength to nod and his arms squeezed around me again and I just gave up.

We ended up in the shower where he washed me again. He probably thinks I'm a complete ass because I just stood there and turned when he told me to and didn't lift a finger to help him.

He smacked my ass playfully and followed me out once he'd taken care of his own shower. He wrapped me in a towel and grabbed another for himself before drying me off.

I started to wonder if maybe I'd escaped into my own head and was still really trapped in that awful basement. Had I conjured him up with my imagination?

No way one guy can be this perfect. Watch, he's going to do something to kill it before the night is over. Bummer!

QUINN

Shit, Quinn you better get your shit together before you scare her off. I'd had her three times in the last hour and a half, but as soon as she dropped the towel and bent over to pick up her clothes from beside the bed my dick tented the towel I'd thrown around my hips.

I moved in behind her and wrapped my arms around her, cupping her full breasts from behind. "I can't stop, I have to have you again. If you're too sore I'll go slow but I have to…"

I stopped talking and just leaned her over the bed. I got down on my knees behind her and opened her red swollen pussy with my fingers to accept my tongue.

She cooed sweetly and pushed back onto my mouth, sending my tongue deeper inside. I had a firm grip on her ass as I tongue fucked her deep and slow.

The more of her taste I got, the more I needed and that damn beast was prowling back and forth in my mind. What is it? Am I supposed to fuck her all night to appease this shit?

I've fucked long into the night before, but never in my life have I recovered this soon. It was as if all I had to do was look at her and my dick got hard.

I brought her off with my tongue because I knew she had to be hurting and I was trying to make it easy on her. But that didn't stop me from getting to my feet and driving my cock into her.

"Oh shit, Quinn." She reached back and held my hip

as if trying to slow me down. I grabbed her hand and held it in mine as I slam fucked her.

My cock looked red and angry as it slid in and out of her. Her juices coated me, making it easier for her to take me, but I knew from the way her tight pussy lips clung to my meat that it was going to be a while before she could take my dick without discomfort.

I didn't want to stay in her too long this time but I needn't have worried. No other woman has ever made me shoot off so hard, so fast before.

It seemed like almost as soon as I got inside her I was ready to cum and this time was no different. I reached around for her clit and brought her along with me as I felt that sweet tingle in my balls again.

"Good, fuck, shit." I gritted my teeth hard to hold back the roar as my cock spat and shook inside her. She drained my balls before her pussy locked me in and I double shot inside her. First fucking time in my life.

When my head cleared I saw that I had her tiny frame trapped between me, and the mattress, and wondered if she was even breathing still. I pulled out and she crawled onto the bed as if trying to escape.

She flopped face down and panted for air and I ran my hand up and down her back soothingly while I too tried to get air into my lungs. If I keep this shit up I'll be dead in a week for sure.

I looked down at my cock in amazement. He'd done

me proud but this fucker need to stay down, she can't take any more and I needed to go.

"I need… to call…my dad. And check on the others. Are they safe with your team?"

I didn't bother asking her how she knew they were my team, with her dad being who he is I'm sure she knew a bit more than most about such things.

"Hold off on that phone call Kelly, I need to debrief you but we need to join the others first."

I helped her up from the bed and her knees buckled.

I picked her up effortlessly like I'd been doing it all my life and held her close to my chest. I was extremely aware of the tread of my heartbeat and my senses, which had been haywire since the night before, had finally settled down now that she was here.

I knew without a doubt that it was her I'd been feeling, sensing. She'd awakened some shit in me that I didn't quite have a handle on yet. But now I needed my beast to lay his ass down and chill the fuck out.

I practically had to hold my breath so that I didn't inhale her scent as I got her dressed myself. I looked back at the bed one last time as I headed out of the room with her in my arms.

As much as I wanted to take her back there and spend the rest of the night between her thighs I knew it wasn't the right time. There was too much shit to do before the night was over.

It was enough for now that I'd had her, marked her and she now wore my scent. She'd accepted me without question, which makes this shit easier.

If she'd rejected me I'd be in a world of hurt, at least I remember that much about the legend. Now I can shift my focus to what was waiting for me out there.

"Have you eaten sweetheart?" I caught myself burying my nose in her hair and told myself to throttle back on the creeper factor. Don't scare her Quinn.

Then again, if fucking her like a centaur three times on first acquaintance hadn't done that I don't think anything could.

"Not really, I pretended to eat the nasty sandwich they fed us because one of the goons was standing over me, but I haven't had anything to eat since yesterday."

Her words sent fire racing through my veins but I didn't give anything away. I'll deal with them soon enough, and they'll pay for everything they'd done to her.

She wasn't harmed that I could see. I knew for a fact the she hadn't been violated, not in the obvious sense anyway. But if anything worse than being held captive had happened to her somehow I knew that I would've known it.

Still, she'd been afraid and alone; I can't let them live. I wanted to question her but held off because she'd have to do it again for the others.

I didn't want her going through that shit twice. I didn't

let myself dwell on her old man and who he was and what that could mean. That was a whole other headache on its own.

Instead I took her to the kitchen and sat her on a stool at the island, before pouring her a glass of juice.

I pulled some meat and cheese from the fridge before getting some bread from the box. I made her a sandwich and waited as she wolfed it down with appreciative groans.

Merciful fuck! My eyes were glued to her lips and those sounds she made had visions of serious hardcore fucking playing through my head.

What the fuck Quinn! Is this what I have to look forward to for the next fifty-sixty years? It was like everything she did had a direct affect on my dick.

My cock throbbed like a persistent toothache and was beginning to hurt just as much. I swallowed hard when she drained her glass and lowered it before running her tongue along her upper lip. Fuck me.

"We have to make sandwiches for the others as well." She said it like an order or more like she knew that I would do her bidding. And so it begins. That shit had my sisters written all over it.

I got to work making a mountain of sandwiches because I didn't know how many of them they were. "How many of you were they do you know?"

"Five, all military brats."

She gave me a look like she was waiting for me to confirm something. "It's dawned on me that that's not a coinkydink, no way those buffarillas just randomly chose five females who all happen to have military dads."

I see her dad shared a lot with her. Her terminology was pure navy. Too fucking smart and that last bit of information, if true, just added another level of fuckery to the shit pile.

I carried on making sandwiches like she hadn't just dropped a bombshell, but I could feel her piercing stare. "And you know this how?"

"I asked." At least she didn't roll her eyes at me but it was implied in her tone. I went back to the refrigerator for more mayo and hid my smile.

I could already see her joining the ranks of my sisters. Somehow instead of putting the fear of hell in me like it should, I somehow find that I was actually looking forward to it. I've lost my damn mind.

My whole world has changed on a dime in the last couple hours and I know it. If I could feel her that strongly before we'd even met, not to mention the old 'curse' coming into play the minute I put hands on her, I am as sure of who she is, as I am of my own self.

She's mine. The one woman that was meant for me. The one I was destined to walk through the rest of my life with. And from this there is no turning back.

I was only a little bit panicked when I realized that I

didn't know what all I should expect from this union. It had been something to shun and hide for so long, that I'd never seriously looked into it.

Now was not the time to dwell on it though, there'll be time enough later and hopefully she won't take my balls in the meantime.

But first things first, there were others in the line of danger now, people who needed my help. Once I'd gotten the whole story and dealt with the others I can focus on my own personal shit.

For now I'll deal with the situation at hand. But later, I'll have to dig through my memory for the old legend so I'll at least have some idea of where my life was headed.

"What else did you find out?" She held her hand out after I'd bagged the food and I thought that's what she was reaching for until she brushed it aside and took my other hand, heading for the door.

She did it so naturally, like she'd done it a thousand times before, and something inside me eased. Shit, now something as simple as handholding is making me giddy. Tyler's gonna have a field day with my ass.

"I thought this debriefing was going to take place elsewhere sailor let's go. I need to make sure the others are safe. Your friends anything like you?"

The shot of jealousy was instantaneous and I pulled back on her hand making her stop. She smirked up at me as if she knew exactly what I was thinking.

"What do you mean?" I could tell from the twinkle in her eye that she knew what was going on with me. It looked like she was straining hard not to laugh.

She wouldn't think that shit was so funny if she knew I was thinking of wringing her damn neck.

She smiled and patted my chest with her free hand before walking on. Meanwhile I was left biting my tongue so we didn't have our first fight.

"Navy, I meant are they navy too. What did you think I meant?" What a little tease. Whatever those words had awakened in me laid its head down and I went calm again.

She was very at ease with me, no doubt more of her dad's training, and I couldn't help but wonder how she was going to fit in with the other women. What role she'd take.

Somehow I don't see her falling in line the way my brothers have been constantly trying to get their women to. I foresee years of running her ass to ground, add them to the mix and damn.

With their track record and her seeming knowhow it won't be good. We've been able to keep them under control somewhat because although Vanessa was military, the baby kind of slows her down. Plus the fact that she's pregnant again. But with this one in the mix I'm not so sure.

"Yes they're navy, let's go meet them I'm sure they're waiting." We walked hand in hand across the yard, and more than just the feeling that had been riding me all day had changed. I felt lighter, in body and spirit. And my heart had come alive in my chest.

Of all the things that I'd expected, this hadn't even made the list. In truth, I'd half expected the omen to have something to do with someone from my past.

That knowing that it was someone I loved, even though I couldn't think of anyone that might be, except for my family who was all here with me had led me to believe it was someone I knew.

It could've been one of my long lost relatives, or a friend from the old days before I signed up. But not once did I ever think it would be this.

And now that she was here, now that I had the answer, it seemed like the most obvious thing. I felt like I'd been waiting for her all my life and it made no sense.

I looked down at her in the moonlight, wondering how I could ever tell her that I loved her before I met her.

That there was some strange anomaly in me that had chosen her for me and I for her, long before either one of us knew the other existed.

I decided it was better to hold off on that for now. She'd already had a rough coupla days. And besides, I need to get my thoughts together before I come across like a raving lunatic.

I don't even fully understand it myself, so how could I

expect her to? But again, she might have some idea seeing as how I've fucked her as often as I looked at her since we met a scant two and a half hours ago.

17

QUINN

We made it to the cottage where my brothers had already started questioning the men. The rescued women were in the other room with blankets and sipping the cups of coffee someone had made.

I passed her the bag of food and indicated that she should take it to them. "In just a minute." She walked across the room and I watched my brothers watch her as she moved.

My skin burned and I gritted my teeth as the men in the room had eyes on her. Okay, I don't like other men near her; check. That might prove to be a problem. Fuck, I'm turning into Cord.

I barely stopped myself from pulling her back when she stopped just in front of them.

"Eenie-meenie-minie." She pointed at Lo, Con, and Dev and seemed to dismiss them before looking at one of the perpetrators.

"Moe." She gave him what I would call a death ray glare then hauled her arm back and socked him in the face. Badass.

"Whoa brother, that's yours?" Dev had moved over to stand beside me.

"Yep." I answered him feeling more than a little proud as we watched her along with everyone else. She shook her hand off and Lo lifted a brow at me.

"Kelly, come here." I held out my hand to her and she came to me and took it without question. The sweet little girl was gone. Her face looked like my brothers' and I did when we were ready to fuck shit up.

"Guys, this is Kelly McCullum, as in Admiral Kyle McCullum's daughter." The only people in the room who didn't react to the name were Lyon and the other civilians in the room.

Even Mancini who we still didn't know if he'd done anytime in the service or not, seemed to recognize the name. There was an obvious shift in the room.

Con's, 'oh fuck'. Was a sentiment I think we all shared. Her old man was one of the CO's best friends. Not to mention his reputation among the SEALs going back forty years.

The men had served together back in the day and he

happened to be on the list we'd found with the codes. I was afraid that this shit had just gone nuclear on our asses.

"Yes and I need to call him soon before we lose most of the western seaboard." She wasn't lying. From what I know of the man he would most definitely level the whole country to find his kid.

"We will." I squeezed her hand in mine before turning back to Lo.

"What have we got?" He looked at her and I got the message.

"You might as well tell him because I already know something's going on. My guess, it has something to do with a run my dad made back in the day with his team."

"I recognized some of the names after I had everyone introduce themselves when we were being held."

She glared at the men again and the one she socked stepped back, trying to disappear through the wall. She gave Lo a look that said she wasn't going anywhere and I couldn't help but admire her guts. Pure trouble!

"Fine, let's get to it." Lo was still looking at her like he expected her to strike. Either that, or he was just plain studying the offspring of a legend.

"Yeah but I have to call my dad first." She actually stared him down with her hand on her hip. The message that she wasn't about to budge came through loud and clear.

"You sure?" Lo's question was directed at me and I knew just what he was asking.

"One hundred percent."

The groans started, as my brothers interpreted the little byplay. "That shit's going to be trouble." Ty grinned and walked over to us.

"Hi I'm Tyler, your new big brother. You're mad-dog's kid huh!"

"Yes sir, but you better not let him hear you call him that. It makes him rabid."

The room cracked up and the tension eased slightly, but I realized that she hadn't called Ty on his big brother crack. Maybe she doesn't know what he's getting at.

"Okay boys and girls, assholes to elbows. We still have that thing and then we have to leave." Connor moved towards the room where the five young girls waited and the rest of us followed.

A cute Latina teenager jumped up from her chair as soon as we entered the room and made a beeline for Kelly.

"Oh thank shit, they said you were okay but I didn't believe them." She glared around the room with a look that in a few years was sure to make some man's balls retract in fear.

The two women hugged and Kelly reassured the girl before she went to all the others and whispered to them.

She gave them the sandwiches and ordered them to

eat, reassuring them in her words, that we were navy and they were safe now.

I noticed she didn't get into too much about who we are though I knew she knew that we were more than that. Her daddy had really trained her well.

It took a couple hours to get the whole story from each of the girls. They were indeed all military brats, some marine and air force.

A pattern was forming. There was no doubt that these men had worked together at some point and whatever it was they'd done, Khalil was at the other end of it.

"Quinn I really need to call my dad."

"I know baby but we have to make sure the call's secure first." When she became distressed I caved.

"I'll make the call." I kissed her temple and told her to stay there even though I was in no hurry to be separated from her.

My brothers followed me out of the room, leaving the girls and the kidnappers behind with Law's crew.

Technically Lyon and Mancini shouldn't be privy to the calls we were about to make but I'm pretty sure that my brothers, like me, knew they'd earned their place by our side.

Of course she followed us out of the room which was good because I'd already begun to feel like there was some shit missing.

It hadn't even been a minute but already I knew, that it

was going to be like this for a long time to come. That being away from her was always going to have an affect on me.

I'll have to brush up on my memory of that part of the old legend, but I'm pretty sure it says she owns my ass now. Fuck me!

As long as Ty never learns about that shit I'm straight. "I thought I told you to stay put lil bit." I took her hand and pulled her along with me, totally contrary to what I was saying.

We headed to the mansion for a secure line to make the call. I could see my brothers were still sizing her up, probably asking themselves some of the same questions that were running through my head.

Her hand was relaxed in mine as she walked silently beside me and I wondered how long it would be before she adrenaline crashed.

For now she seemed to be holding her own though so I'll just keep an eye on her and be there when she falls. And she will fall, unless she'd inherited that hard core her dad was known for.

The women were at the windows of Zak's place looking out but we didn't even acknowledge them for now. Shit had escalated quick and we had to move. Right now the five women that we'd rescued, including her, seemed to be at the center of this whole mess.

We don't know if there were other undesirables in the

area or not, but I was sure my brothers and the others had secured our perimeter while I was tending to her.

She was already disrupting my shit, because I didn't even have a chance to ask them what they'd found out so far. My mind was still wrapped up in her.

Is this what they all felt? It wasn't so much that I was being pulled in two separate directions, but more like there was an internal shift.

Yesterday the Op would've been first on my agenda. In a few scant hours she had taken its place. Now all I can see is her.

I pushed her inside ahead of me and followed Lo into the secure Intel room with the others right behind us.

No one else was allowed in here but I guess we'd come too far with these guys to turn back now.

I reached for the modified SAT phone and tried to work out what the hell I was going to say to this man. He was no longer just a senior officer, but the father of the woman I'd claimed.

I guess Lo had decided to give me point on this one because usually he would've been the one making the call. But he just stepped back in line with the others and looked at me to proceed.

I realized then that we've been doing this same dance with each woman that came into our lives. It was his way of accepting that she was mine, my responsibility. Kind of like passing the torch.

"Put it on speaker Quinn." Lo ordered as I dialed the number she gave me. It was snatched up on the other side before the first ring ended.

"McCullum." That voice was commanding even through the phone. "Admiral sir, this is lieutenant Quinn…."

"You found my kid?" I squeezed her hand in mine.

"Yes sir." He didn't let me finish, but I realized he didn't ask if I had her, but if I'd found her. He knew who I was before I said a word.

I looked at my brothers who'd also caught on. This line was secure, but it ran off the CO's grid, the only way for anyone to recognize the frequency was if the two men had been in regular contact. We'll save that for later.

"Who?" I didn't need him to explain that he was asking me who had taken her, and from his tone I knew he was already whisky tango foxtrot.

"We think it's Khalil with local help and someone high up on the inside, sir."

"This motherfucker. Hang tight, I'm coming to get my kid."

"Ah, you'll have to hold off on that sir I'm taking her in." I held up a hand to silence Kelly when she started to speak. Everyone else in the room was silent.

"Say what again?"

"I'm taking her to a safe place. I'll call you when we

get there and we can make arrangements for you to see her."

There was a long pause on the other end before he asked in the calmest voice.

"What do you mean come see her? I'm bringing her home."

"Negative sir." There was another long silent pause on his end but I heard him loud and clear. He's gonna kick my ass first chance he gets. That's fine but he can't have her. I took the phone off speaker when he started to get personal.

"Boy, what the hell are you talking about?" How can I explain to him that I knew his daughter on sight?

I damn sure can't tell him that I was afraid if she was too far away from me I'd have a fucking meltdown.

Or that my dick hadn't gone soft since I found her on the beach. Now was definitely not the time to have this conversation.

"She'll be safe sir, my life on that." Please don't ask me for any more than that. I'd feel like a complete fucking idiot baring my guts in a roomful of men. Ty was already giving me looks, fucking heel and I was completely out of my depth.

"Give me the phone." She took the phone from my hand before I could say yes or no.

"Daddy, I'm fine, Quinn's taking very good care of me."

She did that girly twirling her hair around her finger shit and even that sent a message straight to my dick. Is this shit for real?

"Quinn is it?"

"Well yeah, that's his name. When we get to where we're going I'll call and you can come out to see me."

Damn he'd raised her too well, she didn't even question the Op. That or she trusted me. I prefer the latter.

But listening to her, it was obvious that she'd accepted that this thing didn't end here, and she was giving her consent to stay and see it through.

Or, she felt the attraction and… For fuck sake it's like walking a fucking maze in my head.

"Didn't you two just meet? Why does it sound like you're staying with him?"

"Daddy he's a SEAL hello."

"Shit."

I couldn't hear his end of the convo but I could imagine. She put the phone back on speaker I'm guessing at his direction. In the background it sounded like her mother came into the room.

"She's safe Isabel."

"Where is she?"

"They're keeping her safe…"

"Kyle McCullum you take me to my child right this second."

"Dammit woman I said she was okay." There were

some muffled sounds which made Kelly roll her eyes but the rest of us were in the dark.

"You're at the CO's place I see. We'll be there in two. Be there or you won't know hell until you've met my other half."

He hung up and the rest of us just looked at each other. Kelly turned back to me and I couldn't quite read the look on her face.

I got it when she leaned into me and whispered in my ear as the men filed out of the room.

"You better have a good story to give dad if you plan on keeping me with you."

Again I was blown away by her easy acceptance.

"You know this is about more than keeping you safe right." She looked me dead in my eyes. I can't remember the last time anyone except my brothers had done that.

"I know." That's all she said before heading out of the room ahead of me. I shook my head and grinned as I walked out behind her.

18

QUINN

We headed back to the others each of us deep in thought. It was obvious we couldn't leave right away like we'd planned to and we were fast losing cover of night.

We had to figure out what to do with the other girls and our new prisoners. Mancini went to his people who had been standing guard outside.

Back inside the cottage Law's brother and his crew had shit under control. The females were in one room and the kidnappers in another.

I looked the men over until my eyes fell on my prey. I have to say, from what we'd learned thus far, they didn't fit.

The men Cord had taken down a few weeks ago were pros. These guys looked like your garden variety scumbags that hung out on street corners looking for their next fix.

"Who the fuck are you working for?" I stood in front of the one who'd manhandled her on the beach. In this new light it was easy to see he was little more than a kid himself, and I'm pretty sure he never saw any action.

If Khalil and whoever he had working for him on the domestic end were using random assholes to carry out their misdeeds, then we were in serious shit.

"I don't know, I already told them." He wasn't looking so brave now and I wondered what Law's boys had done to put that look of fear in his eyes.

There were four of them and five females. I was trying to work that shit out in my head. When we questioned the girls earlier we learned that they didn't all live in the same area, some not even the same state.

Some of them had been snatched the day before the others, but it had been done in a way that the alarm hadn't been sounded.

That twenty-four hour window had given them the time they needed before anyone noticed a pattern. But four men to carry it out would've taken a lot of work and planning and there's no way this kid had that kinda smarts.

He could very well be telling the truth, that he didn't know who he was working for. I don't see Khalil dealing with this bunch, he's way more sophisticated than that. But somebody had given the order.

His cohorts were doing their best to become invisible, but I was sure they all had the same answer.

I needed to think, to put shit together in my head until it made sense. So far we'd dealt with enlisted men, the boys from Langley and a money laundering corporate skell.

Stockton had led us to the hate brigade in Law's neck of the woods, but so far they were the lowest ones on the totem pole, until these clowns.

It was beginning to look like this shit was even bigger than we'd first realized. There were layers and tentacles that seemed to cover all four corners of the damn country. Just what the fuck had we stepped in here?

Just then Kelly yawned from some place behind me and I throttled back. I looked over my shoulder at her and saw the fatigue.

"I'm going to take her home and come back. Maybe I should get the others settled as well. Mancini, they can take a couple hours down before we head out right?"

He looked at his watch and nodded. "So long as we leave under cover of dark we're good and we still have another few hours before daylight."

I hadn't even realized so much time had passed but he was right, it was already well past midnight. Lyon and the others hadn't said a word since this whole thing started and I could only imagine what the hell was going through their heads.

"Come on Kelly." I took her hand and led her into the other room where she rounded up the girls who also looked dead on their feet.

I should probably take them to stay with my sisters at Zak's place, but I knew if I took them there she'd want to stay with them and I wanted her in my house, even though I wouldn't be there with her.

I got them settled and just as I thought, they wanted to stay together. So instead of my bed, she spread some blankets on the floor in the living room and they turned on the TV for some normalcy.

After she'd got the others settled I took her hand and led her from the room to the sound of twitters and murmurings. At least they weren't too traumatized to be annoying ass females. They really do start young.

"You sure you're going to be okay?" I smoothed her hair back and read her eyes for the truth. She did that thing where she turned her face into my palm and even that small gesture went directly to my cock.

She nodded with her head still in my hand, her eyes staring into mine and it was as easy as breathing to lower my head to hers.

The kiss was electric, no other word for it. She zapped me as soon as my lips met hers. It felt as if some strange energy flowed from her to me or me to her, I'm not sure which. But whatever it was, it had me pulling her into my arms until our bodies met.

As with everything else since I found her, it felt like the most natural thing to have her in my arms. That strange tingling started again and my skin felt like it was on fire. "If I get inside you now, we'll both go up in flames." Shit, did I say that corny shit out loud?

I moved to pull back but she ran her tongue along my lip and I ended up hauling her in again. She sighed, I moaned as we deepened the kiss.

Everything about her was superimposed on my brain. The feel of her slight body under my big rough hands, the way she barely came up to my chest. So tiny, so precious.

A well of protective emotion welled up inside me and I was almost tempted to think that she wasn't real, that this wasn't real. Nothing in my life has ever been this perfect, this right.

Maybe I was still trapped in the dream from the night before and all this had been part of it. But I knew as I felt the warmth of her body under my hands, that it was real.

I also knew why a part of me wanted to shy away from it even as I held her closer in my arms. The reason dad had been so against this 'curse' was because as he'd told it, it made a man weak.

He'd become almost a slave to my mother and nothing else had mattered but pleasing her. He'd lost interest in everything else around him and she had become the center of his world.

Funny that I remembered those words now, and sure they did make me think that maybe I should take a step back, assess the situation and come at it again when I had more control.

But I couldn't stand the thought of letting her go. Besides, I was a stronger man than my father had ever been.

Only a weak man would've tried to destroy his own son and I don't see myself ever being that guy. Shouldn't that count for something?

In the end it was only because we needed air that I finally released her lips. I stood looking down at her in amazement, because no matter what, I knew I would never let her go. The die had been cast.

"What are you doing to me lil bit?" Were her eyes really that dreamy or was that too part of my imagination?

There was emotion in her eyes too and I wondered for a fleeting moment if maybe that would be the difference between us and them.

You see, my dad had been an over possessive prick who couldn't bear to let mom out of his sight. But what made it worst, was that she was a jealous, insecure girl when they met and the two negatives fed off each other.

Add to that the fact that mom just never seemed to be

in love as much as she stayed around for necessity's sake after I came into the picture.

I don't think dad was ever sure of her love and that added to his turmoil, which turned him into the man I knew. A man that I'd heard so many times had been nothing like the monster he became after I was born.

From the stories I heard he'd once been a fun loving hard working artist. A man full of light and wellbeing.

I can't remember hearing anything but good things about him, but it all seemed to change when he met and married mom and had me.

For the first time in my life I was beginning to understand him. His own personal weakness had been part of the problem; I see that now.

He'd told me once that this was a curse and no gift. I could see where it could make a lesser man weak, but I was no weakling and the way she looked up at me now, I didn't think it hard that she could fall in love with me.

I'll make damn sure she does before I lose my shit like he did. I'm a fucking SEAL nothing makes me weak. Her ass had better be in love or else. I'm not doing this crazy shit alone.

Where the hell did that come from? I shook my head to clear it and placed one last peck on her lips.

"I gotta go baby, you watch over them until I get back okay. If anything happens, if you need me I'll be in the cottage."

I started to pull away but she tugged me back by my arm. "What is it?" There was a look of uncertainty mixed with stubborn pride on her pretty little face.

"Those women that were staring at us from the windows." She stopped and took a breath before continuing.

"Is one of them…?" Her eyes lost their look of surety and I found that I didn't like her being unsure of herself.

I like the feisty little firebrand who'd socked the enemy in the mouth and looked like she wanted to do much worse.

"No sweetheart, they're my sisters, my brothers' wives. I wouldn't be here with you like this if it were otherwise, if one of them were mine."

I lifted her chin and looked down into her eyes, which had lost that look. "I'm no cheat, that's something you'll never have to worry about ever. We'll talk more when I get back." I kissed her nose and forced myself to walk away and out the door.

Outside I carried her scent with me into the night air. The shit seemed to be all around me now, like wisps of smoke, twirling around and around, ensnaring me.

No doubt this was part of that crazy shit. I guess there's no point in fighting it, I knew at least that the shit was real and I no longer had that fear of becoming a mindless sap.

If things started to go south I'll just have Dev or one

of these others put a slug in my damn head. Shit, I really need to get a damn grip. Each step I took away from her felt like I was severing a damn limb.

I only looked back once before shaking my head at myself and heading back to the others.

We still had to get in touch with the families of the other girls, which I was pretty sure Lo had already got a head start on knowing him.

By the time I met them in the yard between my place and the cottage, Lyon, Mancini, Law and Creed were arguing with Lo and Con. "What's going on?"

"They want to blow the tunnel while we see to our guests."

"Make sense, we're strapped for time and I'm sure they know what they're doing." At least I thought they did.

"See, lover boy here is thinking." Lyon clapped Lo on the shoulder and started to head off. When Lo opened his mouth to argue Law stepped in.

"Best to leave it alone Lo. If Lyon isn't preoccupied with something before long, shit might get hinky.

"What do you mean?" Lo looked in the direction Lyon had taken.

"Well, let's put it this way. He seems cool on the outside, but let's not forget, his kid was in that flesh book. And that little appetizer in the desert, he was only just getting started. Best to keep his crazy ass busy."

We all turned and looked at him as he headed to Zak's. We saw the change when his wife opened the door and stepped out.

We couldn't hear what was going on but it looked like she was giving him hell about something. We did hear his roar of laughter though, and saw the way he picked her up, making her giggle.

"I feel like a damn voyeur." I looked away from the spectacle when he started kissing her like he'd forgotten there was a yard full of men looking on.

"Hey Colt buddy, get a room." I think Ty was the only one who dared. Lyon put his woman's feet back on the ground, patted her ass and pointed a finger in her face before she turned and flounced back inside.

Well as much as any heavily pregnant woman can flounce. Must be something in the water, all the damn women around here were breeding. Oh shit, I came in her over and over again without protection.

Before I could freak the fuck out Lyon made his way back to us. "Come on, what the fuck we waiting for? Let's get this shit going."

He rubbed his hands together and gone was the teasing husband of just a second ago. Guy's a damn chameleon.

19

QUINN

~

"How'd it go with the families Logan, did you reach everyone?" I stepped up beside him as we headed the rest of the way to the cottage.

"I had to do a lot of talking to keep them from coming here. Beyond that, they all know something, I'm sure of it." He looked back to see where the others were.

"I'm sure I don't have to tell you that it's not a coincidence that all these girls are the daughters of the men whose names we just saw in those codes in the CO's little surprise book."

"Nope, and Kelly's already made the connection. I guess we wait until the admiral gets here and see what the hell he knows, unless the old man left anymore clues lying around for us."

"Good luck with that. Once I told each of them who we were, they clammed the fuck up. This is some heavy shit we're dealing with here brother. But before we get into that. She the one?"

I should've known he wouldn't let it go for too long without getting into my shit. I'm positive that it was only because of the situation that it had taken him this long, him and the others.

I had yet to hear from them and Ty hadn't really gotten started on my ass yet with his shit, not that I was looking forward to his brand of fuckery.

"Looks like." Did the others feel this infantile when the rest of us were ragging them about their new relationships?

I felt like a teenage boy who got caught with a pocketful of condoms or some shit.

"Fucking Mad Dog's daughter. That's all we need around here. Fucking reinforcements."

He said it with a laugh in his voice so I didn't take offense, besides, hadn't I thought the same thing?

"It'll be interesting around here that's for sure." Ty's nosy ass was eavesdropping as usual.

"When hasn't it been interesting around here brother? shit. You remember Con after the great fall?" Zak got them going and I just listened as my brothers gave me their blessing in their own special way.

If there's one thing about us, we never question each other's choices. We trust one another to understand that it wouldn't just be as simple as one of us marrying a woman, that that woman would have to fit into our family.

So far we've been lucky. "I think she's going to be perfect. I'm happy for you brother." Dev clapped my shoulder in congratulations but I knew him well enough to catch the strain of longing in his voice.

I didn't forget that only this morning we'd been discussing this shit, or what he'd said. "You're next brother, I held up my end of the bargain."

He opened his mouth to argue but Lo, who seemed to think he could dictate every aspect of our lives put paid to that.

"Of course he's next. It wouldn't be complete without him taking the plunge. We're a team, that's what the fuck we do."

Of course everyone had to have their say once it was realized that Dev was the only one among us who hadn't been snagged.

Lyon of all people was the voice of reason. "Leave him alone, if there's one thing I know about this love shit, it's that you can't escape it. You can't force it either. When the time is right Devon, you'll know trust me." Sounds about right to me. But he wasn't done there.

"Just prepare to never have a moment's fucking peace

for the rest of your life. She'll grab you by the balls and as much as you try to convince yourself that you're still the same man you always were, that you're in charge of shit."

He shook his head here, serious as a judge. "You're not brother. She owns your ass because for the rest of your life everything you do will be about her."

I can't be sure, but I think even Lo was listening to him now. There was a note of truth to his words and I'm guessing we were all thinking, if this guy could cave, then what chance did the rest of us have?

"Then when you finally settle into accepting your fate, she brings in ringers aka daughters and you my man are totally and completely fucked. Don't get me wrong, you'll still walk talk and look like you, but the jig is up."

Dev looked at the others for confirmation and to a man they were all nodding their heads. "Well shit Lyon, I'm not sure if that's an endorsement or a warning." Dev tried to laugh it off but he looked spooked.

"It's neither soldier boy, just the plain truth. I can tell you this though, love doesn't make a man weak like some would have you believe. In fact it's quite the opposite." He looked back at Zak's place where the women were hanging out.

"I don't imagine there's anything I won't do to keep them safe. I'm stronger in here and here, now that I have them." He pointed to his chest and temple.

"Damn Colt, say it ain't so." Ty started his shit.

"What's that Tyler?"

"You're bitch made too." The jackass shook his head in fake wonder as the rest of us cracked up.

It was a nice little change from the last few hours. Insults were shared and the guys took turns getting into my business, giving me their version of what to expect next.

Anyone watching us would have no idea that we were in the middle of hell. I'm accustomed to this easy repartee with my brothers but never shared it with anyone else.

Now we'd added four new members to our crew who'd been so easily accepted. Who knows if we'd have found each other had it not been for this evil we were caught up in the middle of?

But I was sure that when this was all over, we would be in each other's lives forever. Is this her influence I wonder?

Did my heart softening enough to let her in open me up to this way of thinking? I have to say I never once gave a shit about such things.

I thought it prudent to get my ass back on track before I made a fool of myself. Fucking Ty can scent blood in the water.

The last thing I need is for him to see a chink in my armor. "What's the plan? What're we doing with them?" I indicated the door to the cottage where the men were being held.

"Not sure yet. They're still not talking but now that the women are out of the way I'm thinking we can get them to open up a little more." Lo's face had lost the soft playfulness of the last few minutes.

"Let's do it."

20

KELLY

I always knew this would happen. That I would meet a man who's just like my dad and lose my damn mind.

I didn't know my slut meter would go off the charts though. I also never expected that it would happen this way, with him having to save me after being kidnapped and all.

Maybe it was the kidnapping, and coming so close to having my life disrupted in the most horrible way, but I feel freer somehow. Like all my usual inhibitions had been cauterized.

I'm not one for jumping into bed with someone I'd just met, but here I am three bouts of amazing intercourse later. And truth be told, I wouldn't mind a fourth, or a fifth. Oh good grief, I've become an addict.

Maybe that myth about needing to reaffirm that you're still alive after facing trauma had some truth to it.

Because right now, even as I was reassuring the girls that everything was going to be okay, my mind was on him and the way it felt when I was in his arms, in his bed. Oh shit!

His body is so damn firm, so masculine, but what's more I felt safe when I was under him. Like he was shielding me from the rest of the world.

I could still imagine the feel of his body as I ran my hands up and down his back, his chest. I still get a tingle from the memory of him pressed up against me.

I went back into the living room where the other girls were digging into their bowls of popcorn and talking through the movie.

Now that he was no longer here, I was hit once again with the memory of all that we'd been through, how close we came to being sold across the ocean into who knows what hell, and I felt a little unsettled.

There was a slight tension in my body and my nerves were just a little shook as I looked at these young women whose lives could've been ruined forever.

I started to shake as the adrenaline that had been carrying me this long finally crashed and burned, but I knew I had to keep it together for them.

Once I was sure of their safety and they were reunited

with their families, then I can dwell on myself and all that had transpired in the last day and a half.

I was still coming to terms with the fact that it had happened to me, and my mind hadn't quite caught up to reality yet.

I know enough about PTSD to know that though this may not be that on a grand scale, it was bordering on the edges.

The trick was to focus on the here and now and not let my mind go back there to those few hours in the back of that dark hot trailer.

I stared at the screen but saw nothing. Instead of the horrors of the past few hours taking over my mind as would be expected at a time like this, my head was full of Quinn.

I didn't question what I felt for him. Somehow I always knew that when the time came I'd know him on sight. It's the reason I never gave myself away cheaply before.

When I thought of the man I would one day meet and marry, there was always an old world sort of romance attached to my dreams.

When you grow up in a home with a real life hero and watch through the years the love this strong man bore his wife and child, it was easy to weave dreams around such things.

I always knew deep down that nothing but a navy man would do for me, and though I'd met plenty over the years through dad, none had ever touched my heart.

My soldier had always been back there in the shadows, waiting. I couldn't quite picture what he looked like, but I knew what it would feel like to be in his presence. At least I told myself I would.

Now that man has a face and what a face it is. He's every girl's dream of the perfect ten. His dark hair had been allowed to grow out now that they were retired, but I could imagine it the way it's worn shorn close to the head when he's deployed.

His Irish green eyes, I can still see them looking into mine as though he could really see me. See past the face I show the world to the girl hidden inside.

I'm happy that I'd kept myself for him. That I'd believed in the dream enough to hold out. If he's anything like my dad that'll mean a lot to him.

Men of honor seem to put a lot of stock in things like that still, even though they may claim not to. I didn't have to question whether or not he felt the same attraction for me. He'd proved that three times.

Okay time to think about something else. I hadn't showered again after that last time and I could still feel him leaking out of me and it was making me twitchy.

I looked around the living room for a sense of him. His likes, who he was. I'm sure in the next few weeks I'll get a better handle on things as we get to know each other, but I always found that you can tell a lot about a person from their surroundings.

The place was all male but there were a few touches of the feminine as well and I felt a stirring of jealousy until I pushed it aside. Maybe one of his sisters in law were responsible.

I saw an old Afghan that I was sure he used at night when there was a chill in the air, and pulled it around my shoulders.

Cara kept looking back at me, giving me strange looks, but I kept my face neutral. I wasn't ready to answer questions about us. I'm sure the whole situation may seem odd to others.

Hell if anyone else had told me that they met a man and jumped into bed with him on the first date I would've thought them a bit loose.

But I guess when you know you know. Mom had told me that once. During one of our more intimate conversations.

She'd said that when she met dad she just knew in her soul that he was the one for her. I've watched them over the years, and instead of their love for each other waning with time as many so often do. Theirs seemed only to flourish with each passing year.

Mom says it's because dad was gone most of the time

and she got used to missing him so that when he returned it was all the sweeter.

But I think it was more than that. I saw two people who respected each other as much as they loved. That's what I want, with Quinn.

My heart raced at the sickening thought that he might not want the same. What if he wasn't looking to settle down? I know as many navy men who liked playing the field as I do those who get married and raise a family.

Well he'd better be the latter or there'll be no more of that amazing bed wrestling until I trained his ass right.

I felt sudden panic until I remembered the way he'd spoken to dad earlier. No way would he have told dad he was holding onto me if he wasn't more than a little interested.

If there's one thing I'm sure of, no navy man would cross the admiral for any reason unless he had a death wish. And besides, he didn't seem to want to leave me either.

Once I'd convinced myself that his interest was as great as mine, I was able to relax and watch the movie. I mothered the girls a bit, fussing over them each time one of them got nervous.

I'd been so caught up in my own head I'd almost forgotten that their night hadn't ended quite the same as mine.

While I had thoughts of Quinn to overshadow the

horror of what had happened to me, they didn't. It wasn't long before I got them talking, to bring whatever darkness was festering in their heads out into the light.

We started rehashing the night's drama and I got to learn a little more about the girls. We were a family of sorts I realized.

Each of us bonded together by the men who'd fathered us and whatever it is that they'd done together that had gained them a common enemy.

If Quinn is like dad he won't be sharing, but I was pretty sure that those women I'd seen peeping out of windows might know a thing or two. Same as mom.

I just have to wait for things to settle down a little and I'll learn more. But as great as it is that Quinn and his team were taking care of things, this little woman wasn't done with whatever asshole had had her drugged and thrown into the back of a container. Fuck that!

QUINN

We still needed to make arrangements for the girls and getting them to safety. Lo didn't want too much traffic at the compound which made sense so there was no way their parents could come pick them up here.

I was more worried now about getting out than anything else. This place was about to get hot and I didn't want Kelly anywhere near here when shit jumped off.

"Shit, did anyone check on that boat that was waiting for them last night? I forgot all about that shit. Somebody must've sounded the alarm by now." What the fuck I'm off my game.

"I already took care of that. And I think I have an answer to your problem with the girls as well. If I didn't have to babysit you lot I would've handled it myself but this guy is good."

A battalion of fingers went in the air at his cheap shot but he just grinned and ignored them.

"What you got?" I held the doorknob in my hand as I looked back at Mancini who'd made the offer.

"Well, as Logan said, it's not a great idea to send them back to their homes just yet, not until we know it's safe. They can't stay here for obvious reasons and they can't come with us. I know a guy. He's in Washington has a place right on the border."

"This guy has experience handling kids in this type of situation. He has a safe house where he keeps them in the interim between rescue and reinstatement."

"And he's on the level? You know him?"

"Yep to both."

"Name." He gave us a name that didn't sound familiar and I nodded at Dev to go check him out.

"Lo what did you tell their dads?"

"I told them they might be better off for now and because they know we're the commander's they're giving it some thought. We don't know who's watching them or us for that matter. I think it's best to get them out of the line of fire until we get this thing resolved."

"Are we giving this guy a shot or do we have something else lined up?"

"I was playing around with the idea of letting the admiral take them once he got here, but if Mancini's guy checks out it might be for the best. It's obvious the admiral's being watched if they nabbed his daughter."

I nodded my head and opened the door where Law's crew was still standing watch over the prisoners.

I had a feeling things were coming to a head. They'd gone after all the big guns on this one. A SEAL's life is pretty much kept private outside of everyone who was on the team.

For these men to have known and gone after the daughters of the men who'd been part of a singular unit years ago meant that Khalil had an old debt to square.

It could be that it had all been leading up to this, that all the other women who'd been snatched were part of this. And that was a lot of fucking women and girls.

We knew from the book we'd found in Stockton's

place that most of the girls listed had some affiliation with servicemen in some capacity or another, but until now, we hadn't quite understood the pattern.

The fact that the men mentioned in the codes we'd deciphered were all part of the CO's old team when he himself was an active SEAL meant that the shit went back years. But Khalil would've been a kid back then so who? His old man?

I'll have to wait until we'd taken care of our latest hiccup to bring it up with the others, but either way I was sure that whatever we were dealing with had come to a head.

"Well Quinn, I'm thinking it's your time at bat, we'll play this however you say." I knew Lo was giving me lead on this one because of Kelly.

Each man had taken point where his woman was concerned, and it was now my turn. He was also asking if I wanted to eliminate the men who'd put hands on her.

It was a good thought but there were other things worst than death. Like suffering before it and shit.

"We don't have time for what I want to do to these skells, but we have to keep them around until the admiral gets here. I'm sure he'd like to have a word."

"Okay then, let's get the rest of what we need done. We're losing time as we speak. Mancini as soon as Dev gives the all clear call your guy, in the meantime we have a tunnel to blow. I'm coming with so don't even argue." He held up his hand as Mancini prepared to argue.

"Quinn, make sure this guy is safe. No offence but I don't know him and I'm not about to hand over four innocents to someone I don't know, especially after the hell they've been through. The rest of you know what to do."

21

DEVON

"I can't believe you'd do this shit to me bro, that's cold." He didn't pretend not to know what I was talking about. The heat was on for me now and we both knew it.

Once the women find out that he'd found his match there's no doubting what they'll do to me. Damn.

"Look on the bright side. At the rate the rest of us are falling I give you 'til the end of the week before some filly gets her hooks in you too."

He wish. I played along but deep inside I knew that it wasn't in the works for me. I ignored the voice in my head that said 'maybe' and went back to what I was doing.

Thorpe had checked out but since he was still an unknown I was doing another deeper intensive search just to be on the safe side.

Lo and the others had gone with Mancini and the rest because Lo can never let anyone do his job, or that's the way I'm sure he's looking at it.

Quinn was playing it cool but I knew deep down he'd rather be back at his place getting to know his girl than here with me. I also knew why he thought he had to keep me company.

"You don't have to babysit me you know brother, I'm not gonna freak because I'm the last man standing."

"Don't be an ass, I just figured two heads are better than one and time is of the essence. Be glad it's not Ty, that fucker is chomping at the bit to dig into you."

"I bet, asshole's been talking shit all night."

"You know he has to get his licks in or he won't be Tyler. Don't forget we ragged his ass but good when Vicky got her hooks in him. He's looking for payback. I'm sure he's got some shit lined up for me too."

He stopped talking and I looked away from the screen to study him.

"What is it?" He looked uncomfortable as fuck. Not a look I'm accustomed to seeing on my brother.

"You remember what I've been feeling all day? The shit that got me outta bed in the middle of the night?"

I nodded as I went back to the screen. "Yeah, what about it?" I'd forgotten all about that shit with all that's been going on the last few hours.

"It was her." I gave him a questioning look.

"What do you mean? Like you knew she was in danger?" He nodded but looked away almost like he was embarrassed.

I never understood why he had such a hard time accepting his gift. Where everyone else saw it as a bonus, he always seemed to see it as more of a weakness.

"That's fucking amazing bro. You saved them, not just your girl, but those others…and… you might've peeled back another layer of this fuck fest of a puzzle." I let that settle in for a minute.

"If you hadn't sensed something, then we never would've headed down to the beach. We'd probably be halfway to wherever it is Mancini is dragging us off to and those poor girls…"

I stopped and shook my head because the shit was too awful to think about. It's hard being the man I am, the man all my brothers and the men who'd joined us are deep down inside, to see shit like this.

This is the kinda shit you expect to see in third world countries, and even then it's a hard pill to swallow. But in our own backyard? Just feet from where my sisters put their head down to sleep at night? No fucking way.

"Yeah, there's that. But how do you think she's going to feel having a man who can see into her like that? The shit seems even stronger now that she's here. Like I touch her and some kind of electric shock flows through me. I can only imagine that it'll get worst as time goes on."

"You worry too much bro. I was watching her before, she watches you. And the way she reached for your hand back there, that's telling. Plus she's Mad Dog's kid she has to have a strong constitution."

"Yeah fuck, I forgot about that. What the fuck Dev I can't have Mad Dog for a father in law. The guy would make my life a living hell."

"Too late for that bro, you're all the fucking way gone. So you're tuned into her huh. I wouldn't worry about it, I don't see much difference between that and the way the rest of these clowns are with their women."

"You have a point. But though the others seem to have a bead on their women twenty-four seven, this shit is way more invasive."

"I always knew that was the reason for your holdout. I keep telling you, your old man was wrong. What you have is not a curse, I don't know what you'd call it but it's not that. You've saved our skins more times than I can count, how can it be bad?"

He didn't answer right away but from the look on his face I knew there was something else plaguing him.

"What else is bothering you Quinn?" He stood and walked to the windows and looked out. "There's something I never told you, only Logan knows."

Whatever it is must be really bad because I've never seen him hedging this much.

"Part of this…family 'gift' is that the men always

know their women when they meet them. There's some kind of invisible draw or some shit. I never paid too much attention to the stories because dad used to flip his shit whenever anyone tried to tell me."

"Okay, and we've already decided that he was full of shit. What's wrong with knowing the woman you're going to spend the rest of your life with?"

"It's more than that, this knowing…it's like I can see her. I felt her all night and into today but I didn't know it was her, only that someone I loved was in danger. Then when I touched her on the beach, there was this weird connection. When I'm away from her, like now, I feel like something's missing."

I suppose the look he gave me was to check if I was judging him, but nothing could be farther from the truth.

"I don't see anything wrong with what you're describing. If you're telling me that you loved her on sight then I say good for you. As to feeling like something's missing when you're apart, try to remember how your brothers all acted when they first bit the bullet."

"Fucking Cord was a maniac and Ty lost his fucking mind. If you're gonna be worst than those two then hey, at least we've had practice."

He laughed and shut the hell up and let me get back to my own haunting thoughts. My mind was going in two directions at once.

On the one hand the fact that I was the only one left

kinda gave me hope that it could really happen for me too. On the other hand, the same thought scares the shit outta me.

The thing is, it has been so long since I let myself think about love and marriage that I can't even imagine what my woman may look like.

There was a time long ago when I could've at least see an outline of what I wanted her to be, but now, it escapes me.

I couldn't escape the excitement in my gut though. He'd made that shit look so easy it was hard not to have just a little bit of hope that maybe, just maybe I could find my forever too. This was the first time that my brothers and I weren't on the same page.

Obviously I wasn't gonna run out and grab the first woman I met, but what if there really was someone out there for me?

Someone that could love me scars of the past and all. I shook it off and got back to work, but my mind refused to settle. I decided to fuck with him to get my mind off my own shit.

"So what are you planning to do about your new father in law?"

"I'm seriously considering making a run for it. What the fuck am I gonna do if he tries to take her? That can't happen."

"Chill bro, it'll be fine. If anyone knows the kind of

man you are it'll be an ex-SEAL. I think he'll be glad to have you. And from her side of the conversation on the phone I'm thinking that little princess has her daddy wrapped around her little finger."

"Damn, she's going to be just like the others isn't she?"

"Oh it's a given." I grinned when he lost the color in his face.

I went back to work but there was nothing but silence coming from his side of the room. I looked back over my shoulder at him and had to hide my grin.

Damn, can none of them act normal when they're going through this love shit? I've been in life threatening situations with them more times than I can count, but I have to say, I've never seen my brothers lose their fucking minds the way they do when it comes to their women.

"Why don't you go check on her? I can see you're not getting anything done." He'd been staring at the same screen since we stopped talking.

His boyish grin gave me a start. I don't think I'd ever seen that look on his face before. It was almost soft, inviting. What the fuck was going on around here?

"I'll be back in five." He jumped from his chair and headed for the door, leaving me alone to make myself crazy with my own thoughts of what if. I don't need this shit.

There was too much going on for me to waste time

with that shit anyway. Plus with my wingman showing the signs of being bitch made as Ty is so fond of calling them, I had to be on my A-game.

I checked my watch, time was moving fast and there was still a lot to be done here before we could leave.

We really should be getting outta here but we had to wait for the admiral or they'd be hell to pay. For some reason since Quinn's phone call early this morning or late last night, things seem to be on autopilot.

We'd gone with nothing for weeks, chasing our tails, and now things just seem to be falling into place at warp speed.

First the codes, now Quinn, not to mention saving the daughters of fellow servicemen who were the same ones mentioned by the commander in his secret notes. No SEAL believes in coincidence.

We've been going so fast for the past few hours we hadn't even had time to sit down and digest all the nuances as they kept coming at us like fastballs.

My only interest right now is staying ahead and on the right side of this thing. I have to give the others props on their part in all this. Lyon and Mancini especially.

These two never… well Lyon's never served and I still don't know what the fuck Mancini is other than spooky as fuck.

But these guys when they came here weren't

expecting anything but a pick up and drop. Hours later they're still in the danger zone and not one complaint.

Law and Creed have worked with us before but never on domestic soil and that's another problem we're facing.

We can't neutralize these assholes because we're not technically at war so it'll just be murder, unless we gave them a running chance.

That shit would just bring more headaches than we need. The blowing of the tunnel is bound to bring attention and we still can't leave until the admiral gets here, and we have a secure location to take those girls to.

Which is what I'm supposed to be looking into now instead of thinking about my own shit. I went back to my search and tried not to feel like there was a target on my damn back. Fucking women!

Gideon Thorpe looked almost as cagey as Mancini. There were huge gaps in the bios on him online, that only someone who was looking close enough would notice.

On the surface he was a billionaire businessman with his hands in a lot of pies. But if you know where to look those runs he makes into the most out of the way places on earth, spells either criminal, or special Ops.

I'm willing to take Mancini's word that it's something closer to the latter. The fact that I had to use our special equipment to get that much on him told me he was either deep under cover, which was doubtful because there was no military jacket on him. Or he was one of those billionaires who put his money where his mouth is.

I did as in depth a search as was possible before assuring myself that he was solid. Then I went over the decoded file to see what I could piece together with this latest development with Quinn's woman and the others who'd been taken.

There was something there between the lines but it wasn't ready to break loose for me. I just couldn't see it. I think Lo and Quinn might know though, but we haven't exactly had time for a debriefing so I'll wait and see what they got.

I shut it down and went in search of the others suddenly tired of my own company. I met Quinn in the yard on his way back to the mansion.

"Where's everybody?" For all the activity going on around here in the last few hours the place looked and sounded dead.

"Lo, Con and the others aren't back yet from taking care of the tunnel. Zak and Ty are doing one last run through of our equipment and Cord's at Zak's with the wives."

"Of course he is. How're the girls doing?" I nodded in the direction of his house where we'd stashed them for now.

"They're fine, they're passed out in front of the TV. Well all but one, that one's in my bed." He sounded so happy. It was then I realized that that sound had been missing for a while. In fact I've never heard him sound so happy.

"So, you just had to do it, you had to beat me to the punch. Have you any idea what our sisters are gonna do to me?"

I wondered how well Cord was holding up under the Spanish Inquisition. It was for damn sure the women were grilling his ass but good with all the activity going on around here. Poor schmuck.

He clapped me on the shoulder as we changed direction and headed to where Zak and Ty were making sure we had everything we needed for our little trip.

"I'm sorry brother, but like I said, your time in the box is right around the corner. Maybe they'll be too preoccupied with me and my girl to get into your shit."

"My life won't be worth shit until they tie a noose around my damn neck. I thought we were in this shit together bro, that's foul. You might as well had left me in that hole in Fallujah if you were gonna come back here and sell me out like this."

"Nah bro, trust me it's not like that. It's the most amazing feeling in the world. Like all the battles and shit I've been through was all for her." I couldn't even tease him for being a sap because the emotion in his voice was real.

"You really mean that." I know he did.

"Yeah brother, I fucking do. And you know what, I want the exact same thing for you." We were heading into dangerous waters for me so I took his mind off that shit quick.

"Ty is right." I pretended to give it serious thought.

"About what?" He kept step beside me as we headed for Ty and Zak's location.

"You really are bitch made."

"Shut the fuck up Dev you ass."

He threw a punch which I sidestepped and clapped him back one. That weight that had been pressing down on me since his early morning call had lifted. He was okay.

22

QUINN

~

"Don't forget the Macs." The Macmillan one eighty eight is a long range lethal weapon that can take out anything in its path no matter how big or small.

"And the M14 battle rifles." I called out to Ty and Zak as we entered the weapons room we'd set up in the basement of the mansion.

"What do we look like, new fools or some fuck? Get the hell outta here." Zak checked the glock he held in his hand before placing it in the cache with the other weapons he'd already loaded.

It was almost disheartening to see that shit on our homeland. Never thought anyone would bring the fight to us. But we're navy, we're always prepared for whatever.

"If it isn't bitch made number four." I guess he was taking himself out of the equation.

"I'll take that Ty. If this is what it means to be bitch made then I'm all in."

"I'm happy for you brother. She looks solid." Zak bumped my fist and went back to what he was doing.

"Yeah, but in the stakes of in laws you're fucked." Ty was right, their women had just as little to do with their families as we did ours, but there was no mistaking the fact that Kelly and her dad were close.

"Fuck, I'm trying not to think about that."

"He's a SEAL he'll be fine." Dev said as he walked over to help Ty and we switched gears from talk of women to what the hell we were gonna do about the shit that was going on.

Her dad the admiral showed up an hour later with his wife in tow. She made a beeline for her daughter as soon as we opened the gate to let them in, while her husband stood back and watched the two of them.

He barely spared a glance for the rest of us and I had no doubt he knew all our faces, at least the teams' anyway.

I kept my eyes on Kelly the whole time and felt the second she broke. I'd felt the warning just before they appeared at the gate but hadn't had time to investigate, but already I knew it had something to do with her.

Since she was safe behind these walls and I knew there was no force on earth that could get to her with me there, I knew it wasn't physical danger.

I paid attention to the signs now that I knew what her signature was. There are different levels to this shit, kind of like a rating system of sorts.

It had only activated during combat in the past, but hers was off the fucking charts. I really needed to remember that legend and all that I had in store.

There was no one to call so I'll have to wing it on my own. Hopefully there won't be anymore nasty surprises.

This latest one manifested itself as a slight tingling under my skin and I braced myself until I saw her fall into her dad's arms.

As soon as they went around her she burst into tears. I made an involuntary step towards them and he raised his brow at me over her shoulder before turning his attention back to her.

I gritted my teeth and held my ground even though the sound of her tears tore a hole in my gut. Lo gave me a look, like, stand down, and Dev put his hand on my shoulder. Fuck me what is this?

"It's okay pumpkin, you're safe now." He held her until she calmed down and I had to stand there and watch while she fell apart.

I was as surprised as everyone else when she left him and came to me after they exchanged a few whispered words.

There was no mistaking the feeling of pride that swelled my chest, or the way I felt when she took my hand in hers.

I half expected the admiral to object but instead he just shared a look with his wife before turning to the others.

"Right, where you keeping these dead men walking assholes?" Lo took point and showed him the way while the rest of us fell in behind them.

I released her to go to her mother who still needed reassurance that her kid was okay. They looked alike, Kelly and her mom.

And her mom at least looked a little less frightening than her husband, when she looked back at me with a smile.

The admiral made the mistake of telling his wife he thought she should join the other women, but there was no mistaking the look she threw him.

This man of whom I'd heard so many stories of valor just shook his head, sighed and gave up.

Shots fired and she didn't even have to open her mouth.

Damn, I was beginning to understand what my brothers have been dealing with all these months and weeks.

That thought was followed by the sobering realization that this was going to be my life from now on.

We had a little meet while we sent the women ahead of us to wait at the cottage door. We filled the admiral in with a quick summary of what we had so far.

"I know exactly what I'm gonna do with them. I got a few calls before I left the house. Seems that at least one of the daughters of each of the men from my old team were taken. I know you have to have something on this by now, but we'll deal with that later. Take me to them."

"Wait you said you knew what to do with them?" He wasn't planning on killing them was he? It takes time to bury bodies so that even sonar can't find them, and time we do not have.

"I came down The Ditch by boat, they'll be leaving with me. The others are going to meet me and we'll take it from there." By others I took it to mean the other dads, men from the CO's team.

"Lieutenant, you said the girls should go into hiding, you have a place in mind?" I told him about Thorpe and he looked towards Mancini for some reason.

"You I know but who are you?" He looked at Lyon who was reading something on his phone.

"Who me? I'm not that well known. I do all my fighting on domestic soil, never signed up."

He went back to messing with his phone and it was Mancini's turn to ask a question.

"How do you know me?" Mancini asked. It was obvious that the admiral would know Law and Creed, they were military, but I too was interested in how he knew the elusive Mancini.

He just smirked at Mancini who wasn't looking too pleased. "I know your boss."

That seemed to settle Mancini's ruffled feathers not to mention from the look Lo passed the rest of us, sent Mancini up another notch in the trustworthy stacks.

We'd accepted him from what we'd learned so far, but the admiral had all but given him a ringing endorsement with just those few words.

I acknowledged Lo's unspoken statement and we got back on track. "We have to move admiral, time is of the essence." Plus the women looked like they'd had enough of standing around waiting.

It was a different man who followed us into the cottage. Gone was the easy-going father and in his place was pure warrior.

I'd expected him to be older because of his rank and his years in service, but he couldn't be more than early fifties.

He looked much younger, and so did his wife who was her daughter's mirror image. And seeing him here only brought back memories of the CO.

He stood in front of the four men who were still standing against the wall under guard, his stance like that of a shipmaster. It was obvious he'd spent some time at sea.

He studied the men wordlessly for the longest while until he turned to look at his daughter.

"Which one?" Did he always speak in half sentences?

It didn't matter; she knew exactly what he was asking as was made obvious when she pointed out the kid who'd manhandled her on the beach. He stepped in closer until their noses nearly touched.

"You drug my kid?" The guy looked pitiful enough that I almost felt sorry for him.

"I…no, it was…" He looked to the guy next to him.

"You were drugged? You didn't tell me that."

I glared at her and she shrugged. I looked from her to the asshole wishing now that I had done more than rough him up a little.

"How did you know she was drugged sir?"

"Because there's no way any of these punk assholes could've taken her otherwise." He answered me before turning his attention back to his prey.

"I hear you have temporary amnesia. I'm gonna give you five seconds to get that shit gone or I'm gonna pull your lungs through your fucking navel." He cracked his knuckles and started the countdown and no one in the room doubted that he was gonna do exactly what he said.

I guess the kid saw that too because his eyes went wide and he swallowed around a sudden lump in his throat. McCullum made a move towards his throat and he started talking fast.

"Okay-okay, look. I have a cousin in the Midwest." He named the town and my team and all the men who'd been at Law's went on alert. We'd come full circle again.

"He called and asked for a favor." He had to stop before he choked on his own spit and it was becoming more and more clear that this kid was no mastermind.

"Go on." The admiral encouraged him when it looked like he couldn't go any farther.

"He asked me to help this other guy take the girl but I wasn't in charge."

"Who is?" He shifted his eyes to the side and the Admiral moved two men down to the man he'd indicated.

"So, who're you working for?" He looked like he could be trouble but I guess a room full of men who looked like they'd eat his guts for dinner changed his mind.

"I don't know the head guy in charge and that's the truth. I get my orders by phone. They tell me who and where, send me a picture and that's it. We work as a team."

"Keep talking tell me about this team."

"It's usually a two man team. We coordinate with the other teams in different areas and then all the girls are taken to a secure location where another team drives them to the safe house until it's time for them to…"

So that's how they do it. Now it was my turn to do some questioning of my own. "What was the final destination? And don't tell me you don't know."

"Um, I heard some talk. They go all over the place but this last bunch was special, they were going to the Middle-East somewhere and that's all I know I swear."

I looked at my brothers. That was all the confirmation we needed. If there'd been any doubt that Khalil was behind this it was long gone now.

"This bunch? How many of these runs have you made?" Now he was looking real nervous as if he'd had a hope in hell of getting out of this mess.

"A few but we didn't know…"

"If you're about to lie to me don't." Asshole was lucky that we had women and children here and we were strapped for time.

As it stood, we'd already decided to lock their asses away somewhere until this thing was done. There was no doubt that the alarm had been rung by now unless they were complete incompetents.

23

QUINN

Mancini reminded us that we had to go and we helped the admiral load his prisoners on the boat. The sun would be up in another half an hour and we hurried to pack up and head out.

The plan was to ride out to the airfield and board the three planes Mancini had waiting. I felt a whole lot better about this move now that the admiral had given Mancini his stamp of approval.

She'd only cried a little at her parents' leaving and for a second there I thought her father was going to order her to go with them.

I saw the effort it took for him to give her back to me and was grateful I got off easy with just a warning.

Of course being warned that he'd hang my nuts on a

spike if I fucked over his kid was a bit harsh, but it was reasonable.

I'd wanted to take her to meet my sisters, but this would be the last time with the girls she'd saved and I didn't want to rob her of that. She'll have the rest of her life with the others after all.

All the women were going on to Mancini's hideout while we were going with Hank to drop off the girls and make sure this place was legit, or in other words, up to Lo's standards.

I'd just closed the door to leave her to her goodbyes and was on my way to meet the others who were having some sorta powwow.

Apparently Lyon was giving Hank the third degree, since his wife and kids were going ahead of him and he's not in the habit of trusting his family to just anyone.

I walked up in time to hear what I suppose was his last threat. "Anything happen to my woman spook boy ain't enough holes for you to hide in. That's all I'm saying."

Hank, being the smooth operator that he is just calmly reassured Lyon and the rest of us truth be known, that all was good. Besides, Law's crew was going with them.

That didn't necessarily placate Lyon but at least his bark had boiled down to a grumble.

Just then a chopper flew overhead, too damn low for comfort and there was no doubt they were buzzing us.

"What the fuck?" Lo looked up as Zak and Cord took

off running towards the women. Mancini pulled what looked like a glock from under his jacket.

"Get inside."

"Hank, domestic soil." Lo warned him.

"I don't play by those rules." None of the rest of us moved.

The fucker took aim and followed the aircraft as it made a turn. He waited until it was over the water and fired.

The explosion was loud as fuck and we knew any minute the whole place would be swarming with cops. "There were two on board came out of Langley."

"How do you know that?" I asked Mancini as we headed to my place to get the girls.

"My people picked up their Intel while we were inside. The NatSec really needs to do something about their secure broadbands."

"I like this fuck, what's that you're carrying there Hanky?" Lyon, who had been surprisingly quiet at this turn of events jogged up next to him, trying to get a look at the piece he was carrying.

"It's just a little handheld with extra power. I'll get you one." The two of them laughed and Lyon clapped him on the shoulder.

My brothers, Law, Creed and I shared a look and I knew to a man we were all thinking that was not a good idea.

Of course the women heard the explosion and wanted to know what was going on, but we just loaded them up and headed out.

Cord ran back to the mansion and came back with the old man's portrait and the only thing he'd say when we looked at him questioningly was that he'd tell us later.

There were a lot of hurried goodbyes and I had to damn near pry Kelly away from her wards. Her tears I already knew were going to be a problem for me.

I felt like the worst son of a bitch because I couldn't give her what she wanted. And the shit was fucking with my head. Damn!

I introduced her to her new sisters before their plane left and had to drag Ty's ass away from Vicki to get him on the plane with us.

No one was settled and relaxed, least of all me. We'd all just trusted our women to a complete stranger stamp of approval or not.

We got the kidnapped girls settled in the back of the Gulf Stream and strapped in up front. Whoever Mancini is, dude's got the best fucking toys. This G-six held all of us with room to spare.

Just before we went wheels up a screen came on and a female voice came on while it was still black. "Hank are they here? I fell asleep."

"No baby, we have to make a run, I'll be with you in another three hours or so. Are you decent?" There was some wrestling around and it was obvious from the sounds that whoever she was she was in bed.

"I'm up, what's going on?" The screen faded from black to the sleepy face of a very beautiful woman who looked like she was being swallowed by a man's dress shirt.

There was no need to guess who she was from the way Mancini reacted as soon as she came on screen. He did everything but kiss the damn screen.

"Hi baby, say hi to our new friends. Gentlemen Special Agent Cierra Mancini, F.B.I. my wife." Say what now?

"Did we know he was married?" I turned to Lyon who was the one who'd brought him in. "There's someone for everyone, we have to hope that she's stable."

Hank gave us a look and we turned our attention to his wife who apparently was waiting for us and our women at his secret hideaway.

I guess he did that to put our minds at ease and it did. "Go back to sleep princess I'll call you when we land." They shared a look through the screen before it went dark.

"So how does that work? A spook married to an F.B.I. agent? I thought you two were supposed to be like mortal enemies or some shit?"

Damn Lyon, no filter. For the next ten minutes we bullshitted around but it was only a matter of time before things got serious.

It seems Mancini had been making a lot of calls while we were in the cottage with the general. “Okay, two things. That fly over was supposed to drop something on your compound. Not to worry, I have people on it just in case they send in another team.”

My brothers and I shared a look. If’ they’d graduated to taking us out then the chips were down. “You sure Hank?”

“Logan I’ll give you about one more day before you no longer ask me that. Of course I’m sure.”

“They gotta ask spook boy, can’t nobody find shit on you.” Leave it to Lyon to put it so succinctly.

“You said two things.” I was listening in but my mind was already with her. We kept our voices low so that they didn’t carry to the four girls in the sleep room in the back.

“Yeah, you’ve got some heavy hitters involved here. This one goes all the way to the top boys.” We already knew or suspected that to some degree, but having verification changes everything.

“Yeah we know about the asshole senator.” Lyon chimed in. “Who else you got?”

“Generals and a few low key players. And this definitely goes back to your guy in the desert.”

We spent the next forty-five minutes shooting around ideas about the best course of action. “So basically you’re saying Law and I got snagged in his net because we worked for your CO a time or two.”

"Sorry about that boys, but that's the way it's looking. I think this thing started long before any of us came on board though." Since Lo was letting me run this show, I filled the others in on what we'd found.

Now that we'd got the women out of the line of fire it was easy to focus more fully and shit started falling into place.

We didn't know all the men the old man had mentioned in his codes neither did we know where to find them.

If Khalil was exacting revenge for some past wrong we needed to find all these people and make sure they were okay.

We got to our destination in less than half the time it would've taken if we weren't riding in a top of the line Gulf Stream that seemed to just cut through the clouds.

There were a coupla cars waiting for us when we landed and a lone man standing outside the first one. He looked kinda relaxed for someone who'd been dragged out of his bed in the middle of the night.

We got the girls off and kept them between us and him as we walked forward following Hank. As we got closer I saw that this guy was about our age give or take.

"Gentlemen I'd like to introduce you to Gideon Thorpe. Other than myself he's the leading authority on the underground trafficking world. He got dragged into it by default when his wife became a target of sorts."

Thorpe came forward and shook each of our hands, looking at us like he was sizing us up. “Gentlemen!”

“I already told Gideon part of the situation but if anyone wants to add anything feel free.”

“I got all I need.” He whistled and two people stepped out of the backseat of the second car.

“Gentlemen my wife Ashley.” He wrapped his arm around the shoulders of the woman who didn’t look old enough to be anyone’s wife but who was obviously pregnant.

“And her brother Jacob.” A young man held out his hand before the two of them flanked her on either side like they were ready for anything.

“Take the girls to the car Blossom.” He kissed her head and she moved over to the four girls who were standing around huddled together.

“Wait!” I walked over before they could be loaded into the car. I looked them over, especially Cara. “You’ll be safe here until this whole thing is over. Your dads will get in touch with you soon and as soon as we get things settled I’ll bring Kelly to see you guys.”

They all hugged me which was surprising because I didn’t remember doing anything to warrant it. Then they went down the line thanking the others which seemed to embarrass them no end.

We didn’t get to follow to see where they were being

taken which didn't sit very well with us, but this Thorpe guy wasn't taking any chances it seems.

He reassured us that they'd be fine and that he'd keep in contact with us. I didn't know that Mancini had worked it out so that their dads could come to them when the coast was clear.

Back on the plane I laid my head back and processed all that had happened in the last twenty-four hours. Has it only been twenty-four? Damn, felt like a lifetime.

24

QUINN

I must've dozed off because when I woke up again we were landing. I didn't feel bad about rushing to see her since all the others had pretty much the same idea.

I don't know what I'd expected once we got here but I should've known by now that Mancini never did the expected.

It was obvious that we were on an island somewhere but which one it wasn't easy to tell. There was a cliff and waves crashing against the rocks.

Off in the distance there was a mansion, and behind that in what looked like acres of gardens were cottages, or villas, I couldn't tell from this far out.

"Whoa, fuck, I'm not gonna get Kat's ass off this shit." Lyon looked at us like we'd committed a crime before heading for the line of cars that were waiting for us.

We'd sent all our stuff ahead with the women so there was nothing to offload except the cache of weapons.

As we drew up we saw the women sitting out front the mansion watching the kids play. I searched her out and relaxed once I saw her in the midst of the girls.

She was laughing at something Dani was saying, head thrown back and so damn beautiful I ached. She saw me somehow and got up from her chair.

I stopped moving even as my brothers and the others kept going. She ran by them and right into my arms like it was something she did everyday and my beast put his head down.

"Hi baby!" My arms went around her as her legs came around my waist. Our lips met and my beast came fully awake again.

"Are my girls okay?" She whispered in my ear before getting down off of me. "Yeah baby they're good. Their dads are gonna go see them later and once we've got everything cleared up they'll be back home before you know it."

"Then we'd better get to work, they've been through enough already." She took my hand and led me back to the others.

"We…are not doing anything babe, I'll take it from

here." She actually looked over her shoulder and smiled at me.

I kinda thought the smile looked a bit condescending but I wasn't exactly sure until the next words out of her mouth.

"Aw, you're so cute. Your sisters, who I love by the way, told me you'd try something like that. But see, I'm the one who was closest to those freaks so I'm thinking you're gonna need me."

Wait, there's shit she didn't tell me? There was something going on once we got back to the others and from the body language it looked like a girls against boys sorta deal.

"Ah damn, what?" I looked from Lo to Con then to Lyon who seemed to be in a staring match with his wife who ignored him as she rubbed the huge mound of her tummy.

There was only one face I didn't recognize. Mancini's wife looked like a completely different person once she was dressed in her own designer clothes and didn't have bed head.

Ty stepped up to answer. 'Well, far as I can tell. In the time it took us to get here Hank's woman told this lot a little more than we had."

She shrugged her shoulders and sipped her tropical juice like she didn't just open Pandora's box. "No one told me I wasn't supposed to, and since this involves them as well, I thought they had a right to know."

There were groans from all the men including me, but the women looked cool. This shit smacked of a setup, like they'd banded together in the two minutes it took us to get here.

Fucking women, it took us weeks and sometimes months to form a bond as a team. It takes them less time than it does to put on lipstick. All eyes went to Hank to do something about his woman.

"Don't look at me." Mancini backed away with his hands in the air but there was no way to miss the grin on his face as he turned to go inside.

"By the way Quinn congratulations." Dani's comment was followed by the other women's, who once they were done giving me a round of hugs, turned their attention to Devon.

"Oh fu…hell no." He followed Mancini inside leaving the rest of us to deal with our mess. "Kat, time for a nap." Lyon tried pulling his wife up from her seat.

"I'm not sleepy." She didn't budge.

"Babe, you've been up all night those kids need their rest. Speaking of which, where's Mengele?" "Colton, don't call her that in front of company."

"I'm pretty sure they know. It only takes five minutes for those blonde curls and that innocent little girl look to lose it's cover power."

I think everyone else was trying not to laugh, but Kat looked ready to kill.

"I think we all could use some rest."

Lo, either trying to diffuse the situation or trying to waylay the women who actually thought we were going to let them in on what we were doing, piped in.

He wasn't fooling anyone, and when the women all looked around the table I'm sure I wasn't the only one who noticed the nod between Lyon's wife and the rest of them before they suddenly agreed. "Great, you guys can put the kids down for a nap."

She passed Lyon their youngest who'd been resting on Dani's lap and Nessa passed Zakira to her dad.

They made a beeline for the garden and the cottages beyond which apparently had already been divided up.

I counted three men roaming the grounds back there but I'm sure Kelly never noticed them they were that good.

I wasn't sure what just happened back there and why the women had caved so easily, but I wasn't sure I trusted it.

LYON

'This is some place huh!" We were the only couple other than Mancini and his woman who were staying in the big house because of our battalion of kids.

Thank fuck, if I had to stay in one of those match-boxes with my brood I'd lose my damn mind.

Not that I don't love my kids, but damn they can get into some shit. "You been keeping an eye on Mengele right." I put the baby down in the adjoining room and hoped he stayed down.

"Colton, I wish you'd leave our daughter alone."

"Yeah, there's a cliff out there, you won't be saying that shit when she chucks one of your kids off that shit."

My fucking kid; gotta love her. All the way to the SEALs place she must've asked me a thousand questions about what was going on.

All the other kids bought the vacation bullshit we sold them, not her. Her ass was probably listening in at doors and shit and knew that something was up.

Right now I'm more interested though in my wife and what she was up to. That little mini mutiny outside just now smacked of her meddling shit.

"Colton," She hush whispered at me. "Why are you taking off your clothes? We can't have sex here." She looked around the room like there was someone hiding in the corners or some shit.

"Pretty sure they already know we fuck Kat." I pointed at her tummy and she growled. I notice she's been getting worst with each pregnancy. Her hormones are probably outta whack or some shit.

"Maybe you should take yours off, then again better not, sure as fuck one of your nosy ass kids gonna be at that door in the next five minutes. Lucky for you that's all the time I need."

"All the time you need for what?" She scooted back on the bed like that was gonna work. My baby never learns.

I came down on the bed over her, caging her in. It was easy enough peeling the mom jeans off down her thighs and lifting her shirt up over her gigantic amazing tits.

My dick leaked at the sight of her. Her hand came up and played with my cock piercing and my eyes damn near crossed.

When she started stroking me I forgot what the fuck I was supposed to be doing in here, and when she slid down beneath me between my thighs and took the head of my cock in her mouth, I lost all fucking thought.

"Damn baby, shit. Fuck Kat!" Her freaky ass hummed around my meat and sent electric shocks up my spine. She trailed her nails down the back of my thighs and I knew she meant business.

I pulled out of her mouth and went to put her legs on my shoulders. "No Colton I wanna be on top." I looked at her suspiciously but got on my back.

She only likes doing this shit when she wants something. It's her position of power. Uh-huh. Little sneak is up to some shit.

She teased my cock back and forth over her dripping pussy folds before taking me in and sitting herself all the way down on my throbbing cock.

"Damn, how is your pussy still so tight?" I grabbed her hips and fucked up into her, forgetting all about why the hell I'd brought her in here in the first place.

"Ah damn Kat, kiss me." I needed her to swallow my growl before the whole damn island knew what the hell we were up to in here.

She did that clench and release thing with her pussy which was a couple degrees hotter because of the baby in her womb and I started shooting off inside her.

KAT

I gave the others time to get their jobs done before sneaking out of the room. He looked so perfect sleeping there that I was tempted to kiss him, but I didn't want to risk waking him.

I'd had the better part of last night and this morning when we got here to talk to the girls. We've been keeping in touch since meeting over the holidays but it's not the same as being in the same room together.

I'd spent that time wisely. Since my husband and theirs weren't sharing I knew we'd have to go all commando to find out anything.

I would ask Meng…I mean Catalina to spy since she's so good at it, but I'm trying not to do that. The child is scary enough as it is without me encouraging her.

Once we got to meet Kelly who filled in a little bit more of the puzzle, we put our heads together and came up with a plan.

Cierra being a bona fide agent was going to come in handy as well, but it was agreed that we just have to get the men out of the way first.

I've learned and have been teaching them how to work around hardheaded alpha males. I should be a damn expert. I've lived with my nut for the better part of seventeen years. They're newbies.

I snuck out of the room, knowing he was going to be pissed once he wakes up. I figured since they were up all night and us girls had had a few hours down time, they'd be tired once they got here.

Each woman had her job to do and then we were going to meet in the media room where Cierra was going to use her credentials to get us some information.

The only hitch was the kids who were so excited at being at the beach, but Hank had thought of everything and there was a complete staff here, including nannies. If I could just keep Catalina occupied for a while that'd be great.

I snuck along the hallway and down the stairs without seeing anyone else. The Mancinis were on the other side of the house in a separate wing and the others were occupying the cottages.

I wasn't worried about the older kids. Caitlin stays on her phone with Todd, the twins and Caleb are boys who're always into gross but safe things, and Cody's too young to get out of his crib.

But Catalina; there's no getting away from the fact that she needs twenty-four hour supervision. I knew these 'nannies' were some kind of Special Forces.

You can't live around Colton Lyon all these years and not know when someone was carrying, but I have yet to meet the man or woman who can outsmart my kid.

I prayed for peace and waited for the others as I looked out the window. In the distance I saw Catalina and little Zakira on the beach with one of the nannies walking behind.

At least that should keep her quiet for a while. She likes having someone younger than her to boss around since her brothers and sister wouldn't let her, and Cody was too young.

25
DEVON

I escaped into the woods around the property to get away from my sisters and the other women. I knew this shit was going to happen, and now I'm marooned on this damn island with water on one side and a steep cliff on the other.

The only escape was the thick woods way off on the other side in back of the property. I figured they'd had enough time to turn their minds to something else, so once I'd done some recon I decided to head back.

I had my head down in deep thought, wondering if there was any truth to what the others kept saying, that I was next.

A part of me was excited at the thought that there

might be someone out there waiting for me. And then there was the part of me that didn't believe it.

Something, some movement up ahead alerted me. I was about to call out to Dani from my place in the trees but there was something about her movements that tipped me off. "What the hell is she up to?"

I watched her tiptoe away from the door of the cottage taking sneak peaks behind her as if expecting Lo to come after her.

I would've laughed it off but then I saw Gaby and the others acting pretty much the same way and knew I was right, they were up to something. "Well shit!"

I've been riding herd on these women long enough to know the signs and this shit spells trouble. If they weren't so damn cunning this shit would be funny.

The five of them on their own are enough of a headache, but now they have reinforcements, which if anyone had listened to me they would've known to be on their guard for.

But I knew even if my brothers didn't, that getting these women together could be trouble. After they all met at Lyon's place over the holidays, they've become thick as thieves.

I know Lo and Con thought they'd put paid to their sticking their noses into shit that didn't concern them, but I knew better. I saw their faces that night and knew damn good and well they weren't going to leave this shit alone.

Used to be Quinn and I would be the ones to see through their shit since we were the only ones not entangled, but now he'd joined the ranks of the witless.

I wasn't surprised when I saw his woman sneaking out of their cottage and tiptoeing away towards the mansion after the others.

I had one question. Where the hell were their men? I'd left a little over an hour ago after the girls had set their sights on me.

Even though Mancini had the place well surrounded and enough security to protect The Hague, I figured it couldn't hurt to give the place a walk through.

My whole family was here and since my brothers tend to lose their minds when they get caught up with their women, it was up to me to watch their six.

I stood in the tree line for another few seconds trying to figure out what the hell I had just seen, but unless they'd all plotted to off their men in some kinda fucked up scheme, there was some other shady shit going on.

I went to Lo's place first. All the cottages looked alike but his was easy to find. It was the one in the most strategic location.

If an enemy was able to breech the perimeter they'd have to get through him first. That's just Lo. No matter that he now had a woman and a baby on the way. He still won't put his safety before ours.

I could try convincing him that since I was the only

one who didn't have a family to look out for I should be the one taking that position, but I knew that argument would only fall on deaf ears.

We'll all be seventy and Lo would still be standing between us, and danger. It's in his blood. He came to the door wiping sleep from his eyes and looking back into the room over his shoulder.

No doubt he was wondering where his woman had got to. "The women are up to something." He came fully awake and reached down for his shoes that were right inside the door.

"Where are the others?"

"I'm guessing the same place you were."

"Fuck, what now?" He slammed the door behind him and we headed to Con's place next door.

We went door to door rousing the others who all had the same reaction before we headed to the mansion.

We passed the kids running around on the lawn with a battalion of security guards standing watch over them.

Little Zak was having the time of her life with all these new kids to play with and it only brought home the reality of her existence the last few months.

She'd been locked away like the rest of us, her freedom restricted the way no child's should ever be.

It was for her as much as the rest of us that I wanted this shit over and done with. I want her childhood and all my future nieces and nephews to have the sort of childhood I'd enjoyed before my parents were taken from me.

I shied away from thoughts of my parents and that life that was long gone and focused on the here and now, and what new fuckery my sisters were into.

All the men were wide-awake now. "Where's Lyon?" Law yawned and scratched his gut before shaking his head and opening the back door.

Since we didn't know what the hell they were up to we decided to pull a sneak attack. Mancini met us coming down the back stairs with a finger to his lips.

"I'll get Lyon." He motioned for us to follow him and we headed up the stairs and to the other side of the house still no wiser to what the hell was going on.

He knocked lightly on the door before pushing it open. Lyon sat up gun in hand and we all stepped out of the line of fire.

'The fuck is this an invasion?" He looked at the spot next to him and then around the room. "Where the fuck is my wife?"

"Get dressed and come with us. The women are congregating in my media room. It doesn't look good for us." Mancini answered him.

"Fucking Kat." Just then the baby started fussing in the other room and he got off the bed with the sheet wrapped around him.

Mancini closed the door and we waited until Lyon

came out of the room with the baby on his chest. "Okay, I gotta get him settled or he'll scream this shit down."

He passed Ty a bottle and sent him on a mission to heat it up. "That doesn't leave your sight. Forty-five seconds in the nuker. Okay where the fuck we going?"

He addressed this last to Mancini after Ty left on his errand. "We have to wait for him, he'll never find us."

"Ten guesses what they're up to." Con shook his head and said what the rest of us were thinking. "What're we gonna do?" Zak seemed stumped, maybe because he'd been woken out of a deep sleep.

"You don't know that they're up to anything, maybe they're discussing wedding plans or some shit."

"Cord not even you believe that shit." I laughed and slapped him on the back.

"Dammit, I told Susie to stay out of it."

Well shit! All we need is for him to go all caveman and derail our reason for being here. Thankfully Ty was back in five and he got distracted.

We followed Mancini back to his side of the house and into a room that took two doors and codes pressed into three separate keypads to get into.

The place looked like a space station. There were monitors and screens covering the walls and the windows were blacked out.

"Damn Mancini. This is a serious FOB you got here." From the surroundings I'd just cased, the strategic location of the buildings on the property and now this. Fucker even got aircraft back there in the woods.

I'd never seen a setup like this outside the military but could see my brothers and I doing something like it.

It would take a lot of money, but to be this self- sufficient would be well worth it. Not to mention the way shit's going we just might need it.

"This place makes our little compound look like a kindergarten playground doesn't it?" I whispered to Quinn as the others took in our surroundings.

The only one not impressed was Lyon who was busy playing daddy. The kid had his legs wrapped around his dad's arm as if to hold him in place and was going to town on that bottle.

"Mancini, what the fuck are you?" Zak asked the question I think all of us were thinking. As expected he just smirked and took a seat behind the command station.

He pressed some buttons on the computer on his desk and the screens came alive. The women were spread out in the media room.

At first glance it looked like I'd jumped the gun. They had the TV on and it looked like they were watching some kinda wedding planning show.

There were trays of snacks and each woman had what looked like the smallest teacup I've ever seen in their hands.

I was about to apologize for ringing the alarm and

telling myself I was off because of the shit that had gone down last night, but then he hit the volume.

"So, we don't have much time. If I know Colton he's gonna roll over any second and find me gone." "So, what's he gonna do? We're just planning a wedding." That was Kelly, but already I could tell she was being sarcastic.

"Yes, we are, but you don't understand, these men are suspicious by nature. I know Logan is."

"Sheesh, you think your guys are bad. If someone even smiles at me it takes me the whole rest of the day to calm Justice down."

"And by someone I mean anything male. If his suspicions were true, I'd know half the men in our state. He doesn't seem to get the concept that some people just smile and it doesn't mean they want to take you to bed."

Creed flexed his jaw at his woman's words, his eyes dead on the screen. The women all had something to say about their over protective men.

Kat Lyon looked around the room almost as if she could sense her husband's eyes on her. It was like watching a comedy skit.

"I still say we should've done this outside. I don't trust Hank worth shit. I'm pretty sure he has this whole place bugged. You wanna talk about paranoid." Mancini's woman did some looking around of her own.

"Now why would my sweet wife think such a thing about her adoring husband?" Maybe because she knows you? I thought it but didn't say it as Lyon's wife's voice came through the speaker.

"Oh no, we can't risk that. Catalina would snoop and then she'd tell her daddy everything word for damn word. I think he bribes her. Nope this is the safest place. Besides, if you ladies did what I told you, they should be out for a while. It's just Colton…ugh!"

"What about your husband?" Vanessa took a sip from her cup. "He's…different. My little trick doesn't always work on him and that nut takes suspicion to a whole new level, so let's get this started before he wakes up."

"So what is it they did to you lot to put you out for a while?" I looked around at the others in the room with the most innocent expression on my face.

I had to cover my mouth with my hand when they all got twitchy. "Laugh now brother, but your time is fast approaching." Lo grumbled at me.

"Seriously? Why are y'all so intimidated by those men? What are they gonna do? Like, we're grown women." That was Kelly again, the newest addition. Poor thing. I had no doubt the others would soon school her.

"Oh you poor sweet delusional thing. These men are nuts. If we get caught meddling we'll be lucky if they don't lock us in a room for the duration."

"Ah come on Danielle, Quinn's a big old teddy bear. I think he's sweet on me." Quinn took a lot of ribbing over that one and the red flush on his face was damn comical. I'm gonna enjoy this shit.

"And besides, we just met, he doesn't have any control over me."

"Quinn!" Lo's voice stopped him halfway to the door.

"Damn bitch made, you're so easily baited." Ty was talking shit because his girl was the only one actually looking through a bridal magazine and sipping tea.

"I know whatever we're here to do we better make it quick. I am not in the mood for one of Tyler's tantrums. I wanna enjoy the beach before he takes away any more of my privileges."

That started a debate among all the women as they compared their men's tactics. I looked at my brothers and the others in the room and felt pity for them.

"Damn you boys are so fucked." I turned back to the screen when Lyon's woman once again called the meeting to order.

Mancini's woman looked like she was taking notes as each woman went around the room giving what little bit of information she'd gathered from listening into her husband's conversations.

"Damn, they know a lot."

"I tried to tell you." I looked at Lo who looked like he was taking mental notes himself.

"Ok so Kelly, you were the closest of any of us to this mess. What did you hear?"

"Well, like I already told you ladies, I was snatched and held at a place not far from the compound."

Our girls looked at each other and nodded for her to carry on. "My dad's a SEAL, well he used to be active, now he's an admiral so he's more administrative."

"Anyway I get the feeling that whatever this is, it has to do with his team from back in the day, which involved the CO."

"I know a little bit about him but of course dad never got into too much detail, but I heard those men talking. They're working off of some list. All the girls that were taken were the daughters of military men."

"Daughters? Oh shit…that meeting at Law's place last year. Dana, Melissa any of you know what that was about?"

"Same thing, the only one missing was Mancini." Dana Sue answered Kat Lyon.

"I think he met them in the winter. It was the holidays in fact. We'd just got home that night I think and he told me he had to make a run. It was after he came back that he started working on something, I bet it was this."

"Kelly you said they were working off a list what list? And what about daughters? Colton was never in the military." She sounded panicked, like someone who'd just figured out something they wish they hadn't.

"I'm not sure what Colt's part in all this is Katarina,

but when those guys were stupidly talking within earshot, I could've sworn I heard them say their next stop is Cali."

"Shit anyone on the old man's list out there? Mancini do you mind?" Lo went to the computer and since the unit was obviously secure just typed in some code.

The rest of us watched the screen as the names we'd decoded the day before came up and a background search begun.

The women carried on their conversation, Mancini's wife promising to put in a call to someone she knew to see if she could get any information and the others trying to piece shit together. Pretty much the way we do.

"There he is. He lives in the Hollywood hills." "Served with the CO damn, all the way back." "Doesn't say here that he has a daughter though, he has a son."

"What the fuck? It says the kid works for DOD, that can't be right. He's like seventeen, eighteen."

"Give me a minute boys." Mancini moved Con and Lo out of the way and did some fast finger moving shit on his computer.

"Damn, I shouldn't be seeing this." Lo's actions belied his words since he didn't look away from the screen. It looked like we were looking at top- secret documents, and he was right. We shouldn't be seeing this.

"Damn, the kid's a hacker." Law looked over Mancini's shoulder as the rest of us gathered around for a better look.

"Not just any hacker, he's part of Anonymous." Mancini made that announcement.

"Whoa, what the fuck? Is he the one they're after?"

"What or who the fuck is Anonymous?"

"Uh, short version Lyon, an international group of highly skilled hackers. And this little gem right here is the fucker that hacked NASA and the DOD." Mancini tapped his finger against the screen.

"The fucker did it in less then five minutes." Every military man in the room whistled because we knew to a man the type of skill something like that would take.

Mancini on the other hand had a very telling smile on his face. No doubt he was thinking of recruiting the little shit.

"What's his name?" Con asked and Mancini scrolled down the screen

"Track!"

"Oh the irony." Even I had to give the kid his props.

Since the women were still brainstorming and it looked like we'd learned everything they had which wasn't much, except for Kelly's little bombshell, it was our turn to do a little digging of our own.

26

QUINN

Not even a full day yet and already she'd joined ranks with the women. I didn't know if to be pleased about that or pissed that she thought I had no say in what she did.

I'm happy that Lo had stopped me just now though because who knows what I would've done or said if I'd gone down there in a huff.

My brothers were still going on about the kid and trying to figure out where he fit in. So far these boys had gone after daughters, or were they just choosing any kid as long as they belonged to one of the CO's old team?

Lyon was looking quiet and contemplative which is not necessarily a good thing coming from that quarter, but at least he had the baby in his arms.

"Quinn since you've got point why don't you bring these boys up to speed on what we have so far?" "Sure thing Lo."

All eyes turned my way and Mancini turned down the volume so the women's voices were mere drones in the background.

I went through everything we had so far including what we'd found in the CO's little surprise book and the names we'd found there.

It was a testament to how much we trusted them that we were willing to share what could be classified information. But I had no doubt that nothing we said would leave the room.

Plus it was good to have new eyes since the seven of us were so close to the situation. It might loosen something up that we'd missed.

We spent the next hour throwing around ideas, the only common consensus being that we had to go to Cali and grab this kid before those assholes got to him first.

"Where the fuck is Davey?" I'd only just noticed that he wasn't in the room.

"Probably sniffing around my kid. I hope his ass can fly cause I will throw him off that cliff out there."

"Chill Lyon, he's not that kinda kid."

"Dude, I'm pretty sure he's what, eighteen, nineteen? They're all that kinda kid. The only reason I haven't put the fear of hell in his ass is because my girl is already gone over some asshole kid back home."

This guy at some point is going to have to get some kind of medical attention for his psychosis; but that's for another time.

"I think we better keep an eye on him too." My brothers knew what I was talking about but we hadn't shared our suspicions that the old man might be his dad with the others yet.

"So it's settled we're going after this kid."

"Yep, I say we leave tonight. How far are we from location Mancini?"

"About six hours we can make it in three and a half, four."

"Okay we need to get eyes on that house."

"No problem." He pulled up the home on a wall screen and put in some shit on the computer that took us to the front door."

"What the fuck is that?"

"I would think you'd know. The military has been playing around with this little toy for the better part of six months."

It's the first time I'd seen anything like it. It was like Google earth on steroids. You could actually see inside the house and its surroundings in real time, almost like you were there.

"Are we calling ahead Quinn?" I fielded Lo's question and had to think about it. I shook my head as I worked it out.

"No, if they were heading to him that means they already know who he is and might have eyes on his place and who knows what else."

"The first team has been disbanded so it might take them some time to coordinate, not sure what kinda setup Khalil has here. But either way we can't risk it."

"I say we go in at night, take the kid and head back here. Speaking of which I need to call this Thorpe guy, check in on the girls. Kelly would want to know that they're doing ok."

I didn't give any thought to what her dad and his pals might've done to their prisoners, but I wouldn't be surprised if bodies started washing up on the mainland in the next week or so.

"You make that call Quinn. In the meantime, what the hell are we going to do about these women?" The others turned back to the screen at Lo's words while I moved off to the side to make the call.

"Thorpe, Quinn here I'm calling to check on the girls. How's everything going on your end?"

"Yeah, uh Lieutenant I don't know if Mancini told you, but this place is supposed to be kind of secret? I had a visit from their fathers I had a hell of a time convincing them to leave them here."

"And before that the women refused to settle down. They were worried about someone called Kelly; I'm guessing she belongs to one of you. They didn't settle down until after their fathers showed up here."

I could hear the barely restrained frustration in his voice and was thinking from the little time I'd spent with the admiral I could well imagine what Thorpe was facing.

"Serious question. Why is it that you military types are so…?"

"Aggressive?" I tried hard not to laugh at his disgruntled tone.

"No, I was going to say uncultured but that'll work."

"I'm pretty sure you understand the situation. These men… those are their little girls. I'm pretty sure you can cut them some slack."

"I understand, I know. But I also have other people that rely on me and this place. And your boys are just out of control. Another thing, I'm not sure what they were up to before they got here, but it wasn't anything good."

"Now somebody needs to get them out of my place. They say they're not leaving without their kids and Mancini asked me to keep those girls here. The wives are in my damn house eating cupcakes and tea and their fu… their husbands are making me crazy."

"Is that Quinn? Give me the phone." I only lifted my brow at the language on the other end as Thorpe passed the phone to the admiral.

"How's my kid?"

"She's uh, she's okay sir."

"I'm surprised she hasn't started trying to figure this shit out on her own. She's squirrely; keep a tight watch on her. Anything happens to her I don't have to tell you I'll bury your ass."

"Yes sir!" Better Thorpe than me, shit.

"I don't know how secure this line is so I'll let you go. Just make sure you boys check in on the regular. You boys have a run to make, make it. You're expected."

Reading between the lines I took that to mean he knew where we were heading next and that he'd been in contact.

When I hung up the guys were still arguing about how to approach the women and their meddling. "We're on an island in the middle of nowhere, what can they do?"

"Seriously Tyler, are you new?" Lo shook his head and walked around the room like a caged animal. Lyon had the baby on his shoulder burping him and I still didn't trust his ass.

"Cierra is the loose canon. She has contacts, and as my wife, a very far reach. The only good thing we have on our side, is that she doesn't quite know that yet."

"Lyon, your thoughts?" Way to go Con, best you let that shit sleep.

"Watch and learn. Tyler, take the kid." He passed the baby off and headed out the door after Mancini released the locks.

We all watched the screen as he navigated the hallways to get to the media room. It was obvious from the many missteps and all the hand gestures that he was not happy.

"Watch this." Mancini flipped a switch and went to audio. We could now hear Lyon as he traversed the hallways.

"What the fuck! Where am I, in a maze? Mancini you fuck where am I?" He looked up directly into the camera like he knew exactly where it was. Spooky.

"Just go straight ahead and make a left. Head down the stairs and they're in the room at the end towards the back."

He jogged the rest of the way until he stood outside the door. We watched the women jump guiltily when he busted in on them.

He didn't say anything, just stood in the door watching his wife, who started twitching in her seat five seconds in.

"Colton quit it." He still didn't say a word, didn't even move. The other women were now staring back and forth between the two of them, but no one dared say a word.

He didn't move towards her but she acted like he had. You could see the moment she caved, when she looked almost apologetically at the other women.

"Okay…wait, how much do you know?" She gave

him a sneaky look but Lyon just folded his arms and kept that stare trained on her.

"Okay-okay, we were just trying to figure out what was going on." At that point the others started talking over each other trying to protect one of their own.

Cierra Mancini left her post on the chair she'd been lounging on and approached the middle of the room, practically putting herself between the Lyon and his wife.

"What seems to be the problem? We were just giving you guys some time to rest since you were up all night. Here would you like some cake? It's really good."

"Forget it Cierra, he knows. I don't know how he knows but he does." Cierra smiled and shrugged before returning to her seat.

"It was worth a try. Where's that son of a bitch? I knew he had this place wired. Bastard." Lyon still hadn't said anything but the women never shut up.

"We're sorry we won't do it again." Poor Katarina she was still trying. Lyon just crooked his finger at her and waited for her to approach him.

"Where's my son?" Her eyes widened and she looked around as if expecting the baby to appear. "Oh no, I'm so sorry. Isn't he still asleep?" She was back to wringing her hands again.

"I'll go get him."

"No, that's okay I'll take care of him and the rest of my kids who're out there running around a fucking cliff."

"Ohhh, damn Colt that's harsh." Tyler was talking shit but he was looking at his hero with a glint in his eye. Like he needs to be any crazier than he already is.

"Let me ask you something before I go. Are you pregnant?"

"Yes." She hung her head. It's a wonder she has any flesh left on her hands as much as she wrings them together.

"What about these other women here, any of them pregnant."

"Yes." She turned back to the women and mouthed the word 'sorry'.

"Is it good for pregnant women to be stressed?"

"No."

"How many times have you been pregnant?"

"Five, plus this one makes six." Her voice kept getting lower.

"Did I ever allow you to be stressed or do anything even remotely strenuous during any of those pregnancies?"

"No!" Now she was doing the shifting from foot to foot thing I've seen my sisters, do a thousand times.

"But you decided that these three little girls don't deserve the same. I get it."

She went to put her hand on his chest and he moved back out of reach. It was plain to see that that move was the one that gutted her.

Without uttering another word he turned on his heel and left the room. But not before looking into the camera again though. Again, like he knew exactly where they were.

27

QUINN

~

We watched him retrace his steps, jogging up the last set of stairs until he was at the door and Mancini buzzed him in.

"Dude, that was kinda harsh no?" I need to shut up before Ty starts his shit, but damn, I kinda felt bad for the women now.

"Really, what are they doing now?" When we looked back at the screen the women did look kinda miserable.

More than one was wiping their nose or eyes. "I'm sorry I got y'all into this. I didn't mean to get anyone into trouble." Well, it's good to know she had a soft spot.

"Oh Kelly it's not your fault. We've been on this for months. Don't feel guilty." Dani tried reassuring my girl.

"Still, I feel like it's my fault."

"He always does this to me. I know there's something flawed in his logic, but I can never catch it in the moment. He just always sounds so logical you know." Kat sat back in her chair.

She sniffed and wiped her nose with the tissue Cierra passed her. "What I wanna know is how did he know though?"

"Susie, are you serious? Have you not noticed what we've been living with for the past few months? They always freaking know."

Dani apologized for swearing, which made the other women, some who've said worst, cackle with laughter.

"Oh shit, if he knows does that mean…?" The rest of them looked around the room at Vanessa's comment. Now they were the ones looking for hidden cameras.

"Hank Mancini if you're recording our conversation that's a violation of the law in this…well crap those laws don't apply here. He owns the damn island. Bastard!"

That gave us guys something to laugh about as we watched Lyon's handiwork at play. I think we were all holding our breath to see what they would do next.

In that short five minutes we forgot about hunting down assholes and all the other bullshit we had on our plate. It seemed like such a normal thing to do, watching the women get up to their shit.

I for one was glad that we'd made the choice to come here regardless of the doubts I had in the beginning. It felt freer, more relaxed, being away from the compound where we felt like sitting ducks.

Plus, I'm on a secluded island with the girl of my dreams. It's almost the perfect place. I can get in some quality time with my girl without worrying some asshole had me in his scope.

There was movement in the media room once the women settled down a bit. We were going to leave them tonight so it would be good if we were sure they were going to keep their little asses quiet and stay out of shit.

"Ok this is what we're going to do. We're going to go check on the kids. It's almost lunchtime anyway. Then we're going to give the boys everything that we've got so far and then we're going to take a step back." I guess Kat had become dorm leader down there.

She got up from her chair and the others followed suit. "Oh yes, that sounds good. And you know what let's just enjoy the island, it's a beautiful island."

Susie looked relieved and no one had to guess why. Cord is the one most likely to wring his woman's neck out of all of us.

"We'll just make a vacation out of it and leave all that other stuff to the men since they want it so bad."

Gabriella still sounded a bit disgruntled but there was a hint of fear in there somewhere. I guess she was still wondering if Lo had heard them too.

"It's also the perfect place for a wedding." They all stopped on the way out the door and looked back at Kat.

The men groaned, but it was a better prospect than what the hell they were up to an hour ago. It also gave me something to think about.

Am I getting married? I think I already knew the answer, of course I did. But what about her? How fucked up would she think I am if I asked her now?

Not to mention her old man. How happy was he going to be if I married his daughter a few days after we met? Without his consent.

"Yeah, you know what that's right. And there's nothing that says that all six of you can't get married together." Cierra made that suggestion as she put away her little gadget that she'd been using to take notes.

"Oh my gosh that's so perfect." Gaby loves any talk about weddings. Funny!

"Wait a minute six? I just met Quinn like an hour ago. Besides, he didn't ask."

"Oh sweetie, first off, they don't ask. And second, ask these women in here how long they were with their significant others before they found themselves hitched for life, ring or no ring."

There were a lot of heads nodding at Ginger-Lee's words. It was like getting a glimpse into the machinations of the female mind. It's a fucking mind fuck.

"You know what we should do, we should get that movie seven brides for seven brothers."

"Oh yes I could go for a nice old movie right now."
"Ooh Cat on a Hot Tin Roof."

"Oh that's my favorite."

"Some like it hot."

"Oh yeah that's another good one to watch."

"Do we have any of those?"

"I'm sure if we don't Hank will find them for us."

"Shit! Anybody caught all those names?" Mancini was already online looking.

Meanwhile the women walked out of the room talking about movies like nothing.

"Mancini you mind if I have a tape of this? From the time Lyon enters the door till now."

"Yeah I think I want one of those too, damn Lyon how did you do that shit?" Law asked.

"First lesson boys, you can't use logic with women. Go for the emotion every time."

"Isn't that kinda manipulative?" Creed didn't sound like he minded too much.

"The fuck I care? I gotta go put my kid down, fucker's giving me a crick in my arm."

He left the room with his sleeping son on his chest and I'm sure every man in the room was wondering who and what the fuck he was.

"I'm gonna be him when I grow up." Ty joked, but the

truth is he's exactly like that guy. Which is not necessarily a good thing for the rest of us.

Since we were through spying on the women I decided to share the conversation with the admiral. "I think it's safe to say he called Cali already, his exact words were, 'you're expected."

"You think they know what we're dealing with here Lo?"

"I doubt it Dev. I think they would've told us at this point. But I think it's safe to say they know something."

"Especially the admiral. I can't see him holding out with his kid getting nabbed like that. My guess, the old man knew something that the others didn't. But I'm pretty sure from the pattern that Khalil holds the whole team responsible."

"That makes sense but we still don't know what that thing is. I don't think Khalil is gonna give up, and I for one do not want this fucker breathing down my neck for the rest of my life."

"We won't brother, we're gonna take care of this shit once and for all." Each man nodded just as Lyon came back into the room.

"Okay, what's next? You boys need lessons in how to change diapers and shit?" Lyon ragged on us for being newbies to the game and we appreciated the light banter.

Since we weren't leaving until later and the women

seemed to have wound down we decided to spend the rest of the day with them.

They were right about one thing; this place is a perfect getaway. If you didn't have issues of national security to worry about.

They were out on the patio watching the kids run wild. There was a buffet set up with servers waiting to serve. I wonder if the women noticed that the waiters were all strapped?

They looked like a completely different group. In fact they looked lighter than they had when they were plotting.

I think it's easy for us men to expect them not to worry because we're so confident that we have the situation under control.

But the truth is, it's their lives too. I guess I can see things a little clearer now that I had my own woman.

The fact that she'd been touched directly by this makes it easier to understand why she'd want to know more than we've been sharing.

But that's as far as I'm willing to go with that line of thought. The others were right. It's okay for the women to wonder but not for them to get involved.

Except we now have Mancini's woman who's a certified agent and with Vanessa's know how, that whole thing could go south on us.

I hope Lyon's little experiment holds up, because I'm

not sure how long it would take them to find Mancini's toys and use them. Shit!

I put it aside for now when she patted the seat next to her and held out her glass of sunset colored liquid to me.

"Kelly you drinking?"

"No, it's tropical fruit punch and it's the best thing you've ever tasted." She wasn't lying, shit tasted like ambrosia.

The scene was surreal. Happy children running around, laughing. Baby Zak in the mix happy, carefree, the way she's supposed to be.

It was easy to tell that those older boys were Lyon's. The way they watched over their sisters and Baby Zak, and their little brother.

The oldest girl had her head down reading her phone. Every once in a while her fingers would move over the screen at the speed of light. She was texting someone.

Davey was following her around like a lovesick schoolboy, which in essence is what he was and I was about to go save his ass when I saw Lyon glaring in his direction, but Kelly sidetracked me.

"What is it baby?" I nibbled the fingers she'd placed near my mouth to turn my face towards her.

"Nothing I just like looking at your face."

"I spoke to your dad. The girls are okay, their dads are there with them." She got tears in her eyes and I pulled her into my chest.

"They're okay baby, why are you crying?"

"I know, it's just…am I ever going to see them again?"

"Of course you will, I'll make sure of it."

"Are you guys for real?"

"What do you mean?" She shrugged and turned to look at the others with her head still on my chest.

"I don't know. You guys seem so close, so together. My dad used to talk about his old team a lot, but I never really saw them together. I didn't know why because he really loved those guys. I guess I kinda imagine that this is how they would've been if they'd had the choice."

Her words gave me room for thought. Was this thing we were dealing with the reason those men had stayed apart over the years?

It's obvious they'd kept in touch, but she had a point. Why were those men never seen together in almost twenty years? I'll have to remember to bring it up with my brothers later.

For now I just held her close. It was hard to imagine all that she'd been through in the last coupla days.

I'm almost expecting her to break at some point. But then again, if she could join the other women in a coup to fuck me until I passed out she can't be doing all that bad.

"So, where did you go when you left me asleep in the cottage?" She went tense and tried to sit up. I guess the others were being questioned as well because of all the guilty looks they shared with each other.

They must've had some sorta signal worked out between them because no sooner had I seen those looks than they started turning their attention to Dev, who looked like he was ready to bolt.

28

DEVON

~

It was so natural for them. The way they each went to their respective women. I searched my heart and there was no envy, but there was a slight pang of longing, stronger than the others that came before.

I knew it was the surroundings that added to the melancholy. That and the fact that I was the only one without a partner.

But none of that could take away from the happiness I felt at my brothers' joy. Especially Quinn.

He looked so happy it was hard not to smile at the complete ass he was making of himself. For someone who'd sworn to me over and over that he'd never take the plunge, he looked just as gone as the others.

I started getting twitchy when I caught the side eye

looks and the whispering started. I knew what was coming next and knew only one way to save my own ass.

"So, Dani, I walked around this place earlier and you know what? This looks like the ideal place to have a wedding. Did you girls bring your magazines?"

"You've got the beach, these beautiful gardens as a back drop and I think those cliffs would be perfect for pictures at sunset."

My brothers were all giving me what the fuck looks but no fucking way. I'll make it up to them later. For now I made my escape and went to play with Zakira.

I started grinning halfway across the lawn when I heard the arguing start. Then I saw Davey moping around behind Lyon's oldest and remembered the threat from earlier.

Since there was no use pretending that Colton Lyon wouldn't do exactly what he said he would, I thought it prudent to head that shit off.

"Davey, a minute." The girl didn't even seem to notice when he walked out of her shadow. I felt bad for the kid. The girl was absolutely beautiful, but her old man was nuts so there was that.

"Yeah Dev?"

"You're gonna want to leave that alone." I inclined my head in her direction.

"I know but she's so pretty." He said it almost in awe.

"I know, but I think she has a boyfriend, plus the fact

that her dad is not gonna be happy if you keep trailing her like that."

"I know about the boyfriend, she told me. But damn she's gorgeous. There're no girls like her back home and she's smart too."

Because of who we think he is, Davey's like our little brother, he's one of us. And I was the unlucky one who was gonna get stuck leading him through his first heartbreak.

I looked back at the others weighing which was less painful. Letting the girls dig into me about finding a woman, or trying to fix his shit.

"Come with me." I took him towards the water and sat with him on the sand. It was the first time any of us have been able to just relax and talk to the kid since this whole mess started.

Now that we suspected he might belong to the man we'd all looked up to as a dad, makes him that much closer, he and his sister.

Now that Susie was Cord's she'll always be one of us, but Davey might be left feeling a bit left out in the cold, kinda like me in a sense.

"Have you spoken to your mom lately?" We'd basically taken her kids, but we didn't have a choice. It's not that she's a bad mom, some of my other brothers had worse.

But she's going through some stuff of her own and

hasn't really been there, which in itself wouldn't have been that bad if not for the threat against the kids.

"I called her before we left, she's okay; she just misses us a little."

"You'll see her when we get back son, we'll make things right there for you and your sister. Was there anything you needed Davey?" He shook his head no and played with the sand.

It was hard sometimes to remember he was just a teenage boy. We'd sucked him up and kept him away from his friends and everything he's known his whole life but we didn't have a choice.

If something happened to him on our watch we'd never be able to forgive ourselves. Even though we couldn't share our suspicions with him and his sister, they were the only things we had left of the old man.

He may not have served with us, but he's one of us, which is why I can't let Lyon kill him. "So, this girl, she hit you hard huh!"

"Yeah, I guess. I'll get over it though. At least she was nice about shooting me down. Not like some girls her age, she's got class."

Oh damn, the kid had it bad. I tried to remember what it was like at his age, but the truth is, I was never that innocent. None of us were.

"So you think you can handle being here and not…"

What the fuck was I supposed to say here? His nervous laugh saved me from having to say the words.

"Oh come on Dev, I'm a big boy, though the rest of you treat me like a baby. She has a boyfriend, that's who she's been texting all day. I hope when I find a girl she loves me like that."

I put my arm around his shoulders and we gazed out over the water. "You will son, you will." This is why we have to see this shit through, put an end to whatever vendetta the Fox had going on in his sick, fucking mind.

It wasn't only the seven of us whose lives he was fucking with, but these two kids for some reason. The CO had been there for us, had given us more than we deserved, but for some reason wasn't able to be there for his flesh and blood.

Something I'm sure had cut him to the bone. Now it was up to us to make sure they had what he would've wanted for them.

I have no doubt that Cord would see to Susie's happiness, but it might be a little harder figuring out what the hell to do with Davey.

So far he's been getting along fine. It's obvious he sees us as people he can look up to, but what about his future? And how do we keep him from feeling like a fifth wheel?

And why the fuck, do you keep coming back to that?

Maybe I am feeling a little envious. This is the first time I wasn't part of something that my brothers were doing.

I can try to convince myself that it didn't matter, but the truth is, more and more in the last few hours, especially after what happened with Quinn, I've been feeling…off.

As if he could read my mind Davey looked at me with a grin. "So, Quinn has a girl, does that mean you're next?"

"Okay kid that's enough of this." I got up to leave his ass to the waves.

"Oh come on Dev, you guys always do everything together. I don't see why this should be any different. Besides, I heard the women talking back home and your goose is as good as cooked."

"What, what did they say?" At least his mind was no longer on Lyon's kid therefore taking his ass out of the line of fire.

"Well, after they got through talking about weddings and babies." He rolled his eyes. "They decided that you and Quinn needed to settle down. Then once they saw Quinn with his girl, they figured it was a done deal and you were the only one left."

"How did they see Quinn with Kelly?"

"Come on Dev are you serious? They were peeping out the windows and that lady from Law's place, the writer, uh, Ginger, she was reading their body language. At least that's what she said."

I looked towards the women and their men wondering just what the hell they be getting up to. "Anyway, after Quinn went all caveman in the yard, they decided she was his and they started talking about you. I think they plan to find you a girl as soon as we get back home."

"Oh for fuck sake!" I punked out and went to hide out with my niece who was having the time of her life. It did my heart good to see her in her element, running around and laughing happily as we rolled around in the grass together.

As the day wound down the atmosphere changed, even though the guys did their best not to let on to the women that there was something going on.

I'm not sure what excuses they used for our pending absence but by the time we were ready to head out the women were all acting a bit anxious.

Mancini had found them the movies they wanted to watch and he'd done it smooth enough that they still didn't know if their men had been listening into their conversations earlier.

"You know they're gonna figure that shit out right. What are the odds that you'd have all those movies on tap?" I'm still trying to figure out the machinations of this relationship bullshit.

It seems to me each of these men differ in a lot of ways but one; when it comes to their women. Neanderthal comes to mind.

"That's why I got all the movies I could find from that era. This way they'd be left guessing. Of course since my well behaved wife met these other women she seems to think that I'm no longer to be trusted so who knows."

"Did your women try pumping you for information? I think Kelly was trying to figure out if we were listening in on them."

"What did you tell her bitch made?"

"Nothing Tyler, I guess you can say I turned the tables on her."

"Huh?"

"I distracted her Tyler damn, you need me to spell it out for you?"

"Quinn are you blushing?"

"Shut the fuck up Dev."

We ragged the hell out of each other on the way to the airfield. It's always been our way heading into battle.

We keep it light and playful until zero hour, then the masks come off and whoever's on the other end of that shit is fucked.

We made it to the decked out flying palace Mancini calls a plane and filed on. We'd already discussed how we were going in.

Since Quinn had told us we were expected, we figured the retired major in Cali wouldn't shoot us on sight.

The talk turned to world events. Something we hadn't

really had time to delve into since we've been so caught up in our own shit.

Then again, we knew enough to know we had no control over that shit. All we could do is clean up the messes after they'd been made and put shit back together.

This latest horror show was a little more fucked than usual though. And we'd already discussed whether or not we might be called up at some point.

Lyon, who seemed like he didn't pay attention to anything other than his wife and his horde of kids, was the first to broach the subject of traitorous fucks.

"So what's the story on this guy with the leaks and the other one that ran to Russia? I thought you military fucks were supposed to be badass, why are these humps still breathing?"

"What would be your answer Lyon, how should they be handled?" Seriously Con, you have to ask? From the look Lyon threw him and the way Con laughed I'm guessing that shit had been rhetorical.

"They're plants." Mancini took a sip from his bottle of fancy water and grinned at the rest of us. "If they wanted them gone they would've been a long time ago."

For someone who wasn't part of any military outfit he sure did have his fingers on the pulse of shit.

"They're both on somebody's payroll. My money is on the G-eight."

My brothers, Creed, Law and I didn't say anything but

you could feel the tension. The conversation was getting close to shit that was only known by a few and speculated by many more.

"Those fucks get together every year under the guise of global discourse but in reality they're all planning to screw the world as we know it to farther their own fucked up agendas."

"Thought so, damn. Our government is pretty fucked isn't it?"

"They're not the only ones Lyon, it's a concentrated effort between the leaders of the so called free world."

Logan was staring at Mancini like he was trying to dissect his head or some shit. Me, I just kept my lips sealed and my ears open.

29

QUINN

~

I missed her, and I was scared. I finally got why my brothers act so crazy when it comes to their women. Mancini's little island is well guarded true, but nothing beats being there myself to protect her.

I smiled at the memory of our last moments together. After lunch we'd each returned to our cottages under the pretense of resting up before heading out tonight.

I only had one moment of discomfort when Dev waved us off as he hung back with the kids. It's weird but I felt a little off about him being the only one without a girl.

Lo had caught my look since we were trailing the women who all had their heads together up ahead about something. Hopefully it had to do with weddings this time.

"He's going to be fine Quinn, I know it. If he doesn't find someone on his own, I'm pretty sure that gaggle would take care of it. Damn, one day around Lyon and I'm beginning to sound like him."

"Yeah, you might wanna watch that. I don't think Gaby would appreciate you calling her and her girls a gaggle of hens."

"He's got a point though damn, can you believe them? You think they're gonna stay put?"

"Kelly had better if she knows what's good for her."

"It's a constant battle brother you know that. How many weeks, months have we been trying to keep these women outta trouble? Now they have reinforcements. At least Lyon's little guilt trip earlier seems to be working for now."

"Yeah, that's another thing. If the rest of us have to suffer I don't see why Dev should get off so easy." I said it as a way to lighten the feeling of sad that was burning a hole in my gut.

When I thought that I would be doing the single thing with him it had been a little easier to take, even though I wanted him to have what the others already did.

But in the last day after going through all that I had and finding her at the end of the night, which seems surreal now, I didn't want him left out in the cold.

Shit, a day ago I didn't know this would be my new normal. Who the fuck meets their happily ever after like that out of the blue?

Then again the others had pretty much done the same thing. I'll just have to put our whirlwind romance down to a SEAL's life. It seems we do everything at warp speed.

In all seriousness, when you've lived your life on the razor's edge you tend to grab shit when you find it and all the tenets of society don't mean shit.

Lo just clapped my shoulder and reassured me once more that Dev would be fine. I don't know how he expects to fix Dev's love life, but knowing the way his head works I'm sure he believes this too is something he can make right.

"What're you two talking about?" Tyler is about the nosiest fuck. "Quinn's worried about Devon." We all looked back in his direction and saw him deep in conversation with Lyon's youngest girl.

"Yeah, I'm a little worried there too. This is the first time the seven of us haven't been in step on something. He say anything to you Quinn?"

We'd stopped walking and let the women go on ahead, now the rest of my team was listening in to the conversation as well.

I should've known the shit would turn into a crisis meeting. Dev would kick my ass if he knew I was talking, especially with everything else that we have going on. But with all of them staring me down there was no getting out of it.

"He doesn't think he deserves what we have."

"What the fuck and you didn't say anything?"

"Cool it Lo." Zak put his hand on his shoulder and addressed me.

"What exactly did he say Quinn?"

"Something along the lines of it's not for him. He seems to think because of the abuse he suffered at the hands of his uncle that he might be like him, you know, repeat the abuse."

"What the fuck? I'm with Lo, why didn't you tell us this shit before?"

"Because he only told me this yesterday and if you remember Con we had a lot of shit going on."

For some fucked up reason, Ty was the voice of reason in that little skirmish. "Listen we all know how he is. He's one of those show and tell motherfuckers." He looked back towards Dev before turning back to the rest of us.

"I say let the girls put someone in his path, knowing them they probably have a whole stable in mind. He'll find someone and forget this bullshit."

"You might be right but I'd still like to find his uncle and tie his guts around his fucking neck." "Yeah Lo, we got that."

"Tell me Quinn, is this something we have to worry about?" I shouldn't have said shit. Logan's like a dog with a bone whenever something touches one of us. I don't know why I expected this to be any different.

"No Lo; and Dev wouldn't want us taking our focus off the shit we're dealing with here to worry about him. Let's get this shit done and then we can knock some sense into him. I'll keep an eye on him."

"We all will. I still have to deal with you for not telling us what was going on with you yesterday. I don't want any of you thinking that because we're dealing with this shit we let other things fall by the wayside. That's not how we do things."

"Lo's right. You bitch made motherfuckers need constant therapy. I'm all good Lo, just wanted you to know that. My shit's on fleek."

"Tyler, I worry about you most of all."

"What the fuck? What did I do?"

"Plenty, and you and Lyon better not be up to none of your tricks this go round. Con I expect you to keep him under control."

"I got him Lo, he won't be slipping away to pull off any coups this time. I'm not responsible for Lyon though; fuck that. It's like dealing with a general without the fucking stripes."

The talk turned to Lyon as we started walking again.

Law, Creed and their crew had already gone back to their cottages and Lyon was back at the mansion with Mancini.

"I guess Mancini can keep a leash on him. We'll let him know that he's his problem." We split off and went to our respective places.

Kelly had been in the bedroom of the cottage going through the overnight bag we'd brought with us when I walked in.

"Dani and Gaby lent me some stuff to wear but I need to go shopping. There's this beautiful beach here and I don't have a bathing suit." She was nervous as hell.

I didn't have to guess so hard at why she was being so panicky. When we came back early this morning and she'd worked me over in bed so she could sneak out, we hadn't really had time to talk.

Now she was alone with a man she'd only met a few short hours ago. A man who had fucked her within the first few minutes of meeting her, then brought her here away from everything she knew. A man who had all plans on keeping her.

When looked at through the eyes of someone who wasn't under the influence of that ESP shit or whatever it is, this shit really is fucked.

I know each of my brothers except Ty, had claimed their women within days of knowing them. Zak had done the same with Vanessa before they had their little time out.

But it seems to be a trend with us. Or maybe that's just the way it is with all couples? How can you not claim your woman when you know in your gut that she's yours on sight?

Maybe the cavemen had it right after all. Shit sure seems simpler. Whatever the case, it felt right having her here with me. I can't imagine having to leave her behind and coming here.

It's only been a little more than half a day and already I feel like she's a part of me. And I know it has nothing to do with my 'gift' because what the fuck would be my brothers' excuse?

"Come here Kelly!" I stood in the doorway not moving, just watching her. She dropped the piece of cloth in her hand on the bed and came to me.

She wasn't looking so bold now, but I found out why two minutes later. "Quinn, do you think this whole place is wired?" Damn, these women never quit.

"What would make you think that?" I rested my arms around her hips, holding her close as I looked down at her. She picked at the imaginary lint on my shirt and looked up at me through her lashes.

"Oh nothing, what were you guys doing all morning? What made you get up so soon? I thought you were tired for sure." I pulled her head into my chest to hide the fact that I was grinning.

"Ummm, you smell good." She sniffed my shirt and her little arms came around me and I forgot everything else but the feel of her in my arms. I'll take her to task for trying to pull one over on me later.

Now I just lifted her chin with my finger and lowered my head to hers. This kiss was no less hungry than the others but this time I was able to hold myself in check.

She tasted like the ocean and sunshine and the sweet juice we'd shared at lunch. I stripped her standing there, removing her clothes while our lips were still fused together, before walking her backwards towards the bed.

Once she was on her back looking up at me with that hot dreamy look in her eyes, I pulled my shirt off over my head.

"Touch me!" She reared up and put her hands on the tight muscles of my stomach before placing butterfly kisses there. My hand came down and held her head before pulling it back again.

"Release me!" I've never seen anything hotter than the way she looked up at me with need as her hands fumbled with my zipper.

The green cargo pants came apart under her hands and when she lowered her head and licked the place right where the hair on my groin started I had to grit my teeth.

She pushed my pants off down my thighs and her mouth made a trail down the length of my cock until she took the tip between her lips.

I watched my cock grow in her mouth as she innocently sucked more and more of my meat into her throat until she was almost choking.

I loved her innocence, the way she seemed not to know what she was doing but was giving it all she had. But it was the pleasurable sounds she made that made my toes curl and my hand fist in her hair.

I let her get me to the point of no return, fucking in and out of her mouth harder, and weighed cumming on her tongue, before deciding that I wanted inside her more.

The need to cum inside her again, over and over, was overpowering. I could already feel the sensation of my cock shooting off deep inside her.

I pulled her off my cock, pushed her back on the bed and knelt on the floor with her legs pulled over my shoulders. I needed to calm down before I hurt her, so I gave her my mouth.

She giggled from the tickle of the rough growth on my cheeks against her thighs. The sound was so young and innocent it was startling, but as soon as my tongue pierced her that grin became a sexy sigh.

I took my time making love to her with my mouth until her fingers dug deep into my scalp. "Now Quinn." I bit her inner thigh to get her to behave but that only seemed to inflame her more.

She smashed her wet pussy into my face and tried dragging me up her body. My cock was hard and aching but the taste of her was something I'd never get enough of.

I pulled my tongue from her heat and went after her clit, sucking and nibbling on it until she screeched and damn near scalped me.

I went back to her pussy with my tongue, digging deep until her ass shook in my hands and she tightened around my tongue.

When her essence started to dribble down my chin I lifted up and with her legs still on my shoulders slammed into her hard.

Her body shook and she screamed out loud until there was no sound coming from her wide-open mouth, and I freaked.

"Shit, baby, breathe!" I held still, my cock throbbing uncontrollably and smoothed the hair back from her face. I went too deep too fast.

I calmed her with sweet soft kisses at the edges of her lips before taking her tongue into my mouth. She'd settled a little but her heart still beat wildly in her chest.

I started to pull out but she dug her nails into me. "Don't you dare!" I looked into her eyes at her words. If her eyes hadn't been clear except for the cloud of lust I would've pulled out no matter what she said.

She must've read the intent in my eyes because she pulled my head down to hers and consumed me with another one of her heated kisses that threatened to blow the top off my head.

"Okay baby!" Her passion was uncontrollable as she crushed her lips against my teeth and I was afraid she was going to hurt herself.

I tried reining her in but it was no use, the girl was on fire, I was just along for the ride. I held still and let her take what she needed until the need to move became too much.

I tried to hold back, to remind myself that she was new to this, I really did. But years of control just went to hell at the feel of the warm silk of her sex like a glove around my aching cock.

It was her, all her and the amazing hold she had over me. The fact that I was about to leave her in a few hours probably had something to do with the almost desperate way in which I fucked her.

I held her ankles in my hands and fucked into her harder with each stroke. She took my pounding, throwing her hips up at me, keeping pace as she looked up into my eyes.

I brought her off again before pulling out and putting her on her knees in front of me. I slid my cock up and down her weeping slit before forcing the fat head of my cock back into her.

I held her by the waist and pulled her on and off my

cock until her arms could no longer hold her up. When she fell onto the bed I didn't stop fucking, just kept drilling into her until she crooned.

I flipped her onto her back again and this time wrapped her legs around my hips as I slowed my movements and fucked her slowly, softly, gently.

"Pretty girl!" I took her lips, kissing the smile that had formed there. I touched her everywhere I could reach, palming her heavy tit in my hand until her nipple pebbled before taking it into my mouth.

This time when she came it was with a soft sigh as her body trembled and her pussy locked down around me.

Her legs held me in and I felt my cock belch and spit as the feel of her softness, the pulsing of her cunt as she came sucked me under.

I kissed her deeply as I emptied my seed inside her again. I came long and hard, feeling all my energy being sucked through my dick and into her.

Since I had no strength for the next few seconds I stayed buried inside her, my body pressing hers into the mattress as I caught my breath.

I looked down at her face when her body went lax and smiled. It was my turn to put her to sleep it looked like. Poor thing she'd had a rough few days and now she was done. She was asleep before I pulled out of her.

I turned to my side, drawing her into my arms. "I love

you." I whispered the words to her knowing that she couldn't hear me. But my heart felt freer than it ever had.

I kissed her hair and with my arms wrapped safely around her finally got the sleep I needed before facing the night ahead.

30

QUINN

Now I'm on a plane heading away from her for the only reason that could've gotten me out of her bed. To make sure her future was safe. To put an end to whatever this is and make sure that no one else ever gets near her again.

We still had a lot to talk about, a lot we needed to learn about each other. I feel like I already know her, like she's lived inside me my whole life, but I can't wait to know more.

I listened to the others joking around to lighten the mood and closed my eyes, just thinking about her and the amazing day and a half I just had.

My life was changed I know, for the rest of my life she was going to be there. The thought that she was mine, that

I was now responsible for her wellbeing was uppermost in my mind.

I was all the way in from the beginning when it came to destroying this asshole Khalil and whoever else he had working with him. But that shit has taken on new meaning.

I'm pretty sure from Thorpe's cryptic words, that the assholes who'd taken her and the others were at the bottom of the sea or worse by now.

I wasn't sure what was waiting for us at the end of this shit but I knew I was coming back to her. I was convinced now more than ever, though I never really doubted; that we were going to come out on the right end of this thing.

I peeped my eyes open when I didn't hear Dev's voice in the mix. He was sitting alone looking out the window at the dark. Fuck!

I left my seat and moved next to him, but did it in a way that Lo wouldn't notice. I didn't say anything, just rested my head back and closed my eyes. He knew I was there, that's all that mattered.

"Quinn I'm fine."

"What're you talking about? I wanted to get some shuteye but Ty the fuck won't shut the hell up back there."

"You're a lying ass." I smirked but kept my eyes closed and he went back to gazing out the window. If I didn't know for sure that he was going to be okay, I would be worried about him.

But I know that if someone as undeserving as me could find this happiness then he sure can. It wouldn't be right otherwise.

He'd faced enough loss and not enough love in his life. Shit, Ty was right, we all become bitch made when we fall in love. What the fuck am I thinking about?

I should've known that my little seat switch hadn't gone unnoticed. Lo used the others getting ready as cover to corner Dev and I.

"Devon you okay brother?"

"Yep!" Lo looked to me for confirmation and I gave him a silent nod. We both shared a look of understanding before Lo turned and left us alone.

"Quinn what the fuck! what're you thinking? We're in the middle of an Op."

"So? You want the others to rip me a new one if I don't let them know something's up?"

"Stop bitching like an old woman and let's do this shit bro!" He pulled on the last of his gear and headed into the back of the Humvee Mancini had waiting for us.

I think we'd all pretty much given up on trying to figure out how the hell he was able to pull shit out of the hat like that at such short notice. But the fucker did have the best toys.

No one said anything as we headed into the Hollywood hills. At least the two tanks weren't too out of place here. This town was pretty much known for the unexpected and the quirky.

DEVON

I hate fucking Cali. This shit's about to fall off the face of the earth and it's just a weird fucking place. It's the only place we never hung around too long which is weird because SEALs love the ocean.

It was also a strange fucking place. One minute we were in the middle of the city and the next we were in the hills where everything looked different.

It was pitch black outside and without the night goggles we wouldn't be able to see shit. We'd left the huge Hollywood sign a few miles back and were headed into some ritzy residential area that the natives seem to think would get stolen if they put up more than one streetlight.

Each house was bigger than the last and I was starting to wonder what kinda serviceman could afford to live in a place like this. The shits had to cost at least ten million and up.

I pulled up the info on the man we were going to see on my handheld. We'd only given him a cursory glance earlier, just to be sure he was on the right side of this thing. It was his son we were most interested in.

Terrence Samson. There was no real connection between him and the CO, other than the fact that his name had been one of the codes, but as for his time in service, there wasn't really much there.

He did have a high security clearance so that could be the reason for that and until we had the time to do a deep search we wouldn't find more.

It didn't take me long to find out how he could afford to live here though. There was a shit load of information on his public persona that had nothing to do with the military.

He was the son of one of the wealthiest families in the country; oil money. He and his son were filthy rich thanks to his old man and the family assets.

Track Samson was a fucking nightmare. The kid was seventeen and had a sheet that one would not expect for a kid from his background.

It was easy to find the reasons for that too. If you knew where to look. It was a cover. Each time he was taken away for one of these supposed infractions, he turned up at the Pentagon.

It didn't take a stretch of the imagination to figure out what was really going on, since we knew thanks to Mancini that he was a master hacker. It was obvious he was working for the government.

The question still remains, why had he allowed them to catch him? It was obvious that he'd left a trail. Even though he went to great lengths to make it seem like he hadn't.

It sucks to know that our best isn't really that good if they let a kid get the drop on them. I mean it didn't take me long to see the set up.

Or maybe… "Lo tell him to hurry, this kid might be in greater danger than we thought." With his credentials, if he fell into the wrong hands a lot of people would be fucked.

"What have you found?" Lo asked after telling Mancini's expert driver to put his foot on the gas.

"I've been looking into this kid. It kinda bothered me that the DOD caught on to him so easily when no one knows who these people are or where they are and they're usually way more careful than this."

"Go on!" Everyone turned to look at me, and I knew the others in the truck behind us were wired in as well.

"I just went into his file. When he hacked in he left a trail. It was good, but I know we have people on the job who could've spotted that as easily as I did. If he's as good as he seems, why did he let them catch him?"

I let them mull that over. "I think someone knew or had eyes on him. They may not have known that he was part of this Anonymous group, but I think he went digging and someone had a bead on him or was watching him for whatever reason."

"Kinda like while he was watching them they were watching him?" Ty looked confused.

"Or they knew who his dad was and was watching him. Whatever the reason, I don't like it. He was just there a few days ago. I don't like it."

"Khalil!" Con offered.

"Yeah, and whoever he has on the inside. My money's on the general. The kid's good but I don't know if he's that good. But that's not the problem. The question still remains, why did he want in?"

That was the one piece of the puzzle I couldn't quite put my fingers on. Nowhere in the CO's notes did it say anything about the kid. If he was the target, I would've expected there to be something.

The fact that the offspring of the men who'd served with him in one way or another back then were being targeted was obvious to us now, but we'd had to dig to find that shit.

How did this kid know that someone was after him? Had his dad told him something? And if so, how come the others didn't know that their kids were in danger?

"We're still missing a big piece of the puzzle, something's just not adding up. Taking the girls had an obvious motive, but what was he planning to do with this kid?" It didn't bear thinking about.

"If he just wanted to kill him he could've done that a long time ago, something's off. Are we sure it's the kid they're after? Did we miss something? Is there someone else out there that we overlooked?"

"I would give you that it's strange. All the others were female and this kid's hacking into the DOD does raise some questions but we're not going to have any answers until we talk to him."

"Well, Kelly said they were heading here next and the only person in the old man's files that lives in this neck of the woods is this Track's dad. I don't see what else it can be."

"I get that Quinn, but my gut is telling me we're overlooking something. There were only females in that damn book, so where does this kid fit in?"

"If it's some kind of vendetta is it such a stretch that he'd go after this kid as well if his dad had any part in whatever the fuck this is?"

"Yeah but Dev's right. Why didn't the CO mention this boy in anyway? I can see the females, we know what he was doing there, but why this kid?"

"In all fairness he didn't mention any of it. If we hadn't found that book we wouldn't have put this shit together."

"I think he didn't have time. I think he tried to handle the shit on his own and ran into trouble before he had the chance."

"Lo's right. Maybe that's why he was trying to get us to come to him before he died."

"Not died Con, he was fucking murdered."

Everything went silent for a hot minute. It was the only thing that we were still having a hard time coming to terms with.

I know for me personally, it was a hard pill to swallow. Outside of my brothers, the old man was the only other human being who'd treated me like I mattered.

Not since my parents' deaths have I ever felt like I belonged. To know that he'd needed me and I wasn't there is something I'm never going to get over.

It just solidifies for me the fact that I'm no good. I can't be depended on. I wasn't able to save my mother and father and I wasn't there for the old man.

There's a part of me that knows that's stupid, the CO himself would shoot me down for thinking this way, but it wasn't that easy for me to shake.

I'm always going to feel like a failure when it comes to protecting the ones I love. How can I trust myself with a woman the way my brothers do?

As bad as their childhoods were, none of them had seen the shit I had, or experienced the same level of abuse at the hands of someone who was supposed to love and protect.

I feel like shit thinking this way, especially knowing what they went through. But where most of their abuse had been physical mine had been psychological as well.

When you lived most of your life being told you were tainted from birth. That you were little more than a fucking sin because of the color of your skin. It wasn't something you could just walk away from.

I'd come to learn over time that my uncle was full of shit. That when he blamed my birth for the death of my parents he was sick in the fucking head.

But it was still something I'd lived with at the worst time in my life. I'd just lost my parents and was scared and alone.

At fourteen I'd been a pretty sheltered kid. My parents were great, but because of the shit they'd faced because they were an interracial couple, they'd gone above and beyond to protect their only son.

I didn't know much about the real world until they were gone and I ended up in the hands of my uncle. In short the man was a fucking monster. And after years of his bullshit abuse, I'd become hard.

I lost my innocence within the first year after he and his kids had tried to knock the black off my ass. They'd taught me to hate myself, and if not for the great love I bore my parents he would've convinced me to hate them too, just for loving each other.

I learned all about hate and distrust in that house, and by the time I signed up I was damn near an animal. There was no love, no light in me; only hate.

I have that shit in me to this day. It took my brothers and the CO to bring me to some semblance of humanity, but that's where it ended.

It's easy for the others to believe that I would never harm the woman I love if she does exist, but how can I be sure?

I'm not willing to risk it. I can't ask anyone, least of all a vulnerable woman to put up with me and the demons that live inside.

It's not the same with my sisters, I know I would never harm them, or baby Zak. But somehow in my mind it's not the same.

Mancini's voice came through the speakers just then shaking me out of my wayward thoughts. I blame Quinn and his shit for my mind even going there. "ETA five minutes, what do you wanna do boys?"

We were already here, there was no time to learn anything new. It's not like we've never gone in with less information than we had now. But this shit had too many tentacles, and too many unknowns for us to slip up.

If Kelly hadn't overheard those men we wouldn't have known to look here and we might've been too late.

I don't think any of us would've thought his life was in danger, since it was only females being targeted.

We've only had this info for less than twenty-four hours and there was no time to dig deeper than we already had.

My gut told me we were missing something but there was no way we were leaving this kid out in the cold.

"We're going in. We'll figure shit out after we get the kid outta there." I answered Mancini just as we turned the corner and the house came into view up ahead.

The place was almost completely dark with nothing but the stars and the sliver of moon for light.

The house was set apart from its neighbors by a good few hundred yards, which would work in our favor.

We drove past the place and did some recon before parking the vehicles on the path behind the structure. There were trees and brush back there and a steep drop off that led to nowhere.

It couldn't be attacked from behind unless someone wanted to grapple their way up a cliff face and I'm pretty sure there were security measures all around the front and sides.

"Damn, are we all going in there?" There had to be about twelve or more of us.

"No, only the SEALs are going in. The rest of us will surround the place just in case." Mancini answered Lyon's question and the rest of them fanned out.

"Quinn?" He was the one in charge of this run so the rest of us will wait on his word.

"You've got this one Dev, your gut's talking, what do you wanna do?"

"Movement in the window, first floor south side. Two hot bodies, one more upstairs moving around, one pliant, might be asleep. Top floor north side."

Mancini was using one of his toys to see inside. We were armed but no one drew their weapon as we approached.

"We're clear on the perimeter." Lo had gone ahead with Con to make sure while Quinn and I headed for the back of the house before making our way around to meet them.

Zak, Ty and Cord were already in position in the shadows and I didn't see the others as they spread out.

I breathed a little bit easier once it was clear that there was no one else out here with us. But it only raised more questions.

Since we'd botched their plans, and it was obvious from the fly over back at the compound that they knew we were the ones, why hadn't they sent in another team to take over?

I won't believe that they were so inept they didn't have anything else in place. The closer we got to the door the more my gut twisted itself in knots. Some shit was off.

I calmed myself with the fact that they didn't know

Kelly had told us where they were headed, so maybe they thought they had time.

I focused on the door and what laid ahead, putting everything else aside. I had no explanation for the riot going on in my gut, but I stayed on high fucking alert.

We'd decided we were gonna go in easy if there were no impediments, so instead of storming the place, we rang the doorbell; out of respect for the CO and his friendship with the man inside.

One of the shadows in the window moved and a middle aged African American male opened the door a few seconds later.

The smile on his face kinda threw me, until I remembered what Quinn had said earlier about us being expected.

A swift look around the room, showed that there were only two occupants in the room and my body relaxed though my insides remained on high alert.

"I'm guessing from your welcoming look that you know who we are and why we're here."

"Come in. I'm guessing there're more of you out there, tell your friends to come on in."

Lo whistled and the bushes outside came alive as the guys came out of hiding and headed to the door.

31

DEVON

The younger man, who I recognized once his face came into the light as Track, came to stand next to his dad.

It was more like he shielded the older man with his body, but he did it in such a smooth strategic way, that someone without my training would've missed it.

I wasn't sure until now how I felt about the kid, seeing as he was a damn criminal. But that move solidified him in my estimation.

That and the way he sized up the rest of us without seeming to. And there was no fear in him. He kinda reminded me of a younger me after I'd got out from under my uncle's thumb. Puffed up with my own strength.

I moved forward while the others hung back a bit still having that feeling in my gut like something was awry. I didn't feel like we'd walked into a trap, but there was definitely something nagging at me.

"Did you explain things to him?" I kept my eyes on the old man but could feel the tension coming off his son. He wasn't saying shit, but his body said a lot.

"He's not the one you're here for." I sensed as much as heard Lo move behind me.

"I'm sorry? I was under the impression that you spoke to the admiral…"

"Of course I spoke to Mac. Had I not you would've gotten a completely different reception. But like I said, my son's not the one you're here for."

"I don't understand, the pattern here is kids…"

"Yes I know but…." Before he could say more his son all but placed himself between the two of us and got in my face.

"What the fuck do you want with my sister?" I didn't let the surprise show in my eyes, but I'm gonna gut Mancini's ass for sending us in blind. I knew some shit was wrong with this picture.

First off, until his name showed up in those codes we'd never heard of Terrence Samson. We knew the other men or had heard of them in some way over the years, this guy was a complete surprise.

If we'd had more time we probably would've learned more, but there was no use going over that shit again, we were here now.

I finally switched my attention to the boy while the rest of the team came to grips with this new turn of events. I didn't have to hear them to know what they were thinking.

At least it made sense now that he had a daughter, but why hadn't we seen anything about her in the search? Another question for later.

"Calm down young blood we're not here to hurt her." I played it off like we'd known about the girl. Maybe she was one of the warm bodies upstairs and wasn't off somewhere that we'd have to go hunt her down, my ass was tired.

Just as I was about to ask, Mancini uttered the word 'incoming', and there was movement at the top of the stairs.

There was another shift in the room as everyone went on alert and all eyes turned in the direction of the footsteps.

"Track, dad, what's going on?" Shit, that voice sent chills down my spine. It was one of those distinct voices that do shit to your insides and I wondered if the others felt it too. Not good!

It's just a voice Devon for fuck sake chill. But I knew, even before I laid eyes on her, I knew that something was going to change for me in the next few seconds. Maybe Quinn's woo-hoo shit was rubbing off.

I flicked my eyes up and over towards the stairs and she was just there. Her eyes flew open in surprise and there was a hint of fear in them when she saw us. I sensed more than saw her body tense up and had the strong urge to go to her.

She stared back at me and the lightest of smiles crossed her lips before she looked at her family. Her eyes went around the room before coming back to me.

I felt the attraction in my gut even as I told myself it wasn't real. It's not like she was the first woman to get a rise out of me. So I told myself that there was no great mystery.

She just happened to have one of those faces. Like a beautiful movie star that you admire from afar but know you'd never meet, never have. She packed a punch I'll give her that.

I didn't have a ready explanation for the sudden heaviness that seemed to permeate the air and suck all the oxygen out of the room.

Or for the fact that for the barest of seconds it seemed like we were the only two people in that room. I couldn't look away and it seemed neither could she.

I looked at her for so long that my head grew light, and something hit me in the gut. It felt like time stood still, what a cliché.

In the back of my mind I knew what was happening to me, I'd heard my brothers describe this very thing a time or two. But I still couldn't accept, refused to accept that this corny shit was real.

When she finally broke eye contact with me it was as if I came out of a fog. I could hear and feel the others again and my body slowly relaxed.

I knew that no time had passed. That it had only been a matter of seconds, but it felt like half a lifetime.

What the fuck is this? What's going on here? I felt something I hadn't felt in too many years to count just by looking at her; I felt, peace.

My vision blurred and I was shocked to realize there were tears in my eyes. "Fuck me!" I looked back at my brothers. "I'm fucked."

Something must've came across in my tone because Lo and Quinn moved to flank me while I felt my other brothers crowd around me when I turned back to look at her.

Once again I didn't see or hear anything else, in those few seconds, there was just her. Like she had an almost uncanny ability to take me out of myself. I swallowed and tried to get my heart to go back to its place.

She couldn't be real and this couldn't be happening. My life wasn't a fucking Lifetime movie. I'd safeguarded myself against things like this. This isn't supposed to happen to me.

I'd built a wall around myself, a wall that only had

room for my brothers and now their families, but that is as far as I am willing to go.

Besides, look at her, she's so feminine, so delicate. There's no fucking way I can go there. The thought hurt so fucking bad it was like a physical pain. Like I'd taken a beating from a battalion.

I opened my mouth to speak but the words wouldn't come. Before I could say anything the boy headed towards her on the stairs.

Once again he was putting himself between his family and us and I couldn't help but admire his guts. I had no doubt every man in the room was sizing him up.

"Daddy, I'm sorry, you didn't tell me we were having guests." She started to walk back upstairs but his words stopped her.

"No sweetheart don't leave, come here to me." She came shyly down the stairs and did not look at any of us as she walked to his side. She even walked pretty, like her feet didn't touch the ground.

He patted her hand and she put her arm through his and kissed his cheek before leaning her head on his shoulder.

The move was so innocent, so intimate, it reminded me of something baby Zak would do when she was conning one of us out of something she knew she shouldn't have.

She was closer now, close enough for me to reach out

and touch. I could smell her scent, like a Mediterranean garden at night.

Just looking at her made me want things I know I can't have. In all the times I've heard the others speak about how it had been for them when they found their women, I never once believed that shit was real.

That sense of knowing, it was there. It was the wrong fucking time though. I needed to put it aside and do what we came here to do.

But some shit was happening to me in real time, something I couldn't deny. And I'm fucked if I didn't want to turn tail and run.

Had they also felt this fear in the gut the way I now did? Had they questioned everything they'd ever known, ever believed? Just from that one look into their woman's eyes?

And there you have it. The reason Tyler's been calling them all bitch made. I sure wasn't feeling very manly right about now. But if he knew what it was then it was obvious that he felt it too. Idiot!

I was waiting for one of the others to say something, ask the obvious questions anything, since I seemed to have lost my damn senses. But it looked like they were still letting me run the show.

Maybe they hadn't picked up on the fact that I was losing my shit, and I didn't want them to. So I got my shit together and tried to remember at least some of what I'd been trained to do.

But then she looked at me with the most open smile I'd ever seen, and the dimples in her cheeks were the last fucking straw.

I wanted to reach out and touch her, just dip my finger into that pit in her cheek. Dimples are like my weakness. I've always been a sucker for them and hers were fucking perfect.

I shook my head to clear it before I felt Quinn's hand on my shoulder. I steadied myself, wondering the whole time what the fuck was wrong with me.

"Honey, remember what we talked about earlier? No, there's no reason to be afraid." He calmed her when she became flustered.

"These men are here to take you to somewhere safe. I'll come get you soon, it won't be long okay little one? I promise."

"Dad, what the hell are you talking about?"

"Not now son I'll tell you later." The young man didn't seem too pleased with that answer but he had enough discipline to hold his peace.

She looked around at us and there were tears in her eyes. She was obviously an adult, maybe nineteen-twenty, but she seemed way more innocent than someone her age.

There was still one glaring question hanging in the air. How come she didn't show up on the radar?

"And you are?" I reached out my hand for hers and she finally focused on me up close and personal.

My gut went into a spin and I nose dived right into the abyss. She was fucking gorgeous. The tears in her eyes made them shine like some otherworldly creature.

There was a look in them that made my heart melt in my chest. Sadness, fear, confusion. I drew her towards me before I could help myself.

"Ariel!" She said her name like a whisper on the wind and I heard chiming bells and waterfalls. "*Ariel*!" I didn't realize I'd said it out loud until I heard it come back to me on a whisper.

Behind me the others were putting her name into one of our little toys to look her up. I only heard Mancini say one thing, "nothing", which was all the answer I needed. She wasn't in anyone's database.

I looked back at the others again as my mind tried to process. I don't think any of us had expected this twist. There weren't many people who could be off the grid like this, and not many reasons why someone would need to be.

"We gotta go!" I didn't look away from her when I said the words to her dad. Her brother made a move but his dad checked him. "No Track! I'll explain everything but your sister has to leave now."

He wasn't happy when he pulled her away from me

and into his chest. He towered over her and it was only then I realized how little she was.

She barely came to his chest and I had a good two or so inches on him. He whispered something in her ear and she nodded against his chest while tightening her arms around him.

Next it was her dad's turn to hold her before she turned and ran up the stairs. "If you gentlemen would give me a minute of your time."

He headed to the other side of the room and we followed. "I'm sure your commander left information at his place as to what's going on here. I won't say any more for now, not sure how secure this place is anymore."

"There's a lot that I know and some I don't, whatever the CO left will explain it all. Once she's safe let me know and then no contact until everything is done. You'll understand!"

The look he gave me said he knew a hell of a lot more than we did and my fear for her only grew because of what he wasn't saying.

She was back in about five minutes, looking nervous as hell. I passed her luggage to Quinn and took her hand in mine and headed for the door as she looked back at her family one last time.

"Wait!" Track came out the door behind us and stepped in front of me. He actually studied me like he thought he could take me or was giving it some serious thought.

"You take care of her. Anything happens to her I will find you. Come here baby girl." He pulled her away from me again and kissed her forehead before letting her go again.

"You're going to be okay, you know how to reach me no matter what." It was the way he looked at her, like there was some secret only the two of them shared.

The way she clung to him before letting go told me more than words about their relationship. She might be older, but he was a big brother all the way.

I almost felt bad for the little shit when we walked away.

32

DEVON

No one spoke as we headed to the plane that would take us back to the island, and by the time we got there she was half asleep on my shoulder.

She was sitting almost in my lap, scrunched up beside me and I got the sense that she was afraid of all the bodies in the hummer.

She brought out every protective instinct I have. There was just something so…innocent about her. The guys kept giving her questioning looks, but at the moment I wasn't interested in anything other than getting her as far away from there as possible.

No one said anything but it didn't take much to figure out what they were thinking. Who the hell is she? And why did her father keep her so well hidden?

While my brothers played around on their handhelds trying to find information on her, I was busy taking in all the nuances of having her near.

She had a weird calming affect on me, almost like baby Zak does when she's not harassing me about something.

I drew her scent into me and just for now, let myself enjoy having her near. It would be so easy to open that locked off part of me and let this one in.

I gritted my teeth and pulled back when my mind went there. Instead I took her hand in mine as I looked out at the dark.

No Devon, don't do it. She's too delicate, too everything that you shouldn't have. But for one small moment I allowed myself to think what if.

I satisfied myself with a soft kiss on her forehead and closed my eyes as she sighed and burrowed into me.

I caught Logan's look over her head and pulled back again. Fucker stared at me until I looked away and ignored his ass.

I tried rousing her when we reached the airstrip but she didn't budge. Quinn opened my door and waited for me to pass her off to him and I knew I was fucked when I didn't want him to touch her.

He grinned and took her from me and I was out of the car in two seconds flat, taking her out of his arms and holding her close to my chest again.

She felt right there, her hair ticking my nose, her amazing scent intoxicating. There were whispers and murmurings but hopefully they were discussing the case and not what was going on with me.

I had to carry her from the car to the plane and belt her in. How the hell was she sleeping? I sat next to her and laid my head back suddenly tired as fuck. Once again she shifted until her head was on my shoulder.

The whole way, from the time we left her home until we landed on that island I was tense. Because of all the secrecy surrounding her there was a new fear in my gut. A fear that hasn't been there since I was a child.

For the first time in years I let myself think of who I used to be before my life changed so drastically. That boy would've deserved someone like her.

I don't know how I knew it, but I knew that she was all that was good. I could see my sisters corrupting her, tarnishing some of that sweetness, turning her into one of them.

It was a nice thought and again I let myself imagine having something as perfect as her. What would that be like? Just the thought had a sweet warmth rushing through me and I took her hand in mine again.

I honest to fuck had no idea what was happening to me. I tried recalling all the shit my brothers had griped about in the beginning of their relationships, but nothing would come.

I was on my own with this one and it scared the shit out of me. I focused instead on the here and now. On keeping her safe. I'll deal with whatever else comes next when my mind wasn't pulling me in a hundred directions at once.

When the plane landed I waited for the others to file off leaving just Quinn in the cabin with us.

"I'll carry her don't wake her up." He smirked and held his hands up in surrender as he backed away. Ass!

I carried her from the plane to the waiting car and she still didn't wake up. I caught myself before I buried my nose in her hair as I held her close to my chest.

My brothers kept giving me questioning looks which I ignored, I had some of my own. But they'll have to wait. Right now I was more interested in her story and why she didn't seem to exist anywhere.

Once we got back to the grounds I didn't know what to do. The right thing would be to take her to the mansion to one of the many rooms there, but I didn't want to let her out of my sight, I wasn't ready.

Not until I knew what the hell was going on here. At least that's the excuse I gave myself when I realized I actively couldn't let her go.

"I'm taking her with me." I dared them to say

anything with a glare. No one said shit to me as I turned and headed to my little cottage, but I could feel their eyes on me as I walked away.

There was only one bedroom in the cottage so I decided to give her the bed and take the couch in the living room.

Quinn who'd followed us dropped her stuff off at the door while I carried her inside. "You need any help?"

"Get the fuck outta here Quinn." The ass grinned and left.

In the bedroom I laid her on the bed and stood back just looking down at her. I was finally able to breathe a little easier now that she was safe.

She was a tiny little thing. It would be so easy to…No Devon. In all these years I've never given any thought to hurting a woman.

It just wasn't something I had to think about because I'd never come close to finding anyone I wanted for more than a couple hours of bed play.

So why, why did she make me question myself? Why were all these feelings awakening in me now? I was afraid I knew the answer, but it was too dangerous.

Each time I told myself that maybe I could make it work, that sickening fear rose up inside me. I could break her in half with just a snap of my hands.

And even though the very thought of it was repulsive to me, I couldn't risk it. My heart felt like it was bleeding in my chest when I accepted that I couldn't have her, no matter what I was feeling.

I wanted so badly to reach out and touch her in the moonlight that shone through the window, but knew that I shouldn't and the battle raged on inside me.

A part of me wanted to protect her from someone like myself and the other wanted to dive right into her and never look back. "What are you doing to me?"

It was her enticing beauty. It was almost unreal. Her caramel colored skin so beautifully blemish free. The contours of her face, high cheeks bones, lush lips and those pits in her cheeks.

It was almost as if she'd been sculpted from a mold of perfection. I can honestly say I have never seen anything as beautiful as her in my life.

And still there was something so familiar about her. An almost knowing, like maybe we'd met in a past life.

And then it hit me like a punch to the gut, why I'm having such a strong reaction to her. She reminded me of my mom.

She had that quietness about her, an innocence that I remember from my youth. That beauty of spirit and face. Oh shit!

I stepped back away from her and choked up as the sensations hit me from all angles. *Mom*! For the second time that night I felt tears cloud my eyes.

I fought valiantly to hold on to the here and now, not

to confuse the two realities, but it wasn't easy. Why her, why now? Had I dreamed her into existence with my want?

Had my secret yearning for what the others had made her out to be something more than she is? Somehow I don't think so. It was too real.

There's no way I could make myself feel these things. I had no control over the emotions that hit me one after the other and I know I'd never felt anything like this before in my life.

I have to get out of here, I can't breathe. I pulled the sheet up over her after pulling her shoes off, removing the temptation.

I looked back at her once before leaving to go back outside where I knew the others would be waiting. I took a minute to compose myself, but she was still there, inside me, almost as if it was too late.

They were standing on the front lawn when I arrived. I half expected them to rag my ass but they were still in work mode. "Well what the fuck?" Logan was the first to speak.

"I can't figure it out either. I've used every resource and she doesn't show up on any database as his daughter. I mean it's freaky. She's there and that's it. There's no history not even school. No birth certificate, nothing."

"How is this possible? Everybody leaves a carbon print in some way. There's no way she was kept under the radar for this long. She must be what, twenty-one, twenty-two?" Mancini seemed affronted that he couldn't find her with this high tech gadget.

"You'd have to have known the CO and his team Hank to understand it. If anyone could pull this off it was he. The question is why would they go to these lengths to keep her hidden?" Logan answered Hank.

"Shit, I knew it!" Cord who'd been quiet all night caught everyone's attention.

"What is it Cord?"

"Something he said, about the CO leaving something for us that would explain things."

"Well the only thing we found was the book and there was nothing in there that sheds any light on this. Not about her part in it anyway."

"No, the picture I took off the wall. There was something about it." He started heading back to his cottage at a jog as the rest of us were still trying to fit the pieces together.

"Anyone have any idea what's going on here? If no one knew she existed, how the hell does Khalil know she exists?" Justice asked.

"I don't think we're gonna know the answer to that until we get some more information. Hopefully the CO did leave us something because it's fucking nuts." Connor who likes to have all the answers seemed perturbed.

"Okay well what do we have so far? There's always

an answer for everything. And when we figure this shit out I wanna know how it's done."

"I think it's too late for you to go off the grid Lyon. I'm pretty sure you're all over somebody's radar by now. Or a lot of somebodies."

"Fuck you Hank I might need that shit for Mengele, sure as fuck she's gonna end up in jail."

"Oh come on Lyon your little one is something special, she's going to take the world by storm one day."

"Oh yeah, what makes her so special?"

"I saw her reading A Book of Five Rings earlier, what is she like five?"

"What the fuck? Miyamoto Musashi? Where the fuck did she get that?"

"I may have had one lying around the library."

"Your kid is a fucking tadpole." Logan piped in. I guess they'd decided to lighten the mood until Cord returned, since we were all stuck.

"The fuck that mean?"

"It means she's one of them. That's what the navy calls newbies." Mancini laughed and Lyon looked like he was ready to kill.

"Whatever! Somebody gonna tell me what the fuck we have so far? I'd like to get some sleep before my brood wakes up in a few hours and need shit."

"Not to mention I've never been away from my wife as much as I have in the last few days and she's probably counting sheep and waiting to fuck with my ass about some shit."

"So far we know that the daughters of the men who served with the commander have been nabbed or attempts have been made. We didn't know Terrence had a daughter, we only found a son. A son who tricked his way into the DOD." Connor laughed at Lyon as he answered.

"Yeah there is that, we still don't know why he wanted in." I watched Cord return with the life portrait in hand.

We headed back to the mansion and I looked back only once at the cottage, not sure if I should leave her alone. Damn, is this how it starts? What's next, am I going to lose my mind like the rest of these fucks?

We were all tried, it was plain to see by the time we made it back to Mancini's private room with all his unregistered gadgets.

"Okay Cord let's see what you got." Logan took up a spot on the wall with the others but I was literally on top of Cord.

He ran his fingers along the edges of the frame and tapped on the back but there was nothing. "What was it that made you think there was something here?"

He held the portrait away from him and looked at it intently. "The eyes, there was something…" He ran his finger over the eyes and smiled.

"There it is!" He turned the painting over and ripped away the paper at the back. There was a chip in the back of one of the eyes. “Oh shit!” I really hadn’t expected him to find anything.

“Give it here.” Mancini held out his hand and Cord passed it to him. It was a shock when he put it in the computer and the old man’s face came on the wall screen.

I looked around at my brothers and saw the same emotion that was beating in my chest, shining out of their eyes.

33

DEVON

“Hello boys, It looks like I left you in a bit of a quandary didn’t I? I guess you can look at it as our last Op together.”

He grinned that infectious grin that only a few ever had the pleasure of seeing. It was a jolt to the system seeing him like this, almost as if he were here with us.

“I have a lot to tell you, but not a lot of time so why don’t we start at the beginning. If you’re seeing this I guess you know about the general and the fuck up by now.”

“I bet you didn’t know I knew you called him that huh. Fucking hemorrhoid should’ve never seen the inside of the white house, asshole.” The anger was plain to read.

“Don’t be too hard on my old friends, they had no idea

what they were getting into when they agreed to help me all those years ago and now they're paying for it." He took a deep breath and looked away before facing the camera again.

"Alright let's get down to it shall we. This is about Khalil. I took something from him, or at least something he thought belonged to him. His future wife."

"What the fuck?" My brothers all echoed my sentiments. I'm pretty sure none of us were expecting that.

"No you morons not like that, I only ever had one true love but…that too is for later." He cleared his throat on the screen and wiped his eyes before going on.

"About twenty-three years ago, I was part of a special detail for the head of the house of Saud. Yes, the king of Saudi Arabia. He had a delegation to the UN and I was part of his security detail."

"For some reason he liked me, trusted me. For that week and a half I was like his shadow even though he had his own team of course. That's just how it was done back then."

"I never heard from him again, until about a year later. I was on leave at the time so you can imagine my surprise when I heard his voice. I knew it was him because he always called me the American."

"Anyway he needed a special favor. Seems he had a baby girl, newborn, that had been promised to Khalil in marriage when she came of age."

"She was his only daughter. I know, a man with that many wives. He had a million sons and one daughter. He loved that kid, loved her enough to want to save her."

"He found out what Khalil and his father had planned. They were going to use the union to start some kind of war, to reunite the people of the desert and try for world domination or some such crap."

"Khalil thinks he's Salah Ad Din reincarnated or some fuck. Anyway, the old man didn't want that for his kid, so he called me in."

"He asked me to take her away, hide her. It was a daring thing to do. He warned me, told me how dangerous my life would be if anyone ever found out, meaning if it ever got back to Khalil and his father. Even then the little fuck was a terror and he was all of twelve."

"As I said I was on leave, so I went in alone or should I say, I left my team in Tikrit and went into Riyadh alone under cover of night."

"I never kept anything from my men, but with this, I couldn't tell them the whole story because of the danger. Now it's come back to bite me in the ass."

"Anyway once I got her out, I couldn't keep her for obvious reasons. When you find her you'll know what I mean. So I left her with someone I trusted."

"The news was spread that she'd died. It was a big deal all over that part of the world for a while until things died down."

"Right about the time he'd called me, I had met a woman. She was everything I ever wanted and thought I could never have." He swallowed hard here and the look in his eyes, was almost heartbreaking.

"Turns out I was right, but not for the reasons I believed. She got pregnant, had a daughter, the most beautiful little girl you ever saw."

"I loved her more than my own life and was going to marry her mother and give her the family she deserved."

"But after I helped Mustafa things changed. He called me one day about six months later. Khalil's father had found out what I had done."

"I don't know how but he did. Ever since then there was a mark on my back. The old king warned me what could happen. He told me anything I held dear would be in jeopardy."

"So I had to give up my dream of having a family of my own. I had to leave the woman of my heart, even though two years later she gave me a son."

He stopped and took a deep breath before staring back into the camera. "Our relationship had to be kept hidden. Something she never quite understood because I was never able to tell her the reasons why."

"That would be Davey and Susie's mother. Knowing you and knowing him, you've already met my son. Tell them I loved them, tell them I beg their forgiveness, but denying them was the only way I could keep them safe."

"I left everything to you because I trust you; I built you. I chose each and every one of you, because you were throwaways. I thought it was kismet I guess. Your families didn't want you and I couldn't claim mine. But I did grow to love you, each of you, for the man you are."

"I've been proud of you every step of the way and this is why I've done the things I have. I left you the land, but I did not forget my children."

"This portrait holds a lot of secrets. I can only hope that it didn't take you too long to find it and that our enemies haven't finished the job they started."

"I suspected a little over a year ago that Khalil was actively trying to find the girl. He had tried before but didn't have the resources back then, he didn't have the help he needed so his reach didn't extend to the states."

As you know I've spent years trying to rid the world of that fucking blight, but the slippery fuck always found a way to elude me."

"Then after I retired the locals started coming to me with suspicions of something going on down by the water. It never entered my mind that it could be him. But once I started digging I knew in my gut that he was spitting in my face with his shit."

"Once I started tracing the activities down on the water and it lead me to the general it didn't take long for me to realize that he was on the take, that he was in fact working with The Desert Fox."

"I knew my old team, and anyone I worked with was in danger, that's why I called you in that last time. I know the general called you up to keep you away the fuck."

"He was someone I once considered a friend, so I didn't handle that very well. The sense of betrayal kinda threw me off."

"As you know I've had my foot in Khalil's ass forever, not only because I didn't want him to get the girl, but because he is a genuine first grade asshole."

"I never found out how his father knew about my part in taking the baby, and it really doesn't matter. All that matters is that he never gets his hands on her."

"I'm depending on you to make sure she stays safe. It's obvious that they caught up with me if you're seeing this. It's my fault, I lost my head and confronted the general. Asshole!"

"I'm pretty sure I didn't die of natural causes so if that's the shit they're selling don't buy it. The general's specialty is heart attacks, if that's what you were told, don't believe it; and don't trust the general whatever you do."

Mancini and the others were taking it all in and I personally was trying not to lose my shit. I didn't know which I wanted to do first. Go find the general and put one in his head. Or go find this girl wherever she was.

"Now for my kids. If you look closely at the bottom of

this painting you will find something there. You'll need ultra violet lighting to see the writing."

"It's the numbers to my offshore accounts. There should be twenty million there plus interest. No I wasn't on the take you fucks, but the navy paid me well and Mustafa was also very kind though I begged him not to, and most of it I invested."

"That money is to be divided between my kids. You make sure they're okay, that they're safe. And their mother…there's a box in the safe in my office. You'll know the code to get in, no one else knows it."

He looked pointedly at the camera and my brothers and I got the message. It was another one of our secret codes.

"The contents belong to her. Thank you boys for everything you've done over the years and hey, don't be too damn hardheaded to ask for help if you need it, just be careful who you turn to. Call Justice and Law, I think by the time the dust settles they're gonna have a dog in this fight."

"I'm not gonna say too much here just in case it falls into the wrong hands, but I know you'll piece it all together. He's gonna come after you, and maybe anyone else we've ever worked with. As I'm making this I've only reached the tip of the iceberg."

"I did as much as I can thus far but this thing keeps getting bigger and bigger. Watch your six boys, my money's on you. Kick his ass for me will you. I'll see you boys on the other side; be happy."

The screen went dark and he was gone. No one spoke for the longest time and then Mancini broke the silence. "Looks like we have some work to do."

My brothers didn't speak nor did I. Lyon was the one to finally break the silence. "How did my kid get caught up in this? I don't know any of these people."

"Yeah we already established that your connection is the senator, which means the general. Whatever Khalil is doing he's using this trafficking shit as a front."

"Either that or it's just plain revenge. They took something of his, now he's taking something of theirs. I'm not sure what the general and the others are getting out of this, but I think we all know there's a lot of money in that trafficking shit."

At least Logan seemed to be following the tread of this whole mess. I was still stuck on seeing the old man again.

"So his old team didn't know what they were getting into. What does that mean? Did he tell them anything at all?"

"I'm pretty sure he must've given them a heads-up when he realized which way this thing was heading. The question is, why out of all of them was Samson the only one who kept his daughter so well hidden? Did he know more than the others maybe?" Law threw that question out there.

"Maybe he knew enough to know that Khalil would come after her eventually?" Justice who hadn't said much of anything since we left the states was finally heard from.

Pretty soon we were all trying to put the pieces of the puzzle together. We knew more now than we did an hour ago but there was no denying there was still a shit load we didn't know.

"Any ideas on where we start to look for this woman? Would there be anything else back at the compound?"

"Maybe Samson knows something. He did say there were things he couldn't say to us tonight. And we're supposed to call him once his daughter was safe." Speaking of which.

"I'll be right back." I'd been gone for more than an hour. The women and children had all gone to bed and the place was quiet and still.

All I could think of was her waking up in a strange place alone. I needed to find out what her dad had said to her before we showed up, and then I needed to call and let him know she was okay.

Those feelings hit me again as soon as I walked into the room. That gut punch feeling that made me weak in the knees.

She was still asleep, huddled under the covers when I checked on her. I stood over her watching her sleep for a few minutes before turning away. I closed the door softly behind me and left.

I left a little something behind that would alert me once she woke up and had to be satisfied with that for now.

Back at the mansion someone had already set up a board with all that we knew so far. In the middle was the unknown woman that Khalil was apparently after.

Surrounding her were the names of the men who'd served on the CO's team and their daughters. Each of the women in the book had been added as well.

It was easy to follow the trail and see that they all had some connection to someone the old man had either worked with or commanded in the last twenty years.

We didn't need much more to make it clear that this was indeed a vendetta against him. But it was the organization that it took that was surprising. This shit had to be in the works for a long fucking time.

Things got a little confusing once we added the general and the other politicians to the equation. Where the fuck did they fit in?

34

DEVON

We were at that shit for hours. Piecing shit together, moving things around to come up with the answers.

Once we found the right thread and began to tug, it became easier to connect the dots and the picture that was painted was not a pretty one.

“So here, twenty years ago, Khalil was still a kid, but his old man started the search for the girl. It looks like they didn’t know who exactly had taken her, so it took them some time to whittle it down to the commander.”

We’d only got this far because of Mancini and his connections who he’d called for some information going back all those years.

It was tedious work because we had to follow the general going back twenty years and then moving forward again to see when exactly his path had crossed with Khalil's.

Once we found the connection it wasn't hard to pull in the politicians and see their part in the whole filthy mess.

"It was all about money for them. I wonder, did they know who the fuck this guy was when they got into bed with him? I mean, we armed this fuck!" It was safe to say I was beyond pissed.

"This is why I never joined up. No disrespect to anyone in this room, you've all proven to be men of honor, but this shit right here, makes me want to fuck some shit up."

Everyone nodded at Lyon's words. Though I could make the argument that there was a hell of a lot that makes him homicidal, he had a point.

"I hear you Colton, and this isn't the worse of it. This just happens to be the thing we got caught up in, but these men, once they lose their way, you'd be surprised at the shit they get into."

Mancini kept studying the board as he spoke, while the rest of us military men tried to make sense of what the hell we were looking at.

It was hard for me so I was sure it was the same for the others, to fathom selling out our country. But the evidence was right in front of us.

The Desert Fox had set off a shit storm spanning at

least the last ten years in order to find this girl. She would've been ten back then.

"You know what's missing? Nowhere does it show what her old man has been doing in the meantime to make sure she's never found. But I think it's safe to say that he has been doing something."

I looked to Lo for confirmation that he agreed with my analysis. "I'm sure you're right Dev, but what does that mean? Are we supposed to go to him and ask him where the hell he has her stashed?"

"It might not come to that. Let me make a few calls and see what I learn." No one questioned whether Mancini had that kind of reach, by now it was obvious that he did.

"I have one question. Do I have to wait until you've taken care of this Fox guy before I break the senator's neck?"

Lyon was serious as fuck when he said that and it took the whole room to talk his ass down. "You know we can't condone you going after a sitting senator Lyon. You've already taken care of his brother and sister in law…"

"Logan, brother, I don't need you or anyone else to condone shit. When it comes to my kids and my woman everybody's fucked."

"His family didn't have a connection to this guy, he did. And if I find out that your ex-president had anything to do with my daughter's name being in that book personally, he's fucked too."

"Don't waste your breath Lo, I'll talk to him." Law shut Logan down when he started to answer Lyon's threat.

I thought it best to get us back on track before this disintegrated into a screaming match between those two.

Lo has a core of loyalty that runs deep and a huge part of that loyalty is to his country. Until he knows everything and how it all came about, he won't commit to anything.

Especially when it comes to taking out men that were part of our country's leadership. I have to say I'm with Lyon on this one though. These fuckers need to die no matter how or why they got caught up in this shit.

"I'm with Colton. This isn't your garden-variety fuck up, this is some sick shit. They almost had Kelly Lo." Quinn paced the room and looked back at the screen where the CO had been.

"What if it had been Gaby, which we now know could've been a possibility. The only reason she wasn't in that book is because you hadn't met her yet." Lo flexed his shoulders but held his peace.

"But whomever you'd chosen would've ended up in his crosshairs. You can't tell me that doesn't fuck with you."

Quinn was pissed and rightfully so, but now was not the time to lose it. "What are we going to do about the ones who were already taken?" It burned my ass that there were young girls and women who'd already fallen prey to this shit.

"Thorpe, that's what he specializes in. If they're out there, he'll find them. As to the senator, Thorpe already dealt with one of those maybe he would know where to start looking."

"How long ago was this?"

"A couple years ago, why don't I give him a call?" He didn't wait for an answer but called Thorpe right away.

We all listened in as he gave him the bare bones and there was no surprise when he mentioned some names that we had already heard before.

"If they're being held domestically Blade and Jake might be of help there, I'll get my team to look overseas. I'll let you know what we come up with if anything. If you get anymore just shoot it to me. Are the SEALs there?"

"We're here." Logan answered him on the speaker. "Can one of you explain to your admiral that I don't take orders from him? The man's a pain in the ass."

"Why what's he doing?"

"Well for starters, he and his motley crew seem to think that all that's needed is to kill everyone and anything that moves. This is a very delicate situation we're dealing with here, we can't just go blow shit up for fuck sake."

"Why don't you give them something to do? Let them help you out?"

"Because I don't work with unknowns." Another hard ass.

"We'll take care of it Thorpe, and thanks again." He hung up after Lo's words. "Quinn deal with your father in law."

"What the fuck, you're in charge Lo that's your deal." I found my first laugh since we got back from Cali and that little exchange seemed to lighten the mood a bit.

"Okay, so Thorpe's taking care of the ones who were already taken, we have the others secure. All we need to do now is find this woman and then take care of Khalil. Does that sound about right?" I asked the room at large.

"Mancini when are you going to make that call?" He checked his watch. "They're seven hours ahead so it's what, ten in the morning? I say we get some rest and come back at it in a few. I'll make the call then."

We all agreed and the men got to their feet to leave. Mancini pressed some buttons and the board slid into the casing on the wall and disappeared.

"Just in case the girls should find their way in here." Not sure how they would do that seeing as how the shit has more security than Fort Knox, but he was right. These women are resourceful if nothing else.

As the rest of us headed back to the cottages leaving Lyon and Mancini in the mansion, the tension was heavy.

"You know they killed your CO right?" Ah damn Law, not now.

"The rest of you really think I don't want to end these fucks? But what happens if we go after them before we get those girls back? Did any of you think of that?"

That's why he's our fearless leader, because he thinks about shit like that. Me, I say we go take his fucking head and let Lyon loose on the senator. As for the fuck up, that might be a little harder.

"I hear you Lo, but after we've taken care of them he's done."

"Tyler!"

"No Logan, fuck that. We heard it from the old man's mouth. There's no more second-guessing. He's fucked." Ty stormed off in the direction of his cottage.

"Connor!" Logan gritted out the name.

"Yeah I got him. But you know he has that other crazy fuck singing the same tune. I'ma need combat pay."

Con went after Tyler and caught up with him. "We can't go off half cocked here brothers. This isn't some redneck brigade in the fucking hills. We're talking about a senator and a three star general not to mention an ex-president."

"I'll try to rein Lyon in later, but I gotta tell you, if we don't do something soon he's liable to pop his fucking leash. I told you when we first brought him in."

"Yeah you told me but I didn't know the fuck was a renegade. And he and Tyler seem to be cut from the same fucking bolt of cloth. It's a wonder either one of 'em lasted this long as hot headed as they are."

"Lyon's not hotheaded, he might seem to be, but that is one methodical fuck. Personally I think Mancini is the one we gotta watch."

Everyone looked at Justice who was nodding his head. "Think about it. Lyon and Ty might have the anger, but neither of them have the resources this guy has."

"I've been checking out his setup here, and this motherfucker is the real deal. And we all know he has no affiliation with anything as far as we can tell."

"Dammit, how did this get so fucked? Okay, so now it's three of them we gotta watch, fuck my life. Okay, Con has Ty, Mancini has Lyon, but who the fuck is gonna keep his ass in check?"

'That would be you Lo, you're the one in charge." Thank fuck! I don't want to be in charge of shit. I just wanna break some heads and get on with my life.

"I'm gonna fuck Khalil's shit up for this shit alone. The rest of you get some sleep, who knows what the hell is coming next."

"We're gonna owe the girls big when this shit is all said and done." Zak clapped me on the back and moved off.

"And you, we're gonna have a little chat about what the fuck is going on with you." Lo pointed at me before he too walked away.

35

DEVON

I headed back to the cottage and after checking in on her laid down on the couch. It took me a while to fall asleep because she was so close.

My whole body was tense and ready to spring, I was wound too tight to give in to slumber. I tossed on the small ass couch and almost fell on my ass and only gave a passing thought to joining her in bed.

I wonder what she'd do if she rolled over in the morning to find me next to her? The idea was too damn appealing so I had to lock it off quick before I did something I'd regret.

My mind went back and forth between her and the shit we were dealing with. I still didn't know where she fit in, why her dad knew enough to keep her so well hidden, but maybe I'll get those answers when I call him later.

I'd at least remembered to send him a quick text since like he said he wasn't sure how secure his home was, but at least he knew his daughter was safe.

I thought of the CO and the things he'd said, the fact that he'd been murdered, and the rage that I'd held at bay for so long threatened to overwhelm me.

It wasn't just that he'd been taken from us, but the way in which he'd been taken, by those he should've been able to trust.

He'd spent his life in service to his country only to lose it at the hands of traitors. I know Lo is right. That we need to get the women back before we make a move.

But I also know he's full of shit. I'd bet anything if any of us run into that fuck he's as good as dead. If Lyon and Ty decided to make an end run I just might join them.

As it stands I'm the only one who doesn't have anything to lose. I looked towards the bedroom door before the thought faded. She's not yours Dev.

I shut it down but once I blocked out all the other noise my focus went right back to her. I was right back there to that moment when I first saw her standing on those stairs.

The burn in my gut was the same, and that feeling like I was falling off a cliff. Could love really be this potent, this invasive? Or was it just lust?

Somehow that didn't feel right. I've felt lust, even strong attraction before, but nothing ever felt like this. Nothing ever bowled me over. I for damn sure never obsessed over a woman before, not even when I was a teen.

It didn't make sense that she should affect me this way, not with all the safeguards I'd put in place to protect myself and my heart. And why am I going around in circles with this shit?

I'm still in control aren't I? I haven't completely lost my mind like my brothers have, which seemed to be a prerequisite for this love shit.

I'd watched each and every one of them, act in ways I never would've expected once they found 'the one', I wasn't feeling any of that. Am I?

No, but I'm not the same man I was before I walked into that house, that much I will admit to. If I didn't know better I would think that there was something other-worldly at work here.

I'm not the love at first sight type, and I'm not one for fanciful leanings. But sure as fuck something touched me tonight.

The raw emotion she brought out in me was confusing. That soft gentleness about her makes me want to wrap her up in something soft and protect her from everything. Where did she learn to be that fucking angelic?

If that wasn't enough, she's so fucking beautiful it's

crazy. She has that kind of rare beauty that once you've seen it it's hard to forget.

The thought gave me fucking agida. Did other men see her the way I do? Yeah Dev, you're not in love or anything. So why the fuck, do you want to kill imaginary men just for looking at her, for having seen her beauty?

Go to sleep Devon, just go the fuck to sleep, you're not making any sense. I felt a cold shiver run down my spine and straight through to my gut.

Is this how it starts? Quinn that asshole has been acting kinda squirrely since he met Kelly on the beach. It's like he's there, but his mind isn't.

I have no doubt that each of my brothers and the men who'd joined us could and would do the job, but there was no denying that something had changed.

Lo spends more time worrying about Gaby and what the fuck she's getting up to than he does anything else these days, and all the others are pretty much the same.

It's like the women have taken over every part of their brain. Something I used to tease them about until now I find myself on this damn couch thinking about her when I should be trying to figure out where the fuck the Fox is hiding so we could end his stupid ass.

I was able to bring my head back somewhat and focus more on the situation at hand. At least we had all the daughters of the CO's old team accounted for and they were safe.

But the fact that she'd been so well hidden still messed with my head. I could understand her dad going to those lengths if he knew something more than the others, but wouldn't he have shared his fears with the rest of his team?

Why hadn't the others known that something was coming? It was obvious from the CO's video that he didn't have all the information before he was killed.

It seems he'd believed that only he was in danger of Khalil's vengeance, he and whoever is shielding the girl he'd taken out of Saudi Arabia.

Or was it something else? Had she been in danger from another source? I wish now that I had pressed her father for more. It doesn't matter, she's with me now and nothing and no one is going to fuck with her, not on my watch.

My mind went to the faceless girl that Khalil was hunting down. Khalil has to be dealt with no question, but we need to make sure this kid was safe first and foremost.

I could understand the old king's fear and the lengths he'd gone to-to protect his own. I wouldn't want that fuck married to my daughter either, the guy's totally fucking evil.

He's not the first to want to reignite history, Mussolini did that shit when he thought he was fucking Napoleon, but this guy takes that shit to a whole new level.

He seriously believes that he should destroy everyone

who doesn't look and think like him, and unlike the others, he's not playing.

We've gone after Khalil before, more than once in fact. And each time we thought we had him, he somehow slipped away.

The last time we'd been sure we had him, only to have him resurface later. He'd taken Vanessa because she was Zak's and she'd escaped thank fuck, but it's obvious now that all our women are in danger as long as he remains alive.

Our women! Unlike the others I'm not about to jump in with both feet. I have way too much baggage for any one woman to deal with.

The dark shit that had happened to me in the past was easy for me to push aside over the years, but I've always had that fear that that shit lived inside me.

I know about the cycle of abuse, that those who've experienced that shit are more prone to offend, and it scares the shit out of me that I could ever do that.

It didn't matter that I'm so good with my niece and now all the other kids that we've come to know. I'm not with them twenty-four seven. They're not my sole responsibility.

What happens if I take that step and one day my kid cries too hard, or bothers me while I'm busy? Would I snap and hurt him or her? My gut hurt at the thought.

And what about her? I wasn't my uncle's only victim.

He'd beaten the shit out of his wife and kids as well, it was just that with me he had a special kind of hate.

The burns and the beatings were bad enough, but it was the psychological bullshit he'd subjected me to that makes me afraid to put myself out there.

And someone like her, so beautiful, so sheltered, what the fuck would I do to her? The thought makes me physically sick.

To think that I could harm something that fucking beautiful was too much to bear. I can't risk it, can't subject her or anyone else to who I might be.

But that feeling, that knowing in my gut, was it possible to walk away? If it was just a sexual urge to take her, that could easily be dealt with. But the truth is, that was just a small part of it, the least of it truth be told.

The attraction was there no doubt about that. But it was the emotion that had me by the balls. I've been protecting myself since my teens against things like this.

I never want to lose someone I love again in this life. It's one of the reasons I'd held myself back from my brothers in the beginning.

I understand the laws of attraction, I know that shit follows me around and I've never cared enough to find help, because my mind was already made up that I was never going to do the family thing. So there was no danger of me repeating the abuse.

My brothers are grown ass men, they can hold their

own if I ever lost my damn mind. But a defenseless woman, one as little as she is; no fucking way.

I came full circle and was back to her again. I made myself stay where I was when the need to go take one last look overwhelmed me.

She's no longer hidden Devon, she's out there now. What if someone else goes after her? I ran through all the men that were here while my heart beat like a drum.

All married or otherwise attached. I started to calm down until I remembered Mancini's people, are they married? What the fuck, are you doing?

I don't know, but I'm going to make sure no one gets near her. I'll tell Hank in the morning to keep his people away from her. I'll take care of her myself.

I actually laid there worrying about some unknown male getting too close to her. That right there was enough of a red flag for me.

That jealousy shit wasn't something I learned at my uncles fists, that shit was all me. And that's what I feared would lead to the abuse.

It's a no win situation. I'm just not cut out for this shit. I almost wish I'd never met her. Until her I never had these questions, I was never tempted.

But somewhere in the back of my mind I knew that it wasn't going to be that easy. That now that I'd seen her, touched her, smelt her, she was going to live inside me for a long-long time.

36

DEVON

I must've dozed off because the next thing I knew there was movement coming from the bedroom. I sat up and rubbed the sleep from my eyes.

It was ten o'clock local time. I'd had five solid that was good enough. My first thoughts were happy, she was here, and then I remembered that I couldn't have her. "Fuck!"

I headed into the shower and got myself together letting the water beat down on me, clear my head. It was obvious she'd already been in there because of the used towel that was neatly folded over the rack and the condensation on the shower door.

I stared at that towel like a freak for a solid five

seconds before shaking myself out of it. I took my time in there shaving and puttering around, afraid to go out there and face her.

Shit, I didn't think to get my clothes from the bedroom. I looked at the clothes I slept in with distaste, no fucking way. Who are you getting pretty for Dev? Fuck you! Swear to fuck my subconscious laughed at me.

In the end I had no choice but to wrap the towel around me and head back out to the living room. I half expected to find her there but the room was empty.

When she didn't come through the door but instead I heard the springs of the bed as if she sat down again, I went to the door.

I knocked softly, not wanting to scare her, not quite sure what she must be thinking about all this. I didn't want to rush in and start interrogating her but time was of the essence.

"Are you decent?"

"Yes!" Was her voice always that innocent, that soft? Or was it fear? I opened the door slowly, bracing myself for the sight of her, but nothing could prepare me.

In the morning sunlight, she was even more gorgeous than I remembered. Her hair was tousled and sleep sexy. Her lips and face were bare of any enhancements and she looked so young and….sad.

It was the sadness that got to me as I walked into the

room. I stopped a good ten feet away, not invading her space.

"I'll just grab some clothes and be right back." I rifled through the bag which I had yet to unpack for some cargo shorts and a tank.

Back in the bathroom I hurried into my clothes and went back to her. She was sitting exactly where I left her at the edge of the bed with a pillow on her lap.

"Are you okay sweetheart?" She nodded her head and hugged the pillow to her chest. "Yeah, I'm just a little..." She shrugged her shoulders and looked away.

"Would you like to call your dad? Let him know you're okay?" She nodded her head and held out her hand for my phone.

There was an innocence to her that touched something in me. I didn't get the sense that she had any impairments or disabilities, but she was almost childlike in her behavior.

I'd noticed it last night as well, but had been too spell-bound by her beauty to think too hard about it. "Daddy it's me. Yes I'm okay. No I just woke up. Okay!"

She held the phone out to me. "This is Devon." I was sure I didn't need to tell him any more than that. If he was anything like the old man he already knew all he needed to about the seven of us.

"I'll call you later at this number, now's not a good time. Her brother isn't handling this well and I have to take care of him, make sure he doesn't get himself into trouble."

"I'm trusting you to take very good care of her you hear me son? Don't you let those motherfuckers get anywhere near my girl."

"You have my word sir." She watched me intently as I spoke, her eyes almost hypnotizing. So much so that I had to look away as I finished my conversation with her dad.

I didn't learn anything more but at least he knew his kid was safe. Now what to do with her? "Come on sweetie you need to eat something."

She smiled and got off the bed, following me from the room. I was nervous as hell and had no idea why. She was silent as she walked beside me, her head turning this way and that as she took in the beauty of the island.

"Do you live here?"

"No baby, we're just staying here for a few days. Brace yourself, you're about to meet my brothers and sisters."

It was obvious from the way the women were staring in our direction that the guys had filled them in.

Shit, I wonder what hell they were about to put me through. Dani was the first to leave her seat and meet us halfway.

"Hi, Ariel is it? That's such a beautiful name. Oh my word you're gorgeous." She laughed nervously and shook

Dani's hand before we carried on to the patio where it looked like everyone was already seated.

Even the kids were sitting around having breakfast and the atmosphere was light and happy. Anyone looking would think we were on vacation.

I seated her next to me and ignored the stares from my nosy ass sisters as I introduced her around.

She didn't seem very comfortable and I was a little bit surprised when she inched closer to me. The others seemed to catch on and eased up a little.

"What do you like to eat baby?" It would appear that I'd picked up the nasty habit of calling her by those cute little endearments without provocation.

"Fruit, is there fruit?"

"I'll get you some." I loaded up a plate with fruit and got her some juice, placing it in front of her before getting another for myself.

I ignored my brothers and their questioning looks until it became too much. One look at Lo told me he was waiting to hear if I'd learned anything so I just shook my head at him to hold it.

The conversation picked up again and they were talking about mundane shit. The women wanted to go shopping and the men were telling them no. Same old same old.

She was quiet and I had to glare at my family a time or two as they stared at her. "Ariel, why don't us girls show you around?"

Cierra offered and the other women were only too happy to jump from their seats. Nosy fucks! She looked at me as if asking permission and once again I was struck by her innocence.

"It's okay baby I'll be right here." She excused herself to the others at the table and I watched her walk away with the women. For some reason I was tempted to call her back and keep her with me.

"So?" Quinn didn't even let them clear the damn door before he was getting into my shit.

"So what?"

"Come on Dev, is she?"

"Is she what Zak? When the fuck did you lot turn into women?"

"It's obvious you like her, and last night you looked like you were damn near ready to shit bricks, what gives?"

"What gives is that we have a madman on the loose and some female out there whose life is in danger. I don't have time for all that other shit right now."

I didn't even look at Lo who wasn't saying anything but was still saying a fuck of a lot with his staring shit.

"Did you call her father?" Lo finally asked.

"Yes, but he couldn't talk. Track's giving him trouble he said he'll call later."

"Okay!"

"Wait, that's it?"

"You'll talk when you're ready. The rest of you stand down."

Ty mumbled some shit under his breath and then we got sidetracked by Mancini, who came running out the door.

"Where's the girl?"

"What girl who are you talking about?" Quinn asked him.

"Devon's woman."

"She's here safe, why?" I didn't take him to task for his words.

"It's her."

"What's her, what are you talking about?" I was already out of my seat. She couldn't be hurt, she'd only just left my sight like five minutes ago.

"He's after her. I just got off the phone with my contact. She's the one Khalil is after, her father is the king of Saudi Arabia, she's his only daughter."

"Wait that can't be right. She's black not…"

"Her mother was Nubian." I was shaking my head before he was through talking. "It can't be; no."

Fuck not her, not that innocent. I started to go after her.

"It has to be, I just got the same story from my guy that your commander told."

"There was a marriage agreement between the two families. When her father figured out what was going on, how Khalil and his family planned to take over the Arab world and enforce a war, they sent her away for her safety. No one's known where she was all this time."

"So how can you be sure that it's her?"

"It was easy to fit the pieces together. It's why she doesn't show up anywhere. And Terrence Samson never had a daughter, I looked. Believe me I used every resource I have and came to the only conclusion that makes sense."

I looked towards the house again, wanting to go after her. "Is this place safe enough? Who else knows? Who's this guy you talked to?" Why are we just standing here? Didn't they understand the danger she was in?

Where before I thought the place was secure and impenetrable I now felt exposed, like we were out in the open. My mind raced as I looked for a solution, somewhere safe that I could take her.

"No one knows why I was asking it's cool, I've done this before. As to this place being safe my wife is here. Need I say more?" Makes sense, but still…

"Lo?" I knew what I wanted to do, grab her and run. But that's not how we do shit and where the fuck would I go? We can't trust anyone. This is so fucked.

"Bring the kids inside. Mancini we'll use your war room if you don't mind." Lo got to his feet and his ease made me feel less panicked.

If the panic was for myself it would've been easy to deal with, but I kept seeing her the way she looked this morning as she sat on the bed looking up at me. That innocence that I haven't seen in anyone else shining in her eyes.

I felt that shit in my heart and the knowledge that I'm responsible for her now hit me hard. The thought of anything touching her damn near gutted me.

This shit had just gone from zero to sixty and I had a new sense of urgency. We rounded up the kids and after much grumping they were happy enough to hang out in the arcade room Mancini showed them.

Mancini used the intercom to call his woman who appeared out of nowhere. He whispered something in her ear and she went off to join the other women again. I felt twitchy.

She wasn't like the others, she wasn't bold and strong like my sisters; I already sensed that. I didn't want her afraid, I didn't want her without me.

I must've made some kinda sound as I looked in the direction the women were headed in as they moved to another side of the house, because Quinn was on my ass.

"I have to do something, are we sure this place is safe enough?" I'm sure I'd asked that question before but my head was going in and out.

I tried holding onto my training, to look at it as just another Op but that shit wasn't working. If I needed any evidence that she was getting to me this was it.

There was a wild need in me to protect, to shield and

to destroy anyone who posed a threat to her. This wasn't just an Op, this shit was even more personal now than it was an hour ago.

I realized what the problem was, what was so different now. I was scared out of my fucking mind.

37

DEVON

“Calm down Devon, she’s fine, we’re all here. No one’s gonna get to her.” I wanted to yell at Quinn that he didn’t know what the fuck he was talking about, but I knew it was irrational.

The idea that that sick fuck was after that sweet girl turned my guts. I’ve never known such fear in my life and I’ve been in some dicey situations before. But we all knew how formidable a foe we were facing.

Khalil has proven time and again that he doesn’t give up, that there are no lengths he wouldn’t go to- to get what he wants.

“He can’t fucking have her. Somebody knows where this fuck is, where’s the general? Fuck this shit.”

"Lo!" That was Connor.

"I've got him."

"Devon, look at me. I'm gonna need you to rein it in brother. We can't just go after the general, we have to plan and…"

"Why?"

"Because he's a fucking three star general. We start going after these fucks on domestic soil do you know the hell we'll unleash on us, on the women?"

"I don't care who the fuck he is I'm all outta fucks to give. Have you seen her? Have you seen who they're hunting down like a fucking dog in the wild?"

"And there he is. I've been waiting for this."

"Tyler, don't fuck with me right now." The jackass rubbed his hands together and grinned.

I wanted to punch his lights out when he winked at me. It was only the look in his eyes that told me he was only trying to calm the situation that saved his ass.

"Devon, no one is going to get to her. She's ours now. Would I let someone take Danielle? No. No one is taking your woman. Just get your head on straight brother, focus and let's find this motherfucker so we can all sleep at night."

I rubbed the pain in my gut and tried to calm down. I wasn't expecting this but I should've. It all made sense now, the way she'd been so well hidden.

The fact that she doesn't show up anywhere, almost like she doesn't exist. What kind of life has she had? Did she even have a childhood? The shit was heartbreaking.

"I can't…" I felt like I was fucking losing it. It's one thing for Khalil to play his fucked up games with other people's lives, but she was different, what he wanted from her… "Oh fuck no!"

I squeezed my head between my hands to ease the pressure and looked around at my brothers. I need help. I didn't know what to do with the shit that was going on inside of me.

I've never felt more murderous in my life and that's saying a lot. But it was the sense of helplessness that bothered me more.

I'm not afraid for myself, never that, but I never knew what it meant to have someone you care for in danger.

I know that as long as he lives she will never be safe. And we have no idea how many he has working with him on our end.

Kelly had come damn close to being lost, how much more danger is Ariel in? Everything else up to this point was child's play.

She was the main goal. The thing one of the most dangerous men in the world wanted. Fuck me!

"I want his blood in my teeth. I want to find him and rip him limb from limb."

The anger and rage was instantaneous, but there was

no outlet, no way for me to abate it. Nothing was going to make this shit better except Khalil's head on a platter.

Before I wanted him dead because of the CO, but now with her added to the mix, that shit has been multiplied tenfold.

My chest felt like it was about to explode and there was a vise like pressure in my head. It took a monumental effort for me not to walk out the door and go on the hunt.

My control was slipping fast. I could feel it happening but couldn't stop it. I made a move towards the door but a line of bodies stopped me as they stood in my way.

"Get out of my way." I don't know which of them I was talking to because I couldn't see through the haze that clouded my vision. But I knew it was Quinn who put his hands on my shoulders and tried turning me around.

QUINN

Oh fuck, Dev's a madman. Are you shitting me? Not Mr. Cool! How did I not see this shit coming? I should've known he was wound too tight, and trying way too hard to pretend he wasn't affected by this girl. We all saw it.

Last night we'd been excited and high fiving each

other when he was in the cottage getting her settled. The circle was complete and I didn't have that nagging feeling in my gut any longer because my brother wasn't going to be left out.

Now this shit! I know how he feels though, which makes it harder that I have to stop him. I too just want to go find the ones responsible and finish this shit. But Lo is right.

We have to think of the others that had been taken as well as what would happen if we went after the general and shit went south. Our lives would be fucked.

LOGAN

Why the fuck me? From Connor down to Dev they all lose their shit when it comes to their women. I am not looking forward to putting my brother on his ass for wanting to do something I want to do myself. But I'll do it to save him.

"Where are you going Dev?" He glared right through us and didn't say a word, which I knew was more dangerous than the yelling.

It kills me that I can't make this shit right. I'm always the one, they look to me for answers. But there were so many angles at play here, and all of them dangerous.

As the one my brothers look up to, I have to keep a calm head even when I want to just let it all hang out.

Ever since seeing the CO on that recording my blood has been on a slow boil, but going in hot on this would make shit worse for a whole lotta people.

If that's not enough, I have my woman mad at me because she can't have the wedding that she wants, and is making my life a living hell.

Her latest scheme is that sleeping with me outside of marriage goes against everything she believes in. Never mind that half the time she's the one hopping on my dick before I'm fully awake.

My brothers, their women, and now my damn niece is being held hostage and there isn't shit I can do because of some asshole that thinks the world belongs to him.

I know they understand the need for caution, but how can I blame them for wanting to break rank and go vigilante when I'm tempted to do the same on a daily basis?

CONNOR

Well damn, not another one. Between Tyler and Cord I thought we were done with this shit. Zak I halfway expected to be nuts when it came to Vanessa because of their history.

Tyler is always talking shit but I've always known he's crazy since I'm always the one tasked with reining him in.

But I have to say I didn't expect this from Dev. He's always been the most laid back and even tempered of the bunch.

Now it looks like we were going to have to take his ass down. The fucked up thing is that I see his point.

None of the men involved deserve to live, especially the general. I expect asshole politicians to be dirty as fuck. We've cleaned up enough of their messes over the years to know the deal.

But this business of stealing and selling humans was a new low. And now that I looked like he'd found his one, we learn that a madman, one we knew only too well was after her.

This shit had barely touched Danielle and it put the fear of hell in me, his girl is the fucking main event. I don't blame him for wanting to go AWOL.

TYLER

Oh-ho-ho, I knew this shit was coming. I saw the way he looked at her last night, saw the second he fell and fell hard. It's always the quiet ones you have to look out for.

I should be used to this shit by now though. Fucking Connor was nuts, so was Lo and Cord took the fucking cake.

All kidding aside, I can't imagine how he feels knowing that a twisted fuck like Khalil is after his girl, just hours after finding her.

I'm willing to give Lo some leeway here, but if Dev decides to go rogue I'm with him, I don't give a fuck. I know my boy Colton is down, all we need to do is escape the all seeing eye of Lo and his nosy ass.

We've spent way too much time on this shit and as far as I'm concerned, after seeing the CO and hearing what he had to say, I'm done waiting.

"Now that we finally have the answer as to what the fuck is going on here, I say we take care of this shit once and for all. No more waiting."

"Tyler you're not helping." Zak and his peace-keeping ass, is full of shit. "Like you're not thinking the same thing. Which one of us wouldn't feel the same way if she was ours?"

"Not the point Tyler. We're all going to get what we

want, but we have to do shit the right way. Devon, I asked you where you were going."

"You know where. I'm tired of waiting, tired of hiding from this fuck. When is the last time any of us had a good night's sleep? Can you imagine what her life has been like?"

"I don't think she knew Dev. I think Samson kept her well insulated from all that. She doesn't seem…"

"I don't care if she knows or not Lo. The fucking girl has been hidden away her whole life. Not one more fucking day."

"Women have rights, sure her father made the choice for her, but he had reason and we all know that it was the right one. Khalil is a fucking monster."

"Yes he is Dev, but the fact still remains that we can't go running in. We touch the general now everything goes to shit."

"That's what you think, but there's got to be a way to make him talk. He has to know where Khalil is. He's the reason that asshole has always been one step ahead of us."

"Now we know he killed the old man and you want us to do what? Sit around and wait for them to find her?"

"I agree. I have to tell Susie that her father was murdered in the same breath I have to tell her who he was."

"Cord, don't start. Can't any of you see that we can't

go off the rails here? You wait until we get this close to lose your collective minds? I blame you for this."

Logan looked at Lyon whose expression pretty much said he didn't give a fuck and his shrug solidified it.

"I'm sorry but I don't see the problem. This general whoever the fuck he is-is just a man, and apparently not a good one at that. I say take his ass out, after we extract the information we need."

"Yeah see, but that's not how any of this is done. The general isn't just a man, he's a whole fucking army of men. We go after him and miss the shot they will be in our ass and our children's ass for generations to come."

"I still say we can do it. As far as I'm concerned, it's her life or theirs. They were heading to Cali Lo, they either knew she was there or they came very fucking close to knowing."

"They don't know we're here though, so we have the upper hand. I say we lay low and do what we have to-to find whatever hole Khalil is hiding in."

"And once again we're doing shit according to his will. I don't think so. I'm tired of playing his fucking game." Dev pulled away from Quinn but they still wouldn't let him through.

This shit is getting good. It's been a while since I got to cut loose and now it looks like Dev was ready to join me. Go Dev. "Tyler!"

"What Con? I didn't say anything."

"Yeah but your face is saying a lot. Stand the fuck down and don't encourage him."

"Damn Lo, you like to suck the fun out of everything. Very well, carry on."

38

DEVON

"Devon, Dev, look at me brother, right here." Quinn pointed to his eyes. "He will never get through me. Every man in this room will stand in front of her."

"We'll do it for you and for her, but what's more, we'll do it for the CO. It's the last thing he asked of us, to keep her safe, you know what that means."

"He's right Dev, at least we got her before he could. She's never been as safe as she is here with us. We've kept the others safe this far we sure as fuck aren't going to drop the ball now. He had Vanessa remember? I know how you feel."

Damn I forgot about Zak and Nessa and the fact that she had been a prisoner of that sick fuck. "But she's not like Nessa, she's....she's soft, gentle."

"So is Dani, so is Gaby and all the others for that matter. But these women have proven, for all their griping that when it comes down to it, they kick ass." Con took Quinn's place and got in my face.

"That's right, if we've learned anything it's not to underestimate these women. Come on brother we've got this. Don't crack on me now. Besides, I thought you weren't interested?"

"Fuck you Lo." The men grinned as the tension lifted. I felt the fire begin to ease in my gut and my head began to clear.

"Okay-okay, give me a minute." I paced around the room to shake it off. It wasn't easy, not with all the shit that was bottled up inside. Years of injustice had brought me to this moment.

An opportunity to save an innocent, the way no one had saved me. I pounded my fist into my palm as I worked it out in my head.

I reminded myself that she was safe with me. That no one will get to her as long as there's breath in my body. I kept repeating that to myself over and over as I paced the room, always with that picture of her in my head.

When I stopped moving my brothers and the others had crowded around me like they were ready to take me down if need be.

It was the look on their faces that finally broke

through the fog and haze. I was freaking them out. "I'm not going to freak, I'm not Ty." Ty gave me the finger and that stupid gesture for some reason helped settle me down.

"Devon, brother, I know what it feels like to have your woman in that kinda danger, not just the threat of it, but the reality." Lyon put his hand on my shoulder.

"I know what you're feeling, I've been there. Right now, the best thing you can do for her is to work through the fear and the anger, stay calm, stay focused."

"I don't know who this Khalil fuck is, but I guarantee you he's not crazier than me, he doesn't stand a fucking chance."

There were a lot of nods and laughter at Lyon's acknowledgment and I have to admit that for some reason, I believed him. He's that kinda person, a rock. A cross between Lo and Ty!

I nodded my understanding, took a deep breath and let my brothers know that I was fine. "I'm good, I'm cool." Where the fuck did I just go?

"You sure? Maybe we should trank your ass like you fucks did to me?" Trust Tyler to make light of the situation and bring me back down to earth.

"Was I really as bad as him?" I asked the others with a grin that I didn't really feel.

"Nobody's as bad as him."

"Thanks Con you lying fuck. I'm pretty sure I never

spazzed out that bad. Cord might be a close second though."

The men compared notes as to who was the craziest as we followed Mancini up the stairs but my mind was still on her.

There was a new urgency, now that she wasn't just some faceless victim, but the woman who has been tying me in knots since we met.

"Where did you send them?" I asked Mancini as soon as we entered the room. He knew what I was asking and pulled up the media room on the wall screen.

I breathed a little easier when I saw her there with the others, and the way they were fawning over her. Her dimples were on full display as she smiled at something Gaby was saying.

I should've known my sisters and the others would take care of her. But why the fuck, am I so nervous?

I've never doubted that any of the others could hold their own, so why am I so worried about her fitting in?

"I feel like a father taking his kid to school for the first time and leaving her there without me." I hadn't meant to say those words out loud.

"We understand Dev, it's because of the mark on her. Our women are in danger too, but not to the same extent. It's okay, I get it, trust me."

"What the fuck is wrong with me Quinn?"

"Nothing, nothing's wrong with you. It's what we all

feel. I think it's how you know you've found 'the one', you lose your fucking mind."

"Ah damn! Bitch made."

"Is that what that is? I've been trying to figure out for the past seventeen years what the fuck Kat did to me, now I know. I became a bitch."

"Oh no Lyon, say it ain't so."

"I'm afraid so little brother. The right woman gets her hooks into you you're done. Your life is never the same. And like I told you before, once they start bringing in ringers you my friend is totally fucked."

Every man in the room was paying attention. This was Colton Lyon after all. The man was the definition of alpha male and here he was admitting that his wife had him by the balls.

"Like I said before, you boys are new to this shit, but let me tell you, it doesn't get any better, in fact, it gets worst." The others groaned making me laugh.

"Before I found her, I was a fucking beast. I did what I wanted, went where I pleased and fucked shit up on the regular."

"Now each time I get on my ride my first thought is, don't fuck around Colt. Who's gonna take care of Kat and your kids if some fuck happens to you? They're the last thing I think about at night, and the first thing on my mind every morning."

"But I'll tell you what." He looked around the room at

each of us. "You'll never find anything better in your life like the right fucking woman. Hands down the best fucking move I ever made."

No one was talking because I'm guessing they were all feeling the same. "Yeah, and when they're innocent like that and some fuck mess with them, it takes you to a whole other place." Justice looked towards the screen at his girl.

Lo clapped me on the shoulder. "See, there's nothing wrong with you. You've just joined the ranks of the witless."

"Yeah that helps."

"I can tell you for a fact that women make men stupid, and that's all I'm going to say on the subject." Mancini took a sip from another one of his ever-present water bottles as he reclined back in the chair behind the monstrosity of a desk.

"We all have a dog in this fight brother. Our women have each been touched in one way or another behind this. We didn't come this far to lose now."

Law clapped me on the shoulder and I was beginning to feel like a selfish prick. I'd lost sight of the fact that each man in the room had a stake in this. That their women too were targets.

"Fuck no we're not going to lose. That motherfucker's days are numbered. We're coming down to the wire. I can feel it." Zak snagged one of Mancini's water bottles and tipped it to his head.

"I pretty much feel like we've jumped the hardest hurdle. The deal was to find the girl and keep her safe. As far as I'm concerned that's a done deal and the other thing has nothing to do with it. Separate the two in your mind brother."

"We were always gonna go after Khalil, until last night we didn't even know about the girl or why this whole thing was happening. We've already found her and it didn't take much. Now as for taking down this fuck and his whole dirty brigade, that's something else entirely."

"I get what you're saying Cord, I guess I didn't think of it like that." He was right. We'd done the most important part, getting her to safety.

The fact that Khalil was still out there meant nothing. He's always been there and we've always been out of his reach as much as he's been out of ours.

Plus the fact that we now know for sure who is helping him and how, that puts us a little bit ahead of the game.

"Look at them." Mancini brought our attention to the room full of women who were laughing as they sat around talking like old friends.

"She's fine, she's already one of them. You see, we have something Khalil the fuck don't have. We have this."

Tyler indicated the room and the room the women were in.

"We won't let anything happen to anyone here. This is a family, we look out for our own." I nodded at Lo. I wanted to tell them they could stop now, that I got it, but I got the feeling it was as much for them as it was me.

The dynamics had changed and something suddenly occurred to me. "Shit, her being here puts the others in danger. Maybe I should…"

"Don't be an ass Devon; whatever you were about to say, don't. How could you even think that shit?"

"Quinn is right, that's asshole thinking. Now let's get this shit moving." Lo moved across the room no longer standing guard.

"Mancini, you have eyes on that arcade room? It's been way too long since anyone had eyes on Mengele."

"Dude, you gotta stop calling her that." Tyler laughed as Mancini pulled up the room on one of the wall screens.

"See, poor kid's just being a kid." On the screen she was sitting with Zakira reading a picture book. Once Lyon was reassured that his kid wasn't trying to burn the place down it was time to get to work.

"I will bet you any kinda money she's up to some shit."

"Colt, seriously, look at her, she's like the perfect little princess. I can't wait for Cierra and I to have one. She's been going on and on about her ever since they met."

"Remember you said that shit, but mark my words, that is one fucking scary kid. Only thing that gives me the sweats brother."

No one said anything for a hot minute until they realized he was dead serious. "True story." He nodded as Mancini switched off the monitor.

39

DEVON

The men all started to laugh and Quinn sidled up beside me. “So what’s she like?”

“Innocent.” I didn’t even have to think about that shit, it was the one word that summed her up in my mind.

He just nodded as Lo moved to the front of the room. The screen with the women ran in the back with the volume off as all eyes turned forward to Lo.

“Mancini pull up that board again.” Hank worked his magic and the board we’d been working on earlier slid out of hiding.

“Okay, so…we have the target in house. The only thing left is finding the Fox and retrieving the women who’ve already been taken.”

“I already ran the names in the book like you

asked me to Lo. There're twenty girls unaccounted for." Law moved to the board and wrote the number twenty.

"Law gave me those names and I put them through the database." Mancini pulled up another screen on the opposite wall.

"Of the twenty maybe four are still on domestic soil. I've done facial reconstructions, changed hair color and styles just in case."

"Thorpe has a network overseas and he's called in Blade and Jake to handle the domestic side."

"How did you arrive at those numbers?"

"It was easy Logan. Since we're pressed for time I broke into the FBI files and followed their little crumbs. They might be fucked in the head but since meeting my wife I've come to accept that some of them actually know what the fuck they're doing."

"Well if they know where they are why haven't they gone in and got them?"

"Because they don't know Zak, they estimate and that's where we're going to pick it up. Well where those boys are gonna pick it up. Thorpe just needs a general location and he can do the rest."

"The ones who've been taken out of the country are his specialty, believe me, if they're out there he's gonna find them. So are we all cool with this?"

"If you vouch for this Thorpe guy I'll take your word

for it. We've already trusted him this far." That was tantamount to high praise coming from Logan.

"Great, now let's move on then." He pulled up another board and started writing. "Ariel is here, the women are here; all the women are here, including your daughter Lyon." He looked around the room.

"This island can only be approached by air or sea. Anything heading this way without an invite will be shot down or blown out of the water no questions." Mancini assured us.

"I would show you my security measures but then I'd have to kill you and I've grown to like you boys so we'll leave that alone."

He didn't even smile to pretend he was kidding. "Now onto the most important matter here, where is this Khalil fuck? Anyone have any ideas?"

It was Lo's turn to take over. He wrote Khalil's name in the middle of the new board and then a list of places he's been known to hide out.

'The problem with this guy, he doesn't stay in the same place for more than one night. The good thing is he never leaves this general region, he's paranoid as fuck."

"Is there no way to whittle this shit down? You've got him from Baghdad to Kabul, that's a lot of area to cover."

"We know Hank. We've been trying to catch this guy for the better part of five years and each time we think we have him cornered he slips the noose and disappears."

"What about this general? Seems to me he's the answer. Wouldn't he know where he is? And how do we get to the general?"

"That's a good question to both Lyon. But like I said, we can't just go after this guy."

"I'm thinking you might have to rethink that shit Logan. All roads lead to him. You're gonna have to make peace with whatever it is that's holding you back, but so far you seem to be the only one who has a problem going after this hump."

"How many ways can I say this? If we go after him now and don't get what we want, all we're doing is showing our hand. We need to have this shit on point before we move."

"I'm pretty sure we can handle that. So where is he?"

"Fine, the truth is he might know or he might not, I don't know. I don't imagine there's a whole lotta trust between those two. As to where to find him, he's in D.C."

"We can be in D.C. in two and a half hours." I didn't have to look at my brothers to know what they were thinking once Mancini said that.

If we made this move there was a good chance the general would be spending his last day on earth. Now that my anger has cooled I'm not sure we're ready to face this fuck, or if we can let him breathe long enough to give us what we need.

He's responsible for a lot of the shit that had gone

wrong in our lives in the last year and a half, starting with the death of the CO and sending us into a trap that almost got us killed. Had it not been for Quinn's gift in fact, we probably wouldn't be here.

"Give us a minute." Everyone else left the room at Lo's suggestion, leaving just me and my brothers behind.

"We all know what this means if we go there now. I want your word, especially you Tyler, that you'll keep your shit together so we can get what we need from this hump."

"Yeah well I'm not making any promises."

"You're gonna have to brother. I want his blood on my hands as much as you. But if he can lead us to Khalil then we're gonna have to fucking deal."

"He killed the CO what the fuck Devon."

"I know, you think I don't know? Look at her." They all turned to look at the screen.

"She's not like your women. What do you wanna bet her whole fucking life she's been hidden away? She doesn't even exist anywhere, do you know what the fuck that means?"

"If we don't find Khalil and end him now her life is fucked. No one is killing that asshole until we get what we need. Don't make me go against you…"

"Devon!" Quinn's terse voice brought me out of whatever the fuck I'd just stepped into.

"Do you hear what you're saying? Do you really

believe that any one of us would jeopardize her future? The CO lost his fucking life trying to keep her safe."

"You're right, I'm sorry. I don't know what the fuck is wrong with me. I don't… I haven't felt this way since I lost my parents. There's something growing inside me and it scares the fuck outta me."

"That's normal brother, we all have that. It's like Lyon said, it's a sign that you've found 'the one'. I'd like to tell you that it gets easier but it won't. But I promise you, once you get past the fear, the love is…"

"Oh for fuck sake Cord. Listen you, get your head outta your ass. You know what your problem is, you're fighting it." Tyler got in my face. What's with everybody getting in my damn face?

He wasn't done apparently. "I think every man here can tell you it's a losing fucking battle so give it up. You can't control it like you try to do everything else either so give it a damn rest."

"Now, we're going to D.C. and we're gonna beat the shit outta this fuck until he gives us what we want and then Lo's gonna cap his ass and we come back here to our women and get a good night's sleep. I'm tired of having to ride herd on you freaks get your shit together."

"Tyler, anybody ever tell you you're an ass?"

"Yeah, meanwhile I'm the only one of you who keeps a clear head when it comes to this shit." That didn't even warrant a response.

"I still haven't heard what I want from you lot. If we do this, I want your word that none of you will move on this guy until we get what we need."

"Fine, but if he pops off any shit about the CO it's a fucking wrap. His ass is gonna get slept."

"How about we leave your ass here."

"You can try Con, but then where are you going to live?" Tyler smirked.

The fucker is crazy enough to carry out his threats. "Call in the others let's get this shit moving." I could tell that Lo wasn't too happy, but even he had to admit that this was the only way.

It could take us months, even years to pin down Khalil's location. I for one wasn't willing to take that route.

The room really did become a war room once the others rejoined us. Everyone had an opinion on how and when we should go in.

Lyon wasn't saying much, his only interest was in the end result so he just sat off to the side playing on his phone and listening in, grunting out an answer every once in a while.

The other military men were on board with the decision to go in, because as Justice put it, fuck the general if he was involved in this shit. Which is pretty much the sentiment of everyone here.

Every once in a while I'd look at the screen to check up on her, read her body language. "She's tired." What the fuck, I keep speaking out loud when I don't mean to.

The others looked at the screen and we all stretched to work the kinks out after standing around for so long.

"Let's take a break boys, looks like we're just in time for a late lunch. We'll come back to it later. We can't go in until dark anyway."

Mancini pushed away from the desk and stood after releasing the locks and we all filed out of the room. I felt a little more at ease now that we'd made the decision to pay the general a visit.

We joined the women and kids on the front patio for lunch and the difference was like night and day.

For the first time I understood why the guys always go to such lengths to keep things from the women.

It just seemed like none of this should touch them in anyway. Like they should be protected from all the dark shit we'd just waded through.

There were times when I had my doubts about leaving them out of shit, especially Vanessa. Here's a woman who's served her country in battle, had even been taken prisoner and survived on her own.

But when I look at Ariel, her sweet childlike innocence, I don't want her mixed up in any of this. My sisters would probably have a fit and call me a sexist or whatever, but no fucking way.

It's almost ingrained I guess, for men like us to want to protect our women…oh shit. I stared at her as she sat beside me picking at her food while talking to Kat across the table.

Is it really that easy? Does the perfect woman just fall into your lap out of the blue when you're not expecting her? Or am I setting myself up for a fall?

"Stop overthinking shit brother, just go with it trust me." I turned to Ty on my other side about to ask him what the hell he was talking about until I realized they were all watching me.

"Oh for fuck sake!" How could I forget how this works? My brothers are worse than women when it comes to sticking their noses in.

I ignored them after throwing a general finger around the table and pretended an interest in my food. In reality I was highly aware of her next to me.

40

LOGAN

"What's the matter with you?"

"What do you mean?"

"You seem very…happy, downright chipper." What the hell is she up to now?

Only this morning she was giving me shit and now she's all smiles and giggly and shit.

"I don't understand, don't you want me to be happy?"

"Gabriella, what are you up to?"

"Nothing, geez, you're so suspicious. Paranoid much?" She giggled and I tackled her to the bed.

"What are you and your crew cooking up baby? I need you to work with me here. We're almost done, if you and your girls go off the rails that's only gonna set us back." I can't believe I'm actually afraid of this chick.

When we first met she was my sweet little Georgia peach. The damn girl would hardly ever speak above a whisper.

A few months with her new sisters and she's morphed into a whole other being. One sent here to keep me on my damn toes.

Swear to fuck I'd rather do another stint in Abbottabad than walk through that minefield she calls a mind.

"Who says we're up to anything? I'm excited to be on this beautiful island with my man and our friends. Is that so bad?" Oh how I wish I could believe that shit.

I studied her eyes to see if she was telling me the truth, the damn girl is sneaky. "What?" She smiled shyly up at me as I brushed the hair back from her face.

It felt like forever since I'd had the time to just look at my baby. "What-what?" I kissed her nose and felt that familiar clutch in my chest, the one I get whenever she's this close.

"I want you." Her eyes went soft and dreamy and she reached her arms up to me.

"I always want you too Logan."

Fuck! When she says things like that, look at me like that, I want to give her the whole world. And yet I can't even give her the wedding she wants so badly.

I held her eyes with mine as I made my way down her body, pushing her top up with my hands and mouth as I went.

I kissed her tummy where my baby was the size of a peanut and my heart swelled in my chest. Things have been moving so fast around us that sometimes I forget what my life has become.

"Hello little one it's your daddy." I nuzzled the warmth of her tummy and her hand played in my hair, her way of letting me know she liked what I was doing.

I dipped my tongue in her navel before licking my way down her body, removing her shorts as I went. No matter how many times I have her under me, it always feels like the first time all over again.

I gave her my mouth until she was ready to take me before moving up her body and slipping into her heat.

Her legs wrapped around my ass just as I lowered my lips to hers so I could swallow her screams.

DEVON

I didn't know what to say to her now that we were alone. After lunch everyone had split up and gone their way no doubt to get in some special time with their women before the coming night.

How is it possible for a woman to make you feel so

strong and so weak at the same time? I'd brought her back to the cottage because she looked tired, but she was all but bouncing with energy now.

"Are you tired, do you want to take a nap?"

"Can we go to the water?" The question was so tentative, as if she expected to be rebuffed. And again my heart squeezed in my chest at her innocence.

Maybe that's what bothers me. The women in this family demands shit and know they'll get it, while she always seems to expect to hear no.

"We can do anything you want baby." And when this shit's over I'm going to make sure she does. I can't shake the feeling that she'd had to live like a prisoner since her birth.

Everything she does, even the way she speaks, reminds me and for some reason it takes me back to my own childhood.

I almost jumped when she took my hand, as we walked out the door and headed down the path to the beach.

Her excitement was almost palpable and when she dragged me along with her to the water's edge I just followed, never taking my eyes off her.

She was like a child wild and free, the way she laughed and played at the water's edge. "Let's go in Devon."

"Not yet baby, I don't know how safe it is, plus you

need a swimsuit." I wanted to kiss the pout from her lips; she was so cute.

"Can you get me one then?"

"Sure, I'll get you one." She threw herself at me and wrapped her arms around my waist. "Thank you."

My sisters would've insisted and probably raise hell, but not her. She just accepted. She's going to make me cry. I can't get over her sweetness, and I must admit to watching her closely to see if it's an act.

"Let's build a castle." Her eyes were like pennies as she pulled away and ran up on the beach before dropping to her knees.

She looked back to make sure I was following and when I didn't move fast enough ordered me to come. "Come on!"

"Bossy!" I grinned and dropped down next her loving that show of fire. She was very methodical as she gathered sand and patted it into place.

Her tongue was caught between her teeth and she had a razor sharp focus on what she was doing. I watched in amazement as she built damn near a whole village.

There was something about the way she did that shit that gave me pause. "Have you built a lot of these before baby?"

"No, but I always wanted to. Track showed me how on the computer, but the sand feels so much better."

She sat back on her haunches and studied her handiwork while I looked from it to her trying o figure out if she was playing me.

She got to her feet and bent her body over to touch her toes in a stretch, and it was fluidly flawless. There was something niggling at the back of my mind, something about the way she moved, but I couldn't quite put my finger on it.

When she was done she gave me another one of her disarming smiles and held out her hand for mine. I let her drag me down to the other side of the beach, on full alert no matter what Mancini said about the place being safe.

I guess I'm going to be this tense and nervous about having her out in the open until Khalil was taken care of.

So while she played with the water and kicked at the sand, I remained on high alert. She pulled out of my hand and walked ankle deep into the water and I didn't think anything of the look she gave me, until I got a face full of water.

The shit was so surprising I just stood there with my mouth hanging open. And then she laughed and my whole body came alive.

She had one of those laughs that make you want to laugh with her. "Oh so you think that's funny huh?"

She squealed and tried to escape when I cupped my hands in the water and went after her. "No Devon, don't wet my hair."

Holy shit, she's a siren. She gave me the most innocent pouty-faced look as she said this, but it was the light in her eyes that gave her away.

"Too bad!" I let her have it and she howled with laughter before taking off again. I caught up with her and lifted her in the air.

She stretched out her arms and pointed her toes like a ballerina and I just stood there with her held over my head looking up at her.

She had her face raised to the sun and I let her stay up there as long as she wanted until my arms grew tired.

When I pulled her down she slid down my chest until our faces met. "Beautiful!" There I go again saying shit out loud.

She blushed and pushed to be let down and I set her on her feet. She took my hand again and we continued our walk in silence.

Was it natural to feel this tied up in knots just from being this close to her? I tried to remember when I'd ever felt like this and couldn't.

There was so much I could be doing, should be doing to get ready for tonight. But none of it seemed as important as being here with her, letting her have this.

I wanted to ask her a thousand questions but each time I started to, something held me back. I still didn't know how or when to tell her the truth about who she was.

No, let her enjoy these next few days. I don't ever

want to see that light go out of her eyes. Plus there was something else bothering me.

What's going to happen when we get rid of Khalil? Will her real father come back for her? I'd never see her again. The thought left me cold.

"What's wrong Devon?"

"Huh?" She was squeezing my hand and looking up at me as we walked. I'd slipped away in my head and didn't hear a thing she'd said.

"I asked what's wrong, you feel sad." Say what now?

"What do you mean?" She shrugged her shoulders and kept walking but I was still stuck on what she'd said.

How can she tell what I 'feel'? I'm pretty sure I didn't give anything away, I never do. So how? I put it aside and just took her in, the way she was taking in everything around us.

She seemed to have a fascination with the outdoors, stopping every once in a while to pick up a seashell or even some driftwood that washed up on the beach.

By the time I talked her into going back to the cottage I was the one who needed a nap. The girl is exhausting. She gets into more shit than Zakira and gets about just as excited about each new thing she finds.

"Go wash up baby, get that sand off you or you'll be uncomfortable." She kissed my cheek before going into the bedroom and I stood in the same spot like a heel for a good five minutes.

I looked down at my dick and high tailed it outta there. What the fuck Devon? I walked around the cottage a couple times until I had myself back under control before going back in.

She came back into the room dressed in a robe and my dick came back to life. "I'm not tired anymore I think the shower revived me."

Uh-huh, something was revived alright. "That's good honey I'm gonna go take a shower now okay, why don't you watch TV until I get back?"

I never moved so damn fast in my life. I felt like a bastard when I caught myself stroking my cock to thoughts of her in the shower as the warm water washed over me.

Don't do this Dev, she's defenseless and totally dependent on you for protection, you can't jerk off to her fucking legs and don't you dare think about her tits.

But no matter how I tried I couldn't get the sight of her robe opening as she sat, giving me a clear shot up her thigh out of my mind.

My hand stroked faster, out pacing the guilt and I painted the shower stall and almost fell on my ass from the intensity of my orgasm. Once my head cleared I cleaned up and finished my shower before going back out to her.

41

QUINN

"I gotta go babe." I spanked her ass cheek and rolled outta bed. Once again she was sprawled on the mattress fighting for her next breath.

Each time I get her alone I keep telling myself to go slow, at least have a conversation with her before jumping on her; and each time I fail.

This time at least I got a few questions out, like how much longer she had in school and if she was able to finish on line or transfer to the university that was an hour away from the compound.

After asking me why she'd need to do that, and receiving my 'are you serious' look she'd started to get kinda twitchy.

When I apologized for not spending enough time with

her and promising to rectify that as soon as possible she jumped me.

Just left her seat beside me on the couch and straddled my lap with her lips fused to mine. "What the hell were you women talking about anyway?" She seemed horny as fuck to me.

She grinned into my mouth and wrapped her arms around my head. "Nothing!" Liar! I let her kiss me and rub herself against me.

"I'm talking here baby!" I laughed with her as my hands made easy work of her clothes. And that's how we ended up in bed with me buried deep inside her.

We took a nap after round two and I made sure she stayed put this time by wrapping my arms and legs around her.

When I woke to find her so cuddly and warm next to me, it was as easy as breathing to roll her to her back and slide into her again.

Now I have to leave her again because the guys wanted to make a dry run. Her eyes followed me around the room as I got dressed and I leaned over the bed for one last kiss before heading out.

'Try to stay out of trouble okay baby. Use the time to figure out what you need to do to transfer schools, or better yet do your last year online." I left before she could ask me any more questions.

I'd pretty much just told her I planned on keeping her.

I don't know how the others had handled this part of the relationship game, but I wasn't much for asking.

As far as I'm concerned, once this shit is over, my ring is gonna end up on her finger some way somehow and I don't much care how it gets there.

I looked back at her once and couldn't resist going back to her. "Okay I really have to go this time. Stop looking at me like that."

"Like what? I'm just laying her." She stretched on the bed, her arms and legs opening and I got a pretty good view between her legs where my seed was leaking out of her little pussy.

"Well shit!" I didn't get undressed this time, just pulled my pants down below my ass as I climbed onto the bed between her thighs and fed her my cock.

She sighed and wrapped her arms and legs around me as she lifted her lips to mine. I stayed inside her much longer than I'd planned to and by the time I rolled away from her I knew I was going to be late getting back.

"Okay I'm really leaving this time." This time when I kissed her goodbye I didn't look at her body just her damn head before almost running out the door.

In the last couple days it's been getting easier and easier to accept that this shit was real. That something I'd shunned my whole life had led me to her.

And each day I understood why my old man had been so afraid of it. It has a power all its own. It also makes me crave her all the damn time, but I was up for the challenge.

In fact I don't see much difference in what I feel for her than what I see in my brothers with their women. Con damn near disappeared from sight when he and Dani first got together, but things calmed down after a while. I'm expecting us to be the same.

42

DEVON

We'd tried to talk the others into staying back on the island just in case shit got dicey, but none of them would budge.

Lyon had no qualms about pulling the trigger if it came to that and Mancini, well, who knows what his deal is. But it was Justice and Law I was more worried about.

Both of them still had one foot in the military. But they too insisted on coming along. "Do you know how I knew my girl was in trouble Devon?"

"Law's woman told him because one of her girls told her and he called me. Had it not been for that phone call I don't know what would've happened to her."

"This is what we do, we stick together. And those women, we lucked the fuck out there too. So if we have to do this to make their lives safer, then it's on all of us. Not just you."

"I appreciate it Creed." I guess the ball was in my court now since they'd all decided that she was mine regardless of what I say.

Ty the ass had seen us on the beach together and earlier this evening when we'd met to go over the plan one last time he had to open his big damn mouth.

My life was the subject of interest the whole damn evening and then again at dinner the assholes had watched me like we were in high school with Quinn kicking me under the table every few seconds.

He only stopped when I tried to stab him with my fork and then I was able to eat in peace. I had enough on my mind without them breathing down my neck, but at least they were better than the women, more subtle.

After dinner Dani and Gaby had cornered me and just stared for five minutes until I growled at them to cut it the hell out.

Of course they wanted all the details that didn't exist and refused to take no for an answer until I got their men to call them off.

Once I escaped their nosy asses, I took her out on the cliffs alone looking out at the water; where she tried to give me a heart attack by getting too close to the edge. Daredevil.

"Ariel, come sit here with me baby." I held out my

hand for her to join me, pulling her down next to me. "Are you cold sweetie?"

She shook her head no and rubbed her nose in my shirt before settling her head on my shoulder like a kitten and gazing up at the stars.

Why does she do this to me? Just one touch, one whiff of her scent and my dick gets hard while my heart becomes a puddle in my chest.

I swallowed hard when she pulled my arm around her and satisfied myself with burying my nose in her hair for the briefest of moments before pulling back.

I'd brought her out here away from the others for a reason. She'd had a full day to get settled and I could see she was more relaxed so was in no fear of spooking her.

"Comfortable?"

"Uh-huh."

"What did your dad tell you before I came and got you?" She took a few minutes and when I looked down at her face I could see the sheen of tears in her eyes in the moonlight.

"He said I was going to learn why he'd hidden me away all these years." Her voice was soft and sad but I didn't say anything, as it was obvious that she had more to say.

"I knew from a very young age that I was adopted. When I was four or five Track was born and it was then that I realized something was different."

"I never went outside but I didn't know there was anything wrong until Track was allowed to do things I couldn't as he grew older."

"At first I was hurt. I'd scream and throw a tantrum each time he went out somewhere and I had to stay home."

"Then when he got to go to school and I couldn't my heart was broken. Dad tried explaining things but to a nine year old who'd never had a normal childhood his words meant nothing."

"I loved my dad but nothing he said or did could ever make me understand why I couldn't do the same things my brother did."

"As we got older we'd ask but dad never told us and it use to make Track so mad. Once when I was about fourteen and he was about nine, he snuck me out of the house." She had a wan smile on her face.

"Before that day I'd never been farther than the closed in backyard of the house in California. We didn't get far, not even beyond the driveway."

The sadness was back and my heart was hurting for the little girl whose life had been fucked up because of a madman.

"All of a sudden these men came out of nowhere and took us back to the house. Dad was so mad at us, especially Track."

"He still didn't explain but we learned never to try that

again. After that Track became obsessed. He always promised that he was going to find out why I was being held prisoner. His words."

"I'd never looked at it that way before, I just always thought daddy was protecting me from something or someone, after I stopped thinking he loved my brother more than me because I wasn't really his." Well fuck!

"Then when Track met his girlfriend he became even more insistent on finding out what the story was. He said it was because he needed to make sure that I was okay before he could move on with his life."

"He started doing stuff, he never told me what, but I knew he was trying to get answers and that the stuff he was doing could get him in trouble."

"I'd hear him and dad arguing about it late at night. And then my brother started going away for long periods of time but won't tell me where."

That must be all those times he was at the DOD. But something didn't make sense. For all her innocence she was intelligent, graceful and well mannered. And I didn't hear her mention a mom in all this.

"But how did you learn to read and write? Did you go to school?"

"No, I did everything at home online or dad taught me."

"The only people I ever saw were Track and dad after mom passed away. Oh and my uncle."

"Your uncle?" Could she be talking about the commander? "What uncle?"

"Uncle Robert. He's the only one I ever saw except for Track and dad."

"Where is this uncle now?" She shrugged her shoulders and didn't say anything else, just stayed there with her little head on my shoulder as if lost in thought.

"You were very sad weren't you baby?"

"Sometimes." She said it so simply, without any real inflection, and that made it all-the-more-sad.

I kissed her hair and held her closer and decided not to ask her any more questions for now. I'll wait until things were more secure and contact the man she knew as her father.

I did get what I was after though, he hadn't told her who she was. I replayed her words in my head and one thing stuck out for me.

She's never known anyone but her dad and her brother and this uncle Robert. Does that mean she's… a virgin?

Of course it does. The thought sent a shot of fear down my center to my nuts. I stared out over the water as I let that shit marinate in my head.

Not for nothing but I'm not a small man. She's already about half my size so I know she's probably small down there as well. I'd fucking kill her.

No way Dev, for her sake you have to stop taking

these little mind trips into the forbidden. She's not for you for too many reasons.

So why does the thought of never having her make me nuts? Once again that question I had earlier came back again. What's going to happen when the truth is revealed?

And once again I shut it out of my mind. I was afraid I already knew the answer to that and I didn't like it.

How could someone you didn't know, had only just met, cause so much disruption in your well- organized life?

I'm not that guy. I've always known my mind; always known which direction my life was going in. Now one look at her pretty little face and a few minutes of her sweet innocence and everything is turned upside down.

I let myself sit there in silence, taking in the cool night breeze, enjoying the moon's reflection on the water with her under my arm and her head on my shoulder, and it felt so right.

It was as if she'd found a way around my defenses. No walls had been smashed, there's been no fanfare; she took me down without a damn fight.

"Devon?"

"Yes baby?"

"What's going to happen to me now? Who's going to take care of me?" Oh fuck!

I pulled her onto my lap and wrapped my arms around her tight enough to crack a rib. "I am baby I am." I could almost hear the others saying 'that wasn't so hard now was it?'

And the way she relaxed against me as if a weight had been lifted from her shoulders made something inside me ease.

"Have you been worried about this all day baby?" She nodded her head against my chest and I kissed her hair again.

"Why didn't you tell me that this was bothering you? I don't want you keeping things from me okay, next time tell me." Shit, I could swear I've heard Con or Lo say that exact same thing to one of my sisters.

"Okay I will." She patted my chest and snuggled in even closer. Could she be any sweeter? Funnily enough it wasn't her sweetness that I was thinking of now though, but how long it was going to take the others to turn her into them.

43

DEVON

It wasn't easy leaving her again, but Dani assured me that she was going to make sure she had fun while I was gone.

After our time on the cliffs I dropped her off in the media room with the women, which seemed to be their favorite hangout spot.

Even though Mancini had convinced us that this place was safe and secure, none of us, including him, were okay with the women and kids hanging around outside for too long at night.

That left us with another problem though, one we found waiting for us in Mancini's private rooms. "How did she get in?" Hank whispered out the side of his mouth as the rest of us looked over his shoulder at the intruder.

"Where's Lyon?" Law looked back down the hall.

"Not sure, last I saw he was harassing his wife while she was putting the baby to sleep." Con whispered the answer as we watched Lyon's little girl snoop around the highly secure room.

"I'm beginning to see why her father thinks the way he does. Hello Catalina, may I help you?" She didn't even jump when she turned from the desk.

Her little legs didn't reach the floor and the chair almost swallowed her whole. "Hi uncles, can you show me how to turn this on?"

She kept poking at the buttons, but not in some random way like you'd expect a kid her age to, no, there was a methodology to it. Almost like a safe cracker listening for the wheel pack.

"Why do you need to do that?" She looked up at us with the widest eyes and a look of such innocence that had we not all seen her in action before we'd have fallen for it.

"Um, the boys won't let me use the computer downstairs, I wanna watch something." Damn she's good.

"I'm sorry sweetie, it's not that kind of computer."

"Okay, so what kind is it?"

"It's a special kind only your daddy and uncles can use."

"What about mommy and my new aunts? Can they play with it?"

Mancini lifted her from his chair as the rest of us entered the room. The door was left open so as not to spook her but she didn't look like one to be easily spooked.

"Uh, no, this is kind of my own private office."

"Does aunty Cierra have one like this too?"

"Well, hers is being taken care of, you see…"

He looked around at the rest of us when he found himself explaining to a five year old why his new wife didn't have an office in his island home.

"Uh, Catalina, sweetie, how did you get in here?"

"I can't tell you."

"Excuse me?"

"Uncle Hank you told me not to tell my secrets and uncle Ty told me 'trust no one'."

Her impersonation of Ty's voice was comical and I could see we were all trying not to laugh and encourage the little sneak.

"Okay Catalina, can you go join the other kids or your aunties now?" She pouted around the room and folded her arms before making her way to the door where her dad was now entering.

"This is bravo sierra."

"You got that right kid."

Lyon snorted as we watched her leave the room before turning to Mancini.

"What did your woman do Hank? My little angel did not look pleased."

"She's not talking about that Cierra." The room lit up with laughter.

"What the fuck! We got another Cierra running around this bitch that I don't know about?"

"That's Sierra, with an S. It's military speak for bullshit."

"Who the fuck is teaching her this shit? Look, I can barely keep up with this kid in English. The last thing I need is you military types teaching her your shit."

"Too late, that squid is ours."

"What the fuck does that mean?"

"It means she's already well on her way to being some kinda spy or some shit and she might as well be ours." I think Lo was just fucking with him but he had a point, the kid is good.

"Like fuck, she's five."

"Doesn't matter, with her brain some outfit will be recruiting her by the time she hits seventeen."

"The fuck you say Cord."

"Ooh, look who's going all papa bear!" Tyler laughed and clapped him on the shoulder.

"Fuck a bear, you know the name, it's Lyon. And I'll end any fuck who tries to sign my kid up for this shit."

"Calm down Colt, they're just fucking with you." Law tried to diffuse the situation but Lyon didn't look like he believed him.

"What was she doing in here anyway?"

"That's what we're trying to figure out."

"Don't bother."

After Lyon had us search the room for booby traps, which was funny as hell, we got down to business. We spent the rest of the evening fine tuning the plan before it was time to go face the man who might be able to lead us to the Fox.

Now here we are staking out yet another house in the dark while the women waited back on the island.

"So the SEALs are going in while the rest of us surround the perimeter. There's no one in there except the target, the wife is not expected back until late tomorrow, and the staff has already gone."

Mancini sent his people off to get into place before turning back to us. "He's in his study having his last cigar and cognac of the evening."

He pulled that shit up on his handheld and we saw the general sitting in a smoking chair puffing on a cigar.

"We could just take him out through the window and no one will ever know."

"But then we won't get the answers we need Tyler and don't fucking start again."

"Sure we can Lo. We can take his comp, and his phone, there's bound to be something there."

"What if there isn't? Now cut the shit and let's go."

After Ty and Lo got through with their scuffle Quinn disengaged the security and Cord picked the lock so we could get in.

Once inside we made sure there were no surprises waiting for us and made our way to the study. "Uh-uh-uh." Fucking Lo drew down on the general who reached into his desk when he sensed us enter the room.

"Hands on the desk asshole and don't even fucking twitch." So much for a cool head Logan damn. Everyone else stood back and watched the show.

"What are you doing here?"

"We need some answers. We know what you did. So either you tell us what we want to know, or you'll spend the rest of your miserable life in Leavenworth."

The general got slowly to his feet and Lo raised his piece to his head. "Sit down." He dropped back down in his seat and looked around at the rest of us.

"Look I don't know what you think you're playing at here. This is a private home I did not give you leave to enter."

"Cut the crap, you know damn good and well why we're here. Where is Khalil?"

"What the hell are you implying boy?" Even his belligerence was fake it was obvious that he was scared shitless.

"We haven't located him as yet as you well know. You

boys were the last ones tasked with smoking him out of his hole and you failed."

"Not what we're talking about asshole."

"Dev!"

"Had enough Quinn. You, where the fuck is he hiding? We already know that you're in bed with him…"

"I beg your pardon young man, but I resent that baseless accusation. I have received the medal of honor, for valor and patriotism…."

"Being a patriot means giving up your life because you know if it destroys the other guy it's worth it. It does not mean selling out your fucking country for an easy buck."

"I have never betrayed anyone least of all my country."

"What about the commander, remember him? He left proof of your treachery which once exposed just might get your ass put before a firing squad."

"That's a damn lie, your commander and I were friends. I will not stand here and listen to these boundless lies. There can be no proof because it did not happen."

"People usually lie when they're afraid. We're not in the habit of lying. Especially to a fuckwit I won't waste the time to shit on."

"That's insubordination sailor."

"That's lieutenant to you and I'm here to strip your

compromised ass of your title so I really don't give a fuck; general."

Lo got between the two of us and damn near shoved his piece down his throat. "Don't get in his fucking face, now you have two seconds to tell me where Khalil is hiding out."

There was a one second stare off. "Quinn get Admiral McCullum on the phone." I don't know if Lo was bluffing or not.

"No need boys I'm already here." What the fuck? All eyes turned to the admiral and his cohorts as they entered the room.

"Hey traitor, you wanna give these boys what they want? Or do we have to beat it out of you?" Where the fuck is Mancini? No way he didn't know they were coming in.

The general opened his mouth to lie again but the admiral made Lo look soft. He picked the general up by the throat and pushed him back against the wall.

"Who the fuck is running this rat riot? Is it you or Senator Porter? Start talking or lose your balls you gutless wonder."

"A fish rots from the head down Mac, we know whose running this shit. Just get these kids what they want and get them outta here." Terrence Samson was the last one to enter the room.

"Do you have any idea the trouble you have just brought on yourselves? All of you?"

"Too bad you're not gonna live long enough to gloat you dumb fuck. You had someone take my fucking kid. Now talk."

He did more than talk when the admiral squeezed his nuts. In the end he only had a general location, which was about what we expected, but it was enough.

"You kids get outta here." Lo opened his mouth, but we were all out ranked and we knew it. Quinn was the only one brave enough to say anything.

"Uh admiral, maybe…"

"Go boys you don't need to be here for this. We have an old score to settle, don't we traitor?"

We filed out of the room still not sure but I was excited for what came next. We had a general location for Khalil, which meant this shit could be over in a matter of days.

Mancini and the others came out of the shadows once we cleared the door and no one looked back at the sound of furniture breaking in the house.

"Hank did you know they were coming?"

"I called them."

"Why?"

"Because he needs to die Logan and you boys still have too much loyalty to the navy."

He has a fucked up way of thinking but he had a point.

Whichever one of us had taken him out it would've rested heavy on us no matter that he was a traitorous fuck.

"Good call. I still want to go back there and end him myself."

"Come along Ty we've got work to do."

44

DEVON

No one spoke of it on the plane ride back but we were all thinking about what the hell the headlines were going to say tomorrow.

The women and children were long in bed by the time we made it back to the island but we were too pumped to sleep. We finally had a place to start in our search for Khalil.

“So he’s in Doha.” Mancini passed around bottles of water as we took up our usual spots in his private room.

“At least it’s a smaller search area than some of his other hideouts, but I wonder what he’s doing there. That’s not on his list.”

“It’s only an hour and a half from there to Saudi Arabia. Is he about to make some sorta move?”

"If you're talking about him going after the old king Quinn I doubt it. There aren't many who'd risk it and I don't think your guy is that stupid."

"What the fuck are you people talking about? The desert?"

"Yes Lyon the desert."

"We're gonna need someone on the ground…" Lo started speaking but Mancini interrupted him.

"I'll cover that. If this guy's as good as you say he has your faces taped up somewhere believe me."

"We can't ask you to do that Hank, that shit's too dangerous." No one missed the smile that crossed Mancini's face as he assured Logan and the rest of us that he could handle it.

Sheer exhaustion drove us to our beds a few hours later and I snuck in quietly so as not to wake her. I heard the faint sound as soon as I laid on the couch.

I strained my ears until I heard it again and was on my feet and at the bedroom door before my next breath.

I should've looked in on her when I came in but told myself to avoid the temptation. I pushed the door open gently.

There was a swath of moonlight across her face, the covers were down around her ankles and she tossed and turned as she moaned in her sleep.

I moved across the room and stood at the side of the bed looking down at her not quite sure what I should do. I couldn't believe I was afraid to get into bed with her to offer comfort.

When she made another one of those frightened noises the decision was made. I got in behind her and pulled her into my arms.

"Shh, it's okay I'm here."

"Devon?"

"Yeah baby it's me go back to sleep." She rooted around on my chest until she found a place for her head.

I stayed stiff for the first five minutes, literally, until I grew too tired and my body just relaxed into the mattress; it took my cock a little longer to figure out he wasn't getting any play and give me a fucking break.

The sun on my face woke me hours later. I felt her weight on my chest before my eyes came fully open. I came wide-awake when I remembered where I was and got a surprise.

She had her hands folded under her chin and was staring up at me. I didn't think, just wrapped my hand in her unruly hair and pulled her up my chest.

I wasn't expecting the jolt to the system when my lips covered hers. Or the way she melted into me. I rolled, putting her beneath me and deepened the kiss.

I damn near ate her face off. The one time I needed to go easy I couldn't. Her taste was electrifying. And the way she clutched at me with her little hands and pressed herself against me had me pushing her harder into the bed.

I eased her legs open with my hand and settled between her thighs, rubbing my morning wood into her soft flesh until I felt my cock start to leak pre-cum.

Before I knew it I was dry humping her and the only thing keeping her safe were my sweats and her panties.

I pulled my tongue out of her mouth and tried easing away but she let me know she wasn't done with me by pulling my mouth back down to hers.

She made the cutest little sounds as she rubbed herself against me and when she dug her nails into my shoulders and ground herself against me I realized I'd taken her too far.

I came fully awake just when I was about to cum in my damn pants and looked down at her in amazement.

I jumped away from her so fast I almost fell on my ass. "I'm sorry, I'm so sorry, I shouldn't have done that." The look on her face was one of shock and…hurt?

When she flew off the bed and ran into the bathroom I didn't go after her. I needed time to calm down before I went anywhere near her again.

She was in there for a long time but I didn't think anything of it, but guessing that I'd embarrassed her I grabbed some clothes and headed up to the main house to grab a quick shower and get my shit together.

I should've known something was up from the freeze out I received when I joined the others for breakfast later.

"Where's Ariel?" I think I heard a mumbled 'like you care' from Dani before there was a general exodus of women from the table.

"Dude what the fuck did you do?" I looked at Ty like he was stupid. "What, I just got here."

"Yeah but the women are pissed."

A little shadow appeared at my side and I looked down at Catalina who was tugging at my arm. "You made Ariel cry and now she's sad because she's not an aunty and you don't like her."

"What?" I looked at her father for an interpretation. Sixteen grown men were all ears. My mind was still stuck on Ariel and cry.

"Mengele come here." She practically danced over to her dad. She'd be the cutest little thing if not for that gleam in her eye; the shit was almost scary.

"Were you snooping again?" She looked around sharply and her little body got stiff. "What daddy where? Oh you mean now. No daddy I was just listening they weren't trying to be secret or anything so it wasn't snooping."

"And what did you hear?" Again everyone was all ears. She played with the buttons on his shirt and looked at her nails, everything but answer him, and when she did it was a question straight out of left field.

"Daddy don't you like me?"

"What, what kinda question is that? Who told you I don't love you? You're my kid of course I love you." Picture Lyon in a panic.

"But you always call me Mengele."

"Yeah and?"

"He wasn't a very nice person daddy. How would you like it if I called you Hitler? You do act a bit like him you know."

"What the fuck?" He studied her like you would a snake about to strike.

"You playing me?"

"Daddy you said the bad word again." She held out her palm. "Nice try Mengele start talking." She did some fidgeting from leg to leg, tugged at the bottom of her shorts and swung her little body from side to side all before peeping around at all of us.

"Wellllllll. Ariel came running, mommy asked her what's wrong?" She twirled her eyes up like she was thinking really hard.

"Uncle Devon doesn't like her. Aunty Gaby's gonna kill uncle Devon annnndd aunty Cierra and aunty Kelly have a plan."

"You get anything outta that Dev?" Lyon dismissed

her and she went scurrying into the house probably to eavesdrop on the women.

"Yeah, I get it."

"So what did you do and you better have a way to fix it because I'm not too jazzed about my woman giving me the cold shoulder because of one of you fuck-ups."

"Suck it Ty." I put down the coffee cup and rested my head in my hands. I wanted to go find her and explain but what was I going to say?

That I'm afraid, that I don't know how long I'll have her once the threat was eliminated and her father decided he wanted her back?

"What's the problem Devon?"

"There's no problem Cord." I gave him the shut the hell up look. No way am I having this discussion in front of everyone.

"You might as well tell us bro the women are gonna gab anyway."

"Fine, I kissed her okay." I ran my hands down my face and removed them when there was nothing but silence coming from around the table.

"And?" Quinn shrugged his shoulders.

"And what? I shouldn't have."

"Oh shit you didn't tell her that did you?"

"No, I said… I told her I was sorry. Can we drop this now? I need to go see her, make sure she's okay."

"I wouldn't do that if I were you. Give the women time to work their magic and let her calm down."

"No Zak I have to talk to her." I got up and left the table before anyone else tried to talk me out of it.

I heard music coming from the exercise room and was surprised to find the door locked. I knocked hard until Dani opened the door.

"What the hell Dani, what's that look for?"

"Nothing, what do you want?"

"Ariel, I need to see her."

"Not now we're exercising." She slammed the door in my face.

I walked back outside where the others were still sitting. "Well?"

"Con your woman slammed the door in my face."

"Told you. Look, just give them some time to rake you over the coals a bit and then you can try again."

Since when is Zak a damn authority on women? He bosses Vanessa around like a damn drill sergeant and sure as fuck he wouldn't let her hide herself away from him because she was mad.

I said as much to the table at large because they were all guilty of the same shit. "Yeah, but they're our women, we have that right."

"What the fuck does that mean Cord she's… what the fuck are you, women?" I stormed off not knowing what the fuck.

It was killing me that I couldn't see her. That she thought I was trying to hurt her and I wasn't allowed to reassure her. I gave serious thought to breaking down the damn door and hauling her out.

"Dev wait up."

"Not now Quinn." I kept heading down to the beach with him hot on my heels.

"What's going on with you?"

"Nothing, I shouldn't have kissed her, her life's already fucked as it is."

"Devon do you like this girl yes or no?"

"Of course I like her, what's not to like? But I'm not for her. I can never have something that sweet and soft. I'll only end up destroying her life more than that asshole already has."

"How do you know that? And better yet answer me this. If not her, who? I've seen the way you look at her and she looks at you. Can you give her up to someone else?"

"What if I don't have a choice? What about after we take care of Khalil and her father decides he's going to take her back?"

"So what if he wants that, she's an adult, this is America. If you want the girl Dev for fuck sake take her. I know you, if you let her go this is never going to happen for you again, think about that."

"Think about her with someone… whoa-whoa-whoa,

take it easy brother." He stepped back when I rounded on him.

"Don't say that."

"See, that's what I'm talking about. You can't even bring yourself to imagine it. What do you think is going to happen if you let her go?"

"I can't Quinn, she's too good for me." I jogged away before he could say anything else.

45

DEVON

She's not talking to me, well that's not exactly true. She did say 'I'm okay Devon you don't have to worry about me' before disappearing behind the bedroom door and shutting me out.

If I didn't have to hunt down the madman that was after her I would've taken the time to explain to her but time was of the essence.

It hurt like fuck that she wouldn't even sit next to me at lunch and then again at dinner, but it was for the best.

The next day things were a little less stressed. She was back to smiling, but at everyone else but me, and the women were all in a flutter because of some party they were planning, so I was spared the dirty looks.

"Okay my source tells me your guy is indeed in Doha

but I don't have eyes on him yet. It might take a couple days so why don't we spend some time with our women before they mutiny. I think Devon set off some kinda storm and now all our asses are on the line."

"Thanks for putting that shit on me Mancini but you freaks were in trouble long before I came along." We were heading out of the room after another long day, but we were getting closer to the mark.

"So, have you thought of what I said?"

"Leave it Quinn, that shit can only lead to nowhere."

While the rest of them went in search of their women I headed outside and made my way to the water.

I threw myself in after skimming down to my shorts and tried to out swim my thoughts.

QUINN

Hardheaded son of a bitch! It's been two days since that little dust up and shit hasn't changed. That first day we got caught up in the hunt for Khalil, so it wasn't that bad.

Now the other women seem to think that we're all responsible or some shit and so we were getting the big freeze as well.

Kelly tried that shit the first day until I set her ass straight. After we got the last update on Khalil and were now just waiting for the 'go', I had some time to spend with my girl.

The women were planning a party, but Mancini had convinced us guys that it was safe to go into the neighboring town for a night out.

After Lo checked and rechecked the location he finally gave the go ahead and the women were at least smiling at us again.

Plans were made for that coming Saturday which was two days away, so for now we had two days to sit back and relax.

I woke up the next morning with the sun in my eyes and a warm body draped across my chest. Now that my mind wasn't filled with that other shit, I could think of nothing else but her.

I looked down at her sleeping face and wondered again how she came to be. I relived in the next few minutes the day leading up to the night we met.

How I felt her, and how even though I've had to neglect her these last few days that bond has been growing stronger.

When we have to spend hours apart, I check the monitor that Mancini keeps running in the background every few minutes just for a look at her.

And as of last night I have to make sure she never

learns that her father and his cohorts offed a United States general.

I didn't want to think about that now though, I just wanted her. I brushed her hair back from her face and kissed her forehead softly.

"I love you." I whispered the words too softly for her to hear. Not because I didn't want her to know, but because I wasn't ready for her to wake up.

Last night we talked late into the night and I learned about the precocious little girl she'd been. She painted a picture of a happy childhood with two loving parents who doted on her.

I learned that she was a feisty little thing with a beautiful heart. But best of all, I learned that thanks to my sisters and the few hours I've been able to devote to her since we met, that she loved me too; and that she was afraid.

I tried explaining my gift to her without sounding like an ass, and instead of looking at me with scorn or disbelief as I might've expected, she got the biggest smile on her face.

When she tackled me back on the bed and peppered my face with kisses something inside me opened up and gave her another piece of me.

She said that somehow knowing that made her feel less stupid and also gave her peace of mind. It was so contrary to what I expected I'd ended up putting her on her back and sliding into her.

Now I laid there holding her and it felt like I'd been doing it forever. I pulled her fully onto my chest and kissed her awake.

I pushed her hips down and slid into her before she came fully awake with our lips fused together. I held her head in one hand and used the other to push her on and off my cock by her beautiful ass.

"Those women are up to something." Lyon waved his beer bottle in the general direction of the side of the room where the women had congregated.

"What're they doing? They're just talking as far as I can see." I was still feeling mellow from my shower with Kelly before we left the island.

"My wife is nervous."

"Maybe she's just worried about the kids." No one had been happy about leaving the kids behind with some of the staff and more than half the security detail, but Mancini went above and beyond to reassure us.

"Nope, she knows better. She knows I wouldn't leave our kids if I didn't think they were safe, no. That's not her I'm worried about the kids look. That's her 'what's Colton going to do to me when he finds out?' look.

Everyone laughed but I knew we were all on alert now. It's true the women had been acting kinda squirrely since we got here, but they'd promised to behave so I wasn't too worried. Plus I knew if something was gonna go wrong I would've felt it.

The conversation was light for once, though the mood was still the same. Mancini had the whole place covered inside and out and we were trained to see danger, but not one of us let our guards down because of the women who were beginning to make me twitchy.

"What do you think they're up to?" I asked Dev out the side of my mouth.

"How the fuck would I know? Ariel won't even look at me let alone talk, so I don't have a fucking clue."

"Whoa bro, so why don't you talk to her?" I stepped back from the look he threw me. "Just a suggestion brother."

I smirked over his shoulder at Tyler who was acting the damn fool and tried not to laugh because he was rolling his eyes behind Dev's back the way I'd seen Dani or Gaby do with their men.

I didn't pay too much attention when I heard the women hooting and hollering, they're always carrying on about something and it being their first time out anywhere I'm sure they were ready to cut loose.

The tempo of the music changed from some slow

island melody to something a bit more upbeat. "Dev?" What the fuck's wrong with him now?

He'd gone from a relaxed pose to standing on guard, kinda like when a dog's hair stands up on its back. His gaze was focused somewhere over my shoulder in the general direction of the women and I turned to look to see what could possibly have his panties in a twist.

"Oh shit!" Ariel was in the middle of the dance floor and the others were egging her on. I don't know what you'd call what it was that she was doing, but I know for damn sure if I ever saw Kelly do that shit I'd wring her fucking neck.

It wasn't the dance though that was the problem. It was the eyes of the men, some of whom had got closer that sent shit to a whole other place. Devon fucking lost it.

~

DEVON

~

"What the fuck?"

"Oh shit, Quinn get your boy." Ty moved to cut me off even as Logan called out that order.

"Move Ty." I pushed him aside and went for her. I damn near knocked one of the women over in my haste, "sorry Ginger," I steadied her with my hands but my eyes never left Ariel.

"What the hell are you doing?" I grabbed her arm and started to drag her ass outta there."

"Release me!" She might not know she's a princess but she had that shit down. Too bad I ignored her.

"No, you're coming with me. Outta the way asshole." Some enterprising stander-by decided to get brave. My brothers were already in motion so I changed direction.

I stopped short of dragging her outside because of the lingering danger and pulled her into the first dark corner I found.

"What the fuck do you think you're doing?" I totally ignored the voice in my head that told me to pull back. I wasn't swayed by her wide-eyed look; she wasn't looking that fucking innocent two minutes ago.

"I asked you a question. Where did you learn to do that?"

"What's it to you Devon? I'm not yours remember? You can't tell me what to do." That shit didn't even sound like her.

"You… if you ever again in your fucking life do this shit in public, I will heat your fucking ass up."

I had to grit the words out through my teeth because I knew my whole damn family and our friends were standing behind me listening to every word.

I wasn't expecting her to fold her arms and give me

the bitch brow. "You can't threaten me, it's against the rules."

"What the fuck rules are you talking about?"

"Don't you swear at me you…you…man." What the fuck? How long did it take them? Three days?

I glared back at the women who all looked like they were ready to kick my ass if I made the wrong move. I'll deal with them later.

"Come on we're leaving." I met a brick wall when I tried to leave the room. The other people there were going about their night totally unaware of the drama.

"Where're you going bro?" Fucking Logan got in my face.

"Gaby, come here. Take Ariel back over there and you lot behave yourselves."

"Logan…"

"Quiet Dev let the women have their fun." I watched her walk away and was only slightly appeased when she looked back over her shoulder at me.

"Why'd you stop me?"

"Because they played you and you passed the test. Lyon was right they were up to something. Now we know what it was."

"I need a fucking drink."

"No you don't, you need a clear head for what comes next."

"What's that mean?"

"How long you been around these women? You think they're done?"

"If she dances like that again Lo I'll burn this shit to the ground, swear to fuck."

"Calm down Paul Bunyan damn, stop dragging your knuckles on the ground, you're making us look bad."

"Tyler I'm not in the mood." This fucking guy.

"And neither am I. These women haven't seen the outside world in weeks you fuck this shit up that island won't be big enough for all of us."

"I'm not afraid of your women."

"Then you're a damn fool brother." Con piped in as we headed back to our spot.

This time I made sure to stay closer and didn't really relax until the women sat down at their table; the show was over.

"I'd appreciate it if you told your women not to teach her that shit."

"I hate to be the one to bust your bubble bro but she didn't just learn that shit. Only place I've ever seen dancing like that is in a music video."

"Zak's right, she dances like a pro."

"How would you know Law were you watching her?"

"Uh, it was hard to miss bro…okay-okay I'm joking." He probably thinks I'm kidding but I'm in the mood to hurt someone and he'd do just as well.

46

KELLY

"I told you it would work." I high fived the others including Ariel even though she still looked like she was in shock.

I took a quick peek at the guys and toned it down a bit; they were not amused. Oh well! "So, our next move, you're going to completely ignore him."

"I don't know Kelly." Dana-Sue took a sip of her juice and looked back at her man before turning around again.

"Law has that look on his face, the one he always gets when I let Melissa talk me into doing something stupid."

"Hey, my ideas are never stupid. If these cavemen weren't so damn secretive and heavy handed we wouldn't have to go to these lengths. Do you want to know when is the last time I was allowed off the ranch? A damn year ago almost."

"Oh crap, we've only been sequestered a few months but if that shit goes on much longer I'm gonna revolt."

"And Logan will lock your ass away somewhere for good."

"Oh come on Vanessa, you can't tell me you're not going stark raving nuts by now."

"I am, but I understand what they're dealing with. Khalil is not a nice man; trust me I know. I lived in fear for my life everyday since I escaped him, until I came back to Zak. They know what they're doing."

"I have no argument with them knowing what they're doing, but my wedding is getting farther and farther in the distance and that is unacceptable."

""I don't understand why you ladies haven't already done the deed. Law got the preacher to come out and everybody got married in the yard."

Gaby's face was comical. "No way in hell. I've had my wedding planned since I was twelve and each day that Logan makes me wait I'm adding on another expense."

"The way I see it, our boys aren't the problem it's this Khalil person. We have to get his ass taken care of and then we can go back to living."

"I'm working on that."

"Do tell Cierra."

"Not yet girls, I'll let you know how it goes. If all goes to plan this may be taken care of pretty soon."

"That's good for you ladies but Law refuses to let anyone help him find Junior and I don't see us getting early release from prison anytime soon since that little rat is hiding pretty good."

"We already decided that after we take care of this Khalil, we're gonna have our boys help Law."

"Good luck with that, the man is hardheaded as they come."

"Dani take a quick look, is Colton looking at me?" We all turned to look. "Yep!"

"Dammit, I knew he was gonna blame me. Well, in for a penny in for a pound. What's next ladies, and remember, I'm way more pregnant than the rest of you so nothing too strenuous."

"Oh the next part is easy; we all get on the dance floor and strut our stuff." There was a chorus of mumbles and 'I don't knows' around the table."

"Come on ladies, what's the worst that can happen?" They all looked at me like I had a second head growing out of my neck.

"Oh I forgot, she's new, bless her heart."

"I know what that means Danielle."

"Uh-huh that's the least of your problems. You get out there shaking your ass and you won't sit down for a week."

"But you told me to do it."

"Yes Ariel but that was different. Your little exercise was to get a rise out of Devon and bring him to his senses. If we do it, it's just pulling the dog's tail."

"And what's wrong with that?"

'Uh, Victoria weren't you there the night Dani tried that shit and Connor lost his mind?" Dani's face went up in flames as all eyes were on her.

"Do tell!" This was all very entertaining to me. I've seen mom wrap daddy around her finger my whole life and this stuff we were doing was child's play compared to her stunts as far as I was concerned.

"I still say we do it, they can't get mad at us for dancing, they brought us to a club for heck sake."

"You ladies are missing one very important fact here. What is the worst your man will do to you?" Cierra looked around the table.

"My guess is they'll grumble and moan, stomp around a little…"

"Uh Cierra, your Hank seems to be a gentleman, now you've seen Colton Lyon in action." Kat looked over at the men again and waved at her husband who had her dead in his sights.

"You wanna know what he'd do if my pregnant ass get up there and shake my groove thing? Pregnant or not, he'd find a way to heat my ass up. No thanks."

"No way, he's so soft and kind with the kids, especially little Catalina. I saw him spend more than half an hour in a very serious discussion with her this morning, reminded me of me, and my dad."

She spat juice across the table. "What were they talking about did you hear anything? What's the last thing we were discussing in front of her?"

"Calm down Kat, what's the matter with you?" Susie ran her hand up and down Kat's arm. "He picks her for information, I already told you. We are so screwed."

"I wouldn't worry about it. I think she's working for our team on this one. She's not too happy with her uncles these days."

"Why what did they do?"

"They won't let her into their little club." Cierra laughed.

I can't believe the twists and turns my life has taken in just a few short days. I went from facing a fate almost as bad as death to this.

A man who loves me like crazy and a whole bunch of new friends. They were completely different from my friends back home, not better, just different.

And from what Quinn told me earlier, these women are my family now. My head is still spinning and I'm afraid to wake up from this dream.

I never imagined that I'd meet the man who could hold a candle to daddy, but I'm inclined to think Quinn might give him a run for his money.

He's too good to be true, and the fact that he comes with his team of brothers and their women only sweetens the pot. Daddy has given me a great appreciation for strong military men and the brotherhoods they form that last years.

I think it's the presence of the women that's helping me come to terms with this gigantic shift in my life.

Without their stories and their gushing about their brothers, I might've put the reins on; then again I get the feeling that with Quinn I wouldn't have stood a chance.

In the past few days I've barely given any thought to what happened, other than to try to figure out how to make the ones responsible pay. Especially after hearing the other women's stories.

It didn't take much after we all put our heads together, to realize that it was all connected and it had something to do with our men.

Their antics are helping me to overcome whatever lingering fear I might've had because in the real world I should be hiding away somewhere afraid to leave the house.

And at night, when I'm in bed with Quinn, after he's melted my bones, and I drift off to sleep with his scent in my nose and the feel of his strong capable arms wrapped protectively around me, his whispered 'I love yous' makes me feel like anything is possible.

I feel like I'm living in a dream and we haven't even

touched the surface of anything resembling a relationship yet. But somehow I feel in my very core that this is real.

Each time I have a doubt I only have to turn to any one of the women here for some reassurance. Their own story gives me hope, especially Kat, whose relationship is the oldest.

I watch the men with their women and can see the love and adoration with my own two eyes, my daddy taught me how to read people. And if all these couples were lying they should be on a Broadway stage.

I gave Quinn my perfected innocent look while the women debated whether or not we should test the men. I was in the mood to kick up my heels and do a little teasing of my own.

Though for a second there I'd doubted my suggestion that Ariel should get Devon's goat. He'd looked ready to kill, but even then I didn't have that fear in my gut that he would actually do something harmful to her.

"Come on girls, the DJ's going to put on our song soon, so, are we in or not?"

"Ah geez." Kat rubbed her protruding tummy.

"He can't do too much to me, let's go." I threw my hands in the air and whooped as we got to our feet and made a beeline for the dance floor.

I'm sure they were all as aware of their men as I was of Quinn when the music changed and us girls started doing our thing.

We weren't as good as Ariel, she dances like a dream, only for some reason she calls it exercise. For someone who didn't have any formal training she was damn good.

But since it appeared that she and I were the only ones not pregnant, this number was a little less wild. That didn't stop the men from getting into position though.

"You see, this isn't so bad, they're fine."

"Yeah because we haven't started that crazy dance of yours yet. How did I let myself get talked into this?"

"Oh come on Victoria, we're having fun."

"Yeah, you don't know Tyler."

"Look, you ladies have been living like prisoners forever, we're on an island for one night of fun and we're going to have fun dammit."

I can't believe these men would be so bent out of shape if their women danced in a public place. Granted the dance Ariel had done was just a tad seductive, but that was by design.

I'd drifted off with my thoughts so didn't notice the shift until his shadow fell over me. "Let's go Scheherazade."

"What, what's going on?" My mouth was almost to my chin when I realized the other women were already being led to the door. That's what I get for closing my eyes and getting lost in the music.

"Was this your idea?"

"Who me? Why what and why do you think it was?" The look he gave me told me he saw right through me.

Damn, that's not gonna work. I can't have him knowing me that well already, how will I ever get away with anything then?

Was he mad? I couldn't tell, and from the way the others had their lips buttoned I couldn't correctly gauge the situation.

Once we boarded the yacht for the short trip back, I still was none the wiser. Quinn hadn't said anything else and the men didn't appear upset.

In fact they were carrying on a conversation like they hadn't just dragged us off the dance floor. I did notice though, that each of them had their hand on their woman in some way. Including Devon.

The look on Ariel's face was worth whatever was waiting for me once we got back to the cottage. She was so secretive, so reserved it was obvious that there was some serious shit going on there.

So seeing the secret little smile on her face as he held her hand in his made me happy. I caught Quinn studying me as I studied them and smiled.

Resting my head on his shoulder, I squeezed the hand he had wrapped around mine and when he kissed my hair I got tears in my eyes for some stupid reason.

My heart felt so full in that moment that all I could

think was how much I couldn't wait to spend the rest of my life getting to know him. Because what I'd seen thus far only made me need more.

47

DEVON

Unfucking real! I gritted my teeth and held onto my anger and the rail as I looked out over the water as it rushed by below.

Behind me I could hear the din of the others' voices before they were carried away by the wind. I knew it meant something that I could separate her soft murmurs from all the others with my eyes closed.

I knew without my brothers trying to beat it into me that I felt more for her than I was ready to admit or accept.

What I don't know is what the hell I'm supposed to do about it. I took a deep breath and inhaled the sea air as I let myself calm down and relax.

In my mind I could still see the sensuous undulations

of her body as she danced. It wasn't her dancing that made me see red, but the roomful of men enjoying the show.

I don't want anyone else seeing her like that, ever. Shit, the shit made me hard so I can only imagine what it did to the other men in the room. I should go back there and beat the hell out of all of them.

No Devon, better not go there again. You're out here to calm down remember? I took a couple more deep breaths and tried to clear my head.

The one bright spot of the evening was my brothers' and our friends' reactions when their women took to the floor.

The same damn men who'd only just got through telling me I was over reacting had lost their collective shit. I would've laughed had I not known exactly how they were feeling.

I felt her presence behind me and tensed up, as she got closer. I'm not so thick that I don't know why she did it, or why my sisters had put her up to it.

Knowing the way they talk from having overheard way too many of their raunchy conversations when they thought we weren't around, I could only imagine. But the bottom line is it meant she was interested.

It was easier to fight my own feelings when it was just me but if she wants me too… "Go back inside baby it's chilly out here." And you're not wearing nearly enough.

I hadn't said anything earlier because I didn't want to start an all out war, but just who the fuck had given her the little number she was wearing?

I knew the short flouncy skirt with the camisole top wasn't hers. Probably Susie's. One that Cord hadn't destroyed yet. I'll be sure to help him burn the shit as soon as we get back.

Instead of following my order and returning to the others, she came and stood beside me, looking out over the moonlit water.

"Devon, are you mad at me?"

"No baby I'm not mad at you, I just…." Send her away Devon, it's for her own good.

Instead of following my mind I turned to her, looking down at her amazing face. There was so much feeling in her eyes, such vulnerability.

I moved in closer and lifted my hand to her sassy ponytail and her hands came up to rest on my chest. "You're so fucking beautiful." Shit, there I go again.

Her eyes widened and that hint of innocence is the only thing that kept me from pulling her into my arms and just taking her lips. But I couldn't resist trailing my fingers down her cheek. So soft!

As usual, her nearness was having an affect on me and my need for her grew stronger. I tightened my hold on her hair to keep myself from touching her the way I wanted to.

I knew now would be the perfect time to put an end to this once and for all. To crush whatever that was that was growing in her eyes.

But Quinn's words came back to haunt me, and the only thing I could think of, was what would the rest of my life be without her in it.

How would I live knowing that some other man was holding her, loving her…fuck!

"Baby, you don't know what you're asking me to do here."

"But I didn't say anything."

"You don't have to, your eyes say it all." I didn't mention her pebbled nipples that pushed against the soft silk of her top, or the way the pulse beat wildly in her throat.

She didn't answer me, just flicked her eyes up and down before looking back at me with that same intense look and the innocence she was trying so hard to hide.

"Did they tell you what this shit would mean Ariel?"

She bit her lip but still said nothing. "I know they've been filling your head but did they tell you what belonging to me would mean? You just left one prison baby you don't want to exchange it for another."

"You don't have to say these things Devon, I know you don't want me."

"Really, you know that? Well you know wrong. I want

you so fucking bad I can't think straight, but this isn't right, I'm not right."

She didn't blink, didn't look away. Just stared at me with that look that burnt a hole in my gut with need. "I'm trying to protect you here baby, can't you see?"

She bit her lip and I saw the hurt come into her eyes just then and knew that I was only fooling myself. It was too late the second I met her.

That niggling voice in the back of my head warned me that it was too dangerous and once again I found myself battling my need.

"Oh fuck this!" I dragged her against my chest and covered her mouth with mine, holding her head back by her ponytail with one hand while cupping her ass with the other so I could dive into her.

She was soft and sweet and so fucking perfect in my arms. I ate at her lips as she accepted my tongue, her innocence awakening something in me that I'd thought long dead.

I pulled our lips apart when it became hard to breathe, but didn't relax my hold on her.

"I want to have babies with you, lots and lots of babies."

Oh for fuck sake! I only meant to give her room to breathe before going back for more but those words slipped out before I could reel them back in.

I didn't give her a chance to answer, just took her lips again giving my hunger free rein. My heart beat out of time as I held her closer, so close I could feel the hard points of her nipples as they brushed against my chest.

I loved the way she clung to me, like she would be lost if I let her go. "What're you doing to be Ariel?" There were so many reasons why we shouldn't be doing this, most of all the fact that she doesn't even know who she is.

What if she wants that life when the truth comes out? Something inside me revolted at the idea and it was then I realized the truth of what I'd been doing since I brought her back with me.

I've been running from myself. Putting up roadblocks and finding excuses. Fear, it was fear plain and simple.

Fear of losing again, something so precious. The last time had almost destroyed me. When I lost my parents and endured all that had followed, I'd made a vow to myself that I would never open myself to that kind of hurt again.

But so much has happened in my life since then. And I know without a doubt that there's none of my uncle in me. I could never look at her little face and take a fist to it.

Tonight when I'd been so mad at her for dancing in a roomful of strangers it never entered my mind to harm her.

I lifted that face to mine now and took her lips again.

This time I let my hand trail gently along her shoulder and down her arm.

She shivered and got closer and I crushed her body to mine, letting my fingers find their way to her nipple.

Something inside me shifted when she moaned into my mouth and I knew that I would never let her go, not now not ever and not for any reason.

"Are you sure you want this Ariel? There's still a lot that you don't know…" She put her fingers over my lips and looked into my eyes.

"I feel you here." She took my hand and placed it over her heart, which beat wildly under my hand. "Well fuck!"

This time when I covered her lips with mine I didn't hold back but let myself go. I'll protect her heart come what may.

As I fed on her tongue I let myself believe for the first time that this could be real, that I could really have this. Her tongue shyly played with mine only deepening the hole that I'd fallen into.

How could someone so soft, so innocently sweet be mine? If the others are right and this love shit was fate, then how could I deserve her?

I didn't know but I no longer cared. I let myself fall into her, let myself believe that I could have her, for the rest of my life.

"We've got to stop baby." My dick was too hard and I

was just at the point of no return. Wrong fucking place and time.

"Just one more Devon please." She kissed like someone who'd never done it before and her naivety just drew me in even more.

But the strange thing was, as much as I wanted her, I wanted to take my time with her. I want to show her all the ways I can love her.

The idea gave me such a rush. Days spent teaching her all about lovemaking, holding hands as we walked on the beach.

And when we get back home, my home, which she'd never seen, we'd spend all our nights together, wrapped in each other's arms.

I was weaving dreams in my head like one of Tyler's bitch made skells but didn't care. From the very first time I saw her I knew need and want.

She was the first woman to ever make me want more with her and somehow I knew she would be the last.

The fact that she was willing to give herself to me only heightened my senses and I put all other thoughts out of my head as I gave myself over to the rising lust.

I heard footsteps coming and moaned into her mouth, hating to release her. Taking one last nibble of her soft lips I released my hold on her before taking a step back.

Please don't look down baby. If she did she would see

the python straining against the tab of my zipper to get at her and I was sure she wasn't ready for that no matter what my sisters had put in her head.

Her lips were swollen and red and her eyes bright as she looked up at me. I didn't turn to see who was standing there, but instead shielded her body from view. I didn't want anyone else seeing her swollen nipples.

"We'll be there in five Devon." I looked over sharply at Mancini's words. There was something in his voice and the slight shake of his head was all the answer I needed to know that something was up.

"Okay, come on baby let's get you back inside." I shielded her body with mine and led her back inside without letting on that there was anything wrong.

I sat her with the women who weren't even subtle about the fact that they were about to stick their nose in my shit and moved across the room to join the guys.

"What is it?" I kept my voice low so it didn't carry, but I could tell from the looks on my brothers' faces that something was wrong.

"Khalil is on the move." My head whipped around to her and my body went into fight and protect mode. "Where is he?"

"We don't know. My people were lucky enough to catch his movements once he left his place in the hills. All we know for sure is that he's not in the states as yet if this is even where he's heading."

"Oh he's coming here alright, the sick fuck. If he comes anywhere near her…"

"He's not Dev. Not in this fucking lifetime." Quinn's hand on my shoulder helped to calm me but not by much.

This shit can't be happening. I wanted it over, but now that I'd made up my mind to keep her I wanted more time with her. Time to show her and me, what we could be together.

I want to take her out on the cliffs and sit with her doing nothing but holding hands and sharing a few kisses while we look at the sea. Take long walks on the beach; build more castles.

All the things that would make Ty's ass rabid and send him into a frenzy because he thinks I'm getting soft like the others, bitch made as he puts it.

I could see us, she's always smiling and happy and I'm never too far. I could see a baby, my baby in her arms, feeding.

I saw my body covering hers and my dick sprung into action from just that little glimpse of the future and my heart damn near beat me to death.

Oh shit, I'm in love with her. Like really deeply forever and a day kinda shit. "I'm in love with her."

"Uh yeah we know. Wipe the drool off your damn chin McClueless we got shit to do."

"Fuck you Tyler. Did I just say that shit out loud?"

The last was directed at Quinn who just grinned and nodded his head.

This little development had proven one thing to me at least. Whatever doubts and hang-ups I had before were now gone. No one else is going to have her, not ever. I'll find a way to get around the king, but she's mine.

48

ARIEL

~

I know something's coming I can feel it. I've had years of practice reading people. When you've been locked away from the world your whole life, you find interest in a lot of things people take for granted. Like how to use all your senses to read a situation.

It's how I know that I can trust these men and women, even though I've never been exposed to this many people at once before in my life.

It's like being dumped out of my familiar fishbowl and into the real world without gills. And though the fear threatens to overtake me at times, there's one thing here that keeps me grounded. Devon.

I see in him a mixture of the two men in my life. My brother and my dad. There's something gentle and kind in his eyes when he looks at me, but more than that, there's something inside me that comes alive whenever he's near.

My life has been a very sheltered one. I can count on one hand the number of people I've met in my whole life until now, that's including my father, mother and brother.

As a very young child I was happy. I had all the things any little girl could ever wish for. Because I knew no other way, I found joy in the things dad brought to me.

My dad was my whole world. When he wasn't working or off somewhere he spent most of his time with me teaching me. By the age of three or four I could read and so I got all my knowledge of the outside world from books before my first computer at twelve.

When my brother came along and I learned that it wasn't normal for little girls to be shut away from the world it had broken my heart. I couldn't understand why I couldn't do the things my brother was allowed to do.

Until a few days ago, my father would only tell me that it was for my own protection. All the secrecy, the seclusion. Having to travel in the dead of night when we moved between houses. Until that too became too dangerous.

I figured out for myself when I was very young that I was adopted. Not only because I look nothing like my family, but I just didn't feel connected.

Don't get me wrong it was nothing they did. In fact

they went above and beyond to make my life as comfortable and happy as they could given the circumstances.

But there was always something missing. Except with my brother Track. From a very young age he's been my little protector. He's the first human being I loved unconditionally, until now.

He never understood, never accepted the way my life was. Until him, I didn't know to question, because I knew no other way.

The story I told Devon earlier is just one of the many ways in which my little brother had tried to change my life.

While I stayed home all day getting my lessons through the computer, from disembodied voices of the men and women who taught me, he got to go off to school and meet people.

He's the one who started bringing the outside world to me. My parents did their bit there too, but Track was the one who brought me video clips of real people, the kids he went to school with, his friends.

He let me into his life in the most invasive way, sharing everything he could with the sister he loved and did not resent for making his life the disaster it was.

I knew he'd lost out on a lot because of me, only because he refused to take part in anything that I couldn't be a part of, which was pretty much everything.

By the time he was in high school and I was taking

college level courses online, I had come to accept my life while living vicariously through him. But he never did.

He made the days less lonely and gave me hope that someday things will change. My dad for all his love was more reserved. His only interest was in spoiling me to make up for the fact that I couldn't have a normal life.

My rooms were always the most beautiful, and the clothes I never got to wear anywhere were the latest in fashion. I know, because I got to choose them myself from the many magazines dad brought for me to choose from.

I knew from television and later the limited access I had to the Internet that normal people didn't live this way.

By then I'd stopped asking dad about my real parents and this danger that he was protecting me from once I realized that it was stressing him.

Each time I'd bring it up he'd get this pained look on his face and age ten lifetimes. I knew whatever it was it must be pretty bad and as I grew older I learned to be content, somewhat.

Then Track met Valerie, the girl he ran home and gushed to me about. I saw love for the first time. Not the aged comfortable love of my parents, but love in its first blush.

I've read stories, I know all the mechanics of love and where it leads, but I had never seen that fire, that light that shone in my little brother's eyes that day.

That night we talked and talked about his newfound

love and when tears rolled down my cheeks, he'd wrapped his arms around me and sworn a solemn oath that he was going to get me out of there. That one day I too will find love.

He'd never come to terms with my situation and for some reason this new development seemed to galvanize him into action.

Dad had never told him any more than he'd told me, but unlike me, the docile obedient daughter, Track never took no for an answer.

From the time he was old enough, he kept pushing and prodding to get to the truth, but to no avail. And then something changed.

Track had always been good with computers, he even taught me how to do some of the stuff he did. It was fun, a new way to alleviate the boredom.

There was only one thing he refused to teach me until I nagged him. He was never able to refuse me anything and soon he was teaching me the secrets of hacking.

I found a new hobby after that and though we never did anything to harm others, it was fun figuring out the intricacies. I was pretty good at it in no time, but never as good as he.

Like everything else, I knew he was going to marry his teenage girlfriend before anyone else did. He'd told me about her being sick and her dad's neglect. I knew he saw me in her and wanted to save her, and wondered if anyone would ever feel that way about me.

It was not long after that that he started disappearing only to return weeks later looking more and more morose. For the first time he didn't share a part of his life with me.

Then a little over a month ago I noticed a new tension in the air at home. I spend so much time with my dad that I know his every mood, same with Track.

I'd walk into a room and they'd stop talking right away. Whenever we were in a room together the focus was always on me, but that's nothing new, it's always been that way.

But this time was different, this time I was afraid. It was the way they were acting, especially Track this last time he came home from one of his many absences of late.

Then dad sat me down and without telling me much more than I already knew, explained that things were coming to a head and soon I will have all the answers.

I was so afraid after he told me this. Afraid that I'd finally learn the truth and it would change my life. Suddenly I wanted my life to remain just the way it was.

I'd grown used to the way things were. It's not like I never got to see the outside world. My family owns homes in other places around the world, and though I was kept hidden in all of them when we did visit, it was at least a change of scenery and I was allowed more freedom in some of them than at home.

My whole life has been lived through a computer. It's where I was taught, where I did my shopping, where I learned social graces and all the things a young lady should know according to dad.

I lacked for nothing in my life, except my freedom. Yet I didn't feel like a prisoner, and there were times I thought my dad must love me very much to go to these lengths to keep me safe, even though I wasn't his blood.

Now here I am and my life seems to have gone into overdrive in a matter of days. Dad hadn't had time to prepare me for this, it seems things were out of his control. But he trusted these men that much was obvious.

Poor Track, the look on his face when I left. My poor baby brother, my guardian warrior. I remember the first time I held him, the unbridled feelings and emotions that enveloped me then and I knew that he was mine.

Now all these years later I have those same feelings again, but in a whole new way. It happened the first time I saw Devon.

As someone who relies on her senses to tell her what's what, I knew from the first moment that he was mine too, I just didn't quite understand how. Until now!

Now the fear isn't as strong because of him. I like the others too. I've learned what sort of men they are through the women.

I also know they're very secretive because their women know nothing of my situation. I shared what I could with them without putting myself in danger, but in the end I don't know that much either.

They didn't treat me like a freak the way I half expected, but instead drew me into their circle, like I was one of them, with one glaring difference. They each belonged to one of the men here, whereas I was…what am I?

It was them who got the truth of my feelings for Devon out in the open because it was just that easy to talk to them, what with all their prodding.

I tested out all the things I'd learned over the years on them and was never more excited than when I was able to come up with an answer for one of their issues, of which they seemed to have plenty and all surrounding their men.

They're brave these women, brave and strong though I don't think they know it. And it was hard to believe that they hadn't always known each other.

When Kat tells the story of how she met her Lyon and fell in love, it gives me hope that I can have that. The others assured me that it didn't take them long to know that their man was the one.

It gave me hope, though there was no doubt on my part where Devon was concerned. It was his distance that scared me most.

Until Danielle explained that that's how they pretty

much all were in the beginning. And Kelly, who's new like me. She was still coming to terms with her whirlwind romance so I didn't feel so alone. We were alike her and I, though she was a little ahead of me in the game by a few days.

Maybe that's why I'd let her talk me into the dance tonight, why I'd trusted the women that it would work to get Devon to accept his feelings for me.

Feelings his sisters were sure he had but I was still doubting. How could I know he had feelings for me when he wouldn't even touch me, and was always in a hurry to get away from me whenever we were alone?

But that day on the beach I'd seen another side to him. I'd seen the way he looked at me when he didn't think I was watching.

If not for the women I would be scared out of my head. I'd only seen love from a distance or through my brother, but these feelings awakening inside me were all new and oh so frightening.

I was in a new place surrounded by people I didn't know and my life was going through this miraculous change and it all seemed to be happening so fast.

And then he kissed me, and told me he wanted to have babies with me and nothing else matters. I don't know what's going to happen to me, what the big secret of my life is, but I know in my soul that as long as Devon is at my side, it will all work out.

"Well?" Kelly tapped my leg and brought me out of my reverie. I'd drifted away in my head while the others were whispering and laughing at their men and their antics.

"He kissed me." I touched my lips as though I could still feel the pressure of his there. She squealed and the others shushed her even though they too were smiling and clapping their hands.

"Told you it would work, woot."

"Okay-okay-okay shh, they're looking." Kat shushed us and we all took a look across the room at the men who seemed to be deep in conversation about something.

My tummy cramped a little when I thought it might have something to do with me and the reason I'd been brought here. But the look on Devon's face soon calmed me again, only to send the blood heating in my veins.

"Oh my, I hope Hank looks at me like that." Cierra fanned herself and grinned as my cheeks heated up. I couldn't look away from him. I wonder if he knew that his eyes gave away everything?

I finally blinked and when I looked again he was talking to his brothers. "Oh damn I'm jumping Connor tonight."

"As if you'd have to, the man can't keep his hands off you."

"You've got a point Vanessa but good heavens did you see that look? Who knew Devon had it in him?"

"It's always the quiet silent types." Ginger laughed and the rest of us joined in.

"You ladies are forgetting one thing. That dance."

"Oh Kat I'm sure they've forgotten all about that."

"Uh-huh, you ladies have so much to learn. These men don't forget shit. I'd bet you good money if they don't bring it up tonight, some time in the future it will be the topic of discussion and my ass will be on the line."

"Why, you didn't plan it."

"Try telling that to Colton Lyon. As long as I'm anywhere in the vicinity he seems to think it's my responsibility."

"I've noticed that about them, they all seem to have the same school of thought. Melissa's always starting some shit and Clayton ends up blaming me."

"Hey, I'm not the only one. The rest of you pull your fair share of stunts."

"Yes Missy, but not as often and nowhere near as hair-brained."

That set off another one of their playful arguments as to who gets up to the most shenanigans. I've learned so much about who they are and who their men are from listening to their stories of their escapades, but each time I hear one I long to be part of that.

I want to make Devon crazy the way his sisters say

they do their men. I want him to sneak off with me the way Colton does with his Kat when they think no one's paying attention.

Or have him just touch me just because he can't help himself the way all the men seem to with their women.

As I sat there listening to the laughter and gaiety with one eye secretly trained on Devon, I felt alive for the first time in my life.

I felt hope, like all those things he whispered to me out on the deck could somehow come true. My very own fairytale.

49

DEVON

As soon as we got back to the island the women were rushed inside and the kids rounded up to make sure they were all in one piece.

The night was still young since we'd ended it early so the women decided to settle down in their favorite room while the kids went back to what they were doing.

The men headed up to the private room where Mancini made a call while the rest of us waited. "Nothing yet, but we have another problem; her brother."

"Track, what about him?" I'd grown fond of the kid because of the stories she told me about him. Since I knew more about her story than she did, the fact that the kid had gone above and beyond to make her life better made my respect for him grow even more.

"He's been digging his nose in again and he's getting too close. I don't think he understands the danger."

"I'll talk to him." I should've thought of it once we realized what the kid was up to, but I figured since his sister was safe with us he'd give up his quest.

"The search for the general's assassin is heating up. I had my people make a clean sweep after your friends left him so there should be nothing to point to anyone so that's one less worry."

"Lyon, your senator has been getting some interesting communications lately. He's scheduled for a trip to the middle east next week." Mancini gave him a telling look, which we all interpreted.

"What kind of communication?" Logan was the one to ask.

"Well, with the general out of the way the senator and anyone else involved in this mess are going to be trying to cover their ass."

"Devon they still don't know about the girl, but if her brother keeps pushing it might tip them off. So far I don't think they know why he wanted in, you can thank her father for that. He did such a good job hiding her that no one even suspects."

Yes but at what cost? Her whole life is one of secrets and shadows. How am I to know that if given a choice she would've chosen me?

Was I supposed to let her live now? Give her room to

breathe? Fuck that no. Unfair it might be but I can't see myself doing that shit.

I knew in my heart that what I want for her won't be much different from what she was used to. I won't lock her away in a room but she sure as fuck won't have the freedom most women enjoy.

It's the same with my sisters and these other women here. Every man in this room keeps a tight fucking leash on his woman no matter how he couches that shit.

But it's not out of any need to be an abusive asshole, but to protect the thing they hold most dear.

Lyon, the undesignated leader of the husband brigade has been married longer than anyone else here and he still treats his woman like she's gonna disappear if he doesn't know where she is every step of the way.

"How do you guys do it?"

"Do what?" My question came at a lull in the conversation.

"The women Logan, how do you know when to pull back?"

"Pull back from what bro?"

"You know, when to give them space? How to not smother them or keep them from thinking you're a possessive asshole? Because I gotta tell you, knowing what she came from, I don't see much difference in what she'd face as mine."

"Of course there's a difference Dev. We keep our

women sheltered to protect them from the shit we know is out there, but once this shit's over they're going to be free to go anywhere they want to."

"Yeah as long as one of us is there to make sure they're safe right Con?"

"Yeah, what Tyler said."

"But isn't that kinda the same thing? Shouldn't they be able to go out on their own…?"

"Boy, are you crazy? I've had a tracker on Kat and my kids since day one. Not because I'm afraid my wife's gonna cheat on me, but because if some shit goes down I know where to find her."

"That's the world we live in brother. I wish I could fucking lock Caitie Bear in a room somewhere until she's fifty, but that right there would be crossing the line."

"Instead I teach my kid values and shit and hope that some of it takes and when she marries that stupid ass boy I'ma make sure he tags her ass too and if he can't protect her the way I do, he can't fucking have her."

I'm not sure I should be taking advice from Lyon but even Lo was nodding his head. No wonder these women are always getting into shit, their men are crazy as fuck.

"So what's the difference between you lot and the assholes who beat on their wives and kids, never let them leave the house, shit like that?"

The room went quiet as fuck before they all started talking at once. "Whoa-whoa-whoa I'm just asking.

Because you know, she was locked away her whole fucking life. When the dust settles I'm gonna take her back to Georgia and lock her away again?"

"It's not the same thing you ass. In Georgia she'll have the whole compound to roam. I don't think she was even allowed in the backyard at her father's place."

"Yes Tyler but there's more to the world than the compound. What if she wants to travel? Take a cruise? Go to the damn store?"

As I said it I realized that none of my sisters had been let out of our sight alone in months. No wonder they're always rebelling.

"Then that's what we'll do. Things are strained now because of this shit, until Khalil is eliminated their lives have to be this way, but once the danger passes things will relax a little."

"I'm not saying I'm gonna let Gaby run wild but I'm sure as fuck not going shopping with her."

"Same here. But just like Lyon we have tags on them though they don't know it, but it's just to keep them safe. Speaking of which you and Quinn need to get on that shit as soon as we get back."

"So you see nothing wrong with locking them away Con?"

"They're not locked away brother, it just seems that way now. But Dani has a job, so does Gaby, and Vicki, Susie has school and Nessa owes the military what another year or two? As soon as this shit's over they'll go back to their lives, we'll just know where they are at all times."

"What if she wants to get a job? What am I gonna do?" Why is this shit so hard?

"Dude my woman is an FBI agent."

"Oh yeah, that's bad. Shit, how do you deal with that shit Mancini?"

"I'm trying to get her ass fired."

"Okay then so I'm not the only one that's fucked in the head."

"Nope!"

"Damn, I thought the women were in the media room; bitch made motherfuckers. Listen, we have a business, the women have jobs and school. Once we send Khalil's ass to the hereafter, we'll go back to life. She's not going to be locked away brother, unless of course you don't get your head out of your ass and the old king drags her back to Saudi Arabia."

"Tyler what the fuck?"

"Well what do you think is going to happen if you hand her over to him? You'll never see her again I can tell you that much."

"I've already decided that's not gonna happen." That was tantamount to me announcing to the room at large that she was mine.

From the slaps on the shoulder and the congratulations

I guess it didn't go right over their heads. "Welcome brother, now prepare yourself."

"For what Lyon?"

"To never have a moment's peace."

"To sleeping with one eye open."

"To losing your fucking mind." Everyone had something to say.

"Okay I get it." I wonder why the hell they wanted me to take the plunge if it was going to be like that? But the smiles and stupid grins told me they were full of shit.

50

DEVON

After agreeing to meet back here in the morning we left and went back to the women who were sitting around gabbing about who knows what.

I ignored my sisters' knowing looks and sat on the arm of her chair. "Scoot over baby." There wasn't enough room so I lifted her and sat her on my lap.

"Did you have a good time tonight?"

"It was fun, my first party."

"Where did you learn to dance like that?"

"YouTube."

"Seriously?"

"Sure, I learned a lot of stuff that way. Track taught me how to log on without leaving a trace or dad would've skinned us." She smiled and it was so open, so lacking in artifice or any of the things I've grown accustomed to from women.

I had a sudden thought, "you're not shy are you baby?" She couldn't be, not dancing like that in a roomful of people.

"No I don't think so, I like to dance. But not if it's going to upset you."

"It wasn't your dancing that upset me beautiful, I thought you were amazing. It was the men watching you do it that pissed me off."

"Oh so Kelly was right."

"Oh yeah, what did she say?"

"She said it would light a fire under your ass." I could tell from the way she said that that she had no idea she was letting the cat out of the bag. Could she really be that innocent? I decided to test that theory.

"Do you like me Ariel?"

"Yes! I get butterflies in my tummy when you're near and tonight when you kissed me, I thought I could fly."

I stared at her nonplussed for the barest of seconds not quite believing my ears. I looked around at the others but they were busy smooching so I knew my sisters weren't putting her up to this.

"Do you remember what I told you on the yacht?" She nodded her head and pulled at her skirt. "And you're okay with that?"

"I'd love to have a baby!" Did she have any idea of

the shit storm that would follow if I just took her? Of course she doesn't, and she never will.

"And you want that with me?"

"I never wanted it before."

"But you've never been around anyone else before either have you."

"You won't understand."

"Hold that thought, come with me!" I felt sure that the others were too preoccupied to be shoving their nose in my shit when I got to my feet, took her hand and pulled her from the room behind me.

Once outside I removed my light jacket and put it around her shoulders. "Walk with me." I took her hand again and felt the slight tremble as I headed towards the beach.

"What do you mean I won't understand? Won't understand what?"

"My feelings. You think that because my life was so different from yours that I don't know what I feel."

She was right to a point but how does she know that? She can't possibly know me that well. "How do you know that?"

"Because I've been studying you, it's something I'm very good at, reading people. I feel like I know you now. I know you want to protect me because you think I'm wounded. You know why I was shut away don't you?"

She dropped that in there so neatly I almost walked

right into it. "I do, but don't ask me to tell you about that right now. There's still a lot of work to be done."

"Just tell me this. Is whatever it is going to take you away from me?"

"No; never, I won't let it!" I was saying that as much for her as for myself.

"But tell me honestly Ariel, how sure are you about this? You say you've been studying me, and no doubt my sisters have been filling your head with stories, but you have no experience with anything like this."

"All my life, I've done nothing but dream. Dream and imagine what my life would be like if things were different."

"When my brother fell in love, it was eye opening. I'd only seen love in movies, or read about it in books, but I knew that if I ever found it I'd know."

She looked up at me then and I would've given her the world if she asked.

"I said you won't understand because you're like my brother, you and your brothers you're… you think differently, like men. Protectors, providers, you love in a different way."

"But love isn't something you can explain Devon. It doesn't matter if you're someone like me, who've been shut away my whole life, or someone like you who've been free. Love just is."

She pulled my hand to her chest where her heart beat

wildly and I became suddenly tongue tied. She made it sound so easy, could it really be that simple?

"I know because of what I feel when you look at me. Or how my heart races when you're near. I know because I dream about you at night and it makes me sad to think of never seeing you again when this is all over."

"Fuck baby." I took her face between my hands and lifted it to mine in the moonlight. She got up on her toes to meet my lips halfway.

I tested her with soft nibbles of her lips before deepening the kiss the way I wanted to and sank into her. "Don't ever change Ariel!"

I kissed her nose and looked down at her shaking my head. "No matter what your sisters say, don't you ever change you hear me?"

I grinned at her to let her know I was kidding before taking her hand and carrying on. "I don't know anything about sex though so you're going to have to teach me."

I almost fell over my damn feet in the sand. I tried to answer her but there was a frog in my throat, not to mention the python behind my zipper.

"I don't think you're ready for that yet."

"Why not?"

"Why not? Because we just met and you need time to…"

"But Kelly and Quinn had sex the first time they met." What the fuck!

"Don't you want to have sex with me?"

"Baby, haven't anyone ever talked to you about this?"

"Uh-huh, the girls said it's one of the best parts of having a husband. Kat said every time Colton looks at her he mounts her."

"Whoa, okay-okay-okay, baby, don't tell me anything else that the girls say okay." For fuck sake what the hell do these women be getting up to?

"Well don't you?"

"Don't I what?"

"Want to have sex with me?"

"Baby, Ariel…of course I want to have sex with you, but I don't think we should…you're not..."

"I want to have sex with you, but only when you're ready." How the fuck did we get here? Her face looked a bit crestfallen and I felt like a monster.

"Look at me. I'm trying to do the right thing here Ariel. I don't want to rush you…"

"Devon, I don't know what's going to happen to me, I don't even know who I am anymore. And I'm plenty old enough to know I'm not a baby you know."

"I know you're not a baby- baby, but…"

"And you said you want to have babies. Did you know that all your sisters are pregnant? Except for Kelly though she says that as much as she and Quinn do it she just might be because she's not using anything."

Oh man, she really is that innocent. She pulled out of

my hand and ran ahead, skipping and laughing in the sand.

In the background the waves rolled in slowly, gently as she danced in the moonlight. She started to sing and I got choked up.

I stopped moving and watched her as she swayed to the song she was singing. It sounded like Diamonds. I never knew that song was so sensuous.

She moved to the beat in her head, uninhibited, sexy, wanton. She was a confusing mix of innocence and hot sexuality.

I was standing in front of her before I even realized I'd moved. I put my hands on her waist and she jumped up and wrapped her legs and arms around me. "Good girl!"

Her skirt had ridden up over her panties and I cupped her ass in my hands while taking her mouth a little less gently this time.

My cock jumped at the feel of her heat beneath the softness of her underwear. She ate at my mouth in her untrained way and I reveled in feeding her my tongue for her to suck on while she moaned into my mouth.

"I want to fuck you so hard!" Oh for fuck sake I did it again. I started to apologize but her body shook and she pressed herself harder against me before covering my mouth again.

I had visions of taking her down to the sand and driving into her, but I couldn't do that to her, not her first time. Especially when someone might come along any second.

I walked backward a pace before turning and heading onto the path that led to our cottage. I kept one eye on the path as we made it to the door.

I didn't stop at the couch but walked right through to the bedroom and the bed that was waiting there. We stood there for what felt like forever just feeding off of each other's lips.

There was a wet stain on the front of my jeans but I wasn't sure that it was just me. I let my fingers travel down her ass to the slit between her thighs where she had her legs spread and felt the wet spot in the crotch of her panties.

"I'm going to touch you now, don't be afraid." I pressed my finger against her and rubbed until her essence was on my hand and her scent was in the air.

My cock lurched uncomfortably behind my zipper and I needed to get him out of there, but I ran my finger along her heat a little longer, testing her again.

If she showed any fear I'd pull back, give her the time I thought she needed. But she didn't flinch, didn't show any fear, instead she rocked herself harder against my growing cock and pushed down on my finger.

When she whined in frustration at my teasing I knew what she wanted, but I wanted something too. I wanted to, no needed to make her mindless with need so it would be easier for her to take me.

There was a mix of fear and excitement coursing through me as I envisioned getting my long hard cock into her tight little pussy and my head almost exploded at the images that flitted through my mind.

My hunger rose and I bit her lip before licking the sting away with my tongue. I should give myself a minute to calm down before going any farther, before I hurt her. At least that's what I told myself, but it took effort for me to put her down.

My hands were shaking and my heart beat in my cock heavy and strong. When I took my mouth away she followed and whined again, her eyes bright with lust.

I was gentle as I laid her back across the bed, gentle when I lifted her top up over her breasts that I'd been dying to see.

I leaned over her, the roughness of my jeans brushing against the softness of her inner thighs, and took her nipple into my mouth.

She acted like I'd electrocuted her. Her whole body tensed and lifted and her hand came down to hold my head in place as her limbs shook.

I played her nipple with my tongue as I ground my jean covered cock into her pussy, getting us both even wetter.

When she wrapped her legs around me I left one

nipple for the other, sucking it hard into my mouth and giving her my teeth.

Her fresh pussy scent was driving me insane and I wanted to rip her panties in half and bury my head between her thighs, but again I reined it in.

I pushed the top all the way up and pulled it over her head before trailing my fingers along the skin of her soft smooth stomach.

I teased her navel with my fingertip and marveled at my control. In my head I was already inside her, but I knew she needed more, much more.

With her eyes held with mine, I reached beneath her and undid her skirt before pulling it off down her thighs, leaving her only in her panties that were sticking to her cunt from her wetness.

I buried my nose in the wet spot before tasting her through the silk with my tongue. She pulled her legs up and planted them on the bed as she tried pulling my head harder against her.

My heart was a huge lump in my chest as I pulled her panty aside and looked at her pussy for the first time.

It was perfectly bare, fat, pretty. Her gash was one long line between her plump labia, her clit barely peeping out from its hood.

I went after it with my tongue, holding the silk of her panties aside with my hand. The sounds she made echoed in my head as I teased her clit into my mouth.

Her pussy overflowed and I felt her juices run down my chin. I left her clit and licked my way down her gash until I found the hole that I would soon pierce.

I wanted to see all of her so I took the crotch of her panties in both hands and pulled, tearing it in half, but leaving the scraps clinging to her body.

"Open." She spread her legs for me but I pushed them open wider, getting to my knees on the floor between her wantonly spread thighs.

I waited for her to stop me, for her embarrassment to show, but when I looked up at her she was just staring at me with that look of lust in her eyes.

I lowered my head to her again, lathing her with my tongue as I ran it up and down her slit. I could eat her pussy all day it was that good.

Her taste was sweet, untainted, and knowing that I was the first one she'd shared this with only added to the pleasure.

I reached down and released my cock out of her sight giving it some much needed relief. Then I opened her little pussy with my fingers to see just how small she really was.

Her pussy hole was compact and tight and there was no way I was getting the python in there. My head swam with images as I thought of the best way to open her up so she could take all of me.

I dove back into her pussy with my tongue while

easing a long thick finger inside her. I moved it around as best I could while sucking on her clit but her tightness fought me.

I pulled out my finger and gave her my tongue again before trying again. This time I used the sawing action and got my finger deeper inside her.

I don't know where she learned it, maybe it was her natural sexuality but when I looked up her body again, she was pulling on her tits as her head moved from side to side and her hips moved in lustful circles.

Good, she was still with me. I knew by now there was no way to avoid hurting her and I thought it best to get the hard part over with so that I could comfort her afterwards.

If my cock got any harder it'll kill her, not that it could get any harder. It was already harder than it had ever been before and I didn't even know that shit was possible.

I got to my feet and kicked off my jeans while pulling my shirt over my head before laying on top of her.

She accepted me without question, wrapping her arms around my shoulders as she lifted her lips for my kiss.

I wondered how she'd react to her own taste on my tongue but I needn't have, she loved it. She ate at my tongue while I eased my finger in and out of her pussy, stretching her as much as I could.

I was able to get two fingers inside her while my cock revolted. I leaked pre cum all over her thigh and onto the sheets. Copious amounts of the shit, was coming out of me, like someone had turned on a hose.

I used some of it to grease up my length before tapping the entrance to her pussy with the head of my cock, once again testing her.

51

DEVON

Reality tried to intrude, and I had one moment of doubt, before pushing it aside for good. She was nobody's daughter now; no one else had any claims on her but me.

Her eyes widened at the first feel of my cock as the fat head stretched her opening. "It's gonna be okay, just hold onto me."

She nodded her head shyly and her hands came to my shoulders and held on. "Look at me." She opened her eyes on mine and I saw the pain mixed with hunger.

I gritted my teeth against the strain of holding back. I had about half an inch of the fat bulbous head of my cock inside her and it was torture.

I pushed forward a little more until the head popped in

and her pussy had a strangle hold on my meat. "Merciful fuck!"

I thought I was going to shoot right then and there. Her wet heat teased the tip of my cock, while the rest of me was dying to get in.

My cock spat fuck juice inside of her, oiling the way for my length. It took ten minutes of me sawing in and out of her to get the first four inches of my cock inside her.

I teased her clit with my fingers and sucked on her nipples until they were red and sore. I'd brought her off I don't know how many times just to ease the pain of what I was doing to her, and each time it had the added benefit of loosening her up some.

Taking her ass in my hands, I planted my feet on the floor, opened her up wider and drove another three inches into her belly.

I looked down between us at her scream to make sure I hadn't torn her. She was stretched tight around my cock and the sight was almost too much.

I pulled out about three inches and grabbed her hips in my hands before pounding back in. This time I got eight of my thirteen inches inside her, and this time I covered her scream with my mouth as I felt her maidenhead give way under the marauding pressure of my cock.

I pulled her tight against me as her body shook with shock, and soothed her with soft words and even softer kisses.

"Give me your mouth. It's going to be okay." I forced myself to hold still while feeding on her lips. I could feel my cock thumping away inside her as she squeezed around me like a vise.

I ran my rough hand down her ass and around to the place where we met, teasing her with my fingers back and forth.

When one of my fingers touched her puckered little rosebud she went nuts and pushed her ass back against my finger hard.

"You like that?" I did it again only this time I let the tip of my finger slip into her ass. She fucked herself down on my cock.

She was so tight she only got another inch or so but I'd found what I needed. I left my fingertip in her ass and worked my cock in and out of her, opening her up to take more.

Her lips were raw and I had half my finger in her ass by the time I had nine inches in her. "Devon it hurts."

"I know baby, I'm going as slow as I can." I eased my finger in and out of her ass while pulling her down on my cock.

I fucked her with that nine inches while fingering her ass and it was the best feeling in the world. I closed my eyes and just let myself feel.

I opened all my other senses and now I could feel the soft velvet of her pussy as it gloved my cock. The undulations as she clenched and released, and the hot silkiness of her juices.

"Take more baby." I rolled her fully onto her back, which caused my finger to slip out of her ass, but she was too preoccupied with the new fullness inside her as I forced more of my cock home.

"Put your legs higher for me baby." I helped pull her legs up around my waist and lifted her ass again, fucking into her deeper.

'That's it, I'm almost all the way inside you." She hadn't tensed up again so I knew the pain was easing.

I took her nipple between my teeth to keep her mind off of what I was doing to her and the pain I was most certainly causing.

Her pussy made those wet soppy noises each time I pulled out and slid back into her heat. Her hips moved with mine, keeping pace and I was damn near ready to cum.

I pulled out all the way and she whined. Her whine turned into a sigh when I gave her mouth and drank her juices.

My tongue fit a little easier in her cunt this time and I had more room to play. Her body took over and she moved against my mouth as she let herself go.

I gabbed my cock and squeezed off so I didn't waste my seed on the bed. I wanted it all inside her, deep inside her.

I brought her off with my mouth before straddling her and turning her onto her tummy. "Lift." I pulled her ass in the air while pushing her shoulders down all the way with her head turned to the side.

"Spread your legs for me baby." She opened her legs wide and cocked her ass higher in the air. Her pussy peeped open a little and I ran my finger down her ass to her slit.

I pushed first one than two fingers into her and worked them around until she started humping my hand and grunting.

Pulling my fingers out, I led my cock into her, holding it at the halfway point so that I didn't go too deep too fast.

She pushed back in need and I fed her more of my cock, watching as the thick head stretched her open. "Grab the sheets."

Her little hands came out from under her and fisted the sheets. I took her hips between my hands and fucked into her in short hard jabs until my cock slid in easier and easier with each stroke.

She fucked back on my cock and shook her head from side to side as I concentrated on fucking her without tearing her.

I placed a hand under her stomach so I could feel how deep I was in her. The rubbery surface of her cervix rubbed against my cockhead at the ten inch mark and I felt around for that rough patch of flesh that every woman has inside her that drives them crazy.

I knew I'd found it when she yipped and jerked on my cock. Her screams were so loud I had to pull her head back and cover her mouth with mine, feeding her my tongue to muffle the sound.

"Umm, fuck baby you're so tight." I fucked into her harder, letting more of my cock slip into her. Her neck was at an odd angle, pulled back the way it was but she didn't seem to care.

Her ass bounced against my lower stomach each time I pounded into her and she bit my tongue as pussy juice ran down my cock and onto my thigh.

I slid my hand from her tummy to her clit and rubbed it gently as I forced my cock into her womb. She screamed into my mouth and I eased out, but I wanted that tight feeling of her cervix snapping around my cockhead again so I went back in.

I did that over and over again until she got used to it and her screams turned into moans. I cupped her breasts and pulled her back onto my cock until there was just a few inches left.

There was no way I was getting the rest of me into her now, not this first time, not unless I wanted to damage her. But what there was inside her was more than enough.

Once her pussy relaxed and I knew I was no longer

hurting her, well not too much anyway, I let myself go and fed her my cock without hesitation.

I had to release her lips so we could breathe and her head fell forward once again. I leaned over her back and fixed her the way I wanted with her hands planted under mine, back straight and her ass canted.

I slammed my cock in and out of her, butting against her cervix each time, loving the way her pussy juiced all over my cock.

"Cum for me baby I'm close." I teased her clit again and fucked her nice and slow while tugging on her nipple with my free hand.

Her pussy locked down around me and stopped me in my tracks. I felt every movement of her hot cunt as she came. "Let go!"

She had too tight a grip on my cock and I couldn't move. It took three tries with my finger on her clit and her heavy breast being squeezed in my hand for her to ease up on her hold.

"That's it, fuck. I'm sorry baby, I have to…" I broke off and just let go, pounding into her pussy like a crazed beast while she just knelt there and took it, pushing her ass back harder against me, arching her back deeper.

I bit into her neck when I felt my balls tighten and the seed rise in my sac. I should pull out, things were still so uncertain in her life, and I was taking a big risk. But I couldn't.

I wanted to plant my seed in her, could already imagine this sweet innocent with the body made for sin swollen with my child.

My thoughts made me a little bit rough and I bit into her flesh a little harder than intended, leaving my mark as I shot off inside her.

It felt like I was cumming for a good few minutes with no let-up in sight. Each time I thought I couldn't possibly have any more cum in my balls she'd squeeze her inner pussy muscles along my cock and I'd dribble a little more inside her.

Her body gave out and fell limply onto the bed with my cock still lodged inside her. I ran my hands over her ass and around to her tummy, whispering softly to her as we both came down.

I looked at her in amazement that something so little had been able to take me. "Did you get it all in?" She was still catching her breath when she asked.

"Next time baby, you're too small to take all of me." She looked over her shoulder at me and I saw a different person.

Gone was the innocent who'd seduced me with her dance on the beach and in her place was a wild siren. Her hair was all over the place, her lips red and puffy and her eyes sexily dreamy. I'd never seen anything so beautiful in my life.

She pouted prettily at me and her next words had my

cock jumping inside her. “But I want all of you.” The little tease pushed her ass back teasingly, taking more of my semi hard cock.

“Stop that, I can’t take you again tonight.” I pushed into her contrary to my words and let her tease me with her tight pussy as she licked my lips and pushed her tongue into my mouth.

“No baby, we have to stop.” I was already fucking into her again as I spoke. Her ass was a soft enticement against my stomach as I ground my cock into her moving from side to side, batting against what I was sure were her sore walls.

I wanted to hold her, needed to feel her under me in some primal need to dominate her as I looked into her eyes.

With that thought in mind I pulled out and put her on her back before sliding back into her. I closed my eyes against the feelings that overwhelmed me.

This time I fed on her pert nipples, rolling them around my tongue as I surged into her tight pussy. I no longer feared hurting her, she was taking my cock like she’d been born to it.

I felt more and more of my cock enter her, stretching her more around my cock as he went in search of her sweet spot.

Once I found it I made her crazy, nipping her nipples

before easing the sting with my tongue and moving on to the next.

"Fuck yourself on my cock, take what you need." She needed no more instruction as she moved herself on and off my cock, slowly at first until she found her rhythm.

The harder I fucked the wilder she became until I couldn't tell who was fucking who. She used my cock for her own pleasure, cumming time and again while pushing her nipple harder into my mouth.

I slipped and slid into her, her pussy's juice making it easier for me to pound into her. The bed banged into the wall as the wind picked up outside and I was no longer worried about her screams being heard.

I brushed the sweat -drenched hair back from her face and looked down at her lust filled eyes. When she trailed her finger down my cheek I caught it between my teeth before drawing it into my mouth and sucking down hard suggestively.

"I love you." Her eyes widened and the most beautiful smile spread across her face before she pulled my head down to hers and took my lips.

And when she gave me back the words in a soft whisper in my ear, I felt the last bit of doubt leave me. "Mine!"

52

KELLY

~

I pressed my ear against the wall of the cottage straining to hear that sound again. "What are you doing mischief? Don't you think you're in enough trouble for one night?"

I jumped back and away from the wall. "Nothing, nothing at all." What I was doing was trying to see if I'd heard what I thought it was or if it was just the howl of the wind.

If it was indeed what I suspected then it meant my little plan had worked completely. Maybe it is just one of those clichés but since I'd found love with Quinn, I find myself wanting everyone to feel the same.

It was obvious to anyone with eyes that Ariel had the hots for Devon and he wasn't fairing much better the way he eats her up with his eyes whenever they're in the same room together.

I put thoughts of my innocent meddling aside and enjoyed the sight of my half naked man. He'd just come from the shower and was rubbing the water from his hair with one towel while another was wrapped snuggly around his hips.

My mouth begun to water when I saw the tent his cock made in the towel and my hands itched to touch.

He gave me one of his looks as if he could see into my head and read my thoughts and I had to squeezed my legs together and bite my tongue to hold back the moan of lust.

"Come here." He dropped the towel from his hair and I ran and jumped into his arms, wrapping my legs around his hips. His oversized shirt that I'd filched to sleep in rode high on my hips and his towel opened.

"Ummmm!" His hard flesh hit me in the perfect spot and I ground myself against him in need. I felt the wet tip of his manhood brush against my warm thigh and a shiver ran through me.

"I should spank your ass for the little stunt you pulled earlier."

"How do you know it was me?"

"Because the others have learned their lessons well and they know better."

"Do you really want to discuss this now?" I tried

getting his tongue back into my mouth but he nipped my chin and evaded me.

I whined and rubbed myself against him until he gave me what I wanted. I felt his big rough hands on the heated flesh of my ass and my body grew wetter.

It had only been a few hours since we last made love but as the days go by it seems I want him all the time.

The job they're working keeps him away for long hours each day and keeps us apart, but I still look at our time here like a vacation. And once he gets through with this mission, I have another little plot I've been working on with the girls to spring on him.

Right now my only interest though was in getting him inside me. Though his days have been full and mine have been taken up with getting to know my new family, the nights have all been ours.

In the short time we've been together he's taught me a lot. Some of which I never knew were possible, like when he forced his monster cock in my ass and I thought I was going to die, only for the pain to give way to the most intense pleasure.

Or when he brought me off with just his tongue on my nipple, or when I almost scalped him when he gave me his mouth while fingering my ass.

Now he walked us back towards the bed and laid me there. I felt no shame when I spread my legs and rolled the shirt up my stomach until it caught beneath my breasts.

His eyes went right to my pussy and that flash of red slashed across his cheeks as his nostrils flared. I ran my finger teasingly down my middle until I reached my weeping snatch.

His eyes flew up to mine and I knew he was dying to ask me where I'd learned that, but I wasn't about to give away any secrets.

My new sisters were shy in the beginning but once they got going there was a lot to learn and I was an avid learner.

I knew Kat was right, that he liked what I was doing by the way he bit into his lip and looked at me with such hunger I had a mini orgasm.

He dropped the towel finally from around his hips and came to me, spreading my legs even farther. I thought for sure he was going to pound into me and ease the ache that was growing inside but instead he got down on his knees beside the bed and pulled my ass off the edge.

Now I was the one screaming when he drove his tongue into me deep. My eyes rolled back in my head when he pulled his tongue from my body and nibbled on my clit.

I've heard of women having to tell their man what they needed but with Quinn, he had all the bases covered.

Just when I thought how good it would feel to have his finger teasing my ass, he was there ten-steps ahead.

When I wanted his tongue back inside of me he was

there, this time with a finger on my clit, adding to my pleasure.

I was going to die from sensory overload but what a way to go. I tugged hard on my aching nipples and yipped when he bit the inside of my thigh.

"Leave them, it'll feel even better when I take you into my mouth."

"But I want…"

"I said leave them, hands at your sides, or better yet." He lifted my legs and had me hold my ankles in the air while he went back to feasting on my pussy that was now embarrassingly wet.

"Fuck yourself on my tongue until you cum." How could I not? With a finger in my ass and one on my clit pressing down just right, his tongue driving in and out of me, I came screaming over and over until I was exhausted.

He was in a teasing mood, because once I came down with a few laps of his tongue, he went back for more.

"Yes-yes-yes, oh Quinn now please." I wasn't above begging, pleading, crying to get what I want. But the fiend ignored me and kept sucking away at my clit before sticking his tongue inside me again.

"Oh fuck Quinn, now." He spanked my hip and the sting of his hand had me flooding his mouth with my juices. I was amazed that I had any left.

By the time he got up from between my thighs I was a limp noodle, lifeless and completely replete with pleasure.

I came back to life when he plopped down beside me and pulled me over him to straddle his lap and his beautiful cock.

With my lip caught between my teeth in concentration I grabbed his cock and eased it into me inch by inch until my ass met his thighs. I took a moment to enjoy the feel of having him inside me, filling me up.

"Now ride my cock like a good girl." True to his word, he snagged my swaying tit into his mouth and bit down sending me over the edge again.

I hopped up and down on his huge cock, letting him batter my walls as my juices ran down between us.

He chewed on my nipple and that finger found its way in my ass again which was all I needed to have me climbing again until I thought I would go mad with pleasure.

'Too much Quinn, it's too much." My words came out short and choppy.

"Not enough." He threw me to my back, pulled my legs up over his shoulders and slammed into me until I lost what little breath I had left.

If not for the wild wind outside I'm sure the whole island would've heard the racket I made, but I didn't care. I never wanted the pounding to end, never wanted to be without the feel of his hard thick flesh stretching me.

He grunted and moaned as he fed on my tits, his hips moving faster and faster as he pounded his cock harder into me.

"Oh fuck, oh shit." I think this time he's going to kill me for sure. There were times in the last few days when I felt near death when we were making love, but this time I was sure it was going to happen.

No one can survive this much pleasure; it's just not natural. My body bounced off the bed beneath his with each pounding stroke and even the slapping sounds we made as our hips met made my pussy wet.

"Don't stop don't stop don't…I'm cumming." I dug my nails into his ass and pushed my nipple into his mouth as I went up and over.

When I came to he was licking a path of fire down my tummy until he reached my clit and nibbled. "My hot little sailor girl."

"That's me!" I smiled, feeling happier than I ever have in my life.

I wasn't at all surprised when he started all over again, only this time he threw me to my hands and knees once he was through tormenting me with his tongue, and drove into me until I howled and tore the sheets from the bed.

DEVON

She was everything I dreamed of and more and I couldn't believe my luck in finding her. I was still coming to terms with the fact that I could even deserve someone like her.

My little lover was fast asleep in my arms after a torrid night of lovemaking. After the second time I took her I'd gone into the bathroom to run us a bath.

By the time I got back to the bed she was half asleep and so cuddly warm when I lifted her into my arms. I stood over the steaming water in the tub, just holding onto her and wondering still if it was all a dream.

When I stepped into the water and settled her on my lap she curled into me like a kitten and purred at the feel of the warm water rushing around us.

My cock bobbed above her hip, once again ready to get inside her, but I knew she had to be sore so I fought the need.

Her nipples pebbled beneath my hands as I washed her and I took my time and cleaned her there before making my way down her stomach with the washcloth.

"Open." I nipped her ear and pulled her legs open wider so I could soothe her sore pussy with the soft cloth and my fingers.

I got lost in my head and didn't realize what I was doing until she started undulating her hips, pressing her ass back into my cock which was now trapped between us.

I'd been making circular patterns on her clit with my fingers over the washcloth and nibbling on her neck because I could not resist touching her in some way.

She moaned feverishly and turned in my arms, lifting her already swollen lips to mine. I knew better but that did not stop me from lowering my head and taking her lips as softly as I could without hurting her.

My hands found her breasts and hefted their weight before my fingers found her nipples and teased.

I had moved one hand down between her thighs and kept the other on the tit, slipping my finger into her heat as I pinched her nipple a little harder to test her.

She ground herself harder against me and I pushed my tongue deeper into her mouth as I lifted her and sat her on my cock.

She was able to take more of me this way as I leaned her forward a bit with a hand on her shoulder and rocked my hips driving my cock deeper into her.

"Ah fuck, I can stay inside you all night." I wrapped my arms around her middle as she clasped the edges of the tub and slammed her pussy down hard on my cock.

"That's it, bounce on my cock."

"Uhhhhh." She arched her neck sending her head back and rotated her hips round and round, fucking herself on my cock.

I cupped her tits and bit into her neck as she worked my cock in her tight pussy until my balls filled.

I found her pussy under the water and teased her clit while fucking up into her hard. Maybe the water made it easier but she wasn't making those pussy-hurt noises any longer and I took that to mean I could let go.

I had the mad urge to sink my teeth deep into her flesh as her cunt tightened and released around me, and I did.

I marked her everywhere as she creamed all over my cock. Water splashed over the sides of the tub wetting the floor as I pounded harder and faster.

I could see her tits bouncing in the mirrored wall across the room; see the look of utter joy on her face as she took her pleasure.

Her eyes were closed, her head thrown back so she didn't see me watching her and I watched my fill. She was spectacular! Her tits were the perfect size to fit in my hands, or feed my sons.

The thought had me dropping my eyes to her flat stomach and my cock grew inside her at the thought of filling her belly with my seed.

Suddenly I wanted that more than anything else in the world. No one could take her from me then; not that they stood a chance.

After tonight I'm sure I would walk through fire to keep her. Because I knew as sure as I knew my own name that I would never find anyone else like her again.

"I love you so much." I squeezed her hard enough to cut off her circulation but all she did was squeeze down around my cock and lift her hand back and behind my head. "I love you more."

The feelings of love that rushed through me then was unlike anything I've ever known. No achievement, no accolade, had ever made me feel the way she did. And she was all mine.

53

DEVON

I rolled over the next morning to an empty bed. My first reaction was fear that something had happened, that the dream had been snatched away before it had begun. But I reminded myself that had something happened to her my brothers would've told me.

The phone rang as I jumped out of bed and I grabbed it on the first ring. "Yo!"

"Dev you might wanna get over here brother."

"Ariel." I barely got her name past my lips as a lump of cold fear lodged in my gut.

"She's okay but you're needed. Get the lead out."

Since it didn't sound like there was any danger I had a quick shower to get the smell of stale sex off me before hurrying out the door. I missed her already.

I looked in the room where the women like to hang out but she wasn't there and that's when I took the stairs two at a time.

When Mancini let me into the room I came upon a sight that was very confusing. "What's going on what's she doing here?"

Her face fell a little at my harsh tone but she had no place in this room. Then another thought hit me in the gut. "You didn't…"

"No, we didn't, just calm down." Quinn answered me knowing without me having to say that I was asking if they'd told her the truth about who she was.

"Okay then what is she doing here? I don't want her involved in this."

"I'm afraid it's too late for that." Mancini spoke like he was gritting his teeth and I didn't get it.

"Since Khalil resurfaced we haven't been able to get a bead on him. He's even more slippery than in the past, especially since the general was killed."

"Logan…" I started to tell him not to mention that fucker in front of her but then she spoke and I got chills of another kind down my spine.

"I can find him."

"You, how?"

"Does he use the internet at all that you know of? Can you get ahold of anything he's sent over the waves in the last year at least?"

"I can get it." Mancini moved across the room.

"Then that's all I need. I can find him anywhere."

"How did you learn how to do this?" I was afraid I already knew the answer to that. Looks like I'm going to have to have a talk with her little brother.

"My brother taught me. SIGINT is like child's play to me." She grinned at me and knotted her hair at her nape, folded her legs beneath her and flexed her fingers. The girl is a fucking enigma.

I lifted my brow at the others with a silent question of 'what the fuck'. "Ariel go join the other women I'll get you when Mancini has what you need."

She was playing with the computer as if amazed. "Oh can't I just play a little bit? This system is ice." Say what now? That did not sound like her at all.

"Go!" I pulled her up from the chair and walked her out of the room. I stole a quick kiss before sending her on her way.

"Ohhhh, kissy-kissy I see you've decided to stop playing the village idiot."

"Fuck, I forgot this whole place is rigged. Mind your own damn business Ty." Asshole!

"Okay what's going on, how did she know about this shit?"

"Don't look at us, she's the one who came to us."

"What? I don't understand." I'd made it a point not to drop even a hint of this shit in her presence and knew my brothers and the others knew the protocol.

No one approaches another man's woman with this kinda shit, and these fuckers have been claiming she was mine before I took the plunge.

Mancini came back from making his call. "By the way Lyon, I need you to find out what your kid did when she was in here the other day."

"Why what happened?"

"Well, apparently she left something behind and the women were able to listen in on a secure room. I'm sure my wife had something to do with it and I'll be dealing with her shortly."

"Wait, they know?"

"Not all of it thank fuck, but they know enough." Mancini did not seem pleased. But that was probably due to the fact that his woman had somehow outsmarted him.

"And they heard the name Khalil and Nessa filled them in on the rest I'm sure. Now they're back to playing detective." Zak chimed in.

"How the fuck did this happen? She's a fucking princess for fuck sake. She can't get caught up in this Lo."

"She doesn't know that. As to how they know Mancini has some ideas on that."

"They sent in the little one is my guess. Your woman didn't say too much, in fact she didn't give us shit. Only that she could help us find Khalil."

"Well fuck. Did you get what she asked for and how come she can do something no one else in this room can?"

"Because if her brother taught her what he knows, then she's better than all of us combined. And with my equipment she'd be damn near invincible. It'll be a few hours on the other thing I have my guy on it."

"I'm not sure about this. What if she…?"

"You're going to have to tell her sooner or later bro." Quinn answered my unasked question because he knew where my mind had gone. What if she finds out that she was the target and why?

And that's what I was afraid of. How would she react? Yesterday I didn't have this fear in my gut. I hated the idea of losing her for any reason sure, but now after what we'd shared, I couldn't even breathe at the thought.

"Okay what else is going on what did I miss?"

"Nothing much, if she's as good as she says then we should be done with this whole mess before the week is out."

"But we've still got the others that were involved and Thorpe hasn't gotten back to us yet with any news about the missing girls."

"That's all being taken care of, all we need to worry about is this Khalil; everything else like I said is being handled as we speak." Mancini looked around the room before going on.

"Once we've taken care of this asshole, we'll of

course make sure all the women have been accounted for, if not we'll go from there, but for now, we concentrate on cutting off the head of the snake."

"And her father, the old king." I still hadn't worked out in my head how I was going to deal with that part of the equation. All I knew was that she wasn't going anywhere.

"Yeah about that, have you spoken to Samson yet?"

"No, I tried after the last time we saw him but he isn't picking up but I bet we can guess where he is. If he's anything like the CO you know he's not trusting shit, and with his daughter caught in the middle, he's going to be extra careful."

"I have a feeling when the time comes those boys will find you." Mancini said that like he knew something we didn't and of course his ever-present smirk said as much.

"Speaking of fathers, have anybody realized yet that out of all of us Dev is completely fucked?"

"What the fuck are you talking about Tyler?"

"You not only have one, but two fathers-in-law. Not only that but look at who the fuck they are. What? You and Quinn were competing to see who could bag the most hard nosed father in law?"

"Well shit! Lo!"

"Don't sweat it Dev. She's yours, ain't nobody taking what's yours." I see how women make men weak. It has nothing to do with physical prowess, but with the mind.

Until she came into my life a few days ago I never knew this kind of fear. Now I'm afraid of every damn thing. Afraid of losing her, of her being hurt; fear of my life without her. Fuck!

"You know I'm just playing brother, I'm happy for you." Ty slapped me on the neck and went back to arguing with Lyon about who knows what. Those two are worst than an old married couple.

"So what do we do now? Wait around, what about the senator, where's he?"

"Cool your jets Lyon, your pigeon haven't flown the coop."

"What do you plan to do to him anyway Colt?"

"Well Ty my boy, Every normal man must be tempted, at times, to spit on his hands, hoist the black flag, and begin slitting throats."

"Oh shit Lyon, you read Mencken?"

"What's even more surprising Justice, is that you do."

"He had a few good points but he was a racist fuck so I just took what I liked and left the rest."

"Same here. I liked his views on inferior men ruling their superiors cause I'm fucked if our government haven't proven that shit time and again."

We all nodded and changed the subject to something more important. The women and what the hell we were going to do about their meddling shit.

"Colt, looks like you're gonna have to have another talk with your woman."

"Nah brother, a real man always lets his woman show her claws when it's warranted."

"Huh?" Even Ty was confused.

"I thought you said…."

"Didn't any of your women tell you what was going on?"

There were a lot of nopes and head shaking going on. "Well, unlike you chupacabras my woman talks to me. She didn't tell me how she got the information because that would be telling on her girls, but she did tell me they knew some stuff."

"Once I got her to promise me that all they were doing is talking and surmising and that they will stay the fuck outta grown men's business, it was all good."

"The way I see it, they're not doing anything more than what we're doing here. The cat's already outta the bag, and they're not gonna stop until they get what they want. Choose your battles boys."

"What the hell do they want?"

"Cord, do you talk to your woman? What about the rest of you?"

"Yeah, sure…"

"And you still don't know what they want?"

Each man looked around at each other like, 'what the hell did I miss?' And then Ty had the answer. "Weddings."

"You got it. Now see I don't have that problem." Lyon grinned while most of the room grumbled.

"And I'm not wearing no damn monkey suit on the damn beach, shit's just all kinds a fucked up."

"Wait what? What're you talking about on the beach? You mean here?"

"I'm not sharing my wife's pillow talk with you freaks, talk to your women."

"And Hank as to me telling Mengele shit about bugging your place or whatever the fuck it is she did, fuck no you're on your own."

"I haven't had this much peace from her meddling ass since the day she was born. Here, she has a whole smorgasbord to choose from. I haven't caught her listening in at my door in a while. The rest of you…good luck."

"Where is she? Maybe she knows what the women are up to."

"It depends. If her loyalty is to them, and I have reason to believe the little shit is a staunch feminist, then she's not gonna give you shit."

"But she'll tell you."

"Don't kid yourself Connor. She only tells on her mother because she knows her mother's ass would get into trouble if I didn't catch half her shit before it got off the ground. But if those women have their hooks in her you're fucked."

"Then again she does like a good bribe sometimes when she's playing both sides."

"You do realize you're discussing a five year old right."

"If you say so, remember, I warned you."

"Well if all we're doing is waiting and it's still raining outside, I'm going back to bed."

I ignored their frat boy hooting and Ty's kissy faces and left the room. I walked into the room where the women had gone totally silent as soon as I opened the door.

I stopped where I was and crooked my finger at her. No way was I going in there with my sisters looking at me like fresh meat.

"Hi Devon, how are you?" Gaby called out to me when Ariel got up from her seat and came to me.

"Hi Gaby, hi ladies, bye ladies." I closed the door on their laughter. They really are just as bad as the men

"I woke up and you weren't there." I had her hand in mine as we walked in the light drizzle back to the cottage.

"I'm sorry about that, I tried to wait until you woke up but you were taking too long." I'm guessing that was a dig at the fact that she'd put me on my ass after a night of the hottest sex anybody ever had anywhere.

"It's not nice baby, not good etiquette to leave my bed without telling me. I reached for you and you weren't there." What the fuck? I sound like a whiny little brat.

"I'm sorry, I won't do it again." She said in a childlike monotone and lifted her puckered lips up to me for a kiss."

I smooched her and pulled her under my arm feeling happier than any man had a right to. "You're forgiven, just don't let it happen again."

I squeezed her shoulder and grumped and she laughed. It was the most beautiful sound I'd ever heard. The shit went right through me, touched something in my heart and set off sparks. I've become a damn girl.

As soon as we closed the door behind us I had my mouth on hers. "I missed you Devon. I waited and waited for you to wake up."

"Next time just wake me up baby."

"But you looked do peaceful I didn't want to disturb you. Sometimes sleep is the only peace we know."

I looked at her, pleased with her, and happy for us. Her years in seclusion hadn't stunted her the way I first thought.

She's bright and sweet and so what if she doesn't see life the way everyone else does, that's a good thing as far as I'm concerned.

Her innocence was no longer something to bemoan but celebrate. Little nuggets of truth like the one she just made just rolls off her tongue.

So simple and yet so profound! "You're absolutely

right baby." I wrapped my arms tighter around her and kissed her forehead.

"But I want you to wake me whenever you need me. As a matter of fact, no matter what I'm doing, if you need me, you come get me okay."

"Okay Devon. Now did you bring me back here to talk or…" She gave me an impish grin and those dimples sent a jolt straight to my dick.

I growled and she squealed and pulled out of my arms, running towards the bedroom.

I caught up with her and took her down. A long much needed kiss followed before I lifted my heavier weight on my arms and looked down at her.

"You're an extremely beautiful woman Ariel and I'm going to spend the rest of my life making you very happy." I brushed at the wisps of hair at her temple.

"I want to play with you." The rain had picked up outside and was beating against the windows and on the roof, making the place feel cocooned, almost like we were alone.

"Play with me?"

"Yes, I want to take my time and learn your body and teach you mine. Would you like that? Would you like me to learn your body, what pleases you? Teach you what pleases me?"

She nodded her head and bit down on the thumb I

slipped into her mouth while staring up into my eyes. “Then let’s begin.”

So eager! “Tell me if anything I do scares you okay.” She nodded and lifted her arms for me to take her top off.

I leaned in and took her lips first. That little tease back at the mansion had barely wet my appetite. When I’d had my fill I pulled back, “promise me.”

“I promise, but I won’t be scared. I’ve always been curious about sex. It’s the one thing my brother would never discuss with me even though I’m older. He always got so embarrassed.”

“I’m glad, because I want to be the one to teach you, everything.”

“Devon!”

“Yeah baby?” I kissed her nose because I couldn’t resist.

“Stop talking and show me.” Smartass!

54

DEVON

~

"Okay miss curious, first I'm going to bring you off with just my fingers while I teach you how to suck my cock." She tried hiding her face in my chest but I lifted her chin.

"First rule of lovemaking, there's nothing to be embarrassed about when we're together. If there's something you want to try you tell me."

"I have a question."

"Shoot."

"Did you cum inside me?"

"Yes, every time."

The question made my cock jump and reminded me of how innocent she truly was. She didn't say anything else about it so I stripped her and then myself before lying across the bed.

I gave her time to look me over before pulling her down so that she was lying with her head at my cock and her pussy at my mouth, but with her back turned to me.

I ran my fingers teasingly along the slit of her pussy from behind, which was already wet and led her hand to my cock.

I kept her hand under mine and stroked up and down. "Like this." I showed her until she caught on and then moved my hand.

"It's so soft and so hard at the same time." I looked down to see her studying my dick up close and personal.

I pulled her top leg up and open and ran my thumb along her slit before dipping it inside. She moaned and pushed down on my thumb as her hand moved faster on my cock.

I was leaking pre-cum rapidly now and she used that to make it easier for her hand to slide up and down on my rod.

My cock was already steel hard and I was rethinking my idea of showing her the ropes when all I could think of was getting back inside her.

"Okay baby that's good." She was thorough as fuck and I had a lump in my throat.

"Now I want you to just lick the tip. Don't take it into your mouth yet, just use your tongue."

She tongued my cockhead while I pushed my thumb in and out of her pussy slowly, teasingly. I used the four fingers of the same hand to massage her clit and her whole pussy, still with the same slow soft movements.

I pushed the fingers of my other hand into her mouth while she was licking my cock and showed her with my fingers how to suck on my cock.

Her hips were gliding back and forth, pushing back on my thumb, but I controlled her movements. "Slowly!" She slowed down for a minute and concentrated on her technique.

She licked around my cock like an ice cream cone while I fingered her and each time my finger went in deep she'd clench and pull off my cock.

I moved my thumb faster inside her and sped up the four on her clit, easing off when she got close. She whined but her mouth went back to my cock.

'That's what it feels like every time you pull off my cock in the middle of giving me head." She nodded her understanding and made love to my cock in her inexperienced but very effective way.

She licked, she sucked she teased until she had the first few inches in her mouth. "Remember, no matter what you feel, don't stop sucking my cock. If you do I'll take my fingers from you again."

She nodded and kept her mouth tight around my cock as she experimented with sucking hard and then licking around my cock before sticking her tongue in the small slit at the top.

I dug around inside her for her sweet spot and once I found it rotated my thumb over it. I knew she felt it because she scraped my cock with her teeth in her excitement.

I gritted my teeth through the pleasure pain and rewarded her for not pulling off by fingering her to another orgasm. Her hips and ass were moving wildly now against the pleasure of my fingers and she screamed around my cock.

She paused for the barest of seconds but didn't lose her rhythm. Her pussy juiced and clenched around my thumb as she bobbed her head on and off my cock.

I didn't give her any warning when I exchanged my fingers for my tongue. Just pulled her ass back farther, spread her legs wider, and lowered my head to her pussy from behind.

I ate her pussy like a piece of fruit, enjoying the taste and scent of her as I dug my tongue in deep. I loved the way she moved against my mouth like she was trying to get my whole head in there.

She went nuts on my cock, taking more of me into her warm mouth, her head moving faster and faster to keep pace with her hand as it continued to stroke me into her mouth.

I ate her to two more orgasms while holding off my own. When I could no longer hold back I pulled my tongue from her pussy and pushed my fingers back inside her.

"I'm going to cum in your mouth. Keep stroking and sucking but don't forget to breathe or you'll choke."

I took her free hand and led it to my balls that were full and ready to explode. She played with them gently at first until she realized that she wasn't hurting me.

Her hand on my nuts, her mouth on my cock and my fingers in her pussy bringing her scent to me sent me over the edge.

I felt the heat from my seed as it rose and flooded my cock before spilling into her mouth. She tried to get it all but it was too much and was soon running down her chin.

I wrapped my hand around my cock, squeezing off my flow, which was not the most comfortable feeling, but there was something I just had to do.

"Ease off baby. Lie on your back." She did it with a questioning look on her face, but it changed to one of delight when I knelt over her with my cock in my hand and stroked the last of my seed onto her face and tits.

Before she could say anything I took her mouth and pulled her up in a hug. I lied back against the pillows, pulling her over my lap to straddle me.

"Now take me into your hand and lead me into you."

She reached down between us and took my still hard cock in hand, holding it in place for her to sit on.

As soon as her tight pussy closed around the head of

my cock I took her hips in my hands and fucked up slowly feeding her only as much as she could take, until I stretched her to take more.

She wanted to go fast but I slowed her down, using my hands and mouth to inflame her senses while she rode my cock.

"Like this!" I used her hips to pull her up and down on my cock then back and forth and side to side until she caught on.

"Now do whatever makes you feel good." She pulled my hands up to her breasts and held them there while fucking herself slowly on my cock.

She used a variation of everything I showed her until her pussy tightened around my cock and she came.

Pulling her head down to mine I teased her tongue with mine playfully before leaving her mouth to take her nipple between my teeth.

Her pussy spasms and soft moans told me what she liked, how much she enjoyed what I was doing to her.

Her ass felt like heaven in my hands as I squeezed and caressed her firm flesh while fucking my cock up in her slow enough to make us both crazy.

I'd never taken this much time with a woman before. Not that I was a selfish lover, but the women in my past had all been around the block a time or two I made sure of it.

Because I couldn't commit myself one hundred

percent to anyone before, I was always careful not to get entangled.

But now, with her, everything was different. She's the woman I'm going to spend the rest of my life with. The only one I'm going to love until my last breath.

The love welled up inside me and the kiss grew hotter, more passionate and I grabbed the back of her head roughly in one of my hands as I ravished her mouth.

"Give me your tongue." She eased it into my mouth as she moved up and down on my hard cock, her pussy juice and my cock cream making it easier for her to take all of me.

"I love the way your pussy feels around my cock. And your nipples, you have the sexiest nipples. Dark and smooth, like berries."

I trailed my finger around and around her nipple before sucking it into my mouth. I let the fingers of one hand trail a path to her ass and teased her tight puckered rosebud.

Knowing that I'd only ever be able to get half of my cock in there, but knowing before long I was going to try.

"Cum for me beautiful!" I rubbed her clit with the fingers of one hand, slid the finger of the other into her ass and bit down on her nipple while she rode my cock.

Her breathing and pace sped up and so did my fingers and soon she was screaming as her pussy creamed all over my cock locking it off like a vise.

I waited until her pussy stopped its spasms before turning her on her back and with her legs over the crook of my arms, fucked her into the bed.

It was easy to forget that she was new to this. The way she moved beneath me, massaging my cock with her inner walls, as if she were trying to milk my cock and balls of sperm.

I sucked her nipple into my mouth again, leaving a mark as I pounded into her pussy hard. She dragged my head to hers and devoured me with her kiss.

I went in search of and found her sweet spot with the head of my cock and slammed into it over and over before changing up and grinding into her tight cunt.

Her legs stiffened and her back arched off the bed as I felt her warm juices coating my rod. "Fuck, you're gonna make me cum." I pressed down on her clit and her pussy clenched hard around my cock.

She howled and dragged her nails down my back until I felt pain and knew she'd drawn blood but I didn't care.

My mouth was wild on hers and I was sure I bit her but that only made her pussy tighten even more as my cock showed no mercy for her tender flesh.

"Fuck I'm cumming inside you." I didn't think it would be so soon after the first time, but everything about her was ringing my bells.

I tried to go easy, she was already halfway up the bed and I knew I was crushing her, but the way she pulled at me, the way she followed my mouth with hers like she too was starving for the taste of me wouldn't let me.

I fucked her harder, deeper than I had anyone before and when my cock started spitting off inside her I didn't want it to end.

"Give me a baby Ariel. I want to put my baby in you." She wrapped her legs and arms tighter around me, and her pussy flooded again.

I pounded out the last of my cum inside her and held still for minutes after until we could both breathe again.

"I guess that's a yes." I kissed her neck where I'd marked her in the middle of my lust fugue and licked the spot while wrapping her tighter in my arms.

"I'm going to stay inside you until they pry me off." I lifted up on my arms to take my weight off her tiny form and went in for a taste of her lips.

As soon as my tongue touched hers I started grinding my cock inside her again. "I'm going to fuck you nice and slow now. Each time you get close I'm going to stop until you beg me to let you cum."

I moved my hips from side to side with my cock buried to the hilt inside her and my face buried in her neck.

She danced beneath me taking my cock deeper and deeper until I snuck into her womb. I stopped at her flinch of pain giving her time to get used to having me there before pulling out.

I wasn't going to cum again anytime soon and my next deposit was going to be right in there. But if I stayed in there too long it'll only cause her pain so I fucked her pussy nice and slow making sure to catch her clit with my pelvic bone with each thrust.

When her body lifted mine and she bit down on my tongue that was playing in her mouth, I knew she was close. "So responsive."

I'd lost count of how many times I'd made her cum, but each one was as precious as the first.

As her body shook and I felt her clench to cum I pulled my cock out of her wet tunnel quickly and slid down the bed between her legs.

Grabbing her ass in my hands I brought her up to my mouth and dove into her pussy with my tongue. I tasted her nectar straight from the source and wanted more.

Her hands grabbed at my head and she pushed her pussy into my mouth as I fucked her with my tongue. I stroked my cock as I ate her out, keeping it steel hard for when I fuck back into her.

I brought her off in my mouth one last time before climbing back up her body and slipping into her. I brought her to climax time and time again before pulling out and finishing her off with my mouth.

The last time, when I knew that I too was close, I pulled her up and placed her on her hands and knees in the middle of the bed before lining up behind her.

Her pussy opened and closed as I jabbed at her pussy with my cockhead. I teased her with an inch at a time before pulling back.

On the last stroke I fucked into her deep with my hand around her throat to stave off her screams. I could feel my cock in her belly through the hand I had holding her tummy while I fucked her rough and crude.

I didn't touch her like she was a princess. I fucked her like she was mine; my woman, my princess. Once she got comfortable she fucked back at me through the pain and that only made me pound into her harder.

My balls swung into her pussy lips over and over, and I spanked her clit with the flat of my hand. She flung her head back and screamed silently.

Liquids ran out of her and down my thighs and that wet sound from good sex permeated the air each time I fucked into her.

Her ass moved on its own in a natural sexual heat that only spurred me on to fuck harder and harder. She arched her back and rocked back on my length one minute and the next she wiggled her ass from side to side.

When my balls drew up and I felt that sweet tingle that started in my toes and made its way up my spine I slammed past her cervix and started shooting off as soon as the tight ring of her cervix snapped around my swollen cockhead.

Her screams this time rang through the air and thankfully the rain and wind was loud outside. I stayed buried inside her until my cock finally went down and I was able to pull out of her womb without hurting her.

I turned her around swiftly and covered her lips with mine as I held her safely in my arms. “Go to sleep baby, we both need a nap.”

She smiled secretively like she knew she’d put me on my ass again, but I was too worn out to care. Next time I’ll put her little ass to sleep. It was the last thought I had before sleep took me under.

55

QUINN

~

"So when are you going to tell her?" I hated to be the one to burst his bubble. For the past two days he's been a different person.

There were no dark clouds hanging over him and the shadows were gone from his eyes, just as it was with me, and the others.

He was hardly far from Ariel's side; in fact those two disappeared as much as Kelly and I did. We've been waiting to hear back from Mancini's guy and so in the meantime we were laying back and kicking loose.

It had been raining off and on for the past three days so there really wasn't much else to do anyway and I'd enjoyed using the time getting to know my girl.

She'd fit right in it seems which makes my life easier,

and I couldn't detect any lingering fear from what she'd gone through, though I kept prodding. When I wasn't fucking her that is.

But now Mancini had called us in and it was time to get back to fuckery. But first things first, I needed to make sure my brother wasn't tearing himself up in knots the way he likes to.

"I don't know, I guess I'll have to now." He looked miserable at the question, which was understandable. I can't imagine being in his place right now.

There was no getting around the issue of her birth and who she was, and though we'd given him the last few days to enjoy without any interference, Lo had tagged me to get on him now.

We were coming down to crunch time and any minute now she'd be coming in here to do her thing in hopes of tracking down Khalil's exact location.

"It's going to be okay Dev, no matter what, everything is going to be okay." He rubbed his gut and stared off into space.

"I don't know what I'll do if I lost her now Quinn. This whole situation is fucked."

"Are you sorry that you found her?"

"No, of course not. That's the problem. If something goes wrong things will never be the same again. What if she chooses to go back?"

"Where to Khalil?"

"No, to her real dad. I mean fuck Quinn she's probably worth millions. How can I ask her to walk away from that?"

"There's another choice."

"Yeah, what's that?"

"We let Khalil live and he has no choice but to leave her in hiding."

"No way, that asshole must be stopped. Not even for my own happiness would I inflict him on the world any longer than it takes to find his ass and end him."

"I didn't think so. Now get your head out your ass, stop being a defeatist and let's get this shit done. You keep forgetting she's an adult she can make up her own mind."

"Yeah but we both know that that's not how things work in the world she was born into."

"It doesn't matter. He sent her away to keep her safe don't you think he would want her to be happy?"

"We'll see. Anyway you can tell Logan to stop worrying I know this is something I have to do."

"We're just worried about you brother, we know how you like to think things to death."

"Are you boys ready? Let's see what she can do. Go get your girl Dev." Mancini came back into the room where the rest of us were waiting.

I was excited to see what she came up with. My brothers and I have been trying forever to get any kind of line to tug on Khalil with no luck and Dev is a first class hacker.

Knowing what we know about Anonymous, they're way ahead of us to be sure, but he's nothing to sneeze at.

He left the room to go get her and I gave Lo the nod. "How's he doing?"

"He's cool he's going to take care of it soon."

"And you?"

"What about me?"

"He means that since we've been busy with this shit he hasn't had time or opportunity to stick his nose in your business."

"Tyler, shut the fuck up. Pretty much what he said; how are you and Kelly?"

"We're good, your women have been corrupting her so I have a lot to undo once we get back home but other than that, we're solid."

They each tried to convince me that their women were beatified saints, which we all knew was bullshit but at least it was good for a few laughs.

It was true though, I'm not sure if it's just blind luck, or we had someone up there pulling for us, but we each seemed to have found the perfect one.

Fathers in law and international terrorists aside, I don't think any of us could've chosen any better. I used to secretly laugh at the others when they'd lose their minds over their women.

The way they were so overprotective and domineering. I actually used to feel sorry for the girls.

Now I get it, and when we get home, I'm going to ensure that our place is even more secure than it is now. You can never be too careful.

She's strong, she's sweet and she's brave and I have no doubt that she's going to give me hell every step of the way, but whatever it takes I'll do to keep her safe.

Following Lyon's little bombshell I cornered her once we'd broken for the day that first day when the rain started and dragged her back to the cottage.

I waited until I was buried balls-deep inside her to question her. Unfair I know, but whatever works. And that's how we ended up having our first argument while I was fucking her.

She didn't see why she couldn't be part of what was going on since she was the one who'd been grabbed, and almost sold, and I didn't see the need for her to have any part in it now that she was safe with me.

She accused me of being a man, whatever the fuck that means, and some other shit that came straight out of my sisters' mouths.

When I told her that it wasn't up for debate that's when the gloves came off and I saw the admiral's daughter in full form.

She informed me that she was no and I quote 'fucking

shrinking violet and she will not be put in a corner like the others'.

And I informed her that unlike her father who obviously let her run wild, I had no problem taking a switch to her ass.

That's when she dared me. I pulled out, put her over my knee and spanked her ass. I told her it was for being insubordinate, by then I was just fucking with her.

She rolled over, tried to punch me in the eye, I caught her arms, wrestled her to the bed and finished her off with a few hard strokes that was good for both of us.

I gave her another hard fuck just because, but this time she wasn't allowed to say shit to me.

Two days later she's still sulking because she didn't get her way, so yeah we're good.

DEVON

I wish Quinn hadn't brought that shit up now. It kinda tainted the glow of the last few days. Since we weren't doing anything and it was raining cats and dogs I'd dedicated the time to getting to know her.

I learned by watching and listening that even though

she was indeed the innocent I'd first perceived her to be, she was also smart as fuck.

I let her come to me, just to be sure that this truly was what she wanted and not something new that she was fascinated by.

I don't know a lot about being in love, but I took the fact that she loved being close to me, or was always touching me in some way to mean something.

Or the way she likes to climb into my lap to be held when she's tired. In short, I saw in her the same things I was feeling myself.

The cincher was the night I watched her sleep and she called out my name with a sigh before rolling into me and settling against my heart.

If I weren't in love with her before, that would've done it for me. Plus every time I got inside her was better than the last.

So yeah, I kept my thoughts away from the danger outside the door of the little cottage that had become our haven in those two days.

But every once in a while she'd say or do something that reminded me of who she was and I'd think now would be a good time to tell her, but then my guts would hurt and I'd back off.

It wasn't so much fear that held me back, but the disruption I knew was sure to come once the truth was out.

And yeah, I guess there was a hint of uncertainty about whether or not it was right to keep her away from that other life that might be waiting for her once Khalil was eliminated.

I tried in vain to get in touch with her dad, Samson, but for some reason he still wasn't answering the damn phone, and I wasn't about to leave a message.

I spoke to Track who was still pissed, but once I assured him that she was safe he calmed down enough to tell me what it was he was up to.

Apparently the kid hacked his own father and started putting two and two together a year ago. But the old man was too careful to put the most pertinent facts down anywhere, so all he got was that it had something to do with the military.

That's when he came up with the plan to get inside. Meanwhile he told me all this shit in code that no civilian should know and if the wrong people found out about this shit he's FUBAR.

Apparently he knew this too, and I was right, he'd left the trail on purpose. I wanted to know what he planned to do with all the shit he'd uncovered, especially the things that had nothing to do with what we were dealing with here. He just smirked and logged off. Fucking kid!

I did get out of him that his sister knew what she was doing. I asked him why he'd taught her such a fucked up thing, his answer, she needs all the resources she can get and he's going to make sure she's always protected.

"What do you mean by that?"

"Have you seen her fight? No, I'm guessing there wasn't any need to."

"She can fight? What do you mean fight?"

"Ask her, we both learned from one of the best DOJOs in Asia, and an ex Moussad officer. Of course our classes had to be online because my sister as you know, was never allowed OUTSIDE. So I'll teach her whatever the fuck I want to make her feel more empowered. Got it?"

I have to say for all his brashness and total disrespect I liked the kid. I'd probably have done the same thing in his situation.

After he'd logged off I'd gone back to bed where I'd left her sleeping and drew her into my arms. I awakened her with kisses until she opened her mouth to me then turned her on her back and slid into her to the hilt.

She was getting better at taking all of me without too much pain though I knew not to do her rough when I was so deep inside her.

But I didn't want to pound into her, I wanted the sweet slow loving that lasted longer and made my heart trip in my chest.

After she came I'd pulled out and put her on her side, getting behind her and sliding back into her heat, rocking us both to orgasm.

That's how we'd fallen asleep, how I'd awakened this morning, still buried inside her. She slept through my soft caresses and pinching her nipples.

I slipped into her and made love to her while she slept until she awakened and reached her hand back to grab my ass, letting me know she was awake and wanted to play.

Once I put her on her knees and pounded out my morning lust inside her, I was finally drained. I'd put her back to bed after cleaning us both up in the shower and that's where I'd left her before Mancini sent me after her.

She was putting on her shoes when I opened the door. Her dimples winked at me when she saw it was I standing there.

"I was just about to come over, I'm starving." She threw her arms around me like it was the most natural thing in the world and I held her close, already having second thoughts about letting her do this.

"Let's get you fed then baby." I carried her out the door and she found it so funny I carried her all the way to the mansion.

Of course my sisters were sitting outside having breakfast and they had a lot to say about it. "We're not staying." No way was I handling this crowd alone, damn.

"So Devon, how's it going?"

"It's going fine Dani."

"Uh-hmm, uh-hmm, we were just discussing weddings. Are we planning six or seven?"

"Grab your fruit and muffin baby we gotta go, the others are waiting." I glared at Dani and the others who were trying their best to look innocent before getting the hell outta there.

I looked back at the table of laughing women and mouthed the word 'seven', which broke out the hoots and catcalls.

I'll deal with them later for proposing to my woman before I had a chance to. Better yet, I'll let their men handle it.

She munched on a slice of mango and grinned up at me as I carried her into the house. "I'm sorry they did that to you Devon. They don't understand that it's different for men."

"How so?"

"Well, men are more introverted than women it seems. It's true." She carried on at my skeptical look.

"Women can talk about anything, while men seem to think things through in their heads and only grunt out a few words after all is said and done, never really sharing what they really feel."

"And you've learned all this in the last few days of being here."

"Kinda, you've been live subjects but I've noticed it before from reading and stuff."

She says stuff like that with no resentment whatsoever and I wonder how she could be so accepting of her situation, especially since she didn't know the real reason behind it.

"Do you know where we're going?"

"I figure Hank has the information I need?"

"Baby, you don't have to do this." I was chickening out.

Once we walk into that room and she gets involved there's no going back. I was in a quandary here. On the one hand we'd be one step closer to putting an end to Khalil and on the other, I'd be opening Pandora's box and standing the chance of maybe losing her.

It was a choice no one should ever have to make. She turned my face to her and studied my eyes. "This has something to do with me doesn't it?"

I fought myself about telling her the truth but in the end I couldn't lie to her. "Yes!"

'Then I have to do it. And when it's done you'll tell me everything and then we'll move on."

She made it sound to easy. "By the way before I forget, I like solitaires." I didn't know what she meant at first, until she wiggled her finger at me.

I kissed her long and hard, not caring who saw, before heading upstairs where the others were waiting.

My fear came back tenfold and I had to battle it back. There was no turning back now. We'd worked long and hard to get this close and no matter what, it had to be done.

I held her close one last time, enjoying her sweet innocence. The innocence I was sure would shatter once the truth came out.

I hated it for me and for her and if there was any other way I'd do it, but I knew there wasn't. Khalil is such a paranoid fuck no one has ever been able to get into his electronics.

It's a known fact that he has expert techs working for him, some of them ex-military from different countries, some of which had gone after him before.

If she pulled this off, then she'd be one of the top in her field, criminal though it was. "Let's go baby. Are you ready?"

She nodded and clasped my cheek. "Stop worrying, nothing's gonna go wrong. You won't let it." Her faith in me left me breathless and I hoped for her sake she was right.

56

DEVON

"Nice of you to join us lover boy."

"Shut the hell up Tyler." Jackass.

"Hello Ariel, are you ready?" There was a certain reverence in Mancini's voice when he spoke to her and he all but bowed.

I gave him a look and he smiled before taking her hand and leading her to his command center. That's what we'd taken to calling it.

"What do you need from me?"

"Just the number, Devon, you sit here." She scooted over on the chair that was all but swallowing her and I sat.

There wasn't enough room so I pulled her onto my lap and watched over her shoulder as she got to work once Mancini gave her the number.

No one said anything as she concentrated and got to work, but all eyes were on her and the screen. I'm good at hacking, it's my specialty among other things so I'm pretty familiar with most of the methods used by my ilk. The shit she was doing didn't look familiar.

"What code is that?"

"Mine!" She tapped a few more keys.

"Yours!"

"Yeah! I upgraded master locater and added my own backdoors. It's much more sophisticated if I do say so myself."

"And how do you plan on keeping him from knowing that you're in his system or, from sending a trace back this way? I'm pretty sure he's savvy enough or has people who are."

"You see these first few lines here? They work kind of like a firewall. He won't know I'm in there and there's no way to trace."

"Your brother left a trace." Logan said. I hadn't had time to fill them in on my talk with her brother the night before.

"If that's true, then it was deliberate. He never gets caught." She didn't stop in her typing and her focus was razor sharp as she continued adding code almost as if she had it memorized.

"You seem pretty sure."

"Oh yeah, and from the looks of it, your friend here

isn't even close to the hardest I've breeched. He has some great security measures here but nothing I can't handle."

I looked at my brothers, because quite frankly we were never able to get into his system. He changes his phone at least once a month on top of that, and it had been a while since we'd been able to get the latest one. Kudos to Mancini and whoever he had working for him for getting it so quickly.

She did come magic on the keyboard and all I could do was stare at her as information scrolled across the screen.

She doesn't know this, but like I said, this is my specialty and she was totally showing me up in front of my brothers. I've never been more proud of anyone in my life.

The men were all making appreciative noises as they read the information as it unfolded, but I was still mesmerized by her.

Her brain has got to be like a fucking machine to do this shit on this level and I already knew she was better than me because she was already breaking through Khalil's firewalls and shields.

"Time?" I looked over at Quinn who was breathing down my neck almost as excited as I was to see if she could really do it. "Thirty three seconds."

"And we're in."

"What? No, what is this?" Are you fucking kidding

me? The record is a full minute. It takes me a little more than that.

"I not only hacked in but now you can see every number he calls and this…" She tapped a few more keys, "will record what's being said. We haven't perfected the translation code as yet so you'll have to get that some other way."

"You can do that?"

"On no you don't Hank." Fucker had a gleam in his eye. Everyone started talking at once as they studied the screen on the wall.

"Oh man, baby, that was amazing." I kissed her again and gave Tyler the finger because I caught him out the side of my eye making kissy faces.

"Good, so you can go get him now and the girls can get married and be happy." She got a little sullen there at the end and I lifted her chin with my finger.

"Do you want to get married baby?"

"Do you?" She wouldn't look at me, but pulled at the bottom of her shirt.

I had to glare at my nosy ass brothers. "I'm not talking to the rest of you." I got to my feet with her in my arms and headed out the door.

I found the nearest corner that didn't have an obvious camera pointed at us and caged her in with my hands beside her head.

"Yes I want to marry you, more than anything in the

world. Do you want to marry me? Keep in mind no matter what you say we're getting married."

She laughed and kissed my cheek. "That's more like it. The girls keep telling me about what cavemen their men are, and I keep telling them how sweet you are to me. I was beginning to think you didn't feel the same about me as your brothers do their women."

"That is one convoluted statement, but I think I get it. You don't want to be treated with kid gloves, got it."

"Well now, we all want to be treated like a princess, just, you know. Don't treat me like I'm going to break." I studied her after she said that but there was nothing in her eyes, it was just a throw away comment, the princess thing.

"You are my princess and I'll try to remember how tough you are. You just kicked my ass in there in less than a minute so I guess you're not as innocent as I thought."

I meant it as a joke but she seemed to take it as some sort of badge of honor. These women are crazy.

"Where are you taking me? Aren't we going back in?"

"Nope, you're done here. I'm taking you back to the girls."

"Devon…"

"Not this fight baby, you're not gonna win this one." I left her at the door to the media room where the women had moved. They couldn't be up to much since the kids were in there with them.

I made a hasty retreat and got the hell outta there not only because of the women but the look Lyon's kid gave me was kinda spooky.

"Hank you sure this room is secure, you got rid of whatever Catalina left in here?"

"Yeah why?"

"I don't know; she just gave me this look." I mock shivered and took a seat.

"Well her little device was a cheap bug you can pick up at any Sharper Image stuck in gum and left under the desk. Since we're all friends I didn't see the need to sweep, but I won't be making that mistake again."

"Seriously? Who the hell put her up to it?"

"Who do you think? All of them! Apparently they got their tails in a twist because Ariel shared a little bit more of her childhood than she should or that we expected her to at any rate." Damn, no one thought to tell her not to say anything.

"My wife being the fucking spook that she is, decided that there was more to the story and they started comparing notes again. That's when your wife Lyon, decided that your innocent daughter was the perfect fall guy."

"What the fuck are we dealing with here?" Law shook his head

"You didn't think this was gonna happen when you

put them all together here on an isolated island with nothing else to do?"

"Davey, they got to him somehow, because they didn't know shit before."

"Nah, he's been hanging around my people trying to learn the ropes, when he isn't moping around behind Lyon's oldest."

Lyon's jaw twitched and he looked like he was about to spaz the fuck out. "Chill Lyon, I had a talk with him and he knows she's already got a boyfriend."

"Fucking parasite. Say Hank, don't you have another one of those things you took down that plane with? I got a town I'd like to level."

The conversation switched to Lyon and his soon to be son in law, which led to my brothers and I and all the men in the room discussing offspring and their wish to father only sons because girls were too much trouble.

Of course we knew we were just letting off steam because in the next few hours we'd be heading into danger and leaving our women behind.

"Are we telling Susie and Davey the truth now or later?" I'd forgotten that Cord was in the same position as I to a certain extent.

"I thought we decided to do that after this was done."

"I know Lo but what if something goes wrong?"

"Like what Cord, what do you think is gonna go

wrong? Have we ever gone into an Op with anything less than confidence?"

"This time's a bit different Lo, this time we have pregnant women waiting for us to come back."

"Yes Con, that's why this time even more than ever we have to go in with our heads on straight. There's no room for doubt here. Anyone doesn't feel right they can stay back here with the women."

I'd forgotten what a hard ass Lo can be. "Logan I'm gonna let that slide because we're all under tremendous pressure and it looks like we're finally gonna see the light at the end of the tunnel. But don't you ever question my readiness again."

"Oh for fuck sake we're not doing this. Cord, stand the fuck down, you know how Logan is. We have one enemy and he's out there, not in here. Everyone's all tied up in knots because of this shit now that we're this close to ending it, we're not going to disintegrate."

"Logan Susie is Cord's woman, yes she's the commander's daughter and we all feel a certain responsibility to her, but at the end of the day she's his, it's his call."

"And you Cord, you know he gets nervous before every Op, like a fucking mother hen, just ignore his jabs the way we always do. I'm gonna go hang with the women until you fuckers stop acting like you're on the rag."

"Whoa, was that my boy Ty?" Lyon looked after him as he headed out the door.

"Yeah, he gets mouthy when it's time to kill. Only time you can get anything smart outta him." I grinned because this shit never changes.

Cord and Lo hugged and whispered to each other and went back to acting like nothing happened, which is the way with all of us.

Con's gonna be next to show his ass and Quinn and I will keep our mouths shut and grit our teeth. And the rest of us will make sure that Ty stays safe because he's the baby. And also the hothead who likes to put himself in the line of fire. Nothing new here!

I on the other hand had no choice but to tell her the truth for her own protection. It was never more obvious than now why we stuck to our pact in the past. This shit felt like sawing off an arm and leaving it behind.

Only I wasn't just leaving a woman behind while I walked into danger, I was leaving a woman who had no idea that this whole thing was all about her.

"It takes a day and a half to get to Doha from here, when do you want to leave?" Mancini asked the room at large.

"No time like the present. There's a seven hour time difference let's say we go in at nightfall the day after tomorrow." Logan answered.

"That would mean leaving in a few hours." I almost

choked on the words. This is happening. I thought I would be able to handle it but now I need more time.

But the longer he's alive, the longer she remains in danger, not to mention the other women still left on his fucked up list.

"Yeah, so I guess we better let the women know we're gonna be gone." That was Mancini's way of saying we should spend some time with our women before we left.

We headed downstairs to find them and once again I separated her from the herd. "Let's go for a walk on the cliffs."

The rain had stopped and the air was fresh and heavy with the scent of the tropics. The sun played on the blue-green water making it sparkle like diamonds and I remembered the way she'd sung that song so beautifully, the way she'd danced on the beach.

I felt the photo in my pocket the one I'd downloaded from Mancini's computer before leaving his private room.

The next few minutes could decide my future and I was more afraid now than I was of going into enemy territory in a day and a half.

"Have you told me all you know about your childhood?" She'd already told me that she knew she'd been adopted but that was as far as she'd gone.

"Yes, have something happened?"

"No, no, everything's fine. I have to tell you something and I don't know where to start."

She took my face in her hand and turned it towards hers. “Everything has been hidden from me my whole life Devon, always a secret.” I kissed her palm.

“It seems like I’m the only one who doesn’t know the truth. If we are to be happy together, you must never keep me in the dark again. Especially if it has something to do with me.”

“I can’t go back to the way things used to be. These last few days with you and the others have been the happiest of my life. I never knew how bleak my life truly was until now. If I had to go back it would kill me I think. Kill my soul.”

“You’re not going back, no matter what you’re not ever going to be locked away again.” As I said the words I realized how freeing they were.

If I handed her over to her real father, what would her life be like? What am I really keeping her from if I keep her; marry her? Would that really be such a bad thing?

It made it easier to start the dialogue that until a few minutes ago I’d been dreading. I took the printout from my pocket and unfolded it.

“Let’s sit down.” I pulled her down beside me on my lap as I sat on the flat surface of the bluff above the cliffs.

“Do you know this man?” She studied the image looking at it intensely for a few seconds before giving me an answer.

"I think so, take away the robes and the turban and it could be my uncle."

"Your uncle." I was holding a picture of the old king.

"Yes, he came every year that I can remember, at the same time on the date of my birth. I'd awaken to find him in my room just sitting there quietly. He's the only person other than my parents and brother that I was allowed to see. But he looks so different here. Always before he wore a suit and his hair was different."

"Has something happened to him, why do you have his picture?" I took a deep breath and told her the story as I'd heard it on the video the CO had left us from the beginning, making sure to leave nothing out.

57

DEVON

She didn't interrupt but I could feel her body tense and tremble as I carried on with my tale. Once I was done she didn't speak for the longest time and I knew she was crying. Broke my fucking heart.

"Don't baby." I wrapped my arms around her, wishing I could take the pain away. I hadn't thought of this angle, the pain she'd feel at learning the truth.

Why hadn't it crossed my mind? How was I to know that she'd feel guilt, a guilt that was none of her own? Her sobs tore at me, shredding my heart until they turned into sniffles.

"What happened to my mother?" Shit!

"She died after giving birth… no-no-no baby, not like

that. She got an infection and went into septic shock. It wasn't anything you did."

We learned this by digging through old news archives. It hadn't been a secret. We found news of her death as well, the way the old king had staged it back then pretty much lined up with what the CO had said.

It was hard not to feel bad for every one involved and I wondered had I been in his shoes would I have had the heart to do what he did. Personally I would've ended Khalil and his whole fucking tribe from day one, but that's just me.

I vacillated between anger and hope. Anger that her life had been fucked, and hope that now that I'd found her, nothing and no one would try to take her away from me; that we'd be left alone, to live out the rest of our lives in peace.

I want to be the one to show her the world she'd missed. To share all her firsts with her, see that special light come into her eyes when she finds joy in something. Her voice interrupted my inner reverie.

"And this man, this Khalil, he's after me?"

"Yes!"

"And he's bad."

"The worse." I gave her a broad idea of the kind of man he was and the shit he'd been responsible for over the years without going too deep.

He wasn't her problem, was never going to be her

problem. I hated even mentioning his name to her, but she was right. She'd been kept in the dark for too long.

I skirted around a lot of issues, but I forgot about that mind of hers and pretty soon she was putting the pieces of the puzzle together on her own. That's her thing; she listens.

"Was he the one who had Kelly, and the other girls taken?" How the fuck did she know that? Of course, the women had been playing detective.

"Why do you ask?"

"It makes sense. Kelly thinks her kidnapping had something to do with her dad who happens to be one of your… commander's team mates from back then. My dad, he too was in the service. There's an obvious pattern. We just didn't know the cause behind it."

"What else did you ladies discuss?" I should've asked what they hadn't discussed. It was obvious from her words that they knew a hell of a lot more than we thought they did.

Because of her lack of artifice she spoke openly about things I knew my sisters would never in a million years have told my brothers.

I should probably tell her about sharing what I'm sure the others thought were secrets, but I love the fact that she doesn't know how to lie. I give her three months tops before they turn her.

I won't say my sisters lie, but they know how to

manipulate the truth to suit their purpose and I have the feeling my woman would put them all to shame in that department. Her mind scares me.

But I too was listening to her, not just her words but also her body. And I knew what she was doing.

"I know you're scared, I know you're asking me everything but what's really on your mind. Tell me!"

I brushed the hair back behind her ear and placed a kiss there before taking her hand in mine. I didn't know how else to let her know that I was there, that I wouldn't let anything touch her.

"Will he make me go with him?"

"NO! Sorry, I didn't mean to yell, I'm not mad at you baby." I held her tighter as my heart raced with dread. She'd voiced my own fear out loud.

"No one is taking you anywhere. I won't let you go." Even if I had to ghost I'd do it to keep her. This is such a fucked up situation.

I saved her from one prison to bring her this close to another. I have nothing against other cultures and the way they do things, to each his own.

But I can't feel that way about her. I don't care who her father was, or is. I don't care that he loved her enough to send her away to protect her. She's mine dammit.

"Devon."

"Sorry baby!" I loosened my hold on her thinking I

was holding her too tight, but she pulled my arms tighter around her.

"No, tighter, hold me tighter.

My baby was scared and shaking. "Come here baby." I turned her around on my lap and took her mouth in a fierce kiss. "I love you, you'll never be away from me."

I wiped the tears as they fell from her eyes and kissed her cheeks dry until she found my mouth again with hers.

There was a world of desperation in her kiss and her little heart beat frantically against my chest. This is what I'd been dreading. Why I held off from telling her. Words are sometimes not enough and they were all I had to give her for now. "Come on, let's get you inside."

I only planned to lay with her and comfort her until she calmed down. She had a lot to digest and as much as I wanted her as I always do, I needed to take care of her more.

Once inside the cottage I took off her shoes and mine and climbed into bed, pulling the covers up over us both.

I held her against my chest and caressed her back gently, placing intermittent kisses on her forehead and cheeks every so often.

She felt so fragile in my arms. Like the most precious thing I've ever held. And when I felt her warm tears brush against my skin, it damn near broke my heart again.

"Don't do that baby please." I've heard one or more of my brothers claim that their woman's tears fucks with their heads. I never understood the truth of that statement until this very moment.

I rolled with her until she was beneath me. “Hey, look at me. None of this is your fault. Nothing that has happened is your fault.”

Her poor heart; too young, too innocent to carry such a burden. Khalil deserves to die for that alone. For every second that she blames herself for the horrors he’d committed in the name of finding her. I want him dead now more than ever.

“But if I hadn’t been born…”

“Are you kidding me?” I put her hand over my heart. “You feel that? If you’d never been born I wouldn’t be feeling this. I could never have felt this for anyone but you. Would you deny me this?”

“No, never I love you Devon. Please save me.” She wrapped her arms around my head and pulled me into a heated kiss having no idea what her words did to me. “I will, I promise you I will.”

She studied my eyes seeking the truth, and once she found what it was she was looking for, ran her hands up my chest where my heart beat steadily, firm, strong.

“Love me Devon, please love me.” I tried to go slow when I undressed her but she was in a hurry. She tore at my clothes while I worked on hers and once we were both naked, it was she who bit into my chest as if trying to consume my flesh.

I gritted my teeth against the pain but said nothing as she marked me over and over again while I held still. I understood the wild need in her, the need to feel some kind of control in a situation where she had none.

She wrapped her legs around me and tried to get me to fuck her before she was ready. Or at least I thought she wasn't ready.

But when I passed my hand between her thighs and dipped a finger inside her, she was more than ready to take me.

Still I wanted her taste in my mouth. I needed it more than my next breath. I put my head between her thighs and licked her slit until her pussy opened under my tongue.

I licked deep and drew her essence from deep inside before going back for more. I ran my hands up her chest until I held her tits under my hands while eating her out.

She moved beneath my tongue, her hands gripping my hair hard as her legs writhed against the sheets, and she begged me softly to give her more.

~

ARIEL

~

I don't know what's wrong with me. There's a fire burning out of control inside me. Something dark and wild that unfolded as the words came from Devon's lips.

Each word, each new mystery revealed was like a dagger in my heart. Because of one man, my whole world had been destroyed.

I felt anger, hurt, and pain. Why hadn't my 'father' protected me better? Why had so many lives been destroyed because of mine?

As those thoughts ran through my head on the heels of the pleasure Devon caused with his mouth, anger won the day.

I moved against his tongue until that sweet ache had me lifting off the bed as I came with a burst of light that went off like a camera flash behind my closed lids.

I didn't give myself time to come down, but used the momentum of the most spectacular orgasm to reverse our positions.

His look of surprise wasn't lost on me, but the anger was fast becoming hunger as I ran my tongue down the center of his body until I came to the heavy length of flesh between his thighs.

It was so beautiful his manhood. Nothing at all like the aesthetic pictures in the books I'd studied for biology that's for sure.

I teased him with my tongue while holding his eyes the way he'd taught me. I rubbed my face with the liquid that leaked from his tip before taking that tip into my mouth and running my tongue across the slit.

His body jumped and I did it again. His hand came down and fisted my hair. I took more and more of him inside my mouth, using my teeth when my heart beat erratically and the strange hunger and need took me over.

I moved my head from side to side as I swallowed more of his length, regretting the fact that I couldn't fit all of him in my mouth.

My nails dragged along his sides as I sucked more of him into my mouth, stretching my lips around him. Suddenly his taste on my tongue was like the sweetest ambrosia and I wanted more.

His hiss and moans escalated the beats of my heart and I moved my mouth faster, lower until my cheeks hurt and my mouth grew tired. Still I didn't stop.

"Give me Devon." I pulled off long enough to say before speeding up my efforts even when he tried calming me down.

"Shh, baby, easy, easy." He ran his hand lovingly down my cheek, but I didn't want tenderness. I wanted to feel the sweet burn of his flesh pounding into me like he would die if he didn't have me.

When I fondled his balls, his cock jumped on my tongue and I kept it up until I felt the seed fill his balls and they grew hard and drew up close to his body.

He warned me that he was about to cum seconds

before I felt the first spurt hit the back of my throat. I pulled my head back just the slightest bit and the next volley landed on my tongue.

I sucked until there was nothing but dribbles left, and then I climbed on top of him and holding him in place with one hand, lowered myself onto his semi hard length.

It wasn't long before I felt him grow and harden inside me as I rode up and down on his length. His words of encouragement spurred me on to go faster and faster as I chased something inside that seemed just out of reach.

His hands on my hips felt different, stronger somehow; his thick length inside me more filling. I didn't know I was crying until he started crooning softly to me again and kissing the tears from my cheeks.

"Come 'ere, I've got you." He pulled my face down to his with a hand behind my head and took my lips a little more roughly this time as my body undulated over his.

I used him to outrace the thoughts in my head, but no matter how hard I ground myself against him. Or how hard I slammed my hips into his. I couldn't quite catch whatever it was that I was running after.

But he knew! I should've known he would. "I've got you." He whispered the words in my ear as he held my head and rolled us until I was beneath him.

He looked down at me as he lifted my legs around his waist and that's when I found it. From his first powerful stroke, I started to cum.

The look in his eyes: such determination. The strength in his arms, as I gripped them, the feel of his hard length going in and out of me. And most of all the way his body covered and shielded mine blocking out the rest of the world.

We moved together in perfect sync. As his cock butted against that place inside me that makes me see stars, I finally felt fulfilled, like I'd captured whatever it was that had been escaping me.

The void his words had opened, that had widened with each syllable was finally filled and closed. He watched me as if he knew, licking the tears as they fell before they had the chance to flow down my cheeks.

He whispered things in my ears. Sweet things, reassuring things! Things I needed to hear, to believe. Now my heart was full to overflowing.

His hands felt heavy, rough, powerful, as he lifted my ass, bringing me closer to him. My belly was filled with him, and so was the place between my thighs.

And when he bit into my flesh, starting at my throat and making his way down to the tender flesh above my nipples, I felt owned, cherished, loved. "Mine!"

That growl, held such intense heat it made my body respond and I came again, locking off his body inside my own. "My Devon."

"Always." His kiss this time was punishingly rough. I felt his teeth scrape against my lip and teeth as he took my tongue into his mouth, before pushing it out roughly again with his, feeding it to me.

The noise the bed made as it knocked against the wall sent shivers straight to my sex. I loved it almost as much as his growls and sounds of uncontrollable lust.

Those sounds told me that he was totally and completely under my spell. That his need for me was as strong as mine for him.

I spread my legs wider unlocking them from around his waist and holding onto my ankles. Looking down between us I got lost in the sight of his sun bronzed flesh as it slid into me over and over.

I reveled in the sight of my juices that coated him more and more each time he thrust into me. The sight was so primal, so lust inflaming that I began to cum and couldn't stop.

His cock became a blur as he used it to piston in and out of me harder, faster. I felt that sweet burn again as he drove into my belly, hitting something inside me that seemed to have been waiting for him.

He covered my mouth with his hand when my body erupted and I screamed. I bit his palm making him swear and take it away, only to replace it with mouth and tongue.

Now he was bouncing between my thighs, our stomachs meeting in time with our hips as he drove that solid steel length deep into me.

I felt his seed burst inside me. I didn't think you were

supposed to, but I did. I felt its slippery warmth as it splashed against my walls before he snuck into that place that caused me pain mingled with pleasure.

Then his seed seemed to target a secret place inside me that only he knew, only he will ever know. My womb!

58

DEVON

Merciful fuck, what was that? I barely had enough strength left to roll to my side and pull her into me since my cock refused to slip out of her.

I felt like I'd just shared my soul with her. She sure as fuck took something out of me! I pulled her head back and stared down at her in total amazement.

I could see it in her eyes. I'd brought a lamb to my bed but she now stared back at me with the eyes of a lioness. I had the marks on my back and my sides to prove it.

Some of her innocence was gone and I mourned that. But I welcomed this new change. She was going to need to be strong so that we could save each other.

I need her to keep the dark away. If she goes the sun

would cease to shine and my days would go back to being bleak once more.

"I love you princess Ariel." I brought her lips up to mine before putting her on my chest to sleep.

I left her asleep in bed and went to find the others. It seemed we'd all had the same idea since I found them leaving their cottages, headed back to the mansion.

I know the drill. Lo would want to spend the rest of the day doing drills again and making sure we had everything needed to go in and come out without losing anyone.

"I told her." I waited until we were all together in a little huddle.

"How'd she take it?"

"Not well Logan, she blames herself."

"I thought she would; damn."

"She's going to be fine, I'll make sure of it. Once we get rid of this asshole she can breathe easy."

"And what about her father, the old king?"

"She wants to stay with me." And that's what was most important, what I'd learned while she was using my cock to drive out her demons.

It wasn't fear of her being taken from me that had been haunting me, but fear of her wanting to go. Fear; of losing something else precious to me. I knew if that happened I wouldn't survive it this time.

Part of that was because I've seen my brothers' lives change in the last year. All these men who like myself had rough beginnings had found true love.

If I were to fail at this, lose the only woman to ever enter my heart then I would know that happiness wasn't meant for me. That my uncle had been right all along and I was nothing more than a scourge on the rest of the world.

"Dev, where'd you go brother?" I looked sharply at Connor who was staring at me as if he already knew the answer. I started to shake my head but it was no longer my brother standing before me but one of my team leaders.

"Walk with me brother." He didn't wait for me to agree or decline but walked off in the opposite direction from where we were headed.

I didn't even think about not following him, why bother? He'd get me sooner or later and it would be a shit thing to do, going into battle with my brothers worrying about me.

I caught up to him on one of the paths that lead to the beach where he stood waiting for me. "I know your mind went back there again and I know we've all told you more than once that your uncle was a piece of shit asshole who had no fucking brains."

"Yes I think I've heard one or more of you say something along those lines a time or two."

"Who do you trust brother?"

"My brothers."

"So why don't you believe us when it comes to this one thing? Put it away and put it away for good. You deserve the same happiness as everyone else and fuck anyone who says different."

"Dani says she's in love with you."

"Who Dani?"

"No you fuck, Ariel. You know how these women talk, which is good for us that they get along so well, but that also means there are no secrets. It's going to be interesting when we get back home to the compound."

"Anyway, she says the girl's in love with you and you'll be a fool to let anyone get in the way of that. I don't have to ask how you feel, I was there the night you first saw her. I saw the second you were a goner."

"I know the signs, I've been there myself. As to your uncle, he doesn't count with us, we're the only ones who matter and we know your worth so walk it out and let's go get this motherfucker so we can go on with our lives and our women can stop planning to mutiny. Fuck!"

I have to admit to feeling better after his little pep talk. He'd reminded me of things I knew but had lost sight of in the last little while.

The others watched us when we returned and I could

tell from the way they relaxed that they were all worrying.

I had to get my head back in the game for all our sakes, and it was only now that I realized how much what was going on with me really mattered to them.

I should've known though, that no matter what, my brothers would be thinking of me. It's the way it's always been with us. It's like Lo said to Quinn back on the beach back home. If something fucks with one of us, it fucks with all.

We spent the rest of the day doing drills. Mancini tried once to talk Lyon into staying back since he had no military experience and had never been to this part of the world but that didn't go well.

And once again we were regaled with an insight into the psychosis that is Colton Lyon. If I didn't know better I'd swear he gave birth to Ty.

Their minds tend to work alike and it always leads to total annihilation or destruction of whoever it is they've got in their crosshairs.

There was no telling him that he couldn't go because as he saw it, we'd come this far together he wasn't about to punk out because he had to go to the desert. Apparently he'd been there before but I got the feeling we were talking about two different things.

Thankfully Lo had stepped in and calmed the situation since he seemed to understand that craziness that was Lyon better than the rest of us.

When we were done I checked in on her and found her in the shower. When I joined her and she turned to me there were no more tears, though all the sadness had yet to leave her eyes.

Her desperation was tamed when I slipped into her. Fucking her against the shower glass door from behind I could see her reflection.

See the way she closed her eyes and bit her lip in ecstasy. Feel the way she pushed back against me as she got up on her toes, taking me in deep and spreading her legs as if begging for more.

Soon I will have to tell her that I was leaving her again, and why. I'd told her pretty much everything else, but I'd saved this little bit for last.

There was an added burden now. If we missed, it might be her last chance at being free. One way or another she would remain a target, and so would my sisters and the other women out there and in that book.

That night after we'd had a lovely dinner with the others outside under the stars I took her back to the cottage and told her.

"I don't know what's going to happen tomorrow. No…no…no, don't be afraid, no matter what happens you're going to be okay." Fuck Devon way to scare her.

She clutched at me with a sheen of tears in her eyes. "I don't want anything to happen to you either Devon. Isn't there another way? I don't want you and your brothers getting hurt because of me."

I took her little face in my hands and kissed her forehead. How can I feel so much for her in such little time? It still amazes me.

"It's not because of you baby, I told you. You're not to blame for any of this, so put that out of your head. We were set on this course long before we knew about you."

I placed little nibbling kisses along her nose and over to her cheek before making my way to her lips. "Open for me baby." I wanted to take her mind off of it. Didn't want to leave her with that heavy burden on her heart.

Her soft curious tongue played with my lips before I sucked it into my mouth and pulled her tighter against me.

It seems no matter what I do, how much I tell myself that I won't touch her this time just talk and hold her, we always end up here. With this fiery need burning out of control.

I crushed her ass under my hands until she could feel the hardness of my cock digging into her middle. Searching for his favorite hiding place.

I slid her shirt over her shoulders and only broke the kiss long enough to pull it over her head, before removing my own.

"Touch me!" She placed her warm hands on my hot chest and teased circles on my flesh with her fingertips.

I lowered my mouth to hers again and pulled her into my chest so I could feel the pebbled warmth of her nipples as they pressed into me. I wanted to implant each touch, each feel each sense to memory.

The kiss grew wilder, rougher, harder and pretty soon I was grabbing the material of her skirt in my fists as I bunched it up around her ass and hips.

I pulled her between my thighs once again rubbing my aching cock into her before lifting her in my arms and heading for the bed in the next room.

I laid her across the bed and stood back to shed the rest of my clothes. Her eyes were fever bright and out of focus as they followed my hands on the zipper of my jeans.

I paused pushed my shorts down my thighs and revealed my cock to her hungry eyes. I made my way to the bed and came down beside her. "Touch him."

She wrapped her soft warm hands around my throbbing cockmeat and stroked up and down.

While she found her rhythm, I trailed my finger around her navel making her skin quiver.

I covered her lips, distracting her as I removed her skirt and slid her panties down her thighs. "I love your kisses."

I smiled down at her, not believing how happy I was

just to be here with her like this even with the danger awaiting me. Maybe that was the lure of a good woman. What have made men fight and die for centuries.

I pulled back and looked down at her spread out beneath me, my wanton princess. Her body was an astounding thing of beauty. And I made myself take the time look, to enjoy all that was mine.

Though I had no real fear that I wouldn't come back to her, there was no sense in testing fate. I wanted the memory of her like this to carry with me.

High firm breasts, flat concaved stomach, and slightly flared hips that cupped her pretty hairless pussy. Shapely thighs that had I taken the time to really look before I would've noticed were well toned and defined. Dancer's legs.

I held her eyes with mine as I ran my hand over her heated flesh before reaching the junction of her thighs. She opened her legs sensually, inviting me to come to her.

I could feel her pussy's heat the closer I got and although I'd already had her, my hand still trembled when my fingers finally touched her there. Almost as if I still couldn't believe that she was mine.

Her pussy was smooth, fat and honey gold like the rest of her. "Close your eyes baby." I licked and nibbled my way down her well defined thigh putting my shoulders between her legs to spread her open for my mouth.

I studied the flower of her pussy, inhaling her scent,

taking it into me. I opened her with my fingers and looked into her heat at the beauty that would soon encase my cock, before using the tip of my tongue to taste her.

She jumped at the touch of my tongue on her flesh and her legs twitched and spread even wider giving me perfect access to her jewel.

I used my fingers and tongue to bring her to a nice soft climax and watched as her body moved like a wave on the ocean as she gave herself over to me.

I flattened my tongue and lapped at her escaping juices letting her taste rush through me. I had to hold her hips to keep her in place, as I loved her deeper with my tongue.

Her hands came down and held my head in place as she moved beneath my mouth. A quick look showed her biting into her lip to keep her screams hidden, but I wanted to make her let go.

I want her screaming for me, want my beautiful girl to let go and enjoy what I was about to do to her. More, I wanted the sound of her screams of pleasure in my head while I was away from her.

I licked her clit until it came out from under the hood and took it into my mouth. She moaned hoarsely and ground her pussy harder against my mouth but that wasn't enough.

I eased the tip of my finger past her tight folds and into her too tight pussy. "So hot." Her pussy was on fire

I used my fingers and tongue again to bring her to fever pitch before leaving her wanting this time. She smacked my chest and whined cutely and I took her fingers in my mouth as I climbed up her body.

I eased my cock inside her, watching her stretch to accept me. "I'm going to get real deep in you." I worked the rest of my cock into her, giving her time to adjust, until I bottomed out.

She rocked her hips and lifted her ass humping up at me wildly. "Easy baby, easy." I held still until I knew she was comfortable before lifting her ass in my hands and slamming into her once.

"Fuck you're still so tight." And hot and so fucking wet. I pounded her pussy a couple times to see how well she could take me like that and except for a grimace in the beginning, she took it well enough for me to relax and feed her my cock the way I wanted to.

Her nails dug into my ass and her legs went higher around my hips. I was gripping her too hard, sure to leave a mark but I didn't care. Her pussy was making me crazy.

I've never been in anything this tight in my fucking life. The thought that I might never have found her, that she could've ended up in the hands of a madman left me cold.

My emotions raged out of control when I took her lips roughly as I slid my cock out of her until only the head was lodged inside, before slamming my whole length home again.

It was as if I was trying to leave a part of me here with her. And when I came I prayed as I never had before that I had indeed given her a part of me.

It was time to go and I wasn't the only one lingering over goodbyes. The women clung a little harder, because they knew a little more about what was going on.

In the end we'd had no choice but to share at least a little bit with them. They all put on a brave face but it was obvious that they were worried out of their minds.

No one joked around or had anything funny to say. And though they weren't exactly somber, it had a feel of women sending their men off to war.

It was our worst nightmare come to pass, but we had to put it all aside as we boarded the plane. In the last few hours we've been getting updates on Khalil and his movements, which led us to believe that he was about to pull something major.

The trace she had on his phone hadn't as yet intercepted anything useful to us, but at least we knew it worked from what we've seen so far.

No one said much of anything until we were in the air. It was going to be a long ass flight with one stop at the midway point so we didn't have much to do but sit back and rest.

My mind was back there with her, something I knew I would have to change the closer we got. It was never a good thing to go into battle with anything less than a clear head.

I wasn't selfish enough to think that this was more important to me than the others, but it was damn close. My girl happens to be the one that sick fuck is after, the one he'd started this whole mess to find.

I can't help but be a little more worried now than I was in the beginning, which makes no sense when you think about it. When I thought we were ridding the world of one more asshole it was same ole same ole as far as I was concerned.

He's not the first and won't be the last that we've had to take care of over the years and didn't warrant any more thought than the average asshole on every street corner.

But now that she's in the picture my fear level has gone up a couple decibels and that's something I've never dealt with before. I need to get it under control before we land or I stand the chance of putting everyone else in danger.

One thing's for sure though, I now understand Lyon's attitude when it comes to his family and danger. When that shit's personal it's a whole different ballgame.

59

DEVON

We arrived in full dark the next day and immediately went into high gear. This place is crawling with military intelligence and a host of unsavory characters on a good day, so we had to get in and out in as little time as possible without being seen.

Mancini had a station set up in the desert, not sure how he pulled that off, but it looked like any other bivouac we'd ever seen and would cause no undue interest.

In the last few hours before we landed once everyone had rested, some better than others, we'd gone through the plans again.

Only a few of us were going into the camp where the

signals from Khalil's phone were pinging, because it would be too dangerous for us all to go.

Had this been a military Op, it wouldn't have mattered, but some might call what we were doing illegal.

So while we were going in the others were going to stand guard around the perimeter. It wasn't easy choosing who were gonna go in, but in the end it was Lo, Con and Zak who would extract him and bring him back.

We'd decided not to blow him away this time, because that shit never works. The good thing is, we know how he operates because we've been this close before.

The problem is, he always finds a way to slip away and survive whatever we throw at him. This time we're going to have a face to face with asshole number one and put an end to him once and for all. At least that's what we're hoping.

As expected the place was crawling with military but at least there were no locals milling about this late at night.

We checked the signal to be sure it was still working and used that as a guide to finding Khalil's exact location.

We pinpointed his location easily enough. You see, for a desert rat, Khalil can't do without his creature comforts. His tents are like travelling five star hotels wherever he goes which isn't hard to find among the others.

But he's also used them as a trap in the past so we were highly vigilant since we knew that this might be our last chance. If we fucked this up those women's lives won't be worth shit, my woman especially.

While Lo and the others went ahead the rest of us got into position, blending into the dark night as we crawled on our bellies in the dust.

Ty took up his post right above with his scope trained on the tent, while the rest of us took care of the guards one by one.

We weren't there to harm anyone so we used sleepers to put them down. The hardest part was dragging them out of sight after they fell but even that went off without a hitch. Lo's constant drills paid off there.

All in all I was thinking our luck had really changed because the shit was way too easy. When Lo and the others came running out not even five minutes later with Khalil tied and bound, we headed back to the waiting vehicles and raced through the night to the bivouac.

It was well situated away from the others and would afford us the privacy we needed. We didn't plan to be there long anyway, just in and out once we got what we needed.

We weren't interested in interrogating the Fox, after all this time we just wanted to make sure this time that we got him, that there were no more tricks up his sleeve.

This time my brothers and I were all there while the others stood watch outside. We didn't dare make too much light but it was enough to see that the man sitting on the chair grinning at us was indeed Khalil.

Everyone's blood was up and we didn't have a lot of time, it's never too wise to hang around in places like this. So though we each wanted a piece of him we knew it wasn't gonna happen. This was the end of the road.

The only thing we wanted from him now were the names of the men working for him on our end. He was tied, gagged and bound to the only chair in the room.

"Hello Khalil long time no see." Con tore the gag from his mouth. It was easy to see his grin in the dark but he said nothing as he looked around at us.

Lo shone his light in his face and his eyes were either sleep glazed or the Fox was on something. Didn't matter. Lo started the questioning while the rest of us listened and nothing this fool was saying made any sense.

It was like playing a game of cat and mouse. We were getting nowhere and I was seriously beginning to think he was high or drunk when Mancini rushed into the room.

We all went on alert. "What is it, what's going on?" He didn't answer Logan just walked swiftly over to the chair where Khalil was tied in the middle of the room and pulled his head back roughly. Then he slit his throat. He did it so quickly we didn't have time to react.

"What the fuck?" Lo looked at Mancini questioningly.

"He's not Khalil." He opened the dead man's eyes and

removed contacts before pulling his scalp back and dropping it on the floor. There was someone else sitting there.

"Who the fuck is this?"

"I don't know but your boy is on the move we gotta go." As soon as the words left his mouth we were on the move.

"How do you know this?" I questioned Mancini as the others joined us.

"No time to talk now he's heading to the airfield. Shit."

We hopped into the desert buggies we'd left hidden behind a dune and headed back the way we came. We'd been so close, but I can't say I was surprised.

Khalil always seems to be one step ahead of us; only this time there was no way he should've known we were coming.

Once back in the air we turned to Mancini for some answers. "Long story short. Track had a bead on the senator. Apparently he and his sister has been in contact since we left the island."

"An hour ago he picked up noise between the senator and an unknown. I don't know how he knows but he's certain it's Khalil, he has eyes on him."

"What, how'd he do that?"

"Why don't we ask him when this is all done?"

60

DEVON

No one breathed easy as we flew through the night, heading towards the gulf which is where Mancini informed us Khalil was meeting with the senator.

"So that's how he's always evaded us, he uses a decoy." Logan looked around at the rest of us.

"Yep, I guess for the criminal element it pays to be paranoid." Con stretched out his legs and closed his eyes.

"But how did he know we were coming?" Ty dropped his head back and rubbed his eyes.

"I'm not sure he did, but after the move on the general, he must've decided to be extra careful." Mancini filled us in.

"How sure are we that he's the one with the senator?"

"Track seems pretty sure, like I said, he has eyes on

him and they're in a convoy tent. Lots of security so we have to go in hard and fast."

It only took us half an hour to land and we hit the ground running. I'm pretty sure my brothers like me, were hoping that this was it. Sure we'd hit and missed before with the Fox, but we all knew the stakes were much higher this time.

"Lyon, you sure you don't want to stay back? You might get a bit confused in the fog of war."

"No fucking way Tyler, this is perfect. I can kill the senator here and no one would even think about looking at me for it." He actually grinned.

Mancini was right; the place was crawling with military guards. They'd joined a convoy to blend in with people leaving war torn areas heading to safety. It was a smart move, but the only way to pull it off was if the military was in on it.

We went in on foot and since there was no place to hide, had to crawl until we had the place within our scope.

There was more than one tent but it was easy to figure out which one was theirs. That would be the one with all the security on guard.

"They're not military, that's black water, what the fuck are they doing here?" I crawled over to Lo's side to ask.

"Makes sense, the senator is dirty as fuck, he wouldn't want the military tracking his movements here. I count four of them." Ty crawled over to us as the others stayed in place.

Lo spoke into the mike on his collar as we watched the men on patrol. "Ty's going to cover the tent, Zak, Con, take out the guards on three, we're going in."

We fast crawled on our hands and guts just as the first body fell. There was no time for the others to raise the alarm because the others weren't far behind.

Outside the tent we could hear voices inside but couldn't make out what they were saying. Lo held up his hand with the signal for two hot bodies.

A quick look showed that the other tents had not been disturbed, the only sound was the crying of a child a little ways up from us.

We waited a few seconds more to be sure that there were no more guards on duty before climbing to our feet and rushing in.

The two men jumped up from the table they'd been sitting at quite at ease for two dead fucks. "What is this, who are you people?"

I've always believed that if you can't control your fear you should keep your damn mouth shut. The senator looked like a trapped rodent.

"Senator, may I introduce you to SEAL Team Seven." Khalil actually grinned at us like he was in charge of shit. There was no fear after the initial surprise.

We all had our weapons pointed at the two men and of

the two only the senator seemed shook. "What is the meaning of this? Why are you here? This is official business of the United States of America and you gentlemen were not invited. Now if you'll excuse us."

"That's not gonna work senator, we know what you're doing here and it's not official business. What we want to know is who else is working with you?"

"That is none of your concern, this man has been given diplomatic immunity, he now works with the U.S. government in a highly secret capacity, you gentlemen are gonna have to leave."

The whole time this asshole was talking Khalil had a sick fucking smirk on his face like he had us. I had my hand on the trigger ready to blast his ass no matter what the fuck was said, but I waited for Lo to give the order.

"Is that how you do it? He steals and sells American kids and you fucks make a deal with him?"

"Lyon…"

"Fuck that Hank." I was pretty sure from the use of names that those two had no plans on letting these two live. Fine by me.

"Are you going to give us what we want or not?" Just then Mancini's SAT went off on his hip and he turned out of the tent. Lo asked the question again but the senator was still giving us the spiel and time was of the essence.

My only interest was in ending this fuck and getting

the hell back to my girl, and I'm pretty sure from the looks on my brothers' faces they were thinking the same.

"Your commander, how is he?" This fucker. I guess he thought that diplomatic immunity bullshit meant something to us. It didn't. We'd seen enough to know that that shit wasn't worth the paper it was written on.

"I wonder, how did you find me this time? It's only taken you what, five and a half years?" He was talking shit but it was obvious from the dead look in his eyes that he wasn't pleased.

I was about to ask Lo if he was sure we couldn't get the information we needed some other way so I could put one in this asshole, when Mancini walked back in with a smile on his face.

I knew before he spoke that the tables had turned. "We have what you need boys now let's end this and get the hell out of here. There's movement out there and any minute someone's gonna notice the dead bodies lying around."

I wasn't quite sure what he meant by he had what we needed but it sounded good to me. Lo looked around at the rest of us and nodded.

That was all it took for us to open fire. None of us would ever know who made the kill shot, but I'm pretty sure it was Lyon's glock that put the hole in the senator's forehead. He was the only one not carrying a Mac.

Ty planted the explosive devise on the table and we

ran into the night back the way we came. The explosion sounded just as we made it back to our vehicles, scattering all the people who'd ran out of their tents a the sound of the gunfire.

No one looked back as we headed for the plane and the sky lit up behind us. We didn't start laughing until we were safely on the plane and headed back to the island.

"Well that was anticlimactic. After years of trying to bring him to ground, who knew it would be this easy?"

"I hear you Logan but damn I'm glad that shit's over. Is it really over?"

"Yeah, we finally got him Dev, she's free." I felt tears in my eyes and wasn't ashamed of them.

"I still have to deal with the old king."

"Maybe not, I think her father, Samson might be of help there."

"What do you know Mancini?"

"Nothing much until we land, but from what I can tell, he and his son has been running interference. We'll know more once we get there."

It was a long fucking thirty-six hours but once we landed all my fatigue went away as soon as I saw her waiting for me. The others were there as well, but I only had eyes for her.

She ran to meet me as soon as I stepped off the plane and I grabbed her up in my arms. Nothing had ever felt this good. "Is it over?" She had tears in her eyes.

I put her back on her feet and dried her face, my heart breaking just a little at all that she'd had to go through. "It's over baby. Don't cry anymore okay, I can't bear it."

She held my hand to her chest and nodded as the last fear fell. I pulled her into my chest and kissed her forehead before heading after the others.

"Boys I hate to do this to you, but you only have a few hours down time, we have to get back to your compound ASAP."

"What the fuck Mancini, why what's going on there?"

"You'll see when we get there, get some sleep." He just walked away with his arm around his woman leaving the rest of us looking after him.

I was too tired to make love to her so I made her lay with me even though she wasn't tired as I caught up on my sleep. It felt like I hadn't slept in days.

Lo was right, the shit was anticlimactic. After all the time we'd spent hunting down the Fox, for it to end that easily seems almost surreal.

Personally I would've loved to put his ass through a grinder until there was nothing left and feed his remains to a pack of wild dogs, but you take what you can get in these situations.

When I woke up a few hours later she was still there

next to me, watching me sleep. I pulled her down to my chest and rolled with her putting her beneath me.

No words were spoken as I pulled her panties off down her thighs. I felt around between her thighs and found her heat with my fingers.

I slid into her going slow and it felt like coming home when she wrapped her arms and legs around me, holding me close.

There was no haste in my movements as I thrust into her over and over, our mouths sealed together. I felt at peace knowing that she was finally safe and knowing that no matter what, she was mine.

61

DEVON

True to his word Mancini hustled us off the island a few hours later. There was a sense of celebration in the air because the women knew their days of being confined were finally over.

When Mancini said he had what we needed back on the gulf, we took that to mean he somehow obtained the names of all the top-level men involved in the trafficking scheme.

He still wouldn't tell us who or how he knew, all he would say is that we'd know soon enough. So the rest of us just cooled our jets and waited until he was ready. He hadn't let us down thus far and he was one of us now.

It was great to be back here, I was especially excited

to show her-her new home but when we pulled up to the gate it was obvious that we had a welcoming party.

"What the fuck?" Lo swore as we saw the admiral walk out to meet us a soon as the gates closed behind us. There were about six vehicles parked on the grounds, none of them familiar.

The girls who'd been taken with Kelly came running to meet her and I wasn't surprised to see Track come towards me to meet his sister.

They fell into each other's arms and my natural instinct was to pull her away. I checked myself just in time, I guess I'm going to have to get used to at least one other male being that close to her.

He put her away from him with his hands on her shoulders, looking her over. "Are you sure you're okay?" She nodded as tears fell from her eyes and they hugged one more time.

He whispered some stuff in her ear and she nodded against his chest, but it was her sniffles that were getting to me.

I'm going to have to build up some sort of defense against them, because if she ever finds out what her tears do to me, I'm sure she'd own my balls for the rest of my damn life.

"Okay, give me back my girl." I had to damn near wrestle her out of his hands. I think this kid was testing me. I quirked my brow at him because no matter how bad he is at hacking into people's shit, I'm pretty sure I could break him in half easy.

"I'll give her to you for now. Don't forget, you're on probation and I *will* be watching you." He smirked and walked away, back towards the mansion.

"Don't glare at my brother Devon he's just playing. He knows how much I love you he won't interfere. But if you're ever mean to me..." She grinned and evaded my arms.

Her tears were dry now and there was light in her eyes. "Is that a threat princess?" She stopped smiling at my words and I rushed to reassure her.

"My princess, no one else's ever." I kissed her nose and sent her to join the women who were all standing in the middle of the yard talking to the girls.

I went and stood beside my brothers who were watching their women with a new sense of lightness. "Fuck this feels good, look at them."

Lo pointed to the women who were standing out in the open for the first time in who knows how long. Carefree in their laughter and whatever shit they were plotting over there.

"Well boys, I think there's something you're gonna want to see in there." Mancini came up beside us.

"What the fuck Hank, what else you got going on around here? My ass is tired."

"Come along Colt, this concerns you too. We might as

well see it through to the end." No one questioned him as we headed towards the mansion. Zak had stopped long enough to send the women to his place.

The danger might be over as far as we knew, but it was going to take a while for us to get that shit settled in our minds and go back to normal.

We walked through the door, a little bone wary but upbeat nonetheless. We'd just rid the world of a very dangerous threat.

The only thing left now was the fallout from the senator's death, but I wasn't too worried about that. No one knew we were there.

"What the fuck?" I looked up at Quinn's words and got a shock myself.

"Hello boys."

"Commander?" The seven of us moved forward as if in a trance.

"How?" Lo asked as we looked him over to make sure this wasn't some trick. With technology being what it is, you can never be too sure these days.

"It's me, I had to do it this way for everyone's sake."

"You knew?" Quinn asked his father in law who was in the room.

"Nope, not the whole time, I went to his funeral the bastard." He grinned at his friend.

"I had to fake my own death to bring the filth rising to the top. I suspected the general and knowing his close ties to the senator I suspected there were a lot more people involved, but I had to be sure."

"Because of who I suspected was involved, I couldn't afford to make any mistakes. I knew that if I moved before all the players had been smoked out of their holes, I'd only be peeling back one layer and leaving the rest to carry on."

No one else spoke and I know my brothers like me were still coming to terms with what we were seeing. I've never experienced shocked joy before but I can't say I didn't like it.

"I thought I covered my tracks pretty well, but something went wrong and that's when I tried calling you in. When you were sent into a trap, I knew I had to do something or we'd all be fucked, so I came up with a plan."

"I know how the general operates, so when he invited himself here under the guise of friendship I was ready for him. I'd already taken the antidote for his little surprise so when he slipped me the poison I pretended to be dead while he ransacked my place looking for what I had."

"So that's why the closed coffin." Connor asked as he too looked over the commander as if not quite believing his own eyes.

"I had to do it this way boys. I knew once I was gone that you'd take care of it once you got wind of what was going on. I didn't want you involved, but I couldn't get close. They knew me well enough to close ranks and I couldn't find a way in."

"If I didn't want them to kill you off one by one I had to pull back or at least make them believe I had, but leave enough so you'd do the rest."

"Now thanks to this young man we have what we need." He looked at Track who was standing back against the wall in a roomful of fighting men looking way too at ease.

"About that, how did you have eyes on the senator and Khalil?" Mancini asked the kid.

"I switched his glasses."

"Come again."

"The senator is blind without his glasses and he can't wear contacts, they irritate his eyes. I had his glasses switched out for ones with a high-powered recording camera in the lens. Dumb fuck never suspected."

"What the fuck, how do you know these thing? Never mind, I forgot. You ever hack into my shit kid, I'll forget I'm in love with your sister and put one in you."

He gave me his usual smirk and shrugged. I didn't miss the look that passed between the commander and Samson at my words.

"Speaking of which, that's the one hiccup I hadn't prepared for, you and the princess. I don't have to tell you the shit storm that's gonna cause." I opened my mouth to argue but he held up his hand.

"Not to worry, I'll take care of it. It won't be long before he knows that Khalil is no longer a threat and I imagine he'd want to make arrangements to get her back, but I think there might be a way for you to keep her and still keep the peace."

His words had a calming affect on me, plus the fact that I knew there was no way anyone was taking her away from me kept me settled with my feet firmly planted. With Khalil gone I figured I could face whatever roadblocks stood in our way.

The rest of the day was spent playing catch up as we got the whole story out of him and his cohorts. Apparently the commander had got in touch with his friends after Kelly had been taken.

He hadn't known that Khalil had discovered the names of his old team and had thought them out of the other man's reach.

But once he knew that they too were in danger, he'd come out of hiding to get in touch. He'd been there the night the general had been taken out and there was no need to guess who was the one to end him.

The whole thing was almost too much to take in, and the shock of having the old man back hadn't quite worn off. It looks like shit was finally turning around for my brothers and I.

"Wait a minute, what about the compound, the mansion? Now that you're back we..." Leave it to Logan to be thinking about the whole picture, that shit hadn't even crossed my mind.

"No Logan, nothing about that has to change. My will is exactly how I wanted it to be, I just didn't expect it to be read as soon as it was. Think of it as a wedding present for all of you."

"The compound is yours. I plan to ask my woman to marry me and travel the world. I want to see some of those places I never got to enjoy when I was in service."

"Since you've left the mansion as is, I figure we can stay here when we visit but I won't be living here any longer. My kids..."

"They're fine, they don't know yet though, we were waiting to tell them the whole story."

"Well now you don't have to tell them that I died. Hopefully they can forgive me for not being there, maybe they'd understand."

"I'm sure they will commander, if not we'll talk to them."

"Cord, you and Susie."

"Yes sir."

"I couldn't have chosen better for my only daughter."

"I'm proud of all of you, now my friends and I are

going to take care of the rest of this. Track." He came forward and handed over what looked like a chip.

"What's that?"

"It's the conversation between the senator and Khalil on film; everything you need to bring down the whole crew."

"Yes, once we get this into the right hands it'll break the whole thing wide open. I guess there's going to be a lot of destroyed lives and careers." Mancini took the chip and looked it over.

"And you Mancini, how do you play into all this?" Lo asked as yet another layer of our new friend was exposed. When he just smiled without an answer the CO stepped in.

"Better you leave that alone boys. Let's just say your new friend knows all the right people and leave it at that." The CO smiled at us, which pretty much meant that was the end of that.

"And on that note, I think I'll grab my woman and head back to New York. I'll be seeing you boys in about three weeks. I hear there's going to be a wedding on my island."

"Get me the guest list as soon as possible will you. I can't have too many unknowns roaming about my place." I think he actually sneered.

We all got up to thank him and say our goodbyes. "I'll let you know how Thorpe's doing with his rescue mission.

Law, we'll get to your thing soon enough, I have some ideas."

Was there anything this fucker didn't know? We'd already, my brothers and I, decided that we were going to help Law with his little problem whether he wanted us to or not. But I had no idea that Mancini knew anything about that.

"How do you know about my little problem? I don't remember mentioning it." Law looked confused.

"Your wife told mine how else."

Seems the women only pretend to leave shit alone while carrying on behind the scenes. I can't say that I blame them, but like Lyon said back on the island, as long as they kept it to talking and surmising I guess there was no danger.

"I feel like a heel leaving the rest of this up to others now that our women are safe."

"Don't feel that way Devon, that's what these boys do. You boys have been on this for a while now, you should take a break, spend some time with your women and enjoy the fact that you brought down one of the most wanted men in the world."

62

DEVON

~

Three weeks later we were back on the island, which looked like a completely different place. Cierra had shown up a few days early to get the place set up.

There were flowers everywhere leading from the lawn down to the beach and a canopy that looked like it would hold a couple hundred people easy.

We hadn't been let in on any of the plans. After all the threats the women had made about making us help them plan. In the end it was decided that as men we didn't know the first thing about it and were left to our own devices.

We'd used the time to take care of our business and make sure that the people we'd left in charge had done a good job, which they had.

The CO and his boys had been busy in that time and once the news broke about the trafficking ring and all those who were involved, everything was total chaos.

As Mancini had predicted, there were a lot of people with their heads on the chopping block, including the fuck up who couldn't hide behind his past presidency.

People tend to draw the line at selling young girls into sexual slavery. Who knew the world still had a fucking moral compass.

Thorpe had come through, and so had Blade and Jake and though the girls had a long road ahead of them they were all home safe. I don't even begin to know how they did that shit.

Apparently Thorpe was very thorough. He had a medical team that dealt with the kind of trauma the girls had endured, and his place was used as some sort of rehab center where the girls stayed while they were being tended to before going back into society.

His only issue it seems, were the many military men and women who were crawling around his place because they refused to leave their daughters now that they'd been found.

We didn't kid ourselves that that was the end of it. There are always going to be assholes with degenerate minds, but for now, our little stint in hell was over.

The women were bustling around with excitement, and Ariel had blossomed in the last few weeks. She no longer had that haunted look in her eyes like she did when she was blaming herself. I'd taken care of that first thing.

We'd spent the time getting to know each other and she seemed to be adjusting well to life on the outside. The fact that everything was new to her, helped me to see things in a whole new light.

Things that I'd taken for granted over the years suddenly had new meaning. Even something as simple as a butterfly landing on a flower would give her so much joy it was hard not to fall a little deeper in love with her.

She made me laugh, made my heart lighter that it had been since I was a young boy who'd lost his only family. And I no longer saw the world as the fucked up place it once was.

Instead of my sisters corrupting her, she seemed to have an affect on them, though I'm not too sure that was better, they seemed sneakier to me these days.

I had a sneaky feeling between her and Kat that they'd come up with a new strategy on how to deal with us.

I knew I was right the first time I saw Dani diffuse a situation between her and Con that left him with his mouth hanging open and no wiser as to who the fuck had won the argument.

Things were peaceful on the compound, Davey had moved into the mansion since his mother and father had gotten hitched and hit the road a week after we came back.

The CO was like a new man, nothing at all like the straight laced commander we knew and loved. Once he'd broken the news to the kids, Davey claimed he'd always suspected, but Susie hadn't a clue.

Cord had helped her assuage some of her anger at being neglected by her father. In fact she was the one out of her family who had the hardest time accepting.

The other women had accepted him easily enough since they'd heard so much about him already over the past year. And they too helped cool her anger.

It was good to see the others getting back into the groove of things with their women and life settling once more. It was almost sickening how much sappiness was floating around the compound.

Quinn and Kelly were more often than not lost in their own little world and spent a lot of time disappearing. In fact for a time there we only saw them at meals.

I can't say anything because Ariel and I were pretty much the same. I kept remembering a conversation I'd had with Law's boy Clayton who was in pretty much the same predicament as I.

His girl was the daughter of a senator who had no idea that she existed. His advice, get her with child and then there was no question where she'd be staying.

He'd already taken care of that part, but I didn't know if any of the hundred times I'd taken her and resulted in pregnancy.

The CO had only told me that he'd talked to the old king, but he wouldn't say anything more, which left me on tenterhooks for weeks leading up to today.

I couldn't wait to get my ring on her finger before anything could go wrong. I knew once she became my wife there was no way anyone could stop us being together.

EPILOGUE

LYON

"Lyon your daughter is fucking adorable."

"Dude what the fuck, she's sixteen." I glared at Mancini the fuck ready to take him out.

"Not the teen you ass, the little one." That shit made me snort like Kat does. "Oh yeah?" She's been working her con on her new uncles. To a man they melt whenever she bats those lashes of hers at them.

She knows better than to try that shit with me. That ship sailed when the little shit was three and I caught her making her own damn glue to fuck with her big sister's hair.

"What's she doing that makes her so adorable this

time?" I hadn't seen her in a little bit, figured she was with her mom and the other women. Thank fuck. We were here to relax after all and that one don't know the meaning of the word.

"She's reading to Zakira, very hush-hush. Must be some story the way the two of them have their heads together whispering."

I flew out of my chair two seconds later. "Lyon what the fuck?" Tyler and the others looked at me like I was nuts before they came after me.

I held my hand up when we reached the door to the playroom. I don't know what, but I was pretty sure Mengele was up to some shit.

Her mother knows she's not to be left unattended for more than the five minutes unless she needs to use the bathroom; and even then you need a fucking armed guard at the door.

We listened as she seemed to be telling the baby a story. "Okay listen good Kira, you have to remember okay? Daddy won't get me the real stuff like the uncles use, but I know how to make it another way look."

She moved and that's when we saw the line of bottles and bowls she had on the floor in front of them.

"What the fuck?" I whispered the words since I didn't want to give away our position, not yet, not until I knew what the fuck Hitler's youth was up to.

"I found some powder but we don't need that now,

don't breathe okay." She put a mask around Zakira's face and one around her own before pouring some dark powder in a bowl very carefully. "Now we add nitro-glycerine and diato…I can't say the long word but it's okay."

"What the fuck is she doing?" I was at a loss, it didn't sound like her usual recipes. At least I didn't hear anything about sulfuric acid so we were safe.

"Dynamite. The long word is diatomaceous earth. The only thing that's used for is dynamite. I don't know what she needs the gunpowder for though." Mancini answered.

We turned back to hear the rest of her little lesson. "Those bad guys come back we'll be ready."

"Where the fuck? Which one of you taught my kid that shit?" They started backing up hands in the air. "Wasn't me."

"Yeah you're laughing now but you won't be laughing when she blows your house to shit.

It's too fucking early o'clock for this fuckery."

I stormed into the room and the little sneak smiled up at me. "Hi daddy, whatcha doing?"

"The question is what the hell are you doing?"

"Oh nothing, it's a science project."

I looked back at the men who were all laughing their asses off and wondered what the hell I was supposed to do with my kid.

"That's enough science for one day, go outside and

play." Geez this kid! She gave me a put upon pout and took her little friend's hand and led her out of the room.

I heard her greet her uncles who came into the room to join me as we looked over her little stash. "Somebody wanna tell me where the fuck she found this shit?"

"Um, I might have it around somewhere. I guess I'm gonna have to up the security around here since she seems to find her way in and out of places she ought not to be."

"You know Lyon, if you give her to me now I can train her."

"You fancy getting shot in the ass Hank, I can help you out there. Leave my kid alone."

"Let's go see if the women need any help with last minute preparations." Logan slapped me on the shoulder.

"I'm pretty sure they told us to fuck off bro."

QUINN

The wedding is today. There had been a lot of fuss last night when the women tried selling us on some old wife's tale about not seeing the bride the day of. That hadn't gone over well with any of us.

The girls had planned a party on the beach in place of

the traditional bachelor and bachelorette parties and we'd stayed up well into the night.

I spent most of the night watching her as I've been doing ever since we got back from the Gulf and no longer had to worry about being hunted.

She was completely relaxed and at ease, almost as if she'd been part of our little family for years instead of a few short weeks.

It didn't take her long at all to find her footing. In fact she seemed to just jump into life as my woman easy enough without too many hiccups, though sometimes I feel like I'm waiting for the other shoe to drop.

As much griping as the others had done over the last few months when it came to their women I was kind of expecting the worst.

Instead it's been the happiest I've ever been in my life. Even our little skirmishes are funny as hell because we both know there's no way in hell she's ever gonna win, but that doesn't stop her from trying.

I can already see the influence of the other women, and it's funny, but having her has opened my eyes to the fact that these women really do rule us. No matter how we shake it, everything we do is for them, to keep them safe and happy.

It's like she's taken over every aspect of my life and though I find time to do other things, like get back to work, I still spend a good chunk of each day thinking about her, wanting her.

I don't know if it's my 'gift' or just your every day lust, but I don't think a day has gone by that I haven't spent some part of it buried inside her.

Which brings me to believe since she's not on birth control, and I damn sure never used a condom with her, that she might be pregnant. Since she hasn't said anything to me I figured I'd let her tell me herself when she's ready.

I looked down at her head on my chest, still in wonder that something this beautiful could belong to me. It's the same every morning when I wake up next to her.

Sometimes it takes me a minute to remember my good fortune and then that feeling comes over me. A feeling of immense joy unlike anything I've ever known.

I no longer worry about what it had done to my dad, or that I'll lose my fucking mind. Because when I look at my brothers, men that I trust, men that I know are strong, I don't see much difference in the way they treat their women.

I lifted her face with a finger under her chin and kissed her warm lips until she awakened with a sigh. "Morning baby, it's our wedding day."

I rolled her to her back as she stretched and wrapped her arms around my neck returning my kiss as she opened her legs for me to fit in between them.

It was easy to slide into her warmth, her body still wet with my seed from the night before and make love to her slowly for once.

Our mouths stayed fused together as I showed her without words what she meant to me. And when she tightened around me and cried out her love for me I spilled my seed deep inside her.

~

DEVON

~

"Stop being so nervous, everything is going to be fine." We were about an hour out from the wedding on the beach and she was the one reassuring me.

I don't know why, but now that we were down to crunch time I have this fear that some shit is gonna go wrong. Maybe because I know that she's the best thing that ever happened to me.

Or maybe it's because I still don't think I deserve her. Whatever it is, I have this feeling that some shit's gonna go wrong.

"Come 'ere." I wrapped my arms around her and felt myself settle. "I love you, I'm not nervous about marrying you, I just don't want anything to go wrong on our big day." I hope Ty the fuck isn't lurking around somewhere listening to this or he'd ride my ass for sure.

"Nothing's gonna go wrong, now go be with your brothers while I finish getting dressed." Dani and Gaby had been pounding at our cottage door for the last half an hour trying to get me to release her.

The women were getting dressed together up at the mansion and I'm pretty sure like me my brothers were already dressed in their monkey suits, ready to get the show on the road.

I walked her over and withstood the evil glares and hisses before they slammed the door in my face, and headed out front to join the others.

"We look like assholes."

"Give it a rest Zak, it's the price we pay for making them wait. At least we can thank Mancini for letting us use his place since it means no one else will ever see us like this."

A plane came in for landing on the airstrip and my guts went into overdrive. Everyone else was here except the commander and Samson. Their crew was being very hush-hush which only made my nerves go up a couple notches, but when I saw the horde of men in robes filing onto the island I was ready to nab her and bolt.

"Chill brother, the CO said he had this right. He's never let us down before trust him." I tried to accept Quinn's words but I'd never been this afraid in my life.

These last few weeks had shown me what life with her would be like. I knew if I lost that now my shit would be FUBAR. She makes everything worthwhile, including my fucked up past, because it all led to her.

"What if he…."

"He's not." Lo and the others lined up beside me as we watched four men cart what looked like trunks into the mansion.

When the CO and Samson came into view flanking an old man with a cane, dressed in full Saudi royal regalia, I didn't have to guess who he was.

I started to move forward when he went towards the mansion where she was but Logan held me back with a hand on my shoulder. The CO as if sensing my angst, looked back over his shoulder at me and winked.

For some reason that settled me, but the next half an hour was the hardest of my life. I didn't breathe again until I saw her come out the door looking for me.

I met her halfway and as soon as I saw her face my worry disappeared only to be replaced with anger. "What happened, what did he say to you?" I was ready to go pound his ass for making my girl cry.

Her hand on my chest calmed me down and I wiped the tears from her eyes. "I'm fine, we had a nice long talk and everything's okay."

"What did he say? And what the hell were all those trunks?"

"He said to be happy and the trunks are our wedding gifts."

'That's it? He didn't try to get you to go back with him?"

"Of course he did, but I told him if I didn't marry the father of my baby it would bring shame to his family."

"Your what?" There was a ringing in my ears and I stumbled backwards a little bit until I corrected myself. I stared down at her in a daze until I shook myself out of it.

Now I was the one with tears in my eyes. "Why do you think I haven't been nervous this whole time? I knew that once I told him about the baby he'd have to see reason."

"How long have you known?"

"A few days, but the girls and I discussed it and decided it was best to wait to share the news. This close to the wedding they can't come up with any alternatives."

"Do you have any idea how happy you've just made me?" I pulled her back into my arms and looked over her shoulder at Kelly and Quinn who were sharing the same embrace.

From the way he put her away from him and looked down at her tummy before placing his hand there told me that he'd just received similar news.

I looked up at the sky, at the sun high above the clouds, shining down on us and gave thanks that we'd each found our one and only. That something good had come out of the hell we'd lived through the last year and a half.

Kat came outside and called the girls back in. "Okay ladies, your time's up let's go."

"I'll meet you on our cliff in a few Devon." She lifted up on her toes and kissed me before walking away back to the house.

I walked back to my brothers and we looked down towards the water. "Let's get married brothers." We walked down to the beach, seven men whose lives had been intertwined since we met those many years ago.

As we got closer to the place where the women would meet us to say the vows that would bind us together for a lifetime, I felt a cool soft breeze brush against my cheek.

Mom! My life had come full circle.

THE END

Made in the USA
Middletown, DE
29 December 2021

57242063R00383